Resurgence of the Hunt

By
Puja Guha

Book III of the Ahriman Legacy

Resurgence of the Hunt
© 2018 Puja Guha
ISBN: 978-1728804378
All rights reserved. No part of this publication may be reproduced, distributed, or transmitted in any form or by any means, including photocopying, recording, or other electronic or mechanical methods, without the prior written permission of the publisher, except in the case of brief quotations embodied in critical reviews and certain other noncommercial uses permitted by copyright law. For permission requests, write to pujaguha@pujaguha.com
Find out more by joining Puja's mailing list at:
http://smarturl.it/PujaList
www.pujaguha.com
pujaguha@pujaguha.com
Printed in the United States of America
Author photo by Mathew Jacob

Praise for Resurgence of the Hunt

"Guha proves herself with this third installment of the Ahriman series and a strong, female lead. Hers is a well-rounded novel that comes alive with her engaging plot and prose, placing her comfortably in a genre dominated by the likes of Tom Clancy, Robert Ludlum, and John le Carre.

"Guha exerts careful control of the characters and her story, infusing it with humor and a touch of romance while offering a sensitive look at our pasts and the complexities of international relations. Her main characters are portrayed as realistic and human, painted on the page with emotions, flaws, and their own convoluted histories.

"It is a fast-paced read that is powered by non-stop action and a taut, emotional narrative, elevating the story beyond the usual hijinks of the genre novels. It is sure to entertain and please spy thriller fans."
— **RECOMMENDED by the US Review of Books**

"Most thriller writers depend on reference books and the Internet to do their research for their novels. But Puja Guha has 'been there, done that.' She's traveled throughout the world from remote poverty-stricken nations to the boardrooms of high finance in the world's richest cities, and it shows in this excellent novel. Fans of high-paced and action-filled thrillers won't be disappointed."
— **Brendan DuBois, bestselling mystery author, three-time Edgar Award nominee and James Patterson collaborator**

"Resurgence of the Hunt is both a gripping thriller and a nuanced character study. Puja Guha writes with real authority and authenticity."
— **Lou Berney, Edgar Award-winning author of November Road**

"Taut, pacy thriller, with well-drawn characters, believable relationships, and a satisfying plot."
— **Cathy Ace, award-winning author of The Cait Morgan Mysteries, and The WISE Enquiries Agency Mysteries**

Also by Puja Guha
Spy Thriller Suspense Series:

The Ahriman Legacy Book I —
Ahriman: The Spirit of Destruction

The Ahriman Legacy Book II —
Road to Redemption

The Ahriman Legacy Book III —
Resurgence of the Hunt

Contemporary Indian Family Drama / Woman's Fiction:
The Confluence

Find out more by joining Puja's mailing list at:
http://smarturl.it/PujaList

DEDICATION

For Anjna Auntie

Acknowledgment

Normally I write the longest acknowledgments—it's so hard to convey my thanks to all the people that have supported me in becoming the person who I am today, of which being an author is a huge component. To start with, my most important thanks go out to you, the reader. Thank you for reading *Resurgence of the Hunt* and participating in yet another chapter of Petra and Kasem's story. When the two characters first came to me ten years ago, I didn't even know if I could finish one part of their story, and here I am publishing my third novel in the *Ahriman Legacy* series. I know for sure I wouldn't have made it this far without the encouraging feedback I've received from readers around the world. Your perspectives and encouragement have helped to carry me through the moments of my deepest self-doubt, when I've gone down the rabbit hole of believing that nothing I've written would ever see the light of day or be able to touch anyone outside of my own head. I can see the future of the series now, and at last I know how it's going to end—I can only hope that you'll stick with me for the entire journey.

I'd also like to extend my deepest thanks to the *mystery* and *thriller* author community who've been such wonderful comrades in arms. I used to think attending conventions like *Bouchercon* would be stressful due to the extensive networking. I now realize how wrong I was—everyone within the author community has been so kind and welcoming, and we share war stories and empathize with our own struggles. I'm lucky to have stumbled upon such a supportive group of peers. The work that each of you turns out incites both inspiration and a healthy bit of envy, both of which help me to stay focused and on task. Thank you for being mentors and guides to young authors like me who are just starting out.

To my editors, Amy Leigh Owen and Tanya Besmehn of *Bezuki Creative Services*, I may not have agreed with each of your edits and suggestions, but there is no doubt that you've helped to turn me into a better writer. *Resurgence of the Hunt* would hardly be where it is today if it were not for the influence of you both. The same thanks go to my beta readers, Peter Pollak, and my father Pradip Guha. I'm so grateful I can rely on your feedback with everything I write.

My continuing gratitude and thanks:

To John Besmehn of *Bezuki Creative Services* for being so patient and collaborative on cover design and helping me to redo the covers for the entire *Ahriman Legacy* series.

To my parents Pradip and Jayashree Guha for their ever-present love and support. Where would I be without you? I have the luxury to choose my path because of all the work and time you've given me.

To Anjna Auntie—I couldn't find the words in my dedication to say enough about how much your love has helped me to become the person I am today. Your capacity to give, to teach, and to love is something I will carry with me for my whole life.

To my husband, Brendan Snow, thank you for always being so supportive of my identity as a writer. I might never have begun without you.

There are others who I could list out by name, as I've attempted to do in my past books, but I fear I would miss someone—someone I would later recall as a great influence. Instead, I will simply say to everyone who has loved and supported me over the years—we may come in and out of touch, but you are my extended family and I am so lucky to be able to lean and rely upon you when the moment presents itself. I recognize and appreciate your influence every day, in everything I do. Thank you for being such a presence in my life. I am truly grateful.

Prologue

Hai Phong Port, Vietnam – April 2017

Carlos approached the docks with his heartbeat drumming through his ears. He scanned the area for signs that his cover had been blown with his hand resting on his holstered Glock. Something was going to happen today. He could feel it in his bones.

He caught the gaze of his undercover colleague, Vikram, who gave him a slight nod. Agency headquarters had picked up chatter that their mark, Duc Nguyen, knew he had a leak within his crew. Carlos swallowed hard, although his throat still felt like sandpaper. What he wouldn't give for an icy Coke or a cold beer. He and Vik were living on borrowed time, but they still didn't have the necessary evidence to pin the illicit arms deals on Nguyen. His connections with higher-ups in the CIA, at MI-6, and within French military intelligence—*la Direction générale de la sécurité exterieure*—kept him from being targeted, and it didn't hurt that a portion of his profits ended up in Pentagon slush funds like the Red Sea Trading Company. This operation had taken months to set up and it was about to disintegrate. Their only hope was to gain access to the ledger before Nguyen figured out their true identities. With the ledger, they would have an account of every arms sale that Nguyen had orchestrated, along with names of the consultants who had betrayed their respective governments to line their pockets with Nguyen's funds.

Carlos watched Nguyen's posture as they waited for the last of their three containers from the China Star Shipping Company to be unloaded onto the docks. He'd once seen Nguyen hold a gun to a contact's thirteen-year-old daughter based only on the slight suspicion that he'd been compromised. What would Nguyen do now if he were certain that he had been betrayed?

Carlos took a step back and offered Nguyen's business partner, Seymour, a cigarette before he lit his own. He inhaled the smoke deep, feeling his lungs inflate with the delicious poison that he'd tried to quit over and over again. He held it long before slowly exhaling. After one last deep drag, he tagged the butt with a mini GPS sticker and reluctantly dropped it to mark the spot where the containers stood.

The forklift creaked as it placed the last container in front of them. Carlos exhaled as their local contact—a short Italian man whose name he wasn't privy to—unlocked the ranger lock and opened the first container using a door-latch handle extender that was longer than his own torso. Once the door was open, he repeated the same procedure on the other two containers while Nguyen, Seymour, Carlos, and Vik examined the contents of the first one.

Carlos picked up an assault rifle and raised it up to his shoulder to inspect the scope. The rifle felt heavy on his frame, a weapon of precision. He recognized it as the more updated model of one he had seen in training six years earlier. He rarely used such weapons in his life as an operative, but the Agency had made sure to train him and his colleagues in their use. He put the rifle down and examined a set of grenade launchers, followed by a bazooka and a napalm rocket launcher.

Carlos suppressed a shudder. Even with all of this evidence, they had no documentation that directly tied Nguyen to the arms deals. All of the transactions were conducted in the names of his subordinates, and he had an army of lawyers to ensure that he'd never be charged, let alone convicted. Not without the ledger. To the public, Nguyen made his money through private equity investments in holding companies around the world. Those companies owned subsidiaries that made other investments—including illegal arms deals that paid their dividends back to Nguyen and his consultants. Through the operation, Vik had learned that each real transaction was recorded in code in a ledger, and a subsequent, aboveboard lump-sum transaction was created on the company books to account for several of the illicit transactions. Since Nguyen didn't keep electronic records of his transactions, the ledger was the only piece of evidence that could provide incontrovertible proof of his involvement in the arms deals.

As Carlos gripped the napalm rocket launcher, he was catapulted back to his high-school classroom, the day he had learned about the Vietnam War. Images of orange and black smoke from the documentary his world studies teacher showed them filled his head, along with terrifying photos of burn victims. He squeezed his eyes shut, willing the images away and lowered the weapon.

Seymour made eye contact with him. "What do you think, Carlos?"

"Looks good to me," he answered. Carlos quieted an urge to flinch, glad that his training kept those involuntary reflexes at bay. Seymour's hooked nose and nasal voice always cut through to his core. Seymour seemed even more ruthless than Nguyen because he looked at people, even those he trusted and liked, as if they were tools to be manipulated.

Seymour nodded at Nguyen and they exited the container. They followed the same inspection procedure for the other two containers, which held more of the same weaponry. Once the inspection was completed, Seymour handed a wad of cash to the young Italian, who then locked the containers once more.

"Vik, go ahead and transfer the money," Seymour said.

Vik nodded and tapped on his phone, as Carlos watched from a few feet away. When the two of them had started this operation, they could never have imagined how long or extensive it would be. Vik had joined Nguyen's team first, and Carlos didn't even know how the Agency had established his cover. He only knew that Vik had installed himself as one of Nguyen's front men.

Carlos had heard whispers about how they had done it—that Vik first became buddies with one of Nguyen's contacts in Turkey, and slowly segued into the inner circle. Carlos' process was much easier. Vik had given the Agency enough intel to know Nguyen was seeking a specialized weapons expert, and once the Agency had created the cover, all Vik had to do was slip Carlos' cover credentials into the pile. Even so, Carlos was never privy to the inner workings of any of the deals. Vik knew more than Carlos, but he seldom knew the actual locations or buyers until hours before a deal went down.

They had considered an attempt to turn one of Nguyen's men instead of continuing the climb through his close associates, but the Agency had dismissed it as too risky. Nguyen's men appeared fiercely loyal. He kept them in line by showering them with gifts in their chosen vices; women, booze, weapons—whatever ensured their allegiance. While they'd accumulated quite the bounty over time, they were still no closer to securing the ledger.

Once the Italian finished closing up the containers, he scurried down the pier and disappeared into the darkness. Carlos' adrenaline spiked, they were alone again—Nguyen and his inner circle of three. If something were to happen, now would be the time.

Carlos lit another cigarette and stepped to the side as Seymour and Nguyen spoke to each other. He took a few steps to move into earshot but could only catch a few words.

"...from Caspian. He doesn't know..."

"...doesn't know anything...has to be him."

Carlos swallowed the lump in his throat and resisted the urge to bolt down the pier.

Seymour turned toward him, "Carlos, I think we're set. We'll see you at the hotel bar in an hour."

Carlos tried to calm his trembling hand as he brought the cigarette to his lips for another drag. He nodded, desperate to mask his fear, and inhaled deep. "See you in a bit." When he felt as if he were safely out of their sight, he ducked into the shadows alongside another cargo ship and crept back toward the group with his Glock in hand. He still couldn't hear anything from the group that he'd left. *Maybe I was wrong?* His pulse raced, and he compelled his legs forward. Perhaps they didn't suspect either of them, but he had to find out.

He had reached the end of the container ship when he heard the crack of the gun—a single shot. He covered the remaining distance in a couple of seconds, fighting his instinct to break from the shadows to move faster. He stopped behind a supply truck and peaked around the corner. Seymour held a gun in one hand and his phone in the other. Vikram was lying on his back, not moving. "Send a cleanup crew to the docks," Seymour said and hung up.

Carlos waited, his throat constricted, until Seymour and Nguyen disappeared down the dock. He ran toward Vikram's body and dropped to his knees. There was a hole in Vikram's chest and a small pool of blood spread from beneath him. Carlos bit down on his lip until he tasted blood.

"Vik? It's me. It's Carlos." He pressed one hand to the wound and searched for a pulse with his other, but he knew it was futile. "Come on, wake up, buddy. Please…Vik!" he cried out again as he found no pulse.

Carlos scrambled to the edge of the pier and vomited into the water below. *The cleaners are coming.* He retched again and caught his breath as he leaned against a pylon. He steadied himself and staggered back to search Vikram's body for any Agency identification. When he came up empty, he pulled out Vik's phone. He opened the phone sync app on his own phone and touched the two phones together to copy the data and files. When the sync was complete, he wiped the memory on Vik's phone and hurled it into the water. He shut his eyes for a moment. "Bye, buddy," he whispered, "I'm so sorry. I'll make sure they pay for this."

Chapter 1

Kyoto, Japan – Nine years later, April, 2023

Petra Shirazi watched the sun rise to her left as she jogged down the path along Lake Biwa Canal. "I'll race you to the bridge," she said to the man running alongside her before sprinting away.

She covered the three remaining blocks in several seconds and leaned over the bridge rail to catch her breath as Kasem caught up with her.

"I told you I wasn't going to race you," he shook his head.

She flashed a smile and shrugged, "What can I say? I'm not going to stop trying." They spent a few minutes stretching along the rail in silence.

"It still takes my breath away." Kasem put his arm around her waist and the two of them looked toward the water, "I'm so glad you're here with me."

"I'm glad to be here with you," Petra rested her head on his chest and inhaled deeply. A moment later, she stepped away to stretch her hamstrings.

"Do you want to get some breakfast?" he asked.

"Sure, why not?"

Petra followed him toward one of the local grocery stores in the Higashiyama neighborhood. They picked up a couple of green tea and taro flavored rolls, along with two hot coffees and sat down on a bench outside the store. Petra tore a piece off the taro roll and popped it in her mouth.

"I can't believe that's your favorite flavor," Kasem took a giant bite of the green tea roll. "Is there anything that you want to do today?"

"Not really," Petra sipped her coffee and pulled her feet up onto the bench. "You?"

"We can play it by ear," Kasem fidgeted as he finished the roll. "Let's get cleaned up and go for a walk. I want to see the cherry blossoms again."

"Didn't you see enough of them while we were running?"

"Come on. You know it's different. Let's take a stroll and smell the roses. Or in this case, the blossoms."

******

A short time later, Petra stepped into the shower in their traditional Japanese *machiya* house. She turned the water to its hottest and winced as it hit her skin. She adjusted the temperature and leaned against the stone wall of the shower.

Petra splashed water on her face and confronted her dread. Recently she had been avoiding long walks or talks with Kasem. Anything romantic, really, to steer him away from the idea. A ring hidden in his sock drawer? *Isn't that a bit cliché?* She had been trying to find a way to bring it up. She grimaced and wished for the thousandth time that she hadn't gone looking for his navy sweater a few days earlier. He asked her to bring it before she met him at the gym. If only he hadn't asked her to grab it, she never would have been searching in his dresser. She'd opened the sock drawer by mistake, but before she could close it, she saw it—a ring box, barely hidden, tucked in between two pairs of rolled up dress socks. *Did he want me to find it?*

Petra sighed. In another time, maybe in another life, she would have been happy or excited. *If only it were just about the ring.* The ring was lovely. A slim oval shaped solitaire diamond on a platinum band. She had even tried it on. It fit perfectly, both in terms of size and how it looked on her hand. The heart of the issue was that she had no answer for Kasem. She loved him. She had no doubt about that, but how could she marry him? They had never been together in the real world. Their life in Kyoto was like being in a bubble. A beautiful one, but a bubble nonetheless. She missed teaching in Paris. She missed her family in New York. She'd already left so much of her life behind because she'd run from her career as a spy after she caused Kasem to be captured and almost killed. She shouldered the blame for much of what had gone wrong with his life, but she wasn't sure that she could reconcile him—the man that she loved—with all of the terrible things that he had done. After his capture in Iran he had been forced to work as a terrorist and an assassin, and in doing so, had become the Ahriman, responsible for killing hundreds in an attack at the Suez Canal. While he had been tricked into carrying out the Suez attack, he had pulled the trigger numerous other times in cold blood. Petra had even seen him do it in front of her eyes as he executed a Russian operative who had held him captive, an operative whom they could have arrested and turned, who could have helped them capture the real ringleaders of a terrorist attack in Washington DC.

Petra let out another sigh and tilted her head back to wash out the shampoo in her hair. She and Kasem had only scratched the surface on what they had to work through. Could they really build a new life together? Their time as a couple in Kyoto had been nigh-on perfect, but she was petrified of leaving the bubble, no matter how much she wanted to. He was the first man that she'd ever really loved, but when it came to taking the plunge, to trusting in him and what they had, she wasn't sure if she could take that step. His past as the Ahriman lurked in the background, like the elephant in the room.

She shut her eyes and a memory came over her, of the last man that she'd been with before she had fallen in love with Kasem. Even though it was years ago, she could still feel his breath on her neck and how he'd touched her. She'd trusted him implicitly and given in completely, in a way that she still couldn't with Kasem. She felt her heartbeat increase and she exhaled slowly, trying in vain to let go of the memory.

Petra turned off the shower and toweled off. On her way upstairs to the bedroom to dress, she passed Kasem making some more coffee in the kitchen.

"You look great," he said.

She blushed under his gaze. "Thanks."

He put his arms around her and gave her a peck on the lips. "I love you."

Petra wiggled out of his grasp. "I love you, too."

He grabbed her towel so that it slipped off her and she giggled as she tried to retrieve it. He stopped her and kissed her again, deeper this time.

"Come on." She looked up at him with a sparkle in her eyes and led him up to the bedroom.

Chapter 2

Kyoto, Japan

Kasem Ismaili stroked Petra's hair as she lay with her head on his shoulder. *Should I do it today?* He looked toward his dresser where he had hidden the ring. He wanted to ask her, but something in the back of his mind bothered him. They had spent an amazing six months together in Kyoto, but for the past few days, things had been different, although he couldn't quite put his finger on what was bothering him. He turned to Petra and braved the question, hoping a direct approach would work, "Petra, is everything okay?"

She raised her eyebrows and looked up at him. "Everything's fine. Just like this." She nestled further into his chest and closed her eyes.

Kasem exhaled, still unable to quell the uneasy feeling. He lay still and when Petra started to fall asleep, he kissed her forehead and extracted himself from her embrace. He stood up, pulled on his boxers, and padded downstairs. He checked the French press, which had now brewed some very strong coffee, and poured a cup. He grimaced at the bitterness of the first sip but forced the caffeine down his throat. Sleep had been elusive over the past few years, and he had become increasingly reliant on caffeine. Insomnia was still a welcome change from the nightmares that had haunted him when he was living in San Francisco, though. He only wished that he didn't have to hide it from Lila. *Petra,* he reminded himself. Even after all of this time knowing her real name, he still slipped sometimes and wanted to call her Lila.

He sighed. The fact that she had been undercover when they first met was just a reminder of the many obstacles they currently faced. They had so much baggage, and he wanted more than anything to put it all in the past. To shove it into a box. To make it disappear, as if it didn't exist. At least he didn't blame her anymore, although he was certain she still blamed herself.

Kasem poured another cup. *Almost like an espresso,* he thought. He set the mug down and frowned. Their time together in Kyoto had been something out of a dream, better than he could possibly have imagined. Everything with Petra had been fine until a few days earlier. *Did something happen?* He grabbed his laptop from the side table in the living room and opened his calendar. There was hardly anything marked on it, but instinct told him that he was on the right track. His eyes wandered to her laptop charging on the bookshelf, but he redirected his attention to his screen. *No snooping.* His eyebrows narrowed, and he helped himself to the last bit of coffee in the French press. *She started acting weird that day we went out to dinner.* He sat down again and thought through the evening. He'd gone to the gym and they'd met at the restaurant afterward. She had seemed on edge when she handed him his navy sweater. *My navy sweater. From my dresser. Oh boy.* He set the cup on the table and let out a long exhale. He knew exactly what had happened. *Crap.* Petra had been acting uncomfortable ever since that evening. *She must have found the ring. Does she not want me to propose?* It seemed like they were so happy.

Is it because of what I did? After his capture in Iran, Kasem had been duped into working as an assassin for a rogue Iranian general, all because he thought it was the price he had to pay for Petra's ransom. In reality, she had never been captured, and he was manipulated into doing an evil general's bidding, all for nothing. He had sold his soul to General Majed and become the Ahriman, an international terrorist and assassin. After the attack at the Suez Canal, he had tried to stop counting the number of kills on his head—the guilt had become too much of a burden—but he couldn't get the number out of his head. *Three hundred and sixty-seven.* Three hundred and sixty-eight if you included Anatoli, the Russian operative that he had shot rather than capture in Washington D.C.

Kasem left that life behind when Petra told him the truth after they came face to face in Kuwait two years earlier. He was conducting an operation to assassinate the Kuwaiti monarch, and she was there on behalf of the Agency to stop the assassination. He'd kidnapped her before she could expose him, and the shock that she'd never been captured, that General Majed had tricked him into becoming his puppet, was still raw. All his kills, which he had justified on the basis of keeping her safe, had been for nothing. Kasem had been clawing his way back toward a more legitimate life ever since. He had helped Petra on an Agency op in New York the previous year and had hoped that his actions had set him on a path toward redemption. During the op, they had slowly renewed their friendship, along with the romantic connection they had once shared. At the end of the operation, he had asked her to join him in Kyoto to see if they still had a shot at something deeper. He'd hoped they could rebuild their relationship as the people they had become, rather than the fragments of who they were when they first met.

Petra had been hesitant to come, but she surprised him a few months later. The time they had spent together since then had been wonderful, but perhaps she still wasn't willing to let go of her old life?

Before he could go too far down that rabbit hole, Kasem heard Petra's footsteps coming down the narrow stairway. She looked a little disheveled, her wet hair matted, but cute and pretty as always.

"Hey," she joined him on the couch and reached for his coffee mug. "Is there more of that for me?"

"Here you go. Fair warning, though. It's pretty strong. It steeped for way too long." He flashed her a grin.

She leaned over and kissed him, "I hope you think it was worth it."

"No, not at all."

Petra elbowed him lightly and took a sip of the coffee. "Wow," she cringed, "strong is right. Can you make me some more? Something that doesn't taste like battery acid?"

"Sure. We'll go for a walk after that?"

Kasem watched as she paused before she answered, "Okay."

******

A few hours later, Kasem grabbed Petra's hand and walked down the street toward the canal. She gave him a wide smile and he pulled her in closer with his arm around her shoulders.

When they reached the canal, they strolled slowly, once again hand in hand. The sun's rays streamed through the canopy of pink cherry blossoms and danced on the bits of grass and tree moss below, creating playful patterns of light and shadows.

Petra stopped alongside him, "Wow. They're really in bloom today."

"I looked it up online. The weather gods thought they would peak this week."

She linked her arms around his neck, "You're sweet."

Kasem's face lit up as he leaned over to kiss her again, "I want to show you my favorite spot."

"You have a favorite spot?" Petra tilted her head to the side. "Is that where you've been going on your walks?"

"Maybe." He led her down the canal path for a few blocks, and then turned left down Kacho-michi Road.

"Are we going to the park?"

"Just come with me."

They reached Maruyama Park a few minutes later and Kasem led her toward the center of the park. He took her to a path next to a babbling brook nestled within a sea of pink and white tree blossoms.

"Look," Kasem pointed down the lane toward a couple standing about a hundred feet away posing for wedding photos. "Think we could do that someday?" he asked in a tentative voice. Part of him wanted to just ask her—now, here, like he had planned—but his instinct told him not to.

Petra stiffened and dropped his hand, "Kasem, we need to talk."

"I agree. You've been acting strange the past few days. Want to tell me what's going on?"

"I'm not ready."

"You're not ready?"

Petra opened her mouth in obvious hesitation, then blurted, "Okay. Here goes. I found the ring."

Kasem looked around at the setting and nodded, "You thought I brought you here to propose? Why wait until now to tell me you're not ready?"

"I didn't know how. I don't know how to do this. What would the next step be for us? We've been living in a bubble—an amazing one, but still a bubble."

Kasem's shoulders slumped, "This isn't really about not being ready. This is about you. Are you leaving me? I thought you were happy. I thought we were happy."

She shook her head and placed her left hand on his face, "That's not what I'm saying. I do love you, but I don't know what kind of future we can have, or how to figure it out. We've been here for six months, living off the package the Agency paid you, but we can't do this forever. I am so grateful that we've had this time, but we can't keep going like this."

"What do you want to do? Do you miss teaching? We could go back to Paris."

Petra ran her fingers through her hair, "I do miss it, but I don't know."

The tone of her voice told him what she was thinking. "You're not sure we would survive out there. If we left this *bubble*," he said.

"Are you really so sure? Maybe I'm missing something, but we've never been together in the real world. Doesn't that scare you?"

"I think we could figure it out. Or is there more to it?"

"What do you mean?"

"Is this about me? About everything…?" Kasem's voice turned cold and his mind flashed to a vision from one of his old nightmares, with Petra pointing at the flames on the Suez Canal. *Just look at what you've done,* she had said in the nightmare. *She hasn't forgiven me. Maybe she never will.* "There's nothing more I can do, Petra. I can't bring back the people I killed, I can't go back in time and stop myself from working for General Majed. The past is the past. I can't just forget it, and I'm not expecting you to either, but I thought we were at least beyond blaming each other for it. I guess I was wrong." He turned around and walked toward the edge of the park, away from the happy newlyweds and away from her.

Petra jogged to catch up and stepped in front of him. "Kasem, stop. Stop!" She raised her arms to block him, "You're right. I should have talked to you. I wish I had the answers—about you, and me, and us. I don't know where I am with all of this, and that terrifies me. I know that I love you, and I want to try, but I don't know what that means." Her eyes begged for understanding, "As for the past, well there's enough blame to go around."

Kasem met her gaze, shook his head, and started to move around her, when she caught his arm. "Please, Kasem. We have to talk about this."

"If you wanted to talk, why did you wait so long to bring it up?"

"I'm bringing it up now. You can't really be over everything either. You don't sleep. You drink more caffeine than I thought humanly possible."

"I didn't realize you'd noticed." Kasem let out a long sigh and gestured toward a park bench.

They sat down facing each other and Petra reached for his hand, "Don't you ever miss the real world?"

Kasem gave her a pained expression, "I haven't been in the real world for a long time. I guess San Francisco was sort of the real world, but I still wasn't the real me. And it was worse there. I don't sleep these days, but at least I don't have nightmares anymore."

"You never told me about that."

"I had dreams where I remembered the faces. The faces of the people I killed. Where I could see myself doing it again. The worst one was about the Suez. About that night when I thought I was only placing a few bugs, but they turn out to be bombs and then everything bursts into flames, and all those people are dead." He stopped himself from saying the number of kills out loud—Petra knew about the attack, and how he had been tricked into it, but she didn't know how many other attacks he'd been involved in or how much blood was on his hands.

"I'm sorry," Petra gave his hand a gentle squeeze.

"You're there too."

"In the nightmare?"

"You show up before the explosions, asking me what I'd done. Then the bombs go off and you disappear."

Petra looked down at the ground. "I had PTSD too. For a long time. After I thought you died in Tehran, and then again in Paris before the last op. It hasn't been bad since, but I still have moments sometimes. Flashbacks. I can understand why you would rather not sleep than have the nightmares."

"It's not like I was sleeping much then either." Kasem placed his other hand over hers. "You're right, though." He motioned toward the newlyweds who were still posing by the water. "We're not ready for such a big step. *Yet.* But don't you think we're ready to leave the bubble?"

"Maybe." Petra turned to survey the park and pointed toward the sea of gray clouds forming across the sky. "We should get inside. There's a storm coming."

Chapter 3

Kyoto, Japan

Petra glanced behind her at Kasem as the storm clouds darkened overhead. "Hurry." She picked up the pace.

He took several long strides to meet her and grabbed her hand. The two of them covered the remaining distance to their house in a combination of speed walking and jogging. By the time they reached their lane, the streetlights had turned on and the drizzle had transformed into a downpour. The stone pavement was slick and slippery. "Be careful," Kasem said, concerned about Petra's shoes.

"I'm all right." His concern brought a smile to her face. He had always been very attentive, even from the first time they met when she was undercover. Somehow, he still managed to be sweet without being overbearing. She was, after all, a trained operative and could handle slick sidewalks.

They approached the house and her subconscious tensed. *Something's wrong.* She stopped Kasem with her left arm and gestured toward the house. "Someone's in there," she whispered. The string trap that they rigged to indicate if anyone had entered their house had been triggered. Otherwise the house looked normal with the small lamp glowing in the living room that came on automatically when the house became dark. She put her arms around him and gave him a kiss as sheets of rain poured down on them. "It's a pro. No signs of entry other than the string trap, and no shadows in the living room," she said into his ear.

He leaned forward and placed his lips on the nape of her neck. "Drop your purse."

Petra made a show of giggling and let her purse slide off her shoulder and fall to the ground. They both knelt to pick it up as Kasem slipped an out-the-front switchblade out of a holster on his ankle.

"Where's your Colt?" He steadied her shoulders while they stood up.

"Under the bed." Petra's throat tightened. They had gone soft in the months that they had been in Kyoto. She had stopped carrying her gun or any sort of weapon after the first few weeks there. Thankfully, Kasem still wore his switchblade—old habits.

14

He placed his right hand on her face and traced it to her collarbone, "Follow me around to the back. I stashed a baseball bat and a Beretta in the storage box out there when I first arrived." He motioned down the lane and toward the left with two fingers. The houses on their side of the street were nested tightly together, but there were a few access points to the garbage lane that ran behind the houses.

They ducked into the shadows on the side of the street and moved toward the end of the lane. When they reached the end, they turned into a narrow alley that led to the back of the houses. From there they squeezed through the garbage lane toward the back of their house. Petra shivered. The rain had soaked through her dress and the drops stung her eyes as the wind blew them into her face. She kept her gaze focused on Kasem's feet, grateful that his tall form blocked at least some of the wind and the rain. The lights from the houses helped them navigate their way. Every few steps, she counted the number of houses that they had passed. They were staying in the sixteenth house.

Fourteen, fifteen, sixteen. "This one," Petra squeezed Kasem's arm. He nodded, and they took position on opposite sides of the doorway.

Petra pressed her ear to the door. After a few seconds, she shook her head, "I think we're clear, but it could just be sound insulation. I can't make anything out."

Kasem reached down into the shadows on his side of the door and handed her the cold wet grip of a Beretta. She squinted and saw the metallic glint of the baseball bat in his right hand with the switchblade now in his left.

Petra holstered the gun into the belt around her dress, then pulled out her keys and quietly placed her purse on the pavement. She moved slowly to place the key in the lock and prayed that it would be quiet. The lock made a soft clicking noise as she opened the door. With her gun in hand, she leaned sideways to check the hallway. "Clear," she whispered and motioned for Kasem to follow her.

They crept into the house. Kasem shut the door behind them and they moved down the hallway, past the laundry room and the separated shower and bathrooms. The hallway divided after that— left toward the living room, which led to the upstairs staircase, and right toward the kitchen from which you could access the stairway down to the cellar and the second bathroom.

Petra gestured with the gun that she would go left toward the living room. With a nod to the right, she signaled for Kasem to check the kitchen and the cellar.

Chapter 4

Kyoto, Japan

Kasem squinted as he stole past the kitchen. A quick glance at the knife rack showed him that none of the knives were missing, but as he got closer to the staircase leading down to the cellar he stiffened. The stairwell light was off, but he could see the glow of the cellar light at the bottom. He listened in silence and waited at the top of stairs just out of sight. The person in the cellar would have to come upstairs eventually, and he would be there waiting. He knelt slowly and placed the baseball bat on the floor, in the space between the first cabinet and the stairwell wall, careful not to let it roll and make a sound on the ceramic tiles. He wanted the bat to be nearby and available if he needed it, but he preferred to disarm and capture the intruder rather than beat him up—hence the switchblade would be the better weapon for the job.

His patience was rewarded when he heard the bottom step creak and he broke into a sinister smile. *I have you now,* he thought, grateful that the staircase was noisy enough to give him a clear gauge on when the intruder would be upon him. There were fifteen steps down to the cellar—he had counted them when he first moved in—*nine, ten...* He raised his left elbow and readied the switchblade across his body. *Thirteen, fourteen, fifteen.*

As soon as he counted the fifteenth step, he slashed out beyond the stairwell wall with his right forearm, catching his target squarely in the throat. The intruder stumbled and Kasem kicked his knee upward into the man's abdomen. When he doubled over, Kasem grabbed his wrist and twisted it downward to propel the intruder's torso toward the floor. He pushed his right knee into the intruder's back and straddled him, holding the switchblade up to the intruder's throat.

"You better sing like a canary, buddy. Who are you and what are you doing here?"

Chapter 5

Kyoto, Japan

Petra slinked to the side and flattened against the wall leading toward the living room as Kasem disappeared toward the kitchen. She shifted her two-hand grip on the Beretta to get a better feel for the weapon. It was heavier than her Colt pistol, so it would have a larger recoil. She inched her way along and watched the shadows on the other side of the wall, both to make sure that she wasn't giving away her position, and to see if she could spot any sign of an assailant in the living room. Before stepping into the room, she stood still and listened. *No noise at all? Did they see us coming?* She frowned and strode into the room with the gun out and ready, only to find it empty. She moved through it quickly and up the stairs.

When she reached the top of the staircase, she glanced into their bedroom. Everything seemed in order. Even the tatami mats under their mattresses looked as if they were in exactly the same place. *Could they already be gone?* Petra moved to check the other two bedrooms. She slid open the door to the first one and found everything in order before moving on to the second. When she tried to open the door, she found it slightly off its sliding track. *Someone's been up here.* She inched the door a crack to check for any light, but the room was dark. Petra held her breath as she pulled the door open far enough to step inside. She could see a lumpy form under the blankets on the floor mattress. *Sleeping? Seriously?* She moved closer and placed the gun against the back of the person's head. "Who the hell are you and what are you doing here?"

The figure stirred, "Jesus, Petra. It's just me."

Petra let out a long exhale as she recognized his voice and lowered her gun. "Carlos? What are you doing here?"

Before he could answer, they heard a loud thud downstairs. "Don't worry, that's just Nathan," Carlos said.

"You came here with someone else?" Petra turned and sped toward the kitchen. "Kasem, it's Carlos," she called out.

When she made it to the kitchen, she hit the light switch to find Kasem holding his knife to the throat of a young blond guy. "It's okay. He's with Carlos."

17

Kasem lowered his knife and stepped away. "Sorry, man." He retracted the blade with a sheepish expression.

"I'll live."

Petra turned her head as Carlos bumped into her. "Hey, guys, this is Nathan. He's a friend of mine. Nathan, this is Petra and Kasem," he said in a groggy voice. "Sorry about the intro. What can I say? I was jet-lagged," he shrugged and turned his palms upward. "It's good to see you guys."

Petra rolled her eyes, "Let's go talk in the living room. Four people jammed into this galley kitchen is a bit much. But first, Kasem and I need to change out of these wet clothes."

Chapter 6

Kyoto, Japan

Carlos grabbed a seat at the edge of the living room couch to wait for Petra and Kasem to return. Nathan joined him on the other end of the couch. When Petra reappeared in dry clothing, she dragged the loveseat from the corner of the room and positioned it across from them as Nathan's expression changed from dazed to wide-eyed. Carlos stifled his amusement—Nathan had barely spoken to her, but he was staring at her like a doting puppy. She was pretending not to notice, keeping her gaze firmly on the carpet with her arms crossed. They sat in silence until a freshly dressed Kasem squeezed onto the loveseat next to her.

Carlos watched each of them and took a deep breath, "I'm sorry to show up here like this. I couldn't risk tipping anybody off, so I decided not to call first."

Petra raised her eyebrows, "Calling would tip someone off, but flying to Kyoto wouldn't? What's going on, Carlos? When I told you where we were, I thought we agreed that it would be emergency-only contact."

"I'm here because I need your help. I'm here to ask, anyway."

Kasem crossed his arms, "You've helped us out of more than a few jams. I'm sure we can help you."

"Maybe, but this has to be your decision. It's not really about the greater good. Well, maybe it is, but this is different. It isn't about some big terrorist attack or threat that's coming up. It's about an arms dealer. A bad guy who's got his hands in all sorts of shady government business, but we've never been able to tie him to any of the arms deals."

"How did you get involved with this? Aren't you out?" Petra frowned.

"I am. This isn't Agency. It's personal," Carlos blinked twice. "I could really use a drink. You got anything?"

"Babe, could you get a bottle of wine from the cellar?" Petra asked.

Kasem nodded and disappeared into the hallway.

Petra turned back toward Carlos, "Do you want to keep going?"

"Nah, let's wait."

19

After Kasem returned and poured glasses for each of them, Carlos raised his glass. "To old friends. Thanks for hearing me out." He took a long sip and placed the glass on the coffee table. "Back when I was still with the Agency, I went undercover with an organization run by this guy Nguyen—the arms dealer I was talking about—"

"You mean *Duc Nguyen?* The big-time investor?" Kasem interrupted.

"Well, he does that too, but his private equity investments are a front, with a few legitimate ones in the mix. Sketchy acquisitions—not illegal, but they put a lot of people out of work. He's no Buffett, that's for sure. Anyway, I went undercover to get enough evidence to bring him down, but the op went sour and the Agency pulled me out. I vowed that I'd take him down, but I never found a way to do it. Until I met Nathan over here." Carlos took another gulp from the wine glass. "Want to introduce yourself, Nate?"

"Sure, okay. I'm Nathan Goodspeed. I work in anti-terrorist tech."

The nervous stammer in his voice made an amused look pass across Petra's face, "It's nice to meet you, Nathan."

Nathan blushed red under Petra's gaze and he continued in a shaky voice, "Thanks. I'm an accountant, a forensic accountant, that is. I worked in tech ops at the CIA. My team tried to look into Nguyen a few times, but, well, one of the higher-ups always squashed it. I don't know who, but someone kept redirecting us. My team leader, Rachel, was frustrated and sure that Nguyen had someone on the inside at the Company, so we hid some of the intel. We tried all sorts of hacks, but we figured out that the only way we could nail Nguyen was through direct intel. We managed to get an asset on the inside, one of the assistants in his private equity firm. She's been a great source—given us locations of his investments, his travel details, recordings of a few incriminating conversations, along with any records that she's been able to access, but so far, it's not enough. Nguyen doesn't keep electronic records of his deals, but every real transaction is recorded in code in a ledger that he keeps. After that, they aggregate the transactions into legit sums and record it on the electronic books."

"How did you find Carlos?" Petra asked.

"We had Agency records of who had worked on the Nguyen case, and Rachel and I eventually put the pieces together to figure out who it was. That's when I reached out to Carlos a few weeks ago."

Kasem exhaled loudly, "I don't understand. What's changed?"

"There may be a window of opportunity to get to the ledger and take Nguyen down," Carlos said as he polished off his wine and poured himself another glass.

"Exactly," Nathan piped up. "Nguyen is looking for a new finance guy to join his team at the private equity firm. We won't get this opportunity again. We could put someone in his inner orbit."

"The last time we had someone that close was when I was undercover," Carlos added.

"So, you need a finance guy," Kasem said. "What about the asset that you already have?"

"She doesn't have enough access—she's a great asset and her testimony will help put Nguyen away, but like Nathan said, it's not enough," Carlos shook his head. "I need a team. I don't have Agency resources, but Rachel's pulled a few strings to get us some Company budget."

"What's your plan exactly?" Petra asked. "You want Kasem to pose as this finance guy?"

"Yes, but it's more than that. Getting into Nguyen's inner circle isn't just about installing Kasem with his CV. He has to look the part of a suave, privileged kid who's hungry for more. Someone who has contacts that might be worth Nguyen's while."

Petra pursed her lips, "Why the five-man team?"

"Nathan's our tech guy," Carlos answered, "and the forensic accountant to decode the ledger once we have it. Kasem goes in as the finance guy. He'll have some time to develop access. The time to strike, though, is at Nguyen's daughter's engagement party in London. You'll be there with Kasem as our front team. Nathan handles security and Rachel goes in for the ledger. I'll play point from the background and support, if needed."

Kasem leaned in, "When's the engagement party?"

"We've got two months to get you established in their circle and make sure that we have the access we need." Carlos sighed, "Look, I can't make you guys do this. You've got a pretty good setup here, and I know it took time to get to that." He watched and waited as Petra and Kasem exchanged glances.

Kasem stood with a grim expression on his face. "I think the rain's stopped, so I'm going to go for a walk. Clear my head."

Petra looked at him and nodded, "I'll join you in a bit, okay?"

"Sure," he said as he walked out the front door.

Chapter 7

Kyoto, Japan

Petra turned to Carlos, "Don't worry about Kasem. He just needs some time to process. We both do. But I thought I knew all about your Agency history—you never told me about an op with Nguyen."

"You were away on assignment when it happened. When you got back, I guess it was easier to talk about other stuff—lighter stuff."

Nathan squirmed in his seat at the edge of the couch, "I'm going to give the two of you some time to sort this whole thing out. Petra, would you mind if I—if I lie down upstairs? I'm pretty beat from the plane ride."

"Of course," she answered. "Just grab one of the spare rooms upstairs." Her eyes darted to Carlos, "You can take the one that Carlos didn't sleep in. I can't say much for amenities, but the bed's made. Bathroom's down the hall on this floor."

"That's mighty kind of you," Nathan said and disappeared up the stairs.

Petra waited until he was out of earshot, "How are you doing, Carlos? I'm surprised. I didn't think the Agency would be able to reel you in again."

Carlos shook his head, "They're not involved. We could use the resources, but I'd rather not see McLaughry's face again so soon."

"I thought you guys were good after what happened in D.C.," she said with a smile.

"We put a good face on it, but it is definitely not all resolved."

Petra's smile wided, "As if it ever could be with the Agency. I'm glad this isn't an Agency op. It inspires a little more confidence."

"True that."

"True that?" She looked at him with raised eyebrows, "Who are you and what have you done with my old mentor?"

"Very funny." Carlos shrugged.

"How's Diane?"

"She's good. Just running around with her charity work. She's the new communications lead for three different animal shelters in our area. It keeps her busy."

"Does she know you're here?" Petra asked.

"She knows sort of a high-level summary. That I'm working on something to do with my old job, and that I can't turn my back on this one."

"Right," Petra swirled the wine in her glass and looked up. "Carlos, what you tell Diane is your business, but you shouldn't keep secrets from her. Lord knows we've lost enough to this business."

"That sounds like loaded advice."

"I guess so," Petra paused. *There's something he's not telling me.* "I know there's more. How about you save us both a lot of trouble and tell me the rest? You know I'll figure it out eventually and be really mad at you for not telling me in the first place."

He heaved a long sigh, "Kiddo, you're not going to like it."

"It'd still be better to hear it from you now."

"Nguyen killed a friend of mine, Vik, another agent who was undercover with me."

"So, that's why you're so hell-bent to take him down." *Vik?* She had known a Vik, or rather a Vikram, at the Agency once—known him really well, in fact. *It couldn't be...* Petra took a deep breath and nodded again, "Of course, we'll help you. I mean, I have to talk to Kasem, but what are friends for?"

"It's not just that. I think it was my fault."

She frowned, "What do you mean?"

"We had intel that Nguyen knew there was someone selling him out. Vik wanted to pull the op, said that we'd figure out another way, but I convinced him not to. I was so naive. I should have listened to him. We stayed under because we were hoping to access the ledger after we got back from the docks that night. I even made up this ridiculous plan about getting Nguyen drunk at the hotel bar so that his room would be empty, and we could send someone in to grab the ledger." Carlos blinked and looked away. "But one of Nguyen's guys killed Vik on the docks. We never even made it to the hotel."

"I'm so sorry." *So, this is about revenge.*

"That's why I have to do this. That's why I have to nail this guy to the wall, Petra. And it's not just about Vik. This is about justice." Carlos slid out a laptop bag from underneath the couch and removed a tablet device. He tapped the screen and slid it across to her.

Petra's throat constricted as she thumbed through the series of photos. The first one showed a giant red-orange flame cloud on a country hillside. The next three photos were of burn victims, some on stretchers being carried by emergency medical crews and others lying dead on the side of the road. The last photo almost made her sick to her stomach. It showed a child of six or seven being carried off a soccer field. The burns had ripped the flesh from one of his legs and the skin on his cheeks had been replaced by a cluster of pink blisters intermixed with blood vessels. "My God. Nguyen sold the arms that did this?"

"He sold them to the Iraqi government, who unleashed this hell on a Kurdish village in the north."

"We have to take him down." A shudder passed through Petra's spine as she set the tablet on the table. The Vikram that she had known was a specialist in advanced weaponry. *It can't be him.* "The agent that Nguyen killed. Vik? Did I ever meet him?" she fought to keep her voice steady.

Carlos frowned for a second, "I'm not sure. You joined the Agency around the time we went undercover. We called him Vik in the field, but his name was Vikram Jennings. I'm sure you'd remember him if you met him—half-Indian, half-English by blood, but grew up in Durban. Big guy with a booming South African accent."

Petra blinked twice and steeled her reaction as a memory flashed through her head. *Vikram Jennings?* She did indeed remember him—in fact, she thought of him often, certainly more than she should, given her relationship with Kasem. The Drake Hotel in Chicago. The nights before Vikram had gone into deep cover. She had thought of them just that morning, in the shower. They only had a few days together, and they had both known there would never be any real possibilities for a relationship. It was a fleeting moment before she'd met Kasem for the second time in London, but her heart beat faster every time she recalled how much passion and abandon they had had for each other.

Petra swallowed the last few drops of wine in her glass. "Actually, I did meet him while I was in training. He conducted a presentation on investigative ops. I didn't know he was dead." Learning that Vikram was dead brought on an onslaught of memories and she fought to slow her breathing. Walking along the river in Chicago huddled against the wind. Dinner at a hole-in-the-wall taco joint off Lincoln Square. The two bottles of fifty-dollar champagne they had splurged on to drink back in his hotel room.

Carlos tilted his head, "Seems like maybe you knew him better than you're letting on, kiddo."

"I hate that you can read me like that."

"I recruited you, what do you expect? Besides, you've got to give an old fogie like me some credit."

"You're right—we spent a few days together," Petra kept her gaze fixed on the floor. "It must have been right before he left on that op. He only told me that he was going under for a while." She bit her lip, "It's not like we thought that we had a future together, but it just, I just...I can't believe he's gone."

"It's always a shock to hear that about someone you knew, let alone someone you...had that kind of relationship with. He told me about you once."

"He did?"

"Well, I'm guessing it was you. He said there was someone he'd met, that he was really excited about, but he had to cut it off because of the op," Carlos answered with a shrug. "Are you going to tell Kasem about him?"

"I don't know. I guess I have to tell him. It wouldn't be right to keep it from him." She hesitated, "Did you ever figure out what went wrong? How you and Vik were compromised?"

"Not for sure. I traced the leak back to a former Agency asset. Name's Gibran Obaidi. He worked in the arms business. The Agency paid him off, tried to flip him. He brought in intel for a while, but my guess is that Nguyen offered him a whole lot more money."

"Gibran Obaidi?" Petra repeated the name slowly and steeled her expression again.

"Yeah. You heard of him?"

"I don't think so." She fought to keep her expression clear. She really didn't want Carlos to realize she recognized that name. He was an asset she had worked with in Iran, one of the assets that she had paid in her service for the Agency. "You're sure that's who it was? That this was all an Agency op gone wrong?"

"There's no other way Nguyen could have found out that he had a mole."

"But how would a completely separate Agency asset know about your operation?"

"He shouldn't have," Carlos answered. "But after the op went sideways, I went on a crazy spell. That's how I tracked the leak to Obaidi."

"Did you ever find him?"

Carlos shook his head, "He's lucky I didn't."

"What about his handler at the Agency? Did you ever find out who ran him?" Petra blinked. *This is my fault.* The realization struck her to the core. After Kasem's capture in Tehran, she had asked her handler Alex to bring in all of her assets, so they wouldn't be compromised. She had been working with Obaidi at arm's length for a few months at the time. Even though she had never fully trusted him, she still had wanted him out of harm's way. *I brought him into the Agency.* The image of Vikram's face flashed in front of her. *I did this—I'm the reason Vik's dead. I'm so sorry,* she wanted to say to him.

It was too close to be a coincidence. How else could Obaidi have found out about an Agency op? Alex must have assigned Obaidi to someone else to keep running him, and somehow, he found out about Carlos' operation. That was the only way he could have known there was an Agency operative undercover in Nguyen's outfit. That knowledge had gotten Vikram killed. Knowledge Obaidi would never have had if her operations in Iran hadn't come unraveled.

"I never figured out who ran him," Carlos said with a shrug. "In a way, I don't want to know. It doesn't really matter. Obviously, they didn't do this on purpose." He frowned, "You okay? How are you guys doing—you and Kasem?"

"The past few months have been great. We're having a lot of fun together, just being a couple—"

"Now, now, leave out all that dirty stuff—remember, you're like my little sister. I don't want to hear about that," he shuddered.

"Well, you know, the sex has been great." Petra snickered at the pained expression on her mentor's face. "I was going to say that we're good together. Kasem's sweet and funny. Kyoto's quirky with so much personality. Small enough to feel sheltered from the weight of the world, at least in this neighborhood."

"It's a nice town. I'm glad I encouraged you to come here. If I hadn't, Kasem would still be hiding out here on his own. Besides, what would I do now?"

Petra resisted the urge to roll her eyes at him. "Very funny. But yes, you were right. Joining Kasem here was definitely the right move." She pulled her feet up onto the loveseat.

"I'm detecting a 'but'..."

"I don't know," she let out another sigh. "He wants to move forward, to go back into the real world, maybe even get married, but I don't know if I'm ready. We live in this bubble here, where we don't have to really think about who we were before or what we've done."

"That's a load of crap. If you weren't thinking about who you were before, I don't think you would have been in touch at all. But you were, even if you didn't give me much info on what was going on here."

"You could be right."

"Come on, Petra. Didn't your last e-mail say you'd been in contact with that school in Paris? That you were thinking about starting to teach again?"

She opened her mouth and shut it again, "You're right. I guess I've always had one foot back in my old life."

"So why not test it out with Kasem? What are you so afraid of?"

Petra considered how to respond, "What if our relationship can't survive out there? He did so many terrible things when he was in Iran, and I caused him so much pain. I don't know. Maybe I haven't forgiven him? Or forgiven myself? It's not that easy to let all of that go, I guess."

"Someday I hope you will. You can't just forget about everything that happened, but you don't have to forget to forgive him, or to forgive yourself. He's not that person anymore, and neither are you."

"Maybe."

Carlos stood up and clapped his hand on her shoulder, "You're going to be fine, kiddo. Both of you. Now, let's get some more wine going. I haven't seen you in almost a year, and I want to hear all about what you've been up to."

"Can I get a rain check on that? Kasem just texted that he's at a bar down the street. I should go talk to him."

Chapter 8

Kyoto, Japan

Kasem ordered another half-bottle *tokkuri* of cheap, hot sake while he waited for Petra to join him at a bar a few blocks away from their house. He stared at the wall in front of him and pondered what Carlos had said. *Nguyen.* There was a faint memory buried deep in his mind. A conversation that he'd overheard back in Iran when he was working as the Ahriman. He hadn't paid much attention at the time, but the revelation that Duc Nguyen was an arms dealer had brought it to the surface.

When the bartender poured the small *ochoko* cup for him, Kasem gulped it down immediately. The warm liquid passed through him and he felt his body heat up from the inside.

He was on his last cup when Petra came into the bar. She planted a kiss on his cheek and sat down on the barstool next to him, "Is there more of that?"

"You can have the rest," Kasem slid the almost full cup over to her. He waited for her to take a sip before he placed his hand on her knee, "How are you doing?"

"I should ask you that."

"I don't know," he gave her a half-smile. "You want to do this, don't you?"

Petra sighed. "I think we should, but I can't force you. I can't keep asking you to help me deal with my ghosts from the Agency. It's not fair to you."

"Thanks for saying that, but I have a few ghosts of my own that could use some attention."

"What do you mean?"

"You know what I'm talking about. Everything that I did. Maybe putting away this creep would help with that."

"Maybe." Petra gestured toward the bartender to order another sake, "Still, you don't have to do this. This isn't about repaying some debt to society."

"It might be." Kasem gathered his resolve, "There's something I have to tell you."

******

The rain had stopped, and twilight had fallen outside when they left the bar. The streets in the mostly residential neighborhood were quiet as they walked along. Kasem took Petra's hand and they strolled in silence through the lamppost shadows. The city seemed so peaceful with the brownish tint of twilight across the homes. He took in the silence until they reached the main road along the Kamo River. In contrast to the canal path that they had walked earlier in the day, the Keihan Main Line road featured the sound of cars speeding past intermingled with the flow of the river.

"The water level's up today," Petra leaned against the guardrail to look over at the river. "I guess it rained a lot."

Kasem ignored the temptation to stick to small talk. "There's something I remembered. About Nguyen."

"You knew him?"

"Not directly. I think I remember his name, though. I hadn't thought about it in so long," he sighed. "When I was working for General Majed, I ran an op to spy on a group of Kurdish rebels in the north."

"Okay."

"All I could think about was getting Majed to trust me long enough to find a way out. I wanted a mission outside of Iran that I could use as a ruse to get away. It didn't matter what I was doing, or who I did it to, I just followed orders."

Petra nodded slowly, "And your orders were to kill them?"

"Yes. I shot them in cold blood—all of them, twelve men, no arrest, no trial, nothing."

Kasem watched Petra look away briefly before she turned her gaze back toward him, "I know you did some terrible things, Kasem. Any reason you're telling me about this now?"

"After I took care of the leaders, General Majed sent a small infantry to Kurdistan to execute each of their families. Women, children, everyone." His voice caught in his throat, "I wasn't on that mission. I was training with Lieutenant Afshar, but it's not like I was blind. I knew what was going on." Kasem drew in a breath and met her eyes, "I think the weaponry they used was supplied by Nguyen."

"Nguyen sold arms to General Majed?" Petra's posture changed, and a pained look crossed her face.

"I don't know for sure, but I think he might have. So, you're right, maybe this is about repaying my debts. Another chance at redemption? I mean, face it, you haven't really forgiven me, and I have a long way to go before I can ever forgive myself."

Petra bit her lip, "I have forgiven you. That's not what this is about—"

Kasem blinked—he had to hope that she was telling the truth, he clung to that belief, but he wasn't sure. *How could she forgive me?* He leaned in, "It's okay, babe. You don't have to pretend that the past is all in the past. It's too much of a fairy tale. I can't expect that of you, no matter how much I want to." Their lips met in a kiss.

"I mean it, though. I don't care who you were. I care about who you are now."

"That means more to me than you can imagine," he placed both of his hands on her shoulders. "But I'm trying to tell you that I agree with you. I think we should do this. That has to be who I am now. Those people deserve justice." He paused, "Do you think we could use Nguyen to find General Majed?"

"I don't know."

Kasem pushed aside his need for vengeance against General Majed, "Maybe we can't get to Majed, but perhaps we can cut off his supply."

"Are you sure this is what you want?"

"I'm sure. Besides, I know you want to say yes. It's not like we can leave Carlos in a lurch. He's done so much for both of us. We certainly wouldn't be here together without him." He brushed her hair out of her face with his fingers. "I don't know if I have to be on some endless path to redemption, but even the slightest chance that Nguyen supplied Majed with those weapons means that I can't walk away from this. I need to do it."

Chapter 9

Kyoto, Japan

Petra and Kasem returned to the house as twilight dwindled into darkness. The night seemed peaceful and tranquil, as if the rain had washed away any turmoil in the air. They walked into the house and deposited their shoes in the hallway.

"Hey, Carlos," she called out to him, but he had dozed off on the sofa. "No shoes on the couch." Petra shook his shoulder gently. "Wakey, wakey, Sleeping Beauty."

Carlos grumbled and sat up. "We'll see how you like that when *you're* jet-lagged."

Kasem pushed at Carlos' feet to grab a spot on the other end of the couch.

"You can get your revenge on me in a few days," Petra chuckled. "We picked up a couple of bottles of wine and sake. You've got some catching up to do."

"You went drinking without me, and now you're waking me up?" Carlos stretched out with a foggy expression on his face. "How about something to eat? I can't drink much more on an empty stomach."

"Have some wasabi peanuts," Kasem tossed him a bag from the side table. "They're pretty good."

"I'd eat them even if they were stale." Carlos shoved a handful into his mouth. "Not bad," he said as he devoured his second mouthful.

"Easy tiger," Petra refilled their wine glasses and raised hers. "To getting the old team together."

Carlos perked up, "Does that mean you guys are in?"

Petra exchanged a glance with Kasem and nodded, "We're in. Cheers," she said as they clinked glasses.

"To both of you," Carlos added. "Interrupting your romantic getaway to bail out a buddy in need."

"You better be careful reminding us about what we're giving up here. We might change our minds," Kasem said with a grin. "I will need to go over that plan again, though."

"It's simple. I'll get us a charter and we'll head to London in a couple of days. You go under with Nguyen, bond with him and his son. Drink, golf, play squash, whatever you boring finance guys do for fun. You use the connection to get invited to the engagement party, take Petra along as your adoring wife, and she'll make nice with the bride-to-be. That's how you get us access and we'll make our move. Nathan will handle security while Rachel and I go in for the ledger."

Kasem nodded. "Why the engagement party? Just because it's a distraction?"

"Based on Nathan's intel from Madison, the assistant we have inside, Nguyen most likely keeps the ledger somewhere in his country house, Hill Hearst. The party is the perfect opportunity for us to get in there. There's also chatter that Nguyen's expecting a big deal to close after the wedding, which probably means that's when his next big shipment is coming. That's a few weeks after the party, so if we can get to the ledger, we can stop that sale from happening."

"You're sure that the ledger will be enough to put him away?" Kasem asked.

"We need the triple threat—the decoded ledger, Madison's testimony, and the arms themselves. Madison's working on getting us a few leads for storage units he uses in London, so provided that they pan out, once Nathan decodes the ledger, we'll have the evidence we need to shut him down," Carlos answered.

"Right," Kasem pursed his lips and took a sip of his wine.

Petra could tell that Kasem was skeptical. *He's probably right.* Carlos' plan seemed fine, but she sensed that many of the details had to be fleshed out. She didn't know enough about Nguyen or his operations to help refine the plan yet, and they probably wouldn't know most of those details without direct intel from Kasem once he was on the inside.

The thought of Kasem going undercover again scared her. The last time he had helped them, he'd been kidnapped and almost killed. *But it's for Vikram.* She imagined the touch of his hand on her leg and her face flushed. *And all of those children,* she reminded herself. She swallowed her doubts at the thought of the dead child in the picture. *Maybe there really is such a thing as the greater good?* She forced a smile. It wasn't the time to dive into the demons arising from her work for the Agency. "May I just say how glad I am that this is not an Agency op?" she raised her glass once again.

"Hell, yes. We don't have to deal with protocol or all that bureaucratic mumbo jumbo," Carlos agreed. "I've had my fill of that for two lifetimes."

Kasem glanced at both of them, "I can't say I have much to add here."

"That's true, buddy, but I'll tell you one thing that you'll really like. Since this isn't an Agency op, we've got no chance of running into one of Petra's ex-boyfriends," Carlos chortled.

"Carlos!" Petra exclaimed. "What the hell?" *Shut up, damn it.*

"Now, I never met Pepe le Pew—the French guy—but if I never see that blubbering Grant again, it'll be too soon," Carlos shook his head. "That guy's got a few screws loose and he sticks to me like I'm his best bud in the world. Petra, I can't believe you ever dated him. I know I'm just your mentor and I'm supposed to mind my own business, but you need to steer clear of idiots like that—"

"That's enough," Petra interrupted in an icy tone. She grabbed his now empty wine glass before he could refill it. "It's time for bed. Go on. Get upstairs."

She left Kasem on the couch and ushered Carlos upstairs to the room where she'd found him asleep earlier. Once he had crawled under the covers, she handed him a bottle of water. "Drink this. It'll help with the hangover."

"I don't get hungover. I just need something to eat. Don't worry, I'll be fine, kiddo."

"*Old man,* you are lying to yourself. I know you too well. Your filter's gone. That means it's too late for food. The only thing that'll help is sleep and maybe some water. Besides, you're on time-out for bringing up my ex-boyfriends." She chuckled, "When did you become such a lightweight? You used to be able to drink me under the table, and with tequila."

Carlos grunted and turned over.

"Good night, old man. See you in the morning," Petra said.

She made her way back downstairs toward the living room where she took a seat on the floor across the coffee table from Kasem. "How are you doing?" she asked.

"I'll be all right. You?"

"I don't know. It doesn't feel real. I feel like I'm supposed to wake up any minute."

Kasem picked up her hand and planted a kiss on it. "I love you." He pulled her arm gently and she stood to join him on the couch.

"I love you, too."

A loud crack of thunder sounded, and she glanced out the window, "Looks like the storm's back." She watched as a bright streak of lightning lit up the dark sky. "Let's drink some more wine and watch a movie. This might be our last quiet night for a while."

33

Chapter 10

Osaka, Japan

Rachel Fleming stood on the windowsill of the Abeno Harukas building and faced the ground. The street below was littered with the lights of passing cars and pedestrians, which created a staccato noise pattern that penetrated the air even at her position on the fifty-ninth floor. Landing among the cacophony below was her chance at sanctuary. Without it, her whole plan would go sideways. She had to let go of everything behind her to take the next step.

However, her right hand refused to loosen its grip on the central bar of the window frame. She bit her lip and stared at one hand, then the other, willing her right hand to move. The commotion inside the building was moving toward her. Based on her training, she'd been taught that some of the noise had to be from her own psyche—generated by the adrenaline pulsing through her body. She took a deep breath and dissected the sound. At least part of it was from people. People approaching from the inside. People who would capture her. People who would ruin everything.

She stared down at her left hand once again. It was pressed against the side of the window frame. With another breath, she willed it to guide her forward.

Ten seconds. She had learned that trick at training. Counting down to help push her mind to comply.

Her head spun around at the sound of breaking glass in the room behind her. One of the security guards that she had snuck past had found her—she'd stolen his ID, so he'd had to break through the glass pane on the door. *Crap.* He must have seen the log that his card had been used to access the room. *They're coming.* She compelled herself to move, it would be only a few moments before he realized that she was on the windowsill.

Ten, nine. Rachel released two of the fingers of her right hand.

"Get down from there," a voice behind her cried out in Japanese.

She looked back again and saw that the guard had been joined by a man dressed in black, who she guessed was the ranking security officer on duty that night. Reacting on instinct, Rachel grabbed her tranq gun and dealt two shots, catching each of them in the neck through the open window. She watched them collapse to the ground and steadied herself against the window frame, then placed the gun back in her holster. *Back to the countdown.* She had to move quickly now, there was a chance they had already radioed for backup. *It's now or never.*

Eight, seven, six. She released her fingers so that she stood on the ledge with only the support of her left hand.

Five, four. With a grimace, she slid her left hand forward to the corner of the window frame.

Three, two. She redirected her eyes away from the street below, as her body remained on the ledge, unsteady and unstable.

One. She gritted her teeth and leaped forward into the abyss.

******

The ground rushed toward her as she fell. The air flew past her, but the ground was so close. Too close. *So different from skydiving.* It felt like nothing she had ever experienced. A memory flashed through her mind of the cartoons that she had watched as a child, where the characters paused to look down before they realized that they were falling. If only that were possible.

She wanted to scream as she watched the windows of the building pass by her, but instead, she reacted on instinct, as her training had dictated.

Rachel scrambled for her release cord. Half a second later, her body jerked upward when her parachute opened. The movement felt as if it were pulling her from a trance. The greenish-blue hues of the fabric spread out above and she steadied her breathing. The street below was still approaching, but at a much slower pace.

She squinted through the streetlights and steered herself toward the sidewalk, careful to avoid the covered bus stops. *This is going to hurt.* Rachel braced for impact as her feet hit the concrete. She landed in a fast jog and tapped the release button on her chute once again. The chute released behind her in a tangled web of straps. The chute release triggered a mechanism that caused it to contract automatically into a ball and roll up to the side. She picked up the balled-up chute, glad that there were only a few people on the street at three in the morning to watch in amazement. They were taking pictures with their smartphones, but she knew they wouldn't get much with the distance and the shadows of the streetlights.

Rachel maneuvered past the bus stops as if nothing had happened. When she reached the front of the Tennoji Miyako Hotel, she grabbed a cab from the line in front of it. "Airport, please," she said to the driver in accented Japanese. She had a plane to catch before the security personnel at the Sharp Corporation realized what she had taken.

Chapter 11

Osaka, Japan

Petra felt all of her muscles relax as she stretched out in her seat on the charter flight at the Osaka airport. The car ride from Kyoto had been cramped and she welcomed the contrast. She took in the layout with twelve leather seats spread out through the length of the plane. The seat was more comfortable than the first class one she'd enjoyed once after being upgraded on Singapore Airlines. "This is as big as the loveseat in our living room," she said to Kasem with a chuckle.

He nodded, "It's nice."

Petra's brow furrowed, but she kept her thoughts to herself as he sat down next to her. He'd committed to their decision, but he'd been on edge since Carlos' arrival. She tilted her head to the side and nudged him with her elbow. "I know this must feel like falling off the wagon, but let's try to enjoy the easier moments. We'll have plenty of tough ones to deal with in the next few weeks."

"Sure." Kasem pulled out his headphones, "I'm going to zone out for a bit. I'm fine, don't worry."

Petra sighed. Whenever he acted like this, there wasn't much that she could do. He had to process his emotions and he would share when he was ready. It couldn't be easy on him that she had basically turned down his proposal, even though she had stopped him beforehand. She'd tried to talk to him about it, to reassure him that she just needed more time, but she hadn't been able to convince him—she hadn't even been able to convince herself. She crossed the center aisle to sit across from Carlos. "How's it going?" she asked in a low voice, so as not to wake Nathan who was napping in the seat next to him.

"Sorry about the wait. Rachel said that she'd meet us here. I'm not sure what the holdup is."

"No worries. How long have you worked with them?" she gestured toward Nathan.

"A few weeks. They both seem competent. Nate knows his stuff, both the tech and the accounting."

"I'm sure you're super-qualified for that assessment," she said with a grin. She raised her hand to stop his reply, "Sorry, I couldn't help it."

Carlos rolled his eyes and handed her his tablet, "You better study your file instead of mocking me. You need to be Cara Birch by the time we get to London."

"I'll be ready." Petra frowned as she scanned the interior of the plane. "Carlos, how are we bankrolling this? We don't have Agency resources. I know you said Rachel got us some Company budget, but this seems a bit extreme. Is the CIA really funding this?"

"Rachel made the arrangements. She pulled some strings to get us the funding."

"That's great." *But why would they do that?* Petra kept her skepticism to herself and picked up the tablet to skim through the details of her cover. As she looked through it, she jotted down several adjustments she wanted to make. "You already put the ID packages together?" she asked in surprise. "We should have talked about this."

"As if I would? I'm offended, Petra." His face broke into a smile. "Make as many changes as you like. Rachel will put them through after we land in London."

"Great. I'm sure Kasem will have some adjustments too."

"He looked at his last night after you went to bed, but, sure, there's still time to make adjustments."

Maybe that's why Kasem is so tense. Petra returned her attention to the screen while her concerns about Kasem percolated in the back of her mind. A few moments later, she noticed Carlos giving her an amused glance, "Out with it. What's so funny?"

"You've been hiding it well, but you're worried, aren't you?"

"I'm fine," her eyes wandered across the aisle. "It's Kasem. He's been on edge." Petra let out a long exhale. *Maybe we shouldn't be doing this.* She kept herself from saying anything to Carlos, but she could tell from his expression that he already knew what she was thinking.

"If you two aren't up for this, I'll understand," he said in a quiet voice. "It's a lot to ask."

"Come on. We're nervous, but of course we're going to help you."

"Well, I'm grateful. To both of you."

"No need." Petra set the tablet down on the empty seat next to her. "Anything to eat or drink on this flight?"

"Smooth, kiddo. Real smooth." Carlos nodded toward the front of the plane. "There's a galley up there on the right. Help yourself."

"There are sandwiches and some other stuff in the fridge," Nathan piped up. "Personally, I'd go for the fresh bread on the counter and the salami and cheese in the fridge. It's delicious, like having a picnic."

Carlos gave Nathan a bemused glance. "Good evening, sleepyhead. He's right, though—that stuff is delicious. Sorry, there's no service," he shrugged. "I told Rachel to skip the flight staff so that we could talk freely."

"Makes sense," Petra said with a nod.

"Would you like anything, Petra?" Nathan asked. He stood up looking disheveled, but eager to please, "I could make you something. I was going up to get something anyway."

"It's fine. I'll get it."

"Are you sure? I make a really good cappuccino."

She felt her face flush at his persistence, "Maybe some other time." He sat back down and she wandered over to the galley to make herself a cup of tea. When she returned to her seat, she picked up the operation plans and put them down with a sigh. *Maybe I'll doze off for a little while.*

******

Petra sensed someone hovering over her and opened her eyes.

Nathan beamed at her, "I made you that cappuccino. Hope you like it." He gave her a bashful smile and sat down across from her again.

"Thanks." She took a sip and looked over the aisle to where Kasem had passed out in his seat. "How long was I out? When's Rachel getting here?"

"Carlos got a message and said he had to go get her. That was fifteen or twenty minutes ago. I'm sure they'll be here any minute now."

Petra frowned, "How long have you worked with her?"

"With Rachel? Just over ten months. I think she's been with the Company for three or four years, though. I transferred to her team last summer."

"Were you doing tech ops before too?"

"I was more of a pure forensic accountant, but I wanted to get a little closer to the action." He shrugged, "I'm not a field agent, but tech work for field ops is a lot more interesting than just sitting at a desk, you know? At least this way I get to travel a bit."

"I've never met an accountant who wanted to work on field ops."

"I know. I'm a unique breed. Kicking assets and taking names."

A grin spread across Petra's face, "Nice. That's from *Parks and Rec*, right?"

"Yup. The best comedy on TV." He pretended to bow, "They call me Bond. Municipal Bond."

Petra was still chuckling when Carlos reappeared, followed by a tall woman with long blond hair.

"Petra, this is Rachel. Rachel, Petra," Carlos said.

"Hi, Rachel. It's nice to meet you." Petra shook her hand and tried to stop herself from staring. Their newest team member looked like a magazine swimsuit model, with her figure accentuated by a fitted black cat suit.

"One second." Rachel tapped on the intercom to signal the cockpit and called out, "Let's get this bird in the air pronto, before we run into any more delays." She turned her attention back to Petra, "Nice to meet you too. Sorry I got delayed. I had to pick up something important and it took longer than I expected."

"No worries." *Pick up something?* Petra observed Rachel's outfit again, the black cat suit with a small pack on her back. If she had to guess, Rachel had stolen something of value and they needed to get away before they were pursued. *Great.*

Rachel tilted her head and looked over the group, "Would you mind if we did an old team ritual of mine? I'm a little superstitious when it comes to new teams."

Petra exchanged glances with Carlos, "Sure. Why not? I'll wake Kasem."

"Great," Rachel disappeared into the galley.

Petra placed her hand on Kasem's shoulder and shook him gently, "Hey, babe. Wake up. Rachel's here."

His eyes fluttered open and he groaned, "Isn't it the middle of the night? Why do all of you look so chipper?"

"Don't worry. We'll pass out in a bit," Rachel emerged from the galley with a bottle of tequila and a stack of five shot glasses on a tray, along with a saltshaker and a sliced lime. She stepped on a lever next to one of the chairs to release a folded table from a floor compartment. They set up the table and she poured each of them a shot.

"I approve of this ritual," Carlos said. He picked up the saltshaker and scattered some salt on the plate with the limes. "Before you guys do this wrong, the traditional way is to salt the limes first. You take the lime into your mouth and the juice mixes with the tequila when you drink the shot."

"Oh captain, my captain," Nathan made a show of standing at attention.

Rachel followed Carlos' instruction and picked up a lime, "May we live in interesting times, and may we find what we're looking for." She raised her glass and the rest of the group followed suit.

Petra touched her glass to Rachel's and the group of them threw back their shots. The first thing she tasted was the lime, she cringed as the liquid burned its way down her throat.

Kasem set his glass down and whispered to her, "Isn't that toast actually a curse?"

Chapter 12

London, United Kingdom

Petra woke from a deep sleep two hours before the plane was scheduled to land at London Biggin Hill Airport, just within London's city limits. She stretched out and contemplated what to do to kill the remaining flight time. Carlos wasn't in his seat, but the rest of the team was still fast asleep in their flatbed seats. Her muscles felt tight and her head foggy—she could feel the oncoming jetlag.

She meandered toward the back of the plane and found Carlos seated in a lounge area with a movie screen set up in front of him.

"Hey, Carlos," she groaned.

"You look like a princess, kiddo," he said.

Petra rolled her eyes, "There's only one princess on board, and it certainly ain't me." Her eyes wandered back toward Rachel, "She even looks a model when she's sleeping. How does that happen?"

Carlos shrugged and motioned to his right, "There's a shower if you want to freshen up. When you're ready, come join me. We didn't get much one-on-one time in Kyoto."

Petra grabbed her handbag, "See you in a bit."

******

When she emerged from the bathroom, Carlos put the movie screen away and gave her a smile as she approached. "I think you've started to return from the dead." He motioned toward an armchair opposite him, "I've got a fresh pot of coffee." He poured two cups and handed one to her before settling into his previous position on the couch, "What's on your mind?"

Petra sipped her coffee, "The last time I was in London was for a small consulting project through a contact I met when I was teaching."

"I bet you could go back to teaching if you wanted."

"I do, but I already told you I don't know how Kasem fits with that life."

Carlos raised his eyebrows and she could tell that he thought her answer was a cop-out, but instead of pointing it out, he just asked, "Is this about his PTSD? Or yours?"

She shook her head, "I don't have many symptoms these days, but he does. He doesn't really sleep. I'm amazed at how he's been passed out this whole flight."

"Is he still seeing a counselor?"

"No. He doesn't have nightmares anymore, so I guess that's progress, but there's still a long way to go."

"It's not an easy thing to go through."

"I know," Petra said with a sigh.

Carlos leaned forward toward her, "Petra, what's the real problem? As long as he's not attacking you in his sleep, I think it'll be all right. With time. Just get him to see a counselor and keep up his therapy."

"Maybe."

"So, is it more than his PTSD? About all the bad things he did in Iran?"

"You don't know the half of it."

"You haven't forgiven him," Carlos sighed. "You have to let go of your ghosts. You can't have much of a future when all you can see is the past."

"You sound like a fortune cookie. It's not that easy. Sometimes I feel as if none of that past exists. That it's just us and who he is now, and everything's great. But sometimes, I worry the darkness is still lurking, like when he killed that Russian guy in DC."

"That guy tortured him and would have killed him in a heartbeat if the tables were turned. I don't know what I would have done in his shoes." Carlos took another sip of his coffee, "I'd like to think I would have stopped myself, but I don't know. Do you remember what I told you when I recruited you?"

"That your name was Anton?"

"Very funny. No, when you asked me if I'd ever killed anyone. I know there wasn't much else that I could have done, but I still think about the people I've killed. I still wonder if I could have done things differently."

Petra met his eyes, "But that was self-defense, wasn't it? Kasem had already escaped and overpowered Anatoli, but he still shot him in cold blood. We could have arrested him, we could have turned him, and he could have helped us pin the attack on the FSB."

"You're thinking too much like a spy. Kasem was just reacting—he'd been tortured, and he wasn't thinking about how we could turn Anatoli."

"I get your point, but he still pulled the trigger in cold blood. He wasn't in danger. I want to believe that he's changed, that he isn't the same person who did all those terrible things in Iran, but moments like that make me question it."

"Maybe, but that line gets blurry. My kills—they were self-defense, but I shouldn't have been there in the first place. I put myself in a dangerous spot, and I had to kill to get out of it."

"You were in danger though, and he wasn't." Petra turned her gaze to the floor, "Let's talk about something else. My head is too fuzzy for such a deep discussion."

"All right. Are you ready for this? You're crossing the threshold back into spy life."

"Oh, that's so much lighter," she grumbled. "This is temporary, a one-time op. Although we do keep getting pulled back into this life, don't we? Usually, it's my fault, but this time it's all you, old man."

"I'll do what I have to for Vik…and for justice, I guess. I'm just glad you're here. I don't know if I could do this without you. It's good to have someone here who I trust unconditionally."

"Back at you, cowboy." Petra refilled their coffee cups and raised hers. "To Agents Lockjaw and Puppy, back in the game," she said, using their old Agency nicknames. "Seriously, why can't we ever let this go? Is there always going to be some greater good that comes before what we want and our lives?" Her voice quavered, she had a sudden urge to strap on a parachute and storm the door. How could she return so readily when she already had given up so much? She locked eyes with Carlos, afraid that he was reading her mind.

"I don't know. Maybe we can't ever move on. Maybe that's what we signed up for when we joined. All I know is that I have to be here. I have to do this. This isn't about the Agency. This is about me. If we have a chance to get to Nguyen, there's nowhere I'd rather be."

"Even with all the risks?"

Carlos considered, then nodded, "Even with all the risks."

"I hope we can get him. He's managed to elude everyone for so long. He's got so many people on his side." Petra leaned forward with her hand on her chin.

"We can get him. If we're willing to do whatever it takes."

"And what's that? We could get caught. We could get killed."

"Do you think Vik thought about that when we were searching for the ledger? We have to do this. If you guys want out—at any time—it's okay, but I'm in this. I'm all in."

Petra blinked twice, "I've never heard you talk like this."

"I haven't felt like this in a long time." His jaw clenched, "I might have regrets about the men I killed, but if I had the chance to take Nguyen out, I would do it in a heartbeat. No hesitation."

"Because of Vik?"

"He died in front of me because I said we shouldn't abort the op. I'm done with the Agency, but I can't abandon his memory." Carlos grimaced and pulled up the pictures on his tablet that he had shown her in Kyoto, "Anyone who could do this—the world's better off if he's in the ground. I promised Vik."

Carlos watched as Petra's expression melted from concern to understanding, "Okay," she said. "What are you prepared to do?"

"Anything I have to." He hesitated, "You knew him too. Are you with me?"

The expression on her face turned to steel, "I'm with you. For Vik, and for the kids in those pictures." Petra felt a wave of relief as the pilot's voice interrupted their exchange, announcing their descent. She didn't want to think about the pictures, or Vik anymore. Not right now.

Carlos looked toward the front of the plane, "Here we go."

Chapter 13

London, United Kingdom

Kasem stood with his back pressed against the door of the bathroom. He'd been on his way there when he heard Petra and Carlos talking in the lounge.

"You haven't forgiven him…"

"…the darkness is still lurking, like when he killed that Russian guy…"

Kasem stared ahead and replayed the conversation in his head. When the captain announced their descent, he stepped into the bathroom. Before returning to his seat, he gave them a brief wave and disappeared toward the front of the plane.

He reached his seat and put his headphones back in and blasted one of his old favorite songs, *"Waking up at the start of the end of the world…"* The lyrics were so apt as Matchbox Twenty sang about the apocalypse, *"I believe the world is burning to the ground…"*

Kasem resisted the urge to curse aloud. The conversation had confirmed his fears, despite everything that Petra had said to convince him otherwise. *She hasn't forgiven me. Maybe she never will.* How could he ask her to? He couldn't even forgive himself. Yes, he had been duped into setting up the Suez Canal attacks, but the kills that he had made in Tehran, before and after that, were his own. There was no one else to claim responsibility for them, even if he had followed his orders because General Majed was threatening Lila. *Petra.* He sighed.

He wanted to be angry. He wanted to hate her. She had used him as her source and General Majed would never have captured him if it weren't for her job as a spy. However, even though he'd been blackmailed, he had made a choice to follow Majed into the darkness, and now he had to pay the price for it. She might never forgive him. He might never forgive himself.

As the plane started its descent, Petra came over and took a seat next to him, "Did you sleep well? It seemed like you were out." She leaned in to kiss him and he stiffened.

"I did. Much needed sleep," he answered.

"Are you okay?" She frowned as she buckled her seatbelt and took his hand. "How do you feel?"

"Like I'm skating dangerously close to my old life. You know, London, finance guy, all that jazz. Everything that I've had to give up," Kasem answered in a quiet voice. "But I have to keep trying to make things right." She could obviously see that he wasn't okay, and she would continue to press if he didn't say something. It was the truth, just not the whole truth. He sighed and stopped himself from bringing up any of the conversation that he had overheard. He didn't want to, couldn't bear to hear any more of those empty promises—about how she cared about who he was now, not who he was and what he'd done as the Ahriman. It was clear that she did, and he would have to live with that.

******

After landing in London, they went to the apartment that Rachel had rented out. It was just off Regent's Canal, and Kasem felt a lump in his throat after he entered. It was a two-story flat with an updated kitchen, a Victorian fireplace, and a balcony that looked directly out onto the canal. He could only think of what could have been as he observed the view from the chic apartment. His old life beckoned in a way that he had never thought possible. The glitz and the glamor of being wealthy and young in London, with its hedonism and nightlife at his disposal.

Carlos clapped him on the shoulder and shook him from those thoughts.

"You ready for this, buddy?" Carlos asked. "Let's have a toast." He grabbed a bottle of Aberlour scotch from the liquor cabinet along with two scotch glasses and poured them each two fingers. "Thank you again for doing this, for giving up the quiet life in Kyoto," he said as he raised his glass, "we're doing the right thing."

"I bet I could say the same to you for taking a break from your quieter life," Kasem said. "Anyway, I'm at your disposal." He kept his eyes from wandering. Would Petra still be with him if he had refused to be part of this operation? He wasn't sure he wanted to know the answer.

"Did you guys start the party without us?" Petra appeared at the entrance of the living room where she'd just come down the stairs, followed by Rachel and Nathan.

Kasem's chest tightened at the sight of her. He was filled with anger—he was angry that she couldn't forgive him, angry that she had pretended that she could—but at the same time he was filled with longing. He wanted to be with her, wanted to win her trust and commitment more than anything, but he had failed, and failed miserably. What more could he do to show her that he wasn't just the Ahriman? Besides, everything that he had done as the Ahriman had been to save her, to spare her from General Majed. *Why can't she see that? Why can't I make her see that?* He looked away and stared at his whiskey glass until Carlos spoke up.

"I can't always wait for you young'uns. Help yourself," Carlos shrugged.

"I'll skip the liquor," Petra said. "Those tequila shots on the plane did me in."

"Sorry, I couldn't help myself," Rachel piped up. "Besides, it's tradition."

"Hey, Petra, here's some apple juice. There's no alcohol in it," Nathan set a full glass in front of her and retreated to the other side of the table, his eyes averted.

"Thanks," Petra picked up her juice glass and smiled at him.

Kasem caught the bashful shyness of Nathan's expression and frowned. He'd picked up on Nathan's crush earlier, but he'd hoped he would be over it by now. *It's not like she's interested in him,* he reminded himself. He knew that she loved him, but his guilt over everything that he had done, not to mention everything that she had just said, made him doubt the very foundation of their relationship. *She could have anyone,* he recalled Carlos' comment about the number of men that had been running after Petra.

"Before we go into team revelry, we have to commit to this," Rachel said. "I know I'm the biggest proponent of team bonding, but this is serious. Carlos has talked to all of you, but I've gone pretty far out on a limb to put this op together, so I need to know you're committed."

Petra frowned, "We just flew from Japan to London for you. That seems pretty committed to me. Do you have something else in mind?"

"Trackers." Rachel removed a device from her laptop bag that looked like a tranquilizer gun. "I need all of you to have one."

"What?" Petra looked at her in shock. "Are you insane? We're not CIA. I don't know what you guys agree to when you sign on, but this is about trust. We're doing this for Carlos and to put this asshole away. No trackers."

"I'm not going to give the frequencies to Langley, I promise. This is about commitment and safety. I need to be able to find you if something goes sideways."

"Carlos, you can't be on board with this?" Petra turned her palms upward.

"Er, I…"

"This isn't safe," Petra continued. "Any two-bit thug can detect a tracker."

Rachel shook her head, "Not this kind. Nathan designed it specifically to evade scans. Right, Nate?"

"I did," Nathan looked as if he would rather be anywhere else in the world.

Kasem swallowed, *A tracker?* Carlos had clearly already agreed to this, so there wasn't anyone to overrule Rachel. Their only option would be to blow off the op, which was probably the wiser thing to do. The risk of a tracker terrified him. If the CIA ever figured out that he was the Ahriman, a tracker would end him. *And I never want to have to remove one of those again.*

He searched Petra's face. Was she going to go along with this? He could tell that she was wavering, and he wanted to agree with her, but her expression also told him something else. She wanted to take the op, and he was sure that she would respect him more if he went along with it. His only route to her trust and commitment was to show her how far he was willing to go. "Can we have it removed? After the op?" he asked Rachel with concern.

"Of course."

"By a doctor or some medical professional? Or at least a local anesthetic?"

Rachel looked puzzled but answered again, "Of course."

He hesitated, then gave a nod of consent, "Then I'm okay with it."

He could feel the weight of Petra's gaze. After a few long seconds, she let out a loud exhale. "Okay. Let's do this." She held out her left forearm and cringed as Rachel used the device to embed the tracker under her skin.

Kasem held out his arm and shut his eyes as he felt the prick through his skin. This was the point of no return. Whatever his doubts, he had made his bed. Now he had to lie in it.

He took a deep breath, "Let's do this." He raised his glass. "Rachel, do you have that intel on Nguyen's son? I need to figure out how to become his new best friend."

Chapter 14

London, United Kingdom

Kasem smoothed out the front of his tuxedo jacket and looked at himself in the mirror. He hadn't been this dressed up since a colleague's wedding in London more than six years earlier. He looked different now—there were more gray strands through his hair, which he'd grown out along with his beard, and he was wearing contact lenses to lighten the color of his eyes. He picked up the wire-rimmed glasses from his bedside table and examined his reflection. *Amir Birch, son of a wealthy Persian-American businessman. Grew up in New York, worked in private equity investments in New York and London. Looking for new opportunities to invest my family's money.* He certainly didn't look like the Kasem Ismaili who had worked in finance in London.

"You clean up pretty nice," Petra said as she sashayed into the room behind him. She wore a floor-length gown in a deep shade of royal blue. Her hair cascaded in layers over her right shoulder, accentuating the bare skin on the opposite side of her collarbone. She took his breath away.

It took him a few moments to speak, "Wow. I should take you out more often."

Petra spun around to show off her dress, then moved to Kasem, "You look pretty darn dashing yourself." She stepped forward and kissed him. With her heels, she didn't need to stand on her tiptoes as she normally did. "Oops. We better wipe off that lipstick." She handed him a tissue and used another one to fix her lipstick. "If this weren't a mission, it might be kind of fun."

"It would be. Are you good on your cover?"

Petra nodded, "There's just one final touch." She walked past him to their bedside table and removed an engagement ring and wedding band from a jewelry box.

Kasem watched as she slid them onto her left ring finger and held back a sigh. Maybe someday he would have the opportunity to put the same kind of rings on that finger. He took her left hand in his, "Are you ready to go?"

"As I'll ever be."

******

They ventured downstairs where Carlos, Rachel, and Nathan were reviewing schematics of the Orangery venue at Kew Gardens.

"Ladies and gentlemen, the prodigal couple has emerged," Rachel said as she came to the doorway between the living room and the stairs. She made an elaborate gesture with her hand, moving it in circles over her head before bowing.

"Roll out the red carpet," Carlos said in a terrible attempt at a British accent.

Kasem pretended to be offended, "Good heavens," he said in a posh British accent that contrasted with Carlos' feeble attempt. "Shall we, milady?" He held out his arm for Petra and led her to the dining table where the team had spread out the schematics.

Petra followed him in silence and took a seat next to Nathan.

"Petra, you look—wow," Nathan's face blushed red as he spoke.

"Thank you. Not so bad yourself." She pointed toward the map, "I know the main gala is in the central hall. Where will the rest of you be stationed?"

"I'll be at the party, but I'm going to keep my nose down. I plan on staying near one of the food stations that will be over here." Nathan indicated the corner of the building on the map. The redness on his face subsided as he concentrated on the op.

"Beware of all those ladies who will be hitting on you," Petra gave him a gentle nudge. "I bet you'll be one of the few single guys at the party—"

"Right. Can we get back to the plan?" Carlos interrupted. "Since I'm posing as your driver and valet, I'll be out here with the other wait staff while you're at the party. They've erected a small tent in the gardens, which will have some food and snacks for servants, drivers, caterers, etc. Since Rachel is posing as one of the caterers, she'll be in between this tent, the kitchen area, and the main hall."

"Yup. Here are your earpieces. I already set them to the right frequency to communicate with each other. If things go sour, I can help get you out, but I'm sure you both will do just fine," Rachel said. She placed four earpieces on the table and each person on the team grabbed one. "Nathan, since you're posing as another party guest, make sure you stay in my orbit. I know this is your first time being inside during an op. Just don't do too much talking. We only need you to be another pair of eyes. Don't worry, you'll ace this mission."

Carlos clapped Nathan on the shoulder, "You certainly will. Sorry I can't be the one on the inside, but we can't take the chance that Nguyen might recognize me."

Kasem looked at the map and nodded, "Since it's nice out, they'll have the terrace open. That's where I plan to approach Nguyen's son, Jim. He's an LSE alum, and according to my cover, so am I. We did a preliminary review of the campus, so I'll drop in some of those names. He's also a fan of *The Book Club,* one of my old favorite spots, so I might drop that in too if we need more to connect on. Madison's profile says that he joined his father's investment fund a year ago, but he still hasn't managed to bring in any private equity investors and they're running close to their deadline. He's hungry, and always out to get dad's approval, and I'm going to milk that—since Nguyen's legit business sits on top of his arms deals, they can take money from any institutional investor, and that's where I come in."

"Don't you think he'll be a bit reticent given the business they're in?" Nathan looked up from his computer screen.

Kasem shook his head, "Like I said, my money—or rather the Carlson Group's money—is still green, plus there's the urgency of their timeline. They'll have official documentation to back up their legit investments, it's just the majority of the money will be funneled into his arms deals. Since that's where most of the return comes from, nobody's the wiser, or at least they pretend not to be."

"While he's talking to Jim, I'll deal with the phones. That way Madison doesn't have to risk her cover," Petra added.

"Remember, the phone hack will only work if you stay in their proximity for at least thirty seconds. If you need to hack more than one phone, it'll take longer," Nathan explained for the third time that day.

"We've got it sparky," Kasem looked over at him, annoyed at the repetitiveness. For some reason, Nathan seemed to think that he was the only one who could follow basic instructions when it came to using op tech.

"Did you finish the reading on LSE's campus and Grosvenor Hall?" Rachel interjected, referring to one of the many dormitory halls at the London School of Economics.

Kasem made a show of looking shocked. "Reading?" He watched Rachel's expression turn to concern. "Of course, I did the reading. This isn't my first rodeo. Besides, Nathan already uploaded Amir Birch's info into the alumni database, so it's no issue if Jim checks up on me."

Petra rolled her eyes at him, "He'll be all right."

The look of relief that flooded Rachel's face made Kasem chuckle. "I got you, didn't I?" He nodded toward the door, "Come on. Let's get this party started."

Chapter 15

London, United Kingdom

Petra checked her hair and makeup as their car pulled to a stop in front of the Orangery at Kew Gardens. Kasem opened the door for her and she stepped out and linked her arm in his.

The Orangery glowed in the evening light with its walls of windows that emphasized its high ceiling and delicate arches. As they walked toward the entrance, the building looked stunning and appealing, nothing like the apprehension that was building in the pit of her stomach. She might have put on a brave face for Kasem earlier but taking on this operation felt more like a death trap, even if it started with an elaborate gala. They may have been staying in a glamorous flat while working with Rachel's seemingly unlimited budget, but Petra had been an operative long enough to know that this wasn't the norm for spies. As an operative, she lived within a veil of lies that had kept her alternating between loneliness, fear, and even boredom when an investigation seemed to be going nowhere.

She pushed those thoughts aside and resolved to at least enjoy the spectacular venue. *You have to find something good in all of this.* For this cover, the scale of parties and fancy destinations would have to do. She had hoped to enjoy some of that with Kasem, but she could tell that something was wrong. He hadn't been the same since their flight, really since Kyoto, when she had turned down his proposal. The operation obviously had him on edge, as it did the whole team, but in her gut, she felt as if there had to be more to it. She dismissed her concerns and gave him a beaming smile as he kissed her cheek.

"I love you," he whispered into her ear.

Once inside, the main hall was even more dazzling than the view of the gardens. Through the windows, she could see the sun glinting across the trees, with the pinnacled ceiling and chandeliers setting off the table settings and orchid centerpieces on the dinner tables.

Kasem led her toward the hors d'oeuvres and bar on the terrace where Rachel was posing as one of the catering staff. She stopped to offer them glasses of champagne.

"Nguyen is on the east side of the room. I have eyes on Jim. He's at the other side of the hall by the windows. Nathan, can you paint the target?" Rachel moved on with her tray to keep up the appearance of serving the attendees.

"Uh, okay." Even over the earpieces, Petra could hear Nathan's nervousness.

"It's no big deal," she said in her softest voice after making sure there was no one else within earshot. "You're just doing a simple brush pass. You can do this, Nathan."

"I'm on my way."

Petra exchanged glances with Kasem and leaned over the terrace railing. She pretended to take in the view, which was captivating even through her pretense, and sipped on her champagne. Kasem leaned over so that she could whisper in his ear, "I can see Nguyen now—at your three o'clock."

"I, I did it," Nathan's shy voice came across their earpieces again.

"You did good." Petra turned to Kasem, "Do you see Jim yet?"

Kasem scanned behind her and nodded, "He's going into the restroom now. Good job spilling that drink, Nathan."

Petra turned to follow his gaze, "Okay, go say hi."

******

They moved across the ballroom slowly, keeping to the edge of the dance floor. "Are you sure you don't want to go out there and tango?" Kasem whispered.

"Like every crappy spy movie ever made?" She shook her head, "You don't see a lot of tango in a good one like *The Day of the Jackal*."

"Sure thing, Miss Movie Snob."

"Just because I don't like *Transformers*, it doesn't make me an elitist," she protested. They shifted back into operative mode as they neared Jim Nguyen, who had just emerged from the restroom. He had a disgruntled look on his face and was attempting to dab out a wet stain just under his bow tie.

Kasem grabbed another glass of champagne from a high-top table by the wall and handed it to her, then pretended to look surprised as he made eye contact with Jim. "Jim Nguyen? Is that you? Man, it's been ages." He walked over and extended his hand, "It's great to see you. I don't think I've seen you since right before we finished up at LSE. Remember that night at The George? What a crazy night. I don't think I've had that many beers in all the years since then. How are you doing, buddy? Following in the family footsteps?"

Jim looked startled and manufactured a phony smile, "I'm doing great. How are you?"

"Amir, aren't you going to introduce me to your friend?" Petra took Kasem's arm once again after hitting the proximity trigger that would hack Jim's phone when she was close enough to it.

"Of course. Sorry, babe. This is Jim. We were at LSE together. We met through mutual friends at The George one night." Kasem turned back to Jim, "Do you get back there much? I haven't been in ages."

"It's great to meet you, Jim. I'm Cara, Amir's wife." Petra shook his hand, "I've heard so many stories about the old campus. I can't believe I still haven't been to this famous bar after it starred in so many stories from Amir's glory days." She counted the seconds in her head—it would only take thirty seconds for the device to hack Jim's phone.

Jim relaxed his posture and Petra could tell that their bait was working. Even if he didn't remember "Amir," he would play the part until he could check things out. By dropping Kasem's cover name into the conversation, she intended to make Jim more comfortable and give him a way to continue the conversation.

"You haven't taken her to The George? That's one of the first places I took my fiancé when we were dating. I had to make sure she liked it, or she wouldn't be a keeper," Jim chuckled.

"In my defense, we've been living in New York," Kasem said. "We only moved to London a month ago."

"That's great. Did we have any classes together?" The frown on Jim's face made it clear that he was still trying to figure out if he actually knew "Amir."

"I'm pretty sure we had Dev Econ together, but so did a bunch of other students. Such a big class. What was that professor's name? He was brilliant but so obnoxious. Burden? Belgess?"

"Burgess. Right, of course," Jim said. "Brilliant but obnoxious. I like that description. How's the rest of the gang? Are you in touch with any of them?"

Petra braced herself. He was testing them.

"I saw Badger a few weeks ago. Remember him? I tagged along with him to The George that night we met," Kasem answered immediately, naming someone that Jim had known at LSE. They had chosen someone whom Jim was likely to remember, but not a close friend. "You know, we had so much fun drinking those couple of nights at school, I wish we had met sooner and stayed in touch." Kasem clapped his hand on Jim's shoulder, mimicking the motion that Carlos used as a gesture of male bonding and friendship. "So, what are you up to these days? I went into private equity after I returned to New York. That's how I met Cara. Her uncle runs this investment fund called the Carlson Group. I met him at a business meeting and we hit it off. He invited me to a family dinner and the rest is history—"

Jim raised his eyebrows, "The Carlson Group? They've been in our orbit for a while. We don't work as much with energy investments, but they sound like a great fund."

"They are. I really like working with them. I joined the family ship about a year ago," Kasem agreed.

"The family business is definitely the way to go. I joined my dad about a year ago too," Jim looked toward the other side of the room. "Hey, we should get together. I can introduce you to my dad. See if we can work together. We're always looking for new institutional investors."

"And we're always looking for new investments," Kasem said with a chuckle. "Besides, I'm always up for adding to our network." He reached into his inner jacket pocket and pulled out a business card, "Let's set something up for next week."

"Great." Jim gave him a card as well, which Kasem pocketed. "Do you want to meet my dad? He's just over there on the terrace."

"Sure, lead the way," Kasem said with a nod. He turned toward Petra and planted a kiss on her cheek. "Honey, do you want to join us?"

Petra shook her head and slipped the device she had used to hack Jim's phone into his jacket pocket so that Kasem could use it for Nguyen's phone. Her role in this cover was to play the arm-candy trophy wife, much as she abhorred the concept. "You boys go ahead. I'll get some more champagne." She glanced at Jim again, "Is your wife here? I would love to meet her. We can bond over our missing husbands."

"Aren't you sassy? You'll get along famously with Janine." Jim looked over at Kasem and then turned his attention back to Petra. "My fiancé's by the cocktail bar, over there in the dark green dress." He waved at her and she started toward them, "I'll introduce you."

Janine approached them with a smile. "Hi, darling," she said to Jim, "who are your friends?"

"Janine, this is Amir and his wife, Cara. Amir and I went to school together. I haven't seen him since we left LSE. Cara, Amir, this is my fiancé, Janine," Jim said. "Amir and I were just catching up. He's in the investment game too, so I was going to take him over to meet Dad. Maybe you two ladies can keep each other company?"

"Sure. It's nice to meet you both." Janine gave Petra a wide smile, "Cara, why don't we let these boys go talk business and we can go have some fun. I've hidden a few bottles of chardonnay in the back so we don't have to stand in line for cocktails."

Chapter 16

London, United Kingdom

Carlos waited until the party was well in progress before he approached the valet parking lot. He'd taken special care to dress exactly like the other drivers, only wishing that he could cover up his face with a hoodie or a cap of some kind. Since that would cause too much alarm, he'd elected for a thick pair of bright blue rimmed glasses and a wig with a mix of reddish brown and gray hair. He'd also used gum line inserts to fatten up his cheeks—he didn't want to take any chances that Nguyen or one of his people would recognize him. He was probably safe in the valet driver's uniform, it was so far out of context of how they had met him before.

Instead of approaching Nguyen's car directly, he went for the one next to it in the parking lot. Nguyen's driver was smoking a cigarette a few steps away, but he would certainly notice if any of the valet drivers got too close. He approached the driver's seat and fumbled with a set of keys, and then dropped them. While he was on the ground, he placed a small magnetic tracking device just behind the external ring of the hubcap on Nguyen's car. They could use the GPS data from the tracker to help triangulate the storage units that Nguyen used for his weapons when they came through London. Madison had already provided them with a listing of all of the different storage units that Nguyen's company made payments for within the area, but the list was long, and they needed the GPS data to narrow it down. It was far too risky for the overall op to check all of them, and the vast majority would contain only goods that pertained to Nguyen's legitimate businesses, but Carlos' bet was that Nguyen wouldn't spend much time visiting those.

Carlos picked up the keys and stood up again, before he used the remote to unlock the driver side door of the other car. *Gotta love spy tech.* He reached inside and rummaged under the seat for a few moments, keeping an eye out for Nguyen's driver.

He was so busy looking at Nguyen's driver that he didn't notice one of the other valet drivers approaching from the other side. "Hey, you," the driver called out. "What are you doing in there?"

Carlos cursed under his breath and pulled his glasses off of his face and stepped out of the car. "What's your problem, mate?" he inquired, raising his glasses. "I forgot my glasses when I parked the car." He looked over at Nguyen's driver in his peripheral vision—the commotion had attracted his attention, he'd put out his cigarette and was approaching them. Carlos readied himself to reach for his Beretta and sprint away—the stairwell heading out of the garage was only a few meters off. *I could make it.*

"Oh right, sorry," the other driver said. "You can't be too careful, you know?"

"Whatever, mate," Carlos heaved an internal sigh of relief as he shuffled away as fast as he could. The tracking device that he had used could access all of Nguyen's past GPS data and track it going forward, but his original plan had been to retrieve it—Nguyen's past GPS data would probably be enough to get the information that they needed. Even though the device was unlikely to be found, he'd wanted there to be no chance of that. *Best laid plans.* Instead they would be testing whether Nathan's claim that the device was undetectable was worth its salt.

Chapter 17

London, United Kingdom

Kasem followed Jim to the terrace and his heart started to beat faster. He gulped down the rest of his champagne and the crisp, refreshing taste felt like a breath of fresh air, much like the outdoor setting. The sun had dipped behind the trees, setting off the view of the garden in hues of red, pink, and orange. For a moment, he wished that he and Petra could just be out there together to take in the view. With a deep breath, he focused on keeping in step with Jim on their way toward Nguyen.

When they reached him a few moments later, Jim tentatively tapped his father on the shoulder, who then turned to him with a scowl.

"Hi, Dad."

Nguyen was a dapper man in a waistcoat and bow tie who looked to be in his late sixties. When he noticed that Jim was not alone, he immediately slipped into a different demeanor. "Jim, I'm glad you came over. This is an old friend, Sir Caleb. We worked together before I started the company."

Jim held out his hand to greet Sir Caleb, "It's great to meet you. I've heard a lot about your antics together."

"Oh dear. All good things, I hope," Sir Caleb said and shook his hand. "Lovely to finally meet you, Jim."

"Dad, I wanted to introduce you to a classmate of mine from LSE. We ran into each other here, after ages. Amir, this is my father, Duc Nguyen. Dad, this is Amir—" Jim gave Kasem an embarrassed glance, "I'm so sorry, but I just realized I don't remember your surname."

"Not an issue at all," Kasem said, "it's Birch." He shook Nguyen's hand, as well as Sir Caleb's, and triggered the device, "Sorry to interrupt your conversation."

"It's no problem at all. Tell us more about yourself, Amir," Nguyen said.

Kasem nodded, "Absolutely. I was just telling Jim that I joined the Carlson Group about a year ago. I'm enjoying working with renewables. It's been a great transition from the traditional investment banking world."

"The Carlson Group? That's quite an exclusive shop," Sir Caleb said. "Very impressive, especially at such a young age. I don't think they hire anyone for their investment wing who isn't up for partner."

Kasem nodded again and decided to drop a self-deprecating comment to inject some humor into the conversation, "My wife's uncle is one of the founders, so I can't say that nepotism didn't help me out. But they seem happy with how I've proven myself, which makes me feel pretty good."

"I'm sure you have, my boy." Sir Caleb gestured with his hand to summon the waitress, "We'd like four scotches, neat. The best single malt that you have."

"Absolutely, sir," she said before she dashed off to the bar. She returned with four glasses on a tray. Each one had a round whiskey stone centered in the glass with a generous pour of scotch.

"Here you go, sir. This is from a bottle of Macallan Rare Cask that we have in the back. I hope you enjoy it." Sir Caleb took a glass from the tray and she waited while he smelled and tasted it. When he gave her an approving nod, she moved to each of them so that they could take their respective glasses. "My name is Katie," she said, "please let me know if you need anything else, sir."

Sir Caleb watched her walk away, "That's one nice caboose," he said under his breath.

Kasem stopped himself from reacting to the obvious machismo. Instead, he agreed. "You, sir, are right about that," he said and raised his glass.

"Here, here," Sir Caleb raised his glass in turn and the four of them touched them together.

"That's magnificent," Jim said after they each took a sip.

"Sir Caleb, you've outdone yourself. Jim, we were just off to chat about some business opportunities. I wouldn't want to bore you and your friend," Nguyen said.

"I don't mind," Jim said. "Amir, what do you think?"

Kasem shrugged, "I kind of live for business talk, much to the chagrin of my wife."

"I know that problem all too well," Nguyen agreed. "If I take another call at the dinner table, I swear my wife is going to toss my phone straight into our infinity pool."

"We all get by somehow," Kasem chuckled

"Somehow, we do," Nguyen said. "Caleb, as I was saying, this new fund will need to raise another $74 million. How much do you think your contacts will be able to contribute?"

"I have clear interest from parties willing to invest at least $60 million, and the debt should cover the remainder easily, but I will work on getting confirmations so that we know for sure."

Kasem tilted his head to the side, "What's the investment?"

"We're raising money for a major cashew farm and processing center in Vietnam. Processed cashews have a strong global market and there would be a sizeable return, plus we're setting the whole thing up as a sustainable center, with rainwater harvesting, solar panels, the works," Sir Caleb answered.

"That sounds intriguing. Would you be interested in having new blood? I was just saying the other day that I'm interested in expanding Carlson's investment portfolio to other green investments," Kasem said. As Madison had indicated, Nguyen was indeed seeking investors for his new deal, and Jim was particularly hungry to obtain his father's approval. The Carlson Group, as a major investment fund focused on green projects around the world, played right into that scenario. Nguyen might never actually be on board with an investment given the type of business he was actually in—Kasem might not be able to build the requisite trust in the time available—but he certainly *was* going to explore the possibility of having a new major investor.

Nguyen raised his eyebrows, "I'm not sure we'll have room in this particular deal, but let's arrange a meeting in the next couple of weeks. I'll have Jim send you some literature on us in the meantime."

Chapter 18

London, United Kingdom

K asem hung up the phone and looked over at Petra and Carlos with a shrug, "As I expected..."

"What do you mean? What did he say?" Carlos asked.

"Jim said that they're really interested in doing work with Carlson Group in the future, but there isn't room in this particular deal—they already closed the funding gap. He said there might be another opportunity in another six months." *Dammit.* Kasem kicked at the table leg and cursed under his breath.

Petra nodded, "Okay, so we need another plan. What if we just followed the GPS data to the arms themselves? Would we really need the ledger? It would be a lot less dangerous."

"Even if we find out where he's storing the arms, it won't be enough to convict him without the ledger," Carlos shook his head. "Madison doesn't have close enough access to pin him to the actual deals, she can just attest to the funding gap between the actual size of Nguyen's legit investments and what he reports publicly, and what she's heard about how the remainder is used. Without the ledger he could blame the whole thing on whatever name he's got on the paperwork—some patsy or employee. Do you think there's another way to get into their country house to get the ledger?"

"We could break in, but it's risky," Petra said.

Carlos tapped his fingers on the table, "It might be our only option. I'll have Nathan look into the security details when he gets back."

Kasem stared at the ceiling, half listening to them but mostly considering the situation. They did need the ledger, and an invite to the party was the best route for that, at least if the ledger was indeed stored in the safe at the country house. Perhaps he could bond with Jim enough to be invited to the engagement party anyway? They seemed to get along well, but it was late in the game and only a business connection would ensure the invite that they needed. He rubbed the stubble on his chin and an idea occurred to him, "We have four possible storage units under surveillance that Nguyen might use to store the arms."

"You know that—I showed you the camera feeds yesterday," Carlos answered with a frown.

Kasem ignored the comment and continued, "If these were any goods—legit goods—that I was planning to invest in and then sell at a profit, I'd want to inspect my property."

Petra crossed her arms, "Right, that's why we have them under surveillance, so that we can see when Nguyen shows up at one of them."

"Yes, but that probably won't be until after the engagement party, *and* like Carlos said, it won't be enough to convict him."

Kasem's eyes brightened as his idea crystallized.

"What are you getting at, buddy?" Carlos gave him a confused look.

"I'd be willing to bet that one of those storage units already has a sample of the arms that he's buying—a portion of his investment." Kasem's gaze moved between Petra and Carlos, expecting them to comprehend what he was saying, but they still looked bewildered, "Don't you see? When Nguyen makes his investments, he pays a small amount up front, *before* the funds come in from his investors. He uses that to inspect all the goods in the shipment, make sure it's a good deal for his buyer and for him, and then he uses investor money to reach the full amount of the investment."

Carlos raised his eyebrows, "Cut to the chase, Kasem. We're not all specialists in private equity."

"Nguyen already has a portion of the arms in his storage units, so we can change the situation—we can create a financing gap for this deal."

Petra leaned in, "Create a financing gap? You mean steal the arms that he's already received? Would it be enough? You said he only invested a small amount upfront. He could just close the deal for a smaller sale."

"Possibly, but I don't think so," Kasem said. "For someone of his wealth, Nguyen is pretty frugal. Madison said that he spends a couple of hours checking company expenses every week, he even reviews how much they spend on catered lunches from *Pret*. The upfront payment would be small relative to the overall size of the deal, maybe ten percent of the full investment, but for this one, that's still over seven-million dollars. Nguyen didn't get to where he is by being fickle with that kind of money."

"So, you want us to figure out which of the storage units Nguyen already has arms in, and steal them so that he needs your money to make up the difference in the size of the deal? You've got some serious *cahones.*" Carlos' eyes widened as he looked over to Petra, "Have I told you how much I like him?"

Chapter 19

London, United Kingdom

Petra watched the camera feed on her phone screen as a well-dressed Rachel buzzed repeatedly for the security guard at one of Big Yellow Self Storage's locations on the outskirts of London.

"I need help, my car broke down. May I use your phone?" Petra could hear Rachel sobbing over the earpiece. After a few more pleas, Petra saw the guard approach the door to let Rachel in.

"Carlos, Kasem, you're a go," Petra whispered into her com after making sure that she had properly looped the cameras on that part of the facility per Nathan's directions. She wiggled her toes which had started to cramp since she'd been hiding out there for almost two hours. Since Nathan had limited field experience, they had elected to leave him in the van parked half a block away rather than having him serve as lookout. She crouched lower and slid forward on the roof of the storage unit that she was perched on. From the edge she had a good view of the entrance to Nguyen's storage unit and the path leading up to it. There were two streetlamps, one at each end of the path, but they provided limited lighting to the overall area. Petra squinted and watched as Carlos and Kasem came over the fence and approached the unit, keeping to the shadows.

"Unit 84B," Carlos confirmed as they stopped in front of it. "Keep your eyes open, kiddo. You never know what surprises Nguyen might have up his sleeve."

"I've got your back, Carlos," Petra said.

She watched as he took bolt clippers and broke the chain lock on the front of the storage unit, and then moved on to the combination lock, while Kasem moved past him and opened the unit that they had rented across the access lane. They would temporarily be storing the arms that they stole from Nguyen there since it was too risky to try and get them out to the van on the street.

Petra listened as Nathan instructed Carlos on removing the external panel of the lock and wiring it directly to the device that would hack into the computer security chip and break the code. She waited with her heartbeat drumming through her ears as they triggered the device. If Nguyen had laid any fail safes, now would be the time that they were set off. She concentrated on her breathing and counted the seconds in her head, her muscles tense and ready to spring into action.

"We got it," Carlos raised his fist. Petra exhaled in relief as he slid the door to the storage unit open.

"Make sure to scan for any booby traps before you go inside," Petra said.

Kasem glanced up at her and tapped his forehead in a mocking salute as he rejoined Carlos, "We know the drill, babe."

Petra's eyes narrowed, "Fine, sorry." She had to admit that she hated being the lookout, but strong as she was, she wouldn't be able to move the arms from Nguyen's storage unit into the one that they had rented as quickly as Carlos and Kasem.

She waited as they scanned the unit and stepped inside. "Holy mother—," Kasem said. "So, this is how much a few million dollars buys you in arms."

Petra shifted to try to get a better view, but it was too hard to see inside the unit from her position. When Kasem and Carlos carried out a box containing the first bazooka, she whistled softly. *Holy mother indeed.* She let herself smile—she'd been skeptical that Kasem's plan would work, but he'd been right, Nguyen had acquired a sizeable sampling of the arms before the full investments had arrived.

"Heads up, guys. Rachel's on her way out," Nathan's voice came over the com.

Petra looked at her phone again as the guard returned to his desk. He grabbed his flashlight and she realized that he was about to circle the facility again. *Crap,* she sprang into action. Based on her hours watching the facility, the guard made his rounds of the area on the hour. Rachel's distraction had interrupted that process, but they had bet that he would simply skip one set of rounds because of that, but it looked like they were wrong. *Dude, did you have to pick tonight to be employee of the month?*

"The guard's coming," she said as she slid off the edge of the storage unit. "Rachel, can you stall him?"

"I'll do my best."

Petra grabbed the edge of the roof to slow her fall and cringed as her shoulders caught her weight in a dead hang. The ground was only a few feet away, so she let go and landed in a deep squat before she ran over to the storage unit where Carlos and Kasem were still in the process of moving the boxes of arms. "We have to move," she said as she grabbed one of the smaller boxes. "We've got maybe five minutes before he gets here."

They grabbed two more crates and a few boxes and dumped them into the other storage unit, moving as quickly as possible without making too much noise. Petra let go of the box she was carrying and ran back toward Nguyen's storage unit. "Shut the door," she called back to Kasem and Carlos. There were three crates left in Nguyen's unit and there was no way they would get them out in time. She reached into her pack and grabbed a GPS tag and stuck it onto the wood frame of the largest crate. Even if they couldn't steal the last bit of the arms, they could certainly track them.

Petra heard the door to the other unit slide closed as she reached for the one on Nguyen's unit. *Come on, move.* She pulled with all of her strength and got the door shut before she grabbed the frame to shimmy up on top of the storage unit. With one hand on the roof, she attempted to hoist herself up, but couldn't find enough leverage from the door frame. *Crap,* she heard footsteps coming down the lane. She tried to reach her other hand up to the roof to give her the strength to pull herself up, but her left hand wouldn't close on the roof edge. She froze in place as the footsteps got closer, then heard a noise in the distance that sounded like something moving. *Thanks, boys,* she thought as the security guard moved away to check on the noise. With a deep breath, she reached up with her left hand again, this time able to grab the parapet jutting out. The shingles cut into her fingers, but she kept them steady and pulled upward. A moment later she collapsed on the top of the roof panting. *That was too close.*

Chapter 20

London, United Kingdom – One week later

Kasem sat down in the living room of the team's flat on Regent Canal and slid on his dress shoes. His plan had gone in their favor—Jim had called him about a seven-million dollar investment opportunity that had just opened up, and they had set up a time to meet. Kasem could feel the eyes of the rest of the team boring into him as he checked the contents of his briefcase. He had packed a folio with printouts of the materials that Jim had sent him in the main compartment, along with a list of questions, and stashed his pocketknife in a hidden pocket underneath. He wanted to be prepared in case things went sour.

"I know you can do this," Carlos said. His tone didn't match the confidence of his words.

Kasem ignored him and grabbed his spring jacket, as he slipped it on, he caught Petra shaking her head at Carlos. It irritated him that he had to keep proving his competence as an operative, especially when it was his idea that had gotten them this far.

"Don't worry about him," she said in a soft voice.

He nodded at her and leaned against the kitchen island to finish his coffee. Petra had already given him a pep talk earlier while he was getting ready upstairs. Her words had helped to quiet his doubts, but they had been unable to silence them. He felt as if he were on a tightrope at the edge of his old life with this cover as private equity investor. After his capture in Iran, he had spent a lot of time putting this part of his life behind him. He'd accepted that he would never be *that* person again—one who handled clients, structured deals, and somehow brought massive and daunting projects to fruition. He hadn't realized how much he missed that aspect of himself until he looked at the financing materials that Jim had sent him, and it was painful to pretend to be that person again. The critical thinking and analysis came naturally, as if no time had passed, just like riding a bike. He'd wanted to share some of those feelings with Petra, but how would she feel if he brought that up? After all, he probably would still be living that life if they had never met. He didn't want to dredge up their past to share his conflicted emotions.

Instead, he had played it off as nervousness—about the op, about the cover, about their plan, or really lack of one. Not that it didn't make him nervous. It most certainly did. They didn't have concrete intel about where Nguyen kept this supposed ledger, although Madison's information pointed toward Nguyen's country house. Kasem had to figure it out and provide the team with access to it when the time was right. It was by no means a small feat, especially given the limited exposure Kasem would have to Nguyen. He had to bond with the family, and especially with Jim, to even hope for such access, and he had to do it quickly if they were to have any chance at stopping Nguyen before he executed on this upcoming arms deal. While Kasem was confident in his abilities as an operative, developing a relationship with Jim and his family that quickly was a tall order. The phone hacks from the party at the Orangery hadn't yielded anything useful, and until Nguyen went forward with purchasing the remainder of his arms, the surveillance on the storage units wouldn't yield anything. While he couldn't speed up the delivery of the arms, he could help them gain access to the ledger, but only if he could become Jim's buddy and confidant in a ridiculously short time.

"Kasem, are you okay?" Petra placed both hands on his arm, "You kind of spaced out."

"Just getting into the zone."

"Whatever you need to do." As she walked away, she let one of her hands linger on his arm for a second longer.

He appreciated the gesture of support but wished that the rest of the team wasn't just standing around looking at him, waiting. His eyes narrowed, "Don't you guys have anything better to do? I'm prepped and ready. I'll finish my coffee and head to Hay Hill to meet Nguyen. I'll call you as soon as the meeting is over."

Carlos waved his hand at Rachel and Nathan, who both promptly disappeared upstairs to the second floor of the duplex apartment. "Sorry, buddy," Carlos said. "I wish we could get audio support at Hay Hill."

"It would be great, but it's a posh London club." Kasem crossed his arms, "I'll be fine inside. They're not going to kidnap me in front of their lunch guests. Besides, Nathan and Rachel will be on the inside too."

"True, but they have to go on a tour. They won't be able to stay for the whole meeting." Carlos still looked uncomfortable.

"If you're that worried, then they can have lunch there too," Kasem said with a shrug.

"We thought about that," Petra interrupted, "but it's better if we minimize their exposure. We can use them as backup in the future when you go somewhere that isn't as safe as Hay Hill." She stepped closer to Kasem, "Get going before Carlos' worries drown us all."

Carlos' eyes widened in obvious protest, "None of you have seen Nguyen in action. He'll kill anyone he suspects of crossing him. I can't send you into a meeting with him without making sure you have some way out."

Kasem let out a long exhale, "I appreciate your concern. I really do. But we're on this team because you trust us. I know things went balls up last time you dealt with Nguyen, but I can handle this. If it doesn't feel right, I can always say that Carlson Group isn't interested and walk out."

"All right, buddy. You win. It's about time you jump into the fire."

Chapter 21

London, United Kingdom

Kasem hopped out of his Uber at Berkeley Square Gardens and covered the remaining two blocks to Hay Hill on foot. The air was clear and fresh, and the gray clouds threatening rain in the distance contrasted with the greenery of the gardens.

When he reached the entrance to Hay Hill, Kasem exhaled and felt the cool confidence of being on an op set in. Whatever his doubts about himself, his relationship, and the difficulty of the task ahead, he could always rely on his nerves to come through for the op itself. One of his trainers in Iran had commented on how much he excelled at that, that he had nerves of steel when it counted. Kasem put on his most charming smile to greet the pretty redhead receptionist, "Good afternoon. My name's Amir Birch. I'm here for a meeting with Duc Nguyen and his son, Jim. I believe they're booked in one of your meeting rooms."

She looked down at her desk and nodded, "They are. Please follow me."

Kasem followed her through the dining room and down a stairway into the basement bar area, which was surprisingly empty in contrast to the upstairs dining room. They walked to the end of the hall and she opened a sliding door to reveal a circular boardroom with a round table at the center. The seats of the table were already equipped with notepads, pens, water bottles, and glasses. The room felt eerily quiet. "Am I the first one here?" he asked.

"Jim Nguyen is in his office upstairs. I'll let him know that you've arrived, and he'll be down shortly. I'm not sure if his father is with him, but I'll let you know if they expect any delays. While you're waiting, please feel free to order anything you'd like from the bar."

"Thank you." Kasem picked a chair on the far side of the room with a good view of the entrance to the boardroom through the bar. He drummed his pen against the notepad on the table and looked up when he heard someone coming down the stairs.

"Amir, hi," Jim said as he approached. "I hope you haven't been waiting long. Dad's running a few minutes late, but he's with Sir Caleb and they're on their way."

"No problem." Kasem shook Jim's hand, "Good to see you. How are you doing?"

"Great. Just the daily grind. Can I get you anything from the bar?" Jim waved his hand to summon the bartender.

"I'll have a cup of Earl Grey with some lemon, please," Kasem said.

"I'll have an Irish coffee," Jim added. "With Jameson."

"One cup of Earl Grey with lemon and an Irish coffee with Jameson," the bartender repeated. "I'll have those right out to you."

Kasem made sure to keep up the small talk while they waited and sipped on their drinks. He stuck to Jim's interests, which he and the team had researched extensively in preparation for the meeting. They covered the Arsenal Football team, skiing in the Alps, and the London pub scene before they heard Nguyen and Sir Caleb coming down the stairs.

"Amir, my apologies for the delay," Duc Nguyen said. "I trust that I left you in good hands?" He looked at his son and Jim seemed to shrink away.

"Yes, Dad. We've just been chatting," Jim answered. "Now that you're here, we can jump right in."

"Great. Amir, it's good to see you," Sir Caleb said with his hand outstretched. "I must take full responsibility for the delay. I was held up at a meeting at Whitehall, and Duc was kind enough to wait for me."

Kasem stood to shake their hands, "No problem. I've enjoyed my time with Jim. We're both Arsenal fans, so we have plenty to talk about."

"Good to hear," Nguyen's words were warm, but his tone and features were cold and reserved.

Kasem swallowed his apprehension and continued, "I looked at the documents that you sent over on the Thanh Hoa fund. It's an interesting opportunity. I spoke to my team at Carlson and we made a list of questions."

"Very good," Nguyen said. "I always appreciate it when the youth take initiative." He glowered at his son, and Kasem caught the note of disdain in Nguyen's gaze and tone. "Let's go through your questions."

"Absolutely." Kasem removed a list of questions from his folio, "First off, I wanted to know if you already have the exact site mapped out for the farm and power plant investments. To make sure I understand—you're looking at one installation of 40 megawatts of solar panels on a parcel adjacent to the farm itself, with a fifty-fifty debt to equity split, right?"

"That's correct," Sir Caleb said.

Kasem rubbed his chin. He still wasn't sure where Sir Caleb fit into the equation. He clearly had contacts in the upper echelons of British government, but was he also involved in setting up the deal? Or was Sir Caleb purely a financier? Without missing a beat to dwell on the question, Kasem continued, "You're raising $74 million and have already confirmed $67 million, is that still the case?"

Sir Caleb gave him a quick nod. "That's right. Seventy-four is our target raise. We've had statements of interest that cover at least $67 million, but we're waiting on confirmation for the exact investment amounts from each of our partners."

"Do you have written confirmations of that interest?" Kasem asked. "Carlson Group is interested in the opportunity, but we want to make sure that you have enough funds to cover the entire funding gap before we provide a commitment."

"We can provide that for you," Jim said in an enthusiastic voice. "What ticket size are you looking at?"

"We should be able to cover the remaining $7 million in financing, provided that we receive investment committee approval. This investment amount is being raised for Nguyen Capital, which will invest directly into the Thanh Hoa subsidiary. Is that correct?"

"Yes, Nguyen Capital has a great track record of investments around the world." Jim gave his father an eager glance.

"Very good," Kasem said with a nod. "We'll need to conduct due diligence on the company and the investment, but given your track record, I would say that's more of a formality. We can talk about reporting arrangements for the investment, terms, your current operations. Basically, we'll finish up with our due diligence and negotiate terms in one fell swoop."

Nguyen raised his eyebrows, "How long do you expect that process to take? As my son should have told you, we'll be closing this financing round in three weeks. We would have normally given you a more commercially standard turnaround time, but we ran into some unavoidable delays. He's learning the ropes."

Nguyen's expression changed into a creepy smile that almost sent a shudder up Kasem's spine. *Guess I can see what Carlos meant.* Kasem blinked twice and said, "We can work with a three-week timeframe."

"Good. Jim will share the details of our data room so that you can conduct your due diligence, and we can get this moving. I'm choosing to trust you, Amir, and expecting you to deliver on that trust." Nguyen's tone remained cold, and all Kasem could focus on was how quickly the meeting would be over.

"I look forward to a fruitful working relationship," Kasem said. "Subject to our due diligence and negotiations, of course."

Nguyen stood up. "Sir Caleb and I should get going. We have other investors to meet with. Jim can take you through the rest. He's at least capable of that."

Kasem nodded, "Thank you for your time."

"Lovely to speak to you again, Amir," Sir Caleb said. "We'll add the written confirmations from the other investors to the data room in the next few days. Let's schedule another meeting for you to come into the office for the end of next week."

"Perfect."

******

Kasem and Jim passed the next two hours over drinks, first at Hay Hill and then at a pub down the street called The Clarence. The two of them bonded over gin cocktails from the pub's special gin menu, followed by several pints of Guinness and fish and chips. Kasem could feel the alcohol fogging up his head, but he had to keep pace with Jim who was fully intent on getting wasted. After they finished eating and Jim ordered yet another pitcher of Guinness, Kasem asked for some water and downed a glass before taking another gulp of beer.

"I'm so glad you're on board," Jim said, slurring his words. "This is fantastic. I'm bringing an investor into the fund. My dad keeps saying that he can't believe it. You know, he's such a hard ass. I spent some time after university, spent a year working at a ski resort—I just needed a break—and now that's all I'll ever be to him. A ski-bum. What the—?" He followed with a series of expletives.

"Fathers can be tough," Kasem said. He had no real context since his dad had always been easier on him than his mom was, but he played up the angle. "My dad's great and we've always had this easygoing relationship. But my father-in-law? Man, that is a completely different picture. At first, he just didn't like me, and we couldn't figure out why. Turns out, he was being protective. After a while, he realized that I wasn't going away, and things started to get better. I tried so hard to impress him, but it only got better when I said to hell with that—I'm going to be who I am and he has to live with it. That's when he started to respect me." He refilled their beers from the pitcher on the table.

"I don't know. No matter what I do, I can't seem to change his mind," Jim sighed. "The Carlson Group coming into this deal will go a long way, though. I've had loads of meetings with possible investors, but never anyone quite as big."

"Did any of them ever come through?" Kasem asked, although he already knew the answer based on the information that Madison had given them. Jim had come close to raising the final investment required, but the deal had fallen through at the last minute.

"No, we got pretty close, but we never signed a deal."

Kasem nodded, content with how much he'd gotten Jim to open up, "When is Nguyen Capital expecting to break ground on the farm?"

"Dad's planning to make the investment right after my wedding."

"Awesome." If they were going to break ground after the wedding, then the delivery of the arms would happen around that time as well. Now that he had confirmation on that timeframe, he could focus on the bonding aspect of his assignment—the most important part of his role on the op was to gain Jim's trust. Kasem gestured at the bartender to order another round and grinned, "Getting married is tough and stressful. There's so much planning. But being married? Now, that's what it's all about. I'm sure you and your dad will settle down once the wedding is off your plate."

"I hope so. You're right about wedding planning. We're doing this destination thing, and there's so much to organize. I mean, we have wedding planners to help, but we still have to make decisions. Janine wants things a certain way for her family, and my parents want things to be a certain way for them. I had no idea it would be so hard."

"You'll get through it." Kasem raised his glass once again to keep the conversation going. "Janine and Cara really hit it off last week, by the way. We should all go out and blow off some steam together."

Chapter 22

London, United Kingdom

Petra walked to the office building on Baker Street that housed Nguyen's offices and went upstairs to the fourth floor to wait for Kasem. After being buzzed into their office suite, she smiled at the receptionist and said, "My name is Cara. I'm here waiting for my husband, Amir Birch. He's in a meeting with Jim Nguyen."

"Please have a seat."

Petra made a show of hesitating before she asked, "Would you mind if I used your ladies' room?"

"It's right around that corner," the receptionist said as she pointed down the hall. Petra rounded the corner and bypassed the restroom to get a gauge on the offices. Her intuition told her that Nguyen most likely kept the ledger somewhere in these offices or in his home at Holland Park, although Madison had provided intel that Nguyen also kept a highly secured safe at his country house. Offices lined the hallway, most of which had their doors shut, with two glass-door conference rooms in each corner that supplied most of the light in the hallway.

Petra passed by Madison's desk and was surprised not to find her there. They'd never met—Rachel wanted to keep her from knowing too much about their team in case she became compromised—but seeing her there would have been comforting nonetheless. Petra continued her walk-through, not searching for anything in particular. She simply wanted to get a feel for the office and the personality behind the leadership. They still didn't know how many people within Nguyen's organization were aware of the real nature of his investments, or how many of his employees had enough access to even suspect. The closed-door nature of the office supported that theory. Nguyen kept the true nature of his business close to his chest, which had served him well in terms of protection. So, it was doubly surprising that Kasem had been able to get this close to a deal so quickly, even after they had stolen a portion of the arms that Nguyen had already received. If she were a more optimistic operative, she would have rejoiced in how well the mission was going, but her gut told her that it had been all too easy, even with the urgency of Nguyen's timeline. She had done an in-depth review of Nguyen's different investors and they had made sure to pick one that fit the same profile when they'd established Kasem's cover identity, but it was all moving too fast. Either Nguyen was more desperate for money than they'd realized, or he was pulling Kasem in for a purpose.

She tried to shake off her uneasiness. Whatever the situation, the best they could do was keep a close eye on what was happening and react to it before things became too dangerous. She bit her lip and tasted blood as she remembered Vikram. *At least it was quick.* Petra exhaled and turned around before she reached the corridor that led toward the receptionist from the opposite side.

She was halfway back toward the restroom when she heard a nasal voice behind her. "May I help you?"

Petra put on her best confused-face. "Yes. I'm looking for the ladies' room. So sorry, I'm all turned around," she said.

"It's a bit farther down the hall," a tall, skinny man with a hooked nose answered. "Who are you here to see?"

Petra swallowed, "I'm meeting my husband here. Amir's in a meeting with Jim right now, but we're all going to go out afterward."

"A meeting with Jim?"

"Yes."

"Please come with me."

Petra opened her mouth and closed it. "I thought you said the ladies' room was this way," she motioned down the hallway in the other direction.

"It is, but the meeting is this way. Why don't I show you where they are first?"

"Oh, you're so kind." Her heartbeat drummed in her ears and she followed him, attempting to process his demeanor. His eyes had a devilish quality, icy and malignant, but shrewd and deeply intelligent, with a hypnotic element that drew her in—like a snake. There was something about him that put her on edge immediately, made her feel off her game, as if she were supposed to throw herself at his feet and beg for mercy. *What have you gotten yourself into?*

They moved past three office doors to the corner and he gestured to a closed door on his left. "This is Duc Nguyen's office. I believe they're in there. The meeting isn't over yet, so why don't you wait in my office across the hall? I'd like to hear more about you."

Petra quieted her doubts and followed him. When they reached his office, he unlocked the door and motioned toward a plush couch in the corner. He pulled one of the chairs from in front of the desk closer to the couch for himself. Petra shifted in her spot as he retrieved a whiskey decanter from a side table. Without asking, he poured them both a drink and held one out for her to take.

"It's nice to meet you, Cara. I didn't realize that when Jim was bringing his new associate on board, we'd have the privilege of meeting his attractive wife."

Petra steadied her hand and gripped the whiskey glass, her earlier weakness at bay. Part of her wanted to give this womanizer a piece of her mind and the other was scared. Even if he was hitting on her now, her sixth sense told her that this man was dangerous. Very dangerous. Who was he? Why had Carlos never mentioned him? She made a mental note to ask him and turned her attention back to the slime-ball in front of her.

She gave him a shy smile. "I'm not much of a whiskey drinker, but this is great. Thank you." She squashed her anxiety and capitalized on the image of a shy woman in awe of power. "Have you worked with Mr. Nguyen long?"

"I've been with him for more than ten years. We've been to the end of the world together." He shrugged. "Literally, since we've done business in so many conflict zones, investing in the world's most torn apart communities. Figuratively, because he knows I would do anything for him. I just got back from setting up one of our investments in South America, a coffee plantation in Venezuela." He sipped his whiskey. "How long has your husband been with the Carlson Group?"

"About a year." Petra continued to give quick answers as he fired off a series of questions, thankful that she had spent so much time studying both her cover and Kasem's. With the continued questions, her apprehension quelled. Clearly, this was a test, but he hadn't found a hole in their story yet, and she certainly wasn't going to let him discover one. When she finished her whiskey, she stood up tentatively. "I'm so sorry, but I really do need to use the restroom now." She kept her voice meek and apologetic. "I guess Amir and Jim will be out soon anyway."

The man frowned and gave her a curt nod. "Don't get lost this time."

His nasal voice sent a shiver down her spine. "It was great to meet you, Mr.—?"

"I'm Jonathan Seymour. Since your husband is going to be working with us, I suspect I'll see you again."

"I look forward to that, Mr. Seymour."

"Just Seymour, please." He stood up. "I'll escort you to make sure that you don't get lost again."

Petra made a show of thanking him and followed him to the ladies' room. When she was safely away from him with the door shut, she locked the door and leaned over the sink. It took several moments before her adrenaline was in check. Whoever he was, Seymour scared her to the bone.

Chapter 23

London, United Kingdom

Carlos' expression turned bleak. "Seymour? He was there? You met him?"

"So, you do know him?" Petra asked. "How come you never mentioned him?"

"Oh, I know him. He pulled the trigger on Vik." Carlos' chest tightened as he recalled an image of Seymour's hooked nose and unfeeling eyes.

"He's the one?" Petra placed her hand on his shoulder. "Are you okay?"

"I'll be all right. I'm glad you are too after a one-on-one encounter with him."

"Carlos, what were you thinking?" Kasem asked. "How could you not warn us about this asshat? If he's that dangerous?"

"He didn't show up in any of our current research, so I thought he didn't work with Nguyen anymore." Carlos threw his hands out and sighed, "I should have known better."

Petra frowned, "I don't get it. Why didn't he show up in any of the CIA's intel? Where are Rachel and Nathan anyway?"

"They went to pick up takeout. I thought I'd have some food ready tonight since we'll probably be up late planning." Carlos let out another sigh. "They should be back any minute."

Almost on cue, they heard the door to the apartment unlock. "Speak of the devil," Carlos said.

Nathan and Rachel walked into the living room and set two large paper bags on the coffee table.

Rachel cast a darting glance across the room. "Who killed the cat?"

"In all your research and intel on Nguyen, did you find anything about a guy named Seymour?" Petra asked with her arms crossed.

Rachel shrugged, "Sure. He's one of Nguyen's top people. Real cutthroat guy. He's been in South America for the past year."

"He's not in South America," Petra shook her head. "I just met him at Nguyen's offices today. You're right—he's a real cutthroat guy."

82

Rachel raised her hand to her mouth and looked at Nathan. "Any idea how we missed that?"

Nathan looked equally shocked. "All of our intel says that he's working with a subsidiary in South America. Madison never mentioned that he was back, maybe it just happened? Petra, I'm so sorry. I never meant to blindside you—"

"It's fine." Petra gestured with her hands. "I'm not made of glass. You don't have to worry about me. He was testing me, but that's to be expected. I answered all of his questions. It just would have been nice to have a heads up that I might run into him."

"You passed, though. We're okay." Carlos kept his much broader concerns in check and sent a message to check in on Madison. There was no reason to believe that either she or Petra had been compromised, but he was determined to pull the op if there was even a chance that it had happened. *They're not compromised,* he reminded himself. *Maybe we should pull the op anyway if Seymour is still in the game.* Vik had been killed because Carlos had convinced him not to abort.

"We're okay, but I'll need every scrap of intel we can find on him." Petra cocked her head to one side, "We'll have to be ready for the next time we run into him."

"Exactly," Kasem agreed. "I've been invited to the engagement party in two weeks, so that's our next step. Jim mentioned that his father keeps a specialty art collection at his country house, Hill Hearst. Your intel confirmed that he keeps the collection in a safe there. Even if he doesn't keep the ledger there normally, chances are that it will be there while he's there. I bet he likes to keep it close."

"We need to get inside," Petra said. "Nathan, do you think you can make that happen?"

"I've been working on the house's security system for the past couple of days. I can get us in, but I can't remove all traces of the intrusion. If anyone is looking, they'll be able to detect me."

Carlos nodded. "How long will you be able to control the security system?"

Nathan considered for a moment, "Their security protocol includes an internal sweep on the system every thirty minutes. If we stay for longer than that, they'll know I'm in there."

"That should be enough time," Kasem said, "but we still need to get inside the house before then. We have to find the safe and figure out how we're going to access it."

"Doesn't Jim spend some of his weekends out there?" Carlos asked. "Maybe you could get him to invite you over?"

Kasem raised his eyebrows. "Two weeks before his engagement party? I seriously doubt that. Maybe Madison could get inside?"

Carlos checked his phone and heaved a sigh of relief when he saw the all clear message from Madison. "That's too risky. She's not invited to the party, so I don't see how we could pull that off without compromising her. She's okay, by the way—just had to run some errands, that's why she wasn't in the office."

"Good," Petra nodded. "Did she say anything about Seymour?"

"He got back a couple of days ago, but she had no idea how important he was. She was just going to mention it at our regular check in tomorrow." Carlos shifted in his seat, "Maybe we should move her to a safe house—as a precaution."

Rachel's brow furrowed, "Isn't that a bit extreme? She's fine, she just said everything was good. Why would we give up our best source of intel?"

To keep her safe, Carlos sighed and dismissed his internal paranoia. Nguyen hadn't shown any signs of suspecting Madison after they had emptied his entire storage unit, so why would Seymour being on the scene make things any worse? "All right, she stays in," he said with a nod and drummed his fingers on the table. They still needed a plan to get through this op as quickly as possible, and that meant they needed the ledger. "Which still doesn't solve our problem, we need to find a way into that house before the party."

"Maybe I could help with that?" Petra said. "I could see if Janine needs any help getting the place ready for the party."

Carlos raised his finger and pointed at her, "That could work. You have supposedly planned a wedding to Amir. And you could tell her that you did some part-time work in event management, so you want to help out."

"I'll add it to your cover," Nathan added. "Plus, anything else you need, of course. I'm always here to help you, Petra—"

Kasem shot him a glance, "Thanks, Nathan. *We* really appreciate all of your hard work."

Carlos caught the icy exchange and prevented himself from chuckling. Nathan had exhibited an obvious crush on Petra since Kyoto. Kasem didn't seem too bothered by his attitude toward her until now, but it had clearly begun to grate on him. "I think we've figured out some good next steps. Why don't we all take a break, have some dinner, then get back to it. We'll research Seymour, try to find more intel on the house, and see if we can track down what kind of safe Nguyen has, along with any other security measures." He scanned the team one by one. "Think you guys can handle that? A little dinner?"

Rachel gave him a bemused smile. "Sure, boss." She pulled out a series of takeout containers from the paper bags and placed them on the table. "Think you can handle chopsticks tonight?"

Carlos shot her a glance. "Come on. You know I hate those things. Get me a fork from the kitchen."

"No way," Petra said. "What if it were part of your cover? You've got to learn to use chopsticks, and we're all here to help." She handed him one of the takeout containers marked "lo mein" and a set of chopsticks, "I know you can do it." She grinned and grabbed a container herself as the rest of the team did the same. "Chop, chop, boss."

Chapter 24

Hill Hearst, countryside outside of London, United Kingdom

Petra stepped out of the car in the Surrey neighborhood outside of London. The driveway stretched out in front of her for at least two hundred feet and she could see the windows on the turrets of the expansive Victorian mansion glinting at the end of the front drive. "Wow," she said. "I can see why you wanted to have your engagement party out here."

"Actually, having the party here was Jim's idea, since we're having a destination wedding," Janine said. "He wanted to make sure we did something in the London area, and it is stunning."

"Your family owns this place?"

"Jim's does. He used to spend his summer vacations here. You can imagine how great this place is for a kid—they have stables and a few hundred acres."

Petra nodded, "Pretty different from a townhouse in the center of London." She looked out across the green landscape in the distance. "I'm a bit jealous. I can't even imagine spending a week in a place like this."

"Me too. We've been coming out here on the weekends to work on wedding details and I love it. Jim's teaching me how to ride, but it's tough. I thought learning to ride would be so easy."

"I can imagine," Petra said with a smile. "I've always wanted to learn, but I never have."

"After we return from our wedding and honeymoon, you and Amir should come over for a weekend. We can share the misery and soreness of the learning process."

"Janine, that's so sweet. We'd love to do that." Petra held back a sigh. *Like that's going to happen.* She blinked twice and began to wonder how much Jim and Janine knew about Nguyen's real business.

"I can't thank you enough for offering to help out. My bridesmaids don't live in London, and I'm already tired of dealing with the wedding planners. I really wanted to take care of things for the engagement party without dealing with them, but Jim's such a high roller. It's been a bit of an adjustment."

"I understand." Petra gestured toward the mansion, "Come on, let's go see it."

******

After a quick tour of the property, Petra followed Janine into the main hall. "Here's where we're hosting the party," Janine said.

Petra looked around, taking in the dramatic staircase that led down from the entrance into the massive ballroom. "It looks like something out of a fairy tale." Her eyes danced across the decorative wrought iron railings along the staircase that led to the second and third stories, which gleamed under the light of a majestic crystal chandelier in the center of the atrium. "Are any of your guests staying here?" she asked. She needed to gather intel for the party, so she had to focus her attention away from the awe.

"A few friends are coming in from Paris and other parts of Europe, so they'll occupy some of the upstairs rooms." Janine gave her a smile, "I just had the best idea. You and Amir should stay too. It'll be a blast."

"I wouldn't want to impose."

"You wouldn't, not at all. We could stay up as late as we want, spend the night here after the party, go for a ride in the morning, have breakfast on the terrace." Janine motioned toward the curtains at the end of the hallway. She pulled them back and revealed a set of French doors that opened to a massive stone terrace. Past the terrace there was a small lake set off with greenery and a short pier.

"Wow," Petra caught her breath. "Sorry, I don't know how many times I've said that since I've been here."

"Don't worry. I felt the same way the first time I saw this house. It's a shame we don't get more use out of this place. Duc rarely comes up here anymore. I think his bedroom is just a spot to keep his safe."

"His safe?"

"For his art collection. It's like a vault in a heist movie. The door is massive, maybe the size of one of these doors," Janine said as she pointed toward one of the French doors. "I don't even think he comes by much to check on anything. We've run into Seymour a few times when we've been out here for the weekend, but we only really see Jim's parents at their house in the city."

"Seymour?"

"If you haven't met him yet, count your blessings. That guy is insufferable. He's rude and obnoxious, and a total creep. He actually hit on me the first time I met him—can you believe that? Jim was only gone for a minute. He's a womanizing ass, but Duc will never get rid of him. They've worked together for years. Jim hates him too, but there's nothing he can do about it."

"Oh right, I met him at the office the other day. I can't believe I forgot his name—creepy is an understatement," Petra let herself shudder visibly. "And he comes by to check on the house?"

"I don't know what he does. I've only seen him go in and out of Duc's room. He's always carrying something, so I imagine it has to do with the safe, but I have no clue what they even keep in there. Why store something like art in a safe if it means that no one will ever see it? Doesn't that defeat the purpose?"

"I see your point." Petra gave Janine a shy smile and her eyes twinkled, "Can I see this famous, or maybe infamous, bedroom?"

"Sometimes they keep it locked, but I know the code. Let's see if I can get in."

They moved up the regal staircase toward the third floor. Halfway up, Petra stopped along the banister and looked down at the ballroom. "How are you going to decorate for the party?" she asked. "Is there anything that you need help getting? Do you need help with the setup?" Petra paused. "If that invitation to stay here really stands, I could come over a day or two early to help. My wedding wasn't this regal, but I remember how much there was to do. I did work in event management when I was in New York and coordinated a few upscale charity functions. It took an army to tackle everything. No pressure, though—I totally understand if you have it covered."

"Really? I can't tell you how much of a help that would be. We're going to string LED lights along the banisters here and the walls downstairs so that the whole room will twinkle. I have flowers coming in the day of the party for the centerpieces. All of the deliveries are scheduled, and Jim has some people coming to install the lights, but I could use help making sure everything goes smoothly."

"I'd be happy to be your second in command. Put me to work," Petra said as they continued up the staircase.

When they reached the third floor, Janine turned down the first corridor on the left into a short hallway. They passed a lavish bedroom with the door open on the right side and reached a door at the end of the hall.

"This is it," Janine said. She pushed down on the side of the rustic doorknob and a holographic keypad projected from the top of the knob. Petra watched as Janine keyed in a code and the door made a clicking noise before it opened.

Six, seven, three, two, eight, B. Petra repeated the code mentally to commit it to memory and moved into the room behind Janine.

Petra squinted until her eyes adjusted to the dark room. Thick blackout curtains covered the massive floor-to-ceiling windows. Janine drew them back and the sunlight blinded her momentarily. Once her eyes adjusted, Petra approached and took in the view. The window latches were on the inside and they didn't look as if they opened wide enough for someone to get in from the outside. *Rachel might have superpowers, but she can't transform into a six-year-old child to fit through the window.* A grin crept across Petra's face.

"I feel like I'm in a museum." Petra redirected her attention to the rest of the room and strolled in silence. The room looked as if it were out of a Victorian novel. She noted the open door to the walk-in closet, which was larger than the entire living and dining room suite in their so-called fancy apartment on the canal. Only a few items of clothing hung in there, though. At the back of the closet, a large painting adorned the back wall that was set at a slight angle. One look at it told her that the safe was behind it.

"I know what you're thinking," Janine said. "What a waste of an amazing closet. Wait until you see the en suite."

"Seriously. Those shelves are begging for cute shoes to be on them," Petra said, pointing to the left before turning to the right, "and that side desperately needs handbags." They continued on the tour with a weight off her shoulders. She had the information she needed about the safe's location and access points. This trip had been very fruitful indeed.

Chapter 25

London, United Kingdom

Kasem took an enormous bite out of his burger before setting it down to look at Carlos. "How's yours?" he asked.

"Standard chicken club. Nothing to write home about," Carlos answered with a shrug.

"What did you want to talk about?"

"Maybe I'm second-guessing, but I feel like things with this op have been going way too smoothly."

Kasem wiped his chin with his napkin. "It was easier than I thought to get in with Nguyen. Maybe they're just that desperate for money? But that Seymour guy worries me. She handled it, but he really shook up Petra."

"She's not the only one. I'm still a little worried about Madison," Carlos said in a grim tone. "What about you two? How are you dealing?"

"What do you mean?"

"I pulled you out of a vacation and dropped you smack into an op. It would be normal if you had some friction."

"That's kind of personal."

"Not if it interferes with the op. Besides, she's like my kid sister, I'm allowed to check up on her."

Kasem sighed, "We're doing okay." He knew what Carlos meant. He and Petra had certainly had the occasional tiff over the past few weeks since they had been in London. Overall, it wasn't so bad, but there were issues that they were ignoring.

"You don't sound too convincing."

Kasem reached into his jacket pocket, pulled out a flat leather case, and opened it to reveal the engagement ring that he had picked out for Petra. "I was going to propose. When we were in Kyoto."

Carlos nodded slowly, "I see."

"She stopped me. Told me that she wasn't ready for that, which is fine. We haven't been back together that long, and there's still a lot we have to work out. But she doesn't want me to go back to Paris with her either. Maybe I'm going crazy, but I thought being serious was a good thing."

90

"Might not be about your future. What about your history? I don't know the details, and I don't want to know, but it's food for thought."

Kasem felt his torso freeze up, "I had to do some bad things. Before. You know—"

"I get it. We've all been there, trust me. You don't need to explain."

"What if we can't get past it? I've got to admit, sometimes it makes me jealous of the relationship that you two have."

"Have you lost your mind?" Carlos coughed and almost choked on a bit of his sandwich. "The relationship that we have? What you'd rather be her mentor, her brother? I think that's a little bit different from how two people in a couple typically are—"

"That's not what I mean," Kasem chuckled. "I'm talking about how much she trusts you. We need that, but I'm not sure we have it, because of everything I did. What if she never forgives me?"

Carlos took another bite of his sandwich. "I hope that's not true. There wouldn't be a lot of hope for the rest of us. But I'm not the one who you should be talking to about this. Man up, buddy. You're not going to figure this out drinking beers at the pub with me."

"Hey, you asked me to come hang out with you."

"And now I'm telling you to man up and talk to the woman."

"All right, all right. I'll talk to her. Eventually."

"Don't wait too long," Carlos said. "Life is short."

Chapter 26

London, United Kingdom

When Petra returned to the team's apartment, she immediately noticed that it was uncharacteristically quiet. Kasem was out with Jim, and Carlos had decided to visit an old friend and wouldn't be back until later. She wasn't sure where Rachel and Nathan were, but she welcomed the silence. Cramming five people into one apartment, even such a luxurious flat, had been an adjustment. There were only two bathrooms, so they had run into some issues with timing. It didn't help that Rachel loved taking long showers in the middle of the night. The old London pipes creaked and often woke Petra up, and Rachel's pitchy shower concerts didn't help lull her to sleep.

Petra debated between taking a nap or going for a run and elected for the run. She returned thirty minutes later drenched in sweat and rain, which had started to drizzle a few minutes after she'd left. Huddled over the heater, she checked her text messages and saw that Kasem had invited her to join him and Carlos at a nearby pub. One glance out the window where the drizzle had turned into a steady downpour made her reply that she was staying home. She was about to go take a shower, when she heard the apartment door open. *So much for a night of relaxation.*

Nathan walked into the living room in what looked like gym clothes and his face beamed when he saw her. "Hi, Petra. I thought you'd be at the pub with Carlos and Kasem."

"Hi, Nathan. No, I decided not to brave the rain again."

Nathan stood behind the couch awkwardly for a moment, and then shrugged. "Well then, I'll leave you to it."

"You can join me if you want to watch a movie. I was going to shower first, then pick something out on Netflix." She nodded toward the couch, although she secretly hoped he would decline.

"Actually, there's something else that I wanted to ask you about…"

"Sure, what's up?" she turned toward him with raised eyebrows.

"I don't know if you know, but Rachel gave me a couple of self-defense lessons when we were back home. She was supposed to keep it up, but she's been so busy running around doing other CIA stuff on top of this op, so she hasn't had time. She said she was going to ask you or Carlos to help me, but I don't think she's had the chance."

"Oh," Petra masked her surprise, of all the things that she had expected Nathan to ask her, this was certainly not one of them. "Of course. I'd be happy to help. Why don't we do a lesson right now?" *Might as well get it over with, maybe I can still salvage some alone time tonight.*

"That would be great," he perked up.

They moved the dining table to the side so that they had a decent amount of space to practice.

"Okay, so what has Rachel already taught you?" Petra asked.

"We were working on Krav Maga techniques, like extracting from a basic hand grab."

"Makes sense—that's probably the most important thing, to defend yourself long enough to get away. I don't think you'll need a lot of attack training." She picked up a couch cushion and took a step toward him, "I'm going to grab at your wrist and I want you to move with the energy to attack me by kicking at this cushion."

She reached for his wrist with her right hand and held the cushion at ready. Nathan took a tentative step toward her and raised his knee at the cushion, but she could barely feel the impact. "You need to kick harder, Nathan. Don't pull your punches."

He tried it again, this time with some improvement. After they ran the drill a few times, she stepped back and nodded, "That's good, but now I want you to follow the kick with an open hand strike. Kick, then push me away, and that should give you enough time to run."

They repeated the drill and after the fourth time, Petra felt like they were finally getting somewhere, "Your muscles are getting the hang of it, but now I want you to try something else. Push me."

He frowned, "Push you?"

She nodded, and he extended his arms and pushed her at her shoulders. She took a step back, "Good, but this time, take a step closer, and push me again."

He followed her instructions, and when he pushed she had to take two steps back to regain her balance. "Do you see the difference?" she asked. "If you want to attack your attacker, you have to get closer."

"You're right."

They repeated the kick-strike drill, this time with Nathan stepping toward her into the kick. After a few minutes, Petra heard the door open and tossed the cushion aside, "All right, that's a wrap. I'm tired and I need to take a shower."

Kasem appeared surprised as he entered the living room, followed by Carlos. "Hi babe," Kasem frowned, "I thought you were going to have a quiet evening."

"I was, but Nathan asked me to run him through some self-defense drills. We were just wrapping up." Petra gave Kasem a peck on the cheek, "I'm going to go shower." Without waiting for a response, she disappeared up the stairs, not wanting to linger in the unnecessary awkwardness. Halfway up the staircase, she let out a long sigh—if their relationship was so rocky that Kasem was jealous of her teaching Nathan a few self-defense moves, how would he react when she told him about Vikram?

Chapter 27

Hill Hearst, countryside outside of London, United Kingdom

Petra woke up early at Hill Hearst on the morning of the engagement party. She stole a glance into the main hall by opening her bedroom door a crack. Janine had mentioned that the tables and furniture setup would arrive at eight, with the flowers, caterers, and decorators spread out across the next few hours. At just before five in the morning, the house was still quiet.

She shook Kasem awake, "It's time to set up. Come on."

"Why are you so chipper?" His eyes opened, and he gave her a kiss as he sat up. He fumbled past her to the en suite bathroom and emerged a few minutes later, "Hey, when this is all over, there's some stuff we need to talk about, babe."

"That's the first thing you think of at 5:00 a.m.?"

"It's been on my mind a lot actually," Kasem answered.

"Of course." Petra had an inkling of what he wanted to talk about—their relationship, his fears, her fears, where they were heading. She wanted to avoid the conversation since she had no answers for him. Nothing had changed since Kyoto. She loved Kasem, but still wasn't sure how he could fit into her real life. It was tempting to dodge the discussion, but Carlos had warned her that she couldn't continue to do so, not if she wanted him to stick around. Despite her fears and concerns, she did want that. To keep him from reading her expression, she went into the bathroom to brush her teeth. A few minutes later, she emerged and pulled on the riding breeches Janine had loaned her and a T-shirt.

Kasem followed suit and she showed him the corridor that led to Nguyen's bedroom. Part of her was tempted to try to access the safe right now, but she stopped herself. Their original plan was better. The activity of the party would provide a welcome distraction so that Carlos and Rachel could access the safe.

They were on their way back toward the staircase when Petra's heart stopped. Seymour was halfway up the flight of stairs and coming toward them. One look at his face made her blood turn cold.

He knows.

Kasem looked at her with a frown and followed her gaze. When he saw Seymour, he grabbed her hand.

Petra resisted the urge to flee. Why was Seymour so scary to her? He wasn't the first menacing man that she had encountered on an op. She steadied herself and followed Kasem toward the stairs.

"The two of you are up early," Seymour said when they reached him.

Kasem shrugged, "We're going out for an early morning ride."

"I didn't know you were a rider." Seymour's disbelief cut through his tone. "Janine never mentioned you were planning to use the stables."

"She said we could," Kasem answered.

Petra masked her reaction as her instincts kicked in. Thankfully, Kasem actually did know how to ride, but she barely knew her way around a saddle. "I don't really ride," she said in meek voice. "But Amir's going to give me a lesson. I've always wanted to learn, so he asked Janine if we could take out a couple of horses this weekend." She reached out and mussed Kasem's hair to play up the lovey-dovey voice she was using. "He's such a sweetheart."

Kasem pulled her into his arms to further the picture. "You're the sweetheart," he said and planted a deep kiss on her mouth.

Seymour's nose wrinkled at their display of affection. "Be careful out there. Horses can be dangerous. Make sure you stay on the trails. You wouldn't want to get lost on the property."

Petra suppressed a shudder as they moved past him down the stairs. She couldn't get away fast enough.

When they reached the stables, Petra pointed out two of the stalls. "These are the two Janine said we could use. Let's tack them up quickly and get out of here."

He put his hand on her back. "Are you all right? I know that guy is creepy—"

"There's something about him that gets to me, but I'm okay," Petra cut him off. "Let's just go."

They got the horses out and rode down a trail toward one of the country roads that eventually joined the main road that led to the house. Petra was thankful for the vast countryside to help hide their plan and efforts. Within a few minutes of their arrival, Nathan pulled up with Carlos and Rachel sitting beside him.

"Ahoy, there," Nathan said as he rolled the window down.

"We're not on a pirate ship. This is the English countryside," Rachel said. She hopped out of the Peugeot SUV and looked at the landscape with her hands on her hips.

"Tetchy, tetchy." Nathan looked over at Petra, "Where can I park this thing?"

"There's a clearing farther up that has a ditch sheltered by some trees. That's your best bet," Kasem cut in before she could answer.

Petra raised her eyebrows in amusement. "My thoughts exactly. Why don't you follow Kasem over there? I'll take Rachel and Carlos to the house."

Nathan's face shrank, but he nodded and Kasem led him toward the ditch.

Without waiting for them to return, Petra dismounted and led the horse back toward the stables on foot. Rachel and Carlos followed as Petra went over the plan. "Kasem will set Nathan up in the stables so that he's ready to take control of the internal video feed. Nathan should be able to give us enough time to sneak in and access the safe. Rachel, after you set off the distraction, you and Carlos can get upstairs to access it."

"Yep. You've got it," Rachel said. She looked over at Carlos. "Good thing we have a safecracker in the group. I hear you're a regular Mary Poppins with gadgets."

Carlos' expression perked up. "You ain't seen nothing yet, missy."

******

By midday, Petra felt as if her body were already shutting down. She had hoped the adrenaline would hold her together, but the early morning was getting to her. With the help of Janine's different vendor staff and two of her friends, they had directed the various service providers to set up twenty-five round tables, the centerpieces, and the lighting. *When she said she needed the help, she really meant it.*

"Thank you so much," Janine said as she came down the stairs. "I thought it would be easy to handle, but I couldn't have done it without you."

"Come on. You arranged all the vendors and the timing. All I had to do was be here to coordinate. Besides, I had help. Becca and Megha helped out a lot after they got in this morning."

"Good. I'm glad you all got along so well. Are they getting ready?"

"I think so. We've pretty much wrapped up everything here until the guests start to show up." Petra moved her hands outward. "There wasn't a lot to do when you think about it. This room is so picturesque that it really makes the party. Let me show it to you with the lights." She moved to the side wall and dimmed the overhead lighting. The

LED lights that hung across the banisters and the doorways sparkled. The room looked straight out of a fairy tale. Petra couldn't help but be taken in by the grandeur.

"Oh, my goodness. I can't believe you did all this! Seymour told me I was making a mistake having you help out, but I knew he was wrong."

"I don't think he likes me. We ran into him this morning on our way to the stables. I swear he thought we were trying to steal something. I'm surprised he didn't frisk us."

"I can just picture it. I really hate that guy. Like I was going to hire the weirdo he recommended." Janine walked over to Petra and gave her a hug, "Come upstairs and get ready with us."

"Are you sure? That's really for you and your bridesmaids."

"Come on. This is just my engagement party, not the wedding. Besides, it'll be fun. We'll open a bottle of champagne and spread stupid gossip."

Petra couldn't help but smile. Despite the mission and all the tension that it brought, she was actually having fun. She almost sighed, she didn't want to have to screw over Janine's family. *Maybe Janine doesn't know anything about Nguyen's operations? Maybe taking the ledger won't have a big impact on her and Jim?* Petra shook off her concerns and nodded. "I'd be honored. I'll get my things and meet you in your room."

Chapter 28

Hill Hearst, countryside outside of London, United Kingdom

Kasem looked at his watch in apprehension. Since Petra needed to spend time with the bridal party for her cover, she was never alone, so he'd taken over coordinating the team. Nathan and Carlos were set up in the stables, and Rachel was putting out hors d'oeuvres with the catering staff.

He adjusted his tie as he entered the main ballroom. The happy couple had already made their entrance after most of the guests had arrived. Kasem grabbed a glass of champagne from a nearby tray and was in the midst of small talk with Sir Caleb until Jim rescued him.

Kasem made eye contact with Rachel as she brushed past him. He took another full champagne glass from her tray and moved with Jim toward Janine, who was introducing Petra to some other guests.

After crossing to Petra and kissing her on the cheek, Kasem turned to the engaged couple, "I have a surprise for you two. Would you mind if I make an announcement before dinner?"

Jim frowned and shrugged, "Sure, but what's going on?"

"Just something to kick off the party in style. You'll see." Kasem picked up a fork from one of the dinner tables and tapped on his glass before positioning himself in the center of the room. "Hello, everyone. My name is Amir Birch and this is my wife, Cara," he said, stretching his hand toward a smiling Petra in introduction. "Before dinner is served, I wanted to congratulate the happy couple. Jim and I first met briefly in college, but only recently reconnected and had the chance to become close friends. The two of you have been so gracious and welcomed Cara and me into your family, so we planned something special to thank you and congratulate you. Would all of you please follow me out to the terrace?"

Kasem gave Petra a quick nod and watched as the room filed out slowly. When everyone was outside, he looked toward the kitchen and tapped on his earpiece. "Be ready to go in sixty seconds."

"Dimming the lights now," Nathan said through the com system.

Kasem followed the group to the terrace and a moment later, Carlos launched the first set of fireworks. The sky became a garden of crackling and sparkling lights set to Beethoven's Ninth Symphony. A few scattered rockets exploded into little stars in time with the music and lit up the dark sky. The music sped up and a number of firecrackers and sparklers joined the rockets. When the symphony slowed once again, the fireworks display kept pace, adjusting to a series of fountains and then increasing once again. As soon as one star disappeared, another appeared. With the louder major notes, larger rockets took off, setting up a canopy of dripping lights after they exploded. Each time, the backdrop of the trees and countryside became visible in the night sky, set off by the cacophony of falling embers. The music softened, and the fireworks show slowed but built up once again to the next climax. When the music climbed into a long chord, the last set of fireworks launched in line with the drawn-out stopping point. The repeated chords were accentuated by a staggered stream of firecrackers and rockets until the music faded out into a few dispersed notes.

Chapter 29

Hill Hearst, countryside outside of London, United Kingdom

Rachel waited in the hall as the guests went out to the terrace after Kasem's announcement. With a tray in hand, she stopped at a high-top table to clear it of small plates and champagne glasses. She lingered in the shadows next to the stairway in the center of the hall, thankful that it offered enough cover for her to pretend to take several moments just to pick up one table.

Her earpiece crackled as Kasem said, "Be ready to go in sixty seconds."

"Dimming the lights now," she heard Nathan say through the com system.

Rachel watched Kasem walk out to the terrace and close the door behind him. She placed the tray laden with dirty dishes on the floor underneath the tablecloth and counted the seconds in her head. When she reached the end of the countdown, the crowd exclaimed as the fireworks appeared, alongside the first note from Beethoven's Ninth Symphony.

"I'm moving now," she said into her com.

"Deactivating the front door's security system and cameras," Nathan responded. "Carlos, what's your position?"

"I'm in the bushes by the front door," Carlos answered.

Rachel reached the top of the stairs and stopped at the front door as the fireworks outside hit their first major chord. "Ready to go."

"Carlos, the door is ready for you now," Nathan said.

A few seconds later, Carlos opened the door and appeared inside the entryway. Rachel motioned toward the grand staircase to her right, "This way." They moved quickly up to the third floor, past the decorated banisters without bothering to look down at the dramatically decorated hall below.

Once they reached the third floor, Rachel headed toward the hallway that led to the master bedroom with the safe. "We're outside the bedroom door," she said.

"Acknowledged," Nathan said. "Extra security on the door is disabled, so just enter the code when the keypad appears."

Rachel exhaled and waited, "Nothing is happening."

"Stand by." The com link was silent for a few moments until Nathan said, "You should be good to go now."

A slim keypad projection appeared on top of the door handle, and Rachel keyed in the code that Petra had given her. When the door clicked open, Rachel and Carlos entered the room.

Rachel shut the door behind her and checked that the blackout curtains were drawn before she switched on a bedside lamp, while Carlos headed straight for the walk-in closet.

"We have eight minutes and forty-five seconds," she said. "Make it snappy, Mary Poppins."

Chapter 30

Hill Hearst, countryside outside of London, United Kingdom

Carlos moved into the enormous walk-in closet and his eyes widened at the size. *Petra wasn't kidding.* It took him a few seconds to get to the back of the room with the painting that she had described. "Ready to access the safe," he said.

Nathan's voice came over the coms. "I've deactivated the alarm systems in that room. You're all set."

Carlos lifted the painting off the wall and set it aside. "It's a Viking biometric with a rotary combination lock and a fingerprint pad. I guess Nguyen went old school when he had this put in. I can bypass the fingerprint access with the combination." He removed a specialized stethoscope from his jacket pocket and placed it against the surface of the safe as he wiggled the combination lock. "Safe to drill."

He pulled a flat device from his other jacket pocket and clicked its gears into place to assemble the mini drill.

Rachel pursed her lips, "You really are Mary Poppins."

Carlos grunted as she came into the closet to stand beside him. "I need to concentrate. Stay on the lookout."

"Keep your shirt on, Carlos."

Before he turned on the drill and placed the moving bit next to the combination pad, Carlos triggered a switch on the side of the drill that would mask the noise using a rubber dampening structure. He waited until the bit was through, then retracted the drill and widened the opening. With a folded magnetic device-and-mirror combo, he slid the mirror and magnet through the safe wall. Once they were through, he pushed a button and the mirror unfolded so that he could see the other side of the lock mechanism. Using the magnet, he made several adjustments on the lock from the outside to observe changes in the internal mechanism.

Rachel's voice jarred his concentration, "Think you can speed it up? I didn't realize Mary Poppins was such a slowpoke."

"Hold your horses, cowgirl," Carlos grumbled. "Almost there." He adjusted the levers on his end of the magnetic device and heard a louder click as the lock disengaged. "There we go." *This is for you, Vik. We're going to get him.*

He opened the safe door and his heart sank into his stomach. "It's empty. No ledger. Nothing." *Damn it.* He clenched his fists.

Carlos waited for Nathan to acknowledge over their com link. "Nathan, do you read me? The ledger isn't here. We'll meet you at the car. Keep the security deactivated as long as you can. We have to clear out before the fireworks end."

Rachel gave him a frantic look and peered over his shoulder. "What? It has to be here. Our intel…I'm sure." She moved toward the side of the closet and started pushing clothes to the side, knocking some of them to the floor. She did the same to the other side of the closet.

Carlos' eyes danced between the safe and her, "Rachel, stop. We have to get out of here. Put the clothes back the way they were. They can't know we've been here."

"You just drilled the safe. There's no way we can leave without being noticed. Don't you get it, Carlos? He knew to move the ledger. None of us are getting out of here alive."

Chapter 31

Hill Hearst, countryside outside of London, United Kingdom

Carlos took a deep breath and disregarded Rachel's words. He filled the hole that he had drilled with putty and placed a metallic cap on both sides of the hole. A metal scanner would detect the drill hole, but the naked eye would not. He shut the safe door and stood up. His heart was beating off the charts as he checked his watch. *Two minutes to go.*

"Rachel, put the clothes back. Now." He gathered a bunch of the hangers from the floor and hung them up again.

"It's not going to work. We're dead, Carlos," she cried out.

Carlos walked up behind her and wrapped his arms around her torso. She struggled for a moment and then collapsed on the floor in tears. "We're never going to get him," she sobbed.

"We are. Rachel, we are, but right now, we have to go. We'll figure out another way, but first, we need to get out of here before we get caught."

She gave him a slow nod. They picked up the remaining clothes, hung them on the rod, and ran for the main bedroom door. Once they were back in the hall, Carlos could hear the closing chords of their excerpt from Beethoven's Ninth Symphony. "Move."

They sped down the stairs toward the main entrance. When they reached the door, Carlos stopped. *Fifteen seconds.* He clapped Rachel on the shoulder. "You don't have to go back to the event. Cut your losses. Come with me." He could tell that she was still reeling from what had happened upstairs. It was obvious she also had some kind of personal stake in putting Nguyen away. He would have to get clarity on that later, but for now, they just had to get away.

"I'm fine. We might need my catering cover again," she answered. Her voice cracked, but he could see the resolve returning to her eyes.

He nodded and left. Just as the clock wound down and the symphony chords faded away, he ducked back into the bushes. When he was safely out of camera range, he spoke into the com again. "Nathan, I'll meet you at the car."

Again, he was greeted by silence over the com. "Anyone have a twenty on Nathan?" he asked.

Petra's voice came over the link. "What's wrong?"

Instead of answering her, Carlos' blood turned cold. He sped through the shadows toward the stables where Nathan had been hiding. "Nathan, answer me! Nathan?"

Chapter 32

Hill Hearst, countryside outside of London, United Kingdom

Nathan pulled out his earpiece and blew on it before he repeated, "I read you, Carlos. No ledger."

"Nathan, do you read me? The ledger isn't here," Carlos said again. "We'll meet you at the car. Keep the security deactivated as long as you can. We have to clear out before the fireworks end."

"Acknowledged," Nathan said. The earpiece crackled and went completely dead. *Great. Now I can't even hear them.* "Stupid com," he cursed under his breath and packed up his equipment. He threw everything but the laptop into his shoulder bag and checked the clock. *Two minutes, thirty seconds.*

Nathan picked up the computer, leaving it open so that his security hack would remain in place, and checked the lane outside of his stall. It was still dark and empty, so he stepped out, carefully balancing the laptop on his forearm. He shut the stall door and moved toward the stable's entrance. *One thirty-five.*

He struggled with the main stable door for a moment before he put his equipment on the ground to use two hands to open it. As he emerged, he was greeted by the ending chords of the symphony and fireworks show. He shifted his equipment to the ground outside the door and managed to shut it. After grabbing his gear again, he continued around the stables toward the tree cover that led toward the car. He was almost at the cover when the Beethoven chords faded out again. Without thinking, he snapped his laptop shut to make it easier to carry and slid it into his shoulder bag.

Crap. This is why I should have stayed an analyst. As soon as he had done it, he realized that Carlos and Rachel might still need the security hack. He stopped immediately and set up his computer again, figuring that he was close enough to the tree clearing to be out of sight of the lookouts posted around the property.

Before he could get the hack back in place, he felt the cold muzzle of a gun against the back of his head. "Hands up. Who the hell are you and what are you doing here?"

Chapter 33

Hill Hearst, countryside outside of London, United Kingdom

Carlos crossed the clearing toward the stables slowly to keep out of sight. When he reached the stables, he peered through a crack in the door before opening it, careful to lift it so that it didn't creak, and stepped inside. Once the door was safely closed behind him, he ran down the aisle toward the stall where they had installed Nathan. The stall was empty, and his remaining hope shattered, but he rushed back toward the door. *Maybe Nathan was heading toward the car?*

On his way out, he heard a voice in the distance. "Hands up. Who the hell are you and what are you doing here?"

Carlos kept his back pressed to the stable and moved toward its edge. He poked his head around the corner and could just make out the outline of someone holding a gun to someone crouching on the ground. Even in the darkness, Carlos could tell that Nathan was the one on the ground.

He squinted to judge the distance between himself and Nathan's attacker. Depth perception was problematic in the dark and he only had one shot to get to Nathan. Carlos watched as the attacker stepped away and Nathan stood with the gun still pointed at him. *It's now or never.* Nathan wasn't a trained field operative, and Carlos wasn't sure how he would stand up to having a gun in his face.

Carlos took a deep breath and sped toward them, thankful for the dark clothing that kept him concealed. Once he was within reasonable shooting range, he pulled his Beretta out of a holster at his ankle and strode out of the shadows.

"Not so fast," he said in a loud voice. He had to hope that he wasn't within earshot of any of the other lookouts on the property. He had no other choice—he had to risk it for Nathan. "Drop it." He moved closer and motioned with his gun.

The attacker glanced toward him and raised his arms, "I'm putting my gun down."

Carlos blinked several times and advanced toward the guard who was making a slow show of putting the gun on the ground. Nathan was behind the guard, facing Carlos, but he couldn't make out details on Nathan's face.

As the guard was about to place the gun on the ground, Nathan yelled out. "He's got another gun."

Before Carlos could react, Nathan leaped on the man's back and started to pummel him. The guard threw him off and punched him in the gut, while Carlos ran forward to separate them. He grabbed the guard and caught him with a forearm swipe to his solar plexus but dropped his Beretta into the grass in the scuffle.

Carlos caught a punch in his gut and rather than doubling over, purposely dropped to the ground so that he could send a kick at the man's shins. The guard stumbled but remained upright and reached for something at his ankle.

By the time Carlos was back on his feet, the guard had pulled out a switchblade. Nathan lashed out at him and caught a slash across the thigh before Carlos could reach him. The guard dropped the knife under the weight of Carlos' assault and fell to the ground with Carlos straddling him. Carlos dealt a few punches to his head to knock him out.

When he was satisfied that the guard was unconscious, he stumbled over to Nathan. "Nathan, are you okay?" Carlos squinted again to make out Nathan's wound. He was bleeding from his outer right thigh and his breathing was unsteady.

"You're going to be fine, buddy," Carlos said. He peeled off his sweater and pressed it against the wound. "Keep pressure on this." He moved both of Nathan's arms to push his hands against the sweater. Using his belt, Carlos made a makeshift tourniquet above the wound and then tied the sweater around it as a cushion.

"We have to go..." Nathan said in a halting whisper.

Carlos tapped his com and spoke into it. "Nathan is down. Knife wound to the thigh. I need help by the stables."

The com was silent.

"...be...there," a crackling female voice came across the device.

Nathan shook his head, "Coms aren't working."

Carlos steadied himself and stood up. They were still a good five-minute walk through the woods to reach the car under normal circumstances.

"I'm going to have to carry you, but you've got to keep pressure on that wound. Think you can do it?"

Nathan nodded, "I can walk."

"Okay, let me help you up." Carlos wrapped Nathan's arm over his shoulders and heaved him up onto his feet.

They made it a few steps before Nathan started to wobble. "My head."

"Whoa, whoa, buddy. Let me take a look." Carlos lowered him to the ground and checked Nathan's head. He found a bump on the back of Nathan's head and his throat constricted. "Looks like you might have hit your head. Don't worry; it's nothing serious. You're just going to feel hungover for a while."

Nathan's face contorted and he rolled over on his side to vomit into the grass.

"See. Just like you drank way too much." Carlos rubbed his hand over Nathan's back and debated what to do. Vomiting was a clear sign of a concussion, but he had no idea how severe. "Try to keep your right hand on that wound. I'm going to carry you out of here."

Carlos braced himself and hoisted Nathan over his left shoulder. He grunted under the weight and made it into the tree cover some twenty feet away. After a few steps within the trees, he had to put him back on the ground.

"I'm sorry, buddy. I should have spent more time at the gym and less time drinking wine," Carlos panted and tried to catch his breath.

A voice back at the stables caught his attention. "Carlos?" someone was calling out.

Carlos waved toward the stables. "Rachel, over here."

She jogged toward him. "Thank God you're okay. What happened?"

"Nathan has a knife wound to the thigh and probably a concussion. We got into a scuffle with Sir Snores-a-lot back there."

"There's no one back there, Carlos. He's gone..." Rachel gripped his arm. "He must be getting backup. I'll get the car, we need to get the hell out of here."

Chapter 34

London, United Kingdom

Madison fumbled with the keys to her apartment and glanced back at Jonah, the tall muscular blond man waiting behind her. "I'm sorry it's a bit messy," she said in a shy voice as she opened the door.

He followed her inside and slammed the door shut before he pushed her up against the wall and kissed her, hard. When he released her a few moments later, she could barely catch her breath.

"I'm not really looking at the apartment," he said as he caressed her face.

She flushed and felt the need to get some liquid courage. She didn't normally engage in one-night stands, but his rugged charm had swept her off her feet. "Would you like some wine?" she extracted herself from his embrace.

He frowned and shrugged, "How about something stronger?" He pointed toward a bottle of mezcal in her living room.

"Okay," she said. Carlos had given her that bottle as a gift at their last check-in—they were celebrating the upcoming engagement party, after which they would hopefully have the evidence that they needed to take Nguyen down. He'd said that they would drink it together before her testimony, but now was as good a night as any to open it—wasn't it?

Jonah grabbed two shot glasses from the cabinet and set them on her coffee table along with the bottle, "If I had to guess, I'd say you didn't get much use out of these shot glasses."

She shook her head and gave him another nervous smile. She still couldn't believe someone that handsome was remotely interested in her.

"You should leave your hair down," he reached forward and removed the clip that held her hair in a bun. As he moved, she could see the definition in his shoulders and biceps and the muscles in her torso stiffened. Her hair fell to her shoulders in a messy heap and she was about to run her fingers through it to fix it, but his hand stopped her, "Leave it," he insisted.

He poured them each a shot and they took it together, before he moved closer to her and kissed her again.

******

Madison lay on her back panting, still unable to believe what had come over her. *I never do this,* she looked over at Jonah's naked body lying next to her. She touched his arm and hoped that he would ask for her number—was it too much to hope that he might want to see her again?

He gave her a broad smile and sat up and kissed her again, before he asked, "Would you mind getting me some water? I think you wore me out."

She felt her heart flutter yet again as she stood and brought him a glass of water from the kitchen. He drank half the glass in one gulp and handed her one of the shot glasses, "We should keep celebrating."

Her head was already a bit foggy and part of her wanted to say no, but she took the glass instead—*I can't let him think I'm a bore.* "Cheers," she said, before they each downed the mezcal.

This time it tasted different—she wasn't sure what it was, but it burned going down her throat just as before. A few moments later though, her vision grew hazy. "I don't feel so good," she said—her head was pounding, and she felt weak and unsteady. "What did you do?" she looked at her glass, and Jonah's face, he didn't seem surprised at all.

She collapsed onto her elbow, fighting to keep her eyes open, and fumbled for her purse. Her phone was in there, she could call Carlos or Rachel. *They'll help me.* Her fingers reached past the open zipper and closed on the cool plastic case.

Then everything went dark.

Chapter 35

London, United Kingdom

Rachel paced the perimeter of the clinic's waiting area and chewed on her fingernails. "How bad was the concussion?" she asked when she rounded back to where Carlos sat.

"I don't know," Carlos shook his head. "He was dizzy, and his head hurt, then he vomited a couple of times."

"We should have taken him to a hospital."

"Nathan will be fine. He's in good hands. The doctor's affiliated with the CIA, and it's a private clinic, so, like you said, it was the safest choice. Our only choice. Don't second-guess yourself. It's not like it was a gunshot wound. He'd even stopped bleeding by the time we got here."

Rachel swallowed. *CIA-affiliated doctor.* "You're right, but—"

The doctor shuffled into the waiting room and stopped in front of them.

"How serious is it, doctor?" Rachel asked.

"His CT scan came up clean, so there's no evidence of a brain bleed or skull fracture. He does have a concussion, but I think it's mild. We've stitched up the cut on his head," the doctor answered.

Carlos nodded. "What about his leg, Dr. Joplin? I was worried that I made the tourniquet too tight. It was hard to see in the dark."

The doctor sighed. "His leg isn't in great shape. Your tourniquet was fine, but the laceration went deep into the muscle tissue. It will heal, but it'll take time. You can take him home, but you must keep a close eye on him in case any of his concussion symptoms worsen, and only let him sleep about four or five hours at a time. He'll have to be off that leg for a few weeks."

"Thank you, doctor," Rachel said. "Can we see him?"

"Sure."

Carlos looked over at her, "You go ahead. I'll call Petra. They've been chomping at the bit to know how he's doing."

"All right." Rachel followed the doctor into the private room that he'd prepared in his clinic for Nathan.

The room looked bleak because of the gray, early morning sky outside the large window. Nathan was lying on his back in the bed with a bandage wrapped around his head.

When he saw her, he gave her a weak smile, "Hey, boss."

"Hey, champ," she said, returning his smile.

"Hardly."

"Carlos told me you jumped that guy. What were you thinking?"

Nathan answered with a shrug, "I don't know. I couldn't let him shoot Carlos."

"I better tell Petra there's another adjective to add to her description of you. Ballsy. What was it you said? She called you the ass-kicking accountant?"

Nathan chuckled, "Actually, that was me. Kicking *assets* and taking names, you know."

"I forgot how much you love that joke." Rachel grabbed his hand and squeezed it. "The ballsy ass-kicking accountant. I like it."

"Thanks."

"Back at you. I'm going to tell Petra that you saved Carlos' ass last night."

Nathan's smile widened for a moment, but then he let out a long sigh. "I'm sorry you didn't find the ledger. I know how important this is to you."

"We'll get him. Don't you worry. You didn't let me down. Besides, you've kept my secret. That's already more than I could ask for." Rachel looked up as she heard Carlos walk into the room.

"Am I interrupting?" Carlos asked.

Rachel shook her head. "Of course not." She motioned toward an empty chair by the bed. "Have a seat, Mary Poppins. Meet the ballsy ass-kicking accountant."

Carlos rolled his eyes and pulled the chair closer to Nathan's bed. "Keep crunching numbers, buddy. You'll need some more training before you can take up that career in ultimate fighting."

"Real nice." Nathan looked between the two of them. "Do you think Nguyen knew we were coming? Do you think he moved the ledger?"

Carlos shrugged, "Your guess is as good as mine. I'll see if Madison has any ideas. Petra thinks Seymour moved it before the party since so many people would be in and out of the house, but there's no way to know for sure."

"Yes, there is," Nathan said. "We've been so focused on the ledger. What if we went after Seymour instead?"

"You could be on the right track," Carlos said with a shrug, "but right now, you need to focus on getting better. We'll talk about it as a team tomorrow when Petra and Kasem get back. If we're going to get Nguyen or Seymour, we need you clear-headed and on your feet."

Chapter 36

London, United Kingdom

Carlos frowned as he looked up at Madison's window from the bus stop across the street. He'd made two separate passes over the course of the day to see if he noticed any activity—he couldn't wait around loitering in the middle of the street without arousing suspicion—but each time, he hadn't seen anything to indicate that she was home. She hadn't responded to his messages even though she was normally quite good about replying, and it was Sunday, so he couldn't imagine her not being at home the entire day. *She would have said something if she were going out of town.* When the #23 bus pulled up in front of him, he hopped on and rode it for a couple of stops. He would have to wait until after dark to return. If there was still no sign of her at that point, it would be time to sound the alarm.

******

When he returned to Madison's apartment building after dark, Carlos' heart sank once he saw that none of her lights were on. *Something has to be up.* He followed another resident into the building to access the main door and trudged up the three flights of stairs, praying that no one else would be in the hallway if he had to pick the lock. His luck held out, and he stepped into the apartment a few minutes later. He walked into the living room and almost collapsed against the wall, resisting the urge to vomit. Madison was lying naked on the floor in front of the couch, her head against the coffee table. In front of her was the now empty bottle of mezcal that he had given her, a half-filled shot glass, and an open bottle of aspirin.

No, no, he wanted to scream. He rushed toward her and felt for her pulse—he knew it was no use, he knew she was already gone, but he checked anyway. "Madison, no," he cried as he slid to the ground next to her. He put his arm around her and shook her, wishing that that was all it took to wake her. Underneath her head he found a short suicide note, written to her brother. *Dammit. Damn you, Nguyen.* The scene in front of him had clearly been made to look like a suicide, but he knew better. He'd spoken to Madison three days earlier and she'd been fine—there was no way she was suicidal, and Nguyen had to be involved. He just had to be.

Carlos sat there on the floor trying to collect himself, before he felt able to stand. He checked the apartment for any clues as to what had tipped Nguyen off about Madison's involvement. Her purse was lying open on the floor, but her phone was still there. He had to assume that Nguyen already had any data she'd stored there, but he synced it anyway, just in case. *Thank god we used an encrypted message system.* To an outside observer, Madison had used Snapchat a few times to message friends, but the messages had been sent over an encrypted server and had already disappeared. He didn't know how Nguyen had figured out that Madison wasn't to be trusted, but it wasn't because of their messages.

After checking the rest of the apartment, Carlos wiped his fingerprints and removed any trace of his presence. On his way out, he paused and turned back toward Madison's body. He bit his lip and blinked several times. "I'm so sorry, Madison," he whispered. "I'll make him pay for this." He stood there frozen, in the living room doorway, unable to move as images of Vik's dead body flashed in front of his eyes. He could see both bodies there now, lying in front of him, taunting him. He would never be able to catch Nguyen, never be able to avenge their deaths. Carlos squeezed his eyes shut and took control of his emotions. *I will make sure that he pays. I will make sure.*

Chapter 37

London, United Kingdom

Carlos was tempted to bang his head against the wall while he listened to his team members argue. They'd been at it for the better part of an hour and showed no signs of slowing down.

"We should get a new tech guy," Kasem said for the third time. He was the only one keeping a somewhat even temperament. "Whatever we decide to do, there's no getting around that. We can't gallivant off on an op with Nathan like this."

"But Nathan wants to see this through," Rachel persisted. "We can't just boot him off the team. Besides, how many tech specialists do you know who are also forensic accountants? We'll need him once we bring in the ledger."

"How on earth are we going to do that?" Petra asked. "Your intel said the ledger would be at Nguyen's country house and in that safe. Either he knew we were coming, in which case this has all gone to shit anyway, or he keeps it in another location and we have no idea where that could be. Or maybe there is no ledger. Nguyen could have created this myth about a ledger as a red herring for anyone trying to bring him down. For all we know, he just keeps his records in code, aboveboard. Regardless, we're back at square one. Besides, our entire strategy is dead in the water—without Madison's testimony we won't have enough to put Nguyen away, even *if* we find the mythical ledger. Why can't you just admit that, Rachel?"

"Do you really think the ledger might not exist?" Carlos interjected before Rachel could respond. His eyes moved between his two female team members as he thought through what Petra was saying. *Could it really all be a ruse?*

Petra sighed, "I don't know. We don't have confirming intel on where Nguyen keeps it much less any details about it—what it looks like, what size it is, if it's red, black, or covered in Disney Princess stickers, for God's sake. Rachel, your intel hasn't given us *anything*, and Madison was never sure about it either. So, yeah, I think it's entirely possible it's an urban legend. For me to even consider continuing this op, we need tangible proof that it at least exists. We need an eyewitness." She met his gaze, "Did you ever *see* a ledger?"

Carlos blinked several times. His mind returned to those days when he and Vik were undercover. They had heard about the ledger, talked about the ledger. Vik was the first one who brought it up.

Remembering what Vik said during that conversation sent a shiver up Carlos' spine. *The reason no one can ever catch him is this ledger. He doesn't keep real records of his transactions anywhere else, doesn't trust computers. The ledger is written in code, but if we could get to it, we could decipher it.* Vik had made it sound so simple. Carlos exhaled and shook his head as he opened his eyes, "I never saw it, but I think Vik did. He was leading that op and he was deeper undercover in Nguyen's organization. The way he talked about the ledger…he was always certain there was one. He had to have seen it."

Petra moved over to the couch to sit next to him and placed her hand over his. Her expression told Carlos what she was thinking but wouldn't say in front of the group. *It's not your fault.* He noticed something else in her face, as if she were carrying her own guilt, but he couldn't understand why. He nodded at her and looked up at the rest of the team. "Look," he said, "maybe there is no ledger, maybe I was wrong about that—"

"But my intel—" Rachel protested.

Carlos waved his hand to cut her off. "Let's say we don't know for sure that the ledger exists. Even if that's true, there must be records of these deals somewhere. Nguyen doesn't run a multimillion-dollar arms operation without some sort of records. We have Nathan's hacks on his financial data, but that didn't give us anything. But there must be records—evidence—somewhere. It could be a spiral notebook or a Hello Kitty diary. Doesn't matter because it's hidden somewhere. We just have to find it."

Petra crossed her arms, "Even if we can find it, like I said before, the ledger won't be enough."

"What do you mean? We'll have the ledger, and the arms," Rachel narrowed her eyes.

"To take Nguyen down, he has to be prosecuted. It has to be legal. A stolen ledger won't be enough. We need real human intel on his operations, on his arms deals. We won't have Madison's testimony to say that Nguyen purposely misreported the size of his legit investments. Besides, she never saw one of the arms deals go down, so even that might not have been enough."

"We could capture Seymour and force him to turn on Nguyen," Nathan said.

Carlos sat up straighter, "Is that what you meant, Petra? I'm not sure we could turn that scumbag."

"Not really. When you and Vik were undercover, did you ever see one of the deals go down?"

Carlos shook his head, "We were at the beginning of one. I saw Nguyen buy the arms, but I never saw him deliver them."

"So how does he do that?" Petra glanced at Rachel. "Did your intel tell you anything about how he's covering up these deals? He's getting help from somewhere."

"We already know that," Carlos said with a frown. "He has loads of connections—MI-6, CIA, French intel."

"If you know that government and law enforcement have been corrupted, then you need first-person intel," Petra said. "That must be why you and Vik were under in the first place. I don't think this was ever about the ledger."

"What are you proposing?" Rachel's tone sounded icy.

"I'm proposing that we get inside one of the arms deals. Kasem already has a connection with the Nguyens. He can get our first-person intel."

Carlos picked up his mug and glanced across the coffee table for Kasem's expression. He couldn't read Kasem's perfect poker face. He wasn't sure Petra had discussed what she was proposing with Kasem before she brought it up, but either way, she had a point. "Kasem, what do you think?" he asked. "If this was a go, you'd be on your own. Petra could help you a little, with her connection to Jim's fiancé, but setting up the deal…that would all be on you." *We already lost Madison to this,* Carlos swallowed. *But this might be the only way.*

"I don't know," Kasem answered in a quiet voice. "I think it could be done, if that were really the only way."

As soon as he said that, Carlos could tell that Petra hadn't spoken to him about this before dropping it on all of them. *What are you thinking, kiddo?* Carlos silenced the urge to confront her immediately. "Here's what I propose. We already have backing from the CIA to get the ledger. If it does exist, we can use it to bring in Nguyen." He shot a glance at Petra so that she wouldn't interrupt. "Maybe it's a ledger, maybe it's a computer program, maybe it's some kind of mini book. Whatever it is, Nguyen has some way of keeping these records. Our job is to find out what that is and get to it. That's plan A. If we come up empty, or decide we need more to take him down, we can move onto plan B—that's when we'll revisit having Kasem work his way into Nguyen's arms deal."

Petra nodded slowly, "Okay, but how do we execute plan A?"

"The same way you were going to get in on the arms deal," Carlos said with a shrug. "Just a little less risky. Janine invited you to the wedding, right?"

"She did."

"We know the deal is going down shortly after that. If we're going to catch him, that's our best shot, but that gives us a little bit of time before we have to make that call," Carlos continued.

"So we're off to Madagascar," Rachel said. "We have to go there to take him down—"

"Hold up, cowgirl," Carlos interrupted. "I know this is tough. We were supposed to be decoding the ledger right now, but we're nursing an injured team member and grasping at straws instead," his voice caught, "and Madison's gone." He looked around the room, pausing to catch each person's gaze. "I propose we take a break. Go for a walk, run, swim, whatever. Play some video games, have a drink, decompress. We have time to get everything ready. Nathan's coming with us and we'll make do. In two weeks, we head to Madagascar. So, take the rest of the night off, come back tomorrow with a cool head, and we'll get to work."

Rachel sighed, "I've got to go back into the office. We need to keep these pesky purse strings flowing. I might need your help on a side project."

Chapter 38

London, United Kingdom

Kasem got into bed and turned away from an already sleeping Petra in silence. He and Carlos had spent the last few hours helping Rachel on a recon op for something separate that the CIA had assigned to her. He'd been glad that Rachel had asked Petra to stay home to watch Nathan—he still wasn't sure if he could stomach being around her.

He was still reeling from the team's conversation that afternoon. *She volunteered for me to go undercover without even asking me. How could she do that?* Part of him wanted to tell her how hurt and angry he was, but he resisted. In the heat of the moment, he didn't want to say things that he wouldn't be able to take back. She had been looking at him with her big eyes, obviously waiting for him to bring it up, but he wasn't sure if he could handle it right now.

He felt her hand on his shoulder and his heart started to melt. Whatever she had said or done, he did love her.

"Kasem?" she said softly. "I'm so sorry."

He sighed and sat up to face her. "It's okay."

"It's not."

"Why didn't you talk to me first?"

"It wasn't planned, I swear. I didn't even think of the idea until we were debriefing, and it just slipped out. I was riled up and my mind was racing." She leaned over and kissed him. "I really am sorry."

Kasem nodded his acceptance but avoided eye contact. "Is that what you want? For me to go undercover on the arms deal?"

"That's not what I want, but…"

Kasem watched her face. Something in her eyes told him that she was keeping something from him. "Petra, everything you told me about why you left the Agency was about how they always put the greater good over the operative or asset. That's what you did today with me—the man you say you love—and you did it without talking to me." He imagined other things he could say. *Is this because you don't see me as anything but an asset? Is this because of what I did?*

"I do love you. I just wasn't thinking, and I want to catch Nguyen. You've seen those pictures that Carlos has of what Nguyen's caused. All of those children. He's a monster."

"He is a monster, and so is Seymour. It might be worth it to bring them down, but I wish you had talked to me about it first."

"The words were out of my mouth before I could stop myself. I regretted it the minute I said it." Petra caressed his face. "I don't know what I'd do if anything happened to you."

Kasem studied her features. Whatever she was keeping from him, she wasn't ready to tell him yet. He decided to cling to the fact that he knew that she loved him. He planted a kiss on her forehead. "I love you too. Don't worry, we'll figure out us after Madagascar."

Chapter 39

London, United Kingdom

Petra watched Kasem fall asleep. She needed to tell him about her past with Vik so he might better understand why she had been so compelled to avenge his loss. She looked up at the ceiling. *Why can't I tell him? He would understand.* She couldn't believe that she'd brought up an idea like sending Kasem undercover into an arms deal without talking to him first. She sighed and for a second she could remember Vikram—his hand grazing hers when he'd taken her out for a harmless drink before they had both acknowledged their flirtation. Petra blinked twice and lay there with her eyes closed. Perhaps if she pretended to sleep for long enough, she would actually fall asleep.

******

Petra opened her eyes and looked over at the man laying next to her. She pulled on a bathrobe from the hotel room closet and padded to the floor-to-ceiling windows. The view of the nightlights over Chicago was magnificent—the architectural marvels in every direction, with the river snaking in between. "Vikram, wake up," *she whispered with a nudge.* "You've got to see this."

He squinted at her and grabbed her hand and pulled her back into bed, "The only view I'm interested in is the one right here."

She giggled and kissed him as he untied the bathrobe and tossed it to the side.

When she fell back onto the bed, she looked up and she was somewhere else—her old apartment in Tehran. What? She tossed the covers aside and stood up, fully dressed. Her phone buzzed and she picked it up.

"It's Nasser," *a voice said from the other side of the line.* "Is Sarah there?"

Petra sat up straight and answered, "You have the wrong number." *She hung up, grabbed her purse, and headed straight for her car, parked outside within the French embassy compound. The call meant that Gibran Obaidi had time sensitive intel that he'd left at their designated drop point. Normally she wouldn't go there outside of her scheduled weekly stops, but whatever it was, she needed to get to it immediately. Before she left the compound, she took a wad of cash from the hidden storage compartment under her* seat. If Gibran had indeed dropped off new intel, then her agreement was to pay him.

Her car sped out of the gate and suddenly she was somewhere else again, she was at a port, and it was the middle of the night. She looked around for any indication of where she was and caught a sign post under a streetlight that read "Hai Phong Port." She frowned—Vietnam? How did I get here?

She heard a voice that sounded familiar and moved toward it, Carlos? She was tempted to call out, but instinct told her to keep silent. She passed several massive containers before she saw them—Carlos, Seymour, Nguyen, and Vikram. She ducked down to stay out of sight and peered around the container, but couldn't get a good enough view, so she hoisted herself onto the top of the container instead. She belly-crawled across the top and looked out over the edge from above. Carlos was walking away from the group and a knot formed in her stomach as she saw Gibran Obaidi approaching from the other side. WTF?

Gibran stopped next to Nguyen and whispered something that she couldn't catch, and then a moment later he was gone.

Nguyen turned toward Vik and nodded at Seymour, who raised a gun to his head. "Vik, I don't take kindly when people betray me. Do you have anything to say for yourself?"

Vikram opened his mouth and protested, "Duc, I've been loyal to you for a year. Are you going to believe some rat you just pulled off the street?"

Nguyen waved his finger and a large crack sounded over the docks. Petra watched in horror as Vikram fell to the ground with a bullet hole in his chest. She jumped off the edge of the container and a sharp pain shot up through her right knee, but she ignored it and stumbled toward Vikram. Nguyen and Seymour had disappeared, but she didn't even notice where they had gone. She shook Vik's body and started to sob. "Vikram? Vikram!"

His eyes shot open and he spoke to her in a raspy voice, "Why did you do this? You recruited Obaidi, you brought him in to the Agency. Why did you do it?"

Petra opened her mouth and tried to speak, but the words failed to form. Vikram held her gaze for a few seconds before his eyes glazed over. She put pressure on his wound, but a moment later he was gone. She checked his pulse, still sobbing and looked down at her hands, stained red with his blood.

******

Petra sat up panting and doubled over, attempting to catch her breath. She looked to the side and saw Kasem next to her, fast asleep, and a tear rolled down her cheek. *I messed everything up. For him, and for Vikram.* She crawled out of bed, threw on a robe, and headed downstairs.

After pouring herself a glass of wine, she stretched out on the couch and sipped on it slowly. The initial shock of the nightmare had subsided, but she didn't want to think about it so she focused on the operation instead. So much rested on this potential plan in Madagascar. Petra still didn't think that a bookkeeping record would be enough to put Nguyen away, though. *Unless the CIA has other plans for him?*

She heard a noise on the stairs and glanced toward the hallway adjacent to the living room. A moment later, a grumpy looking Carlos fumbled his way into the living room. "Hey," she said.

"I thought I heard somebody downstairs," he said as he took a seat across the coffee table from her, glanced at the label on the wine bottle, and then guzzled half of it. After setting it back on the table, he wiped his mouth, crossed his arms, and looked at her. "Well, Lockjaw..."

She raised her eyebrows, "Yeah, Puppy?" She could tell that a scolding from her old mentor was in the cards.

"What happened today?"

"I don't know. It just slipped out."

"So, you didn't talk to your boyfriend before you offered to shove him into the frying pan? I guess I did read the room right."

Petra ducked her head and sipped from her wine glass. "If I'd thought of it earlier, I would have, but like I said, it just slipped out. I wasn't thinking."

"That's one big ass understatement. How'd he take it?"

"How do you think?"

"Ah, so that's why you're down here drinking by yourself in the middle of the night."

"You can read a room pretty well, old man."

Carlos' eyes bore into her and she shifted in her seat. "You still haven't told Kasem about your relationship with Vik, have you?"

"I don't know how to bring it up. This op—" she shook her head, "I keep thinking about him. I even had a nightmare about him, about watching him die."

"An op like this is bound to stir up some of that stuff. Just tell Kasem. It's not like he thought you were a nun before you met him, kiddo. It'll help him understand why you're so invested in nailing Nguyen."

Petra scoffed, "I'm sure he'd be happy to know that's why I'm so invested. Then if he lines up the timing that I was with Vikram around the same time that I met him, well, he'll be even more thrilled. Kasem was just my asset, so that's not a betrayal at all. No big deal."

"Snapping at me isn't going to fix anything. Vik was a fling, not a relationship. And he's dead, so he's not exactly a threat. You're just scared and it's going to eat you alive if you don't tell him." Carlos scooted forward on the sofa to grab the wine bottle, "You're not giving your boyfriend enough credit if you don't think he'll understand why it's important for you to stop Nguyen. Try having some faith in him. Kasem would go to the ends of the earth for you, so give him a chance to prove that. Again."

Petra frowned and stared at the floor.

Carlos took another swig of wine from the bottle and stood. "If you two don't want my advice on your relationship drama, fine, but quit talking to me about it instead of each other. This isn't high school. Besides, we need your heads in the game for this op. You both volunteered to be here, so sort this out and get focused. Don't screw this up."

******

"Petra, wake up."

Petra squinted and opened her eyes slowly. Rachel was hovering over where she had fallen asleep on the couch, "Trouble in paradise, huh? Usually, it's the guy who gets kicked out of the bedroom." She placed a large glass on the table in front of her that was filled with green sludge and a celery stick poking out of the top. "Drink this. Wine will give you a killer hangover if you're not careful."

Petra glowered at her, "I'm fine. I didn't have that much to drink."

"I see two empty bottles that beg to differ." Rachel moved the green sludge an inch closer to her, "Drink up."

"Carlos drank some of that." Petra frowned at the glass on the table, "What is that?"

"My own specialty hangover cocktail. A bunch of vegetables, loaded with vitamins and minerals to replenish your system, along with a couple of other goodies."

Petra considered protesting again, but the effort of creating the words seemed far too daunting. She leaned forward and took a sip of the green juice. The first sip tasted exactly like it looked—green slime—but the second sip was a little less revolting. *Maybe she's right.* Petra grimaced and managed to swallow the rest of the drink.

"Good job. In ten minutes, you'll be right as rain. You'll see. I've got to get going—I get to deal with another crapshoot that Langley thinks I have time for since this op isn't going anywhere."

"Isn't that a little harsh? We may not have found the ledger, but we did deliver them a boatload of sophisticated illegal arms," Petra stood up and groaned, not really bothered to hear Rachel's answer.

"Oh, right, yeah. I guess that helps a little."

Rachel's tone sounded odd, but Petra ignored it and groped her way up the stairs to the bathroom. After a quick shower, she started to feel human again. She checked the bedrooms and saw that both Carlos and Kasem were still fast asleep. With a frown, she checked the hall clock and almost cried out when she saw that it was six thirty in the morning. *Why would she wake me up so early?* Petra was tempted to stomp downstairs and give Rachel a piece of her mind, but her hangover had cooled enough that she kept herself from throwing the tantrum. Instead, she glanced into Nathan's room.

"Hi, Petra," he said.

"I'm sorry. I didn't mean to wake you. I just wanted to check on you."

"No worries. How are you?"

"I'm all right," Petra said with a shrug. "I might have hit the wine a bit too hard last night. I was only going to have a glass, but I ended up having a wee bit more."

Nathan chuckled, "You should have Rachel make you her green hangover cure. It tastes awful, but I swear it'll beat the worst hangover in less than ten minutes."

"I certainly hope so. She just force-fed it to me, the most miserable three minutes of my life."

Nathan raised his eyebrows, "I guess you guys don't get along that well."

"I don't know. We haven't really spent any time together other than the op. She seems like she knows what she's doing."

"She's not so bad once you get to know her. Give her a chance. She's been through a lot."

"Haven't we all?" Petra frowned as she detected something behind Nathan's statement. "Anything in particular?"

Nathan's face froze for a second, but then he shook his head. "Oh, just the ordinary trials and tribulations for a field agent or team lead, I guess."

"Of course," Petra could tell that he was covering up for something. "I'll let you get some more rest," she said and retreated into the hallway. Petra contemplated whether to head downstairs but decided against it. Instead, she slid into bed and placed her head on

Kasem's shoulder. His eyes fluttered, and he pulled her in closer. She shut her eyes and drank in the peacefulness of the moment.

Chapter 40

In flight to Madagascar

Carlos directed the team to gather around the table in the lounge area shortly after they boarded the plane to revisit their plan. "I wanted to run through the plan again before we get to Madagascar." The last two weeks had been grueling—Rachel had put them to work on a series of side ops for Langley, which had kept them running around in separate small groups doing recon, checking drop sites, and gathering incriminating evidence on three staff at different embassies around London to help the CIA build a case for them to provide future intel. She'd even put them on report duty—writing out detailed accounts on each of the assignments that she'd forcibly drafted them onto. *We've got to get the bills paid somehow,* she'd said. They had been on so many distinct side ops that Carlos hardly felt like he was still working to take Nguyen down, even though they'd gone over their plan a number of times. Now that they were all stuck on the plane together, he wanted to take the opportunity to reorient them around their original mission, especially since tensions had been running high since the strategy fracas after the engagement party. Petra was still tiptoeing around Kasem and had distanced herself from much of the planning. Rachel was a lone wolf, as usual. She had taken care of filing their flight plan and reporting to the CIA, but kept her distance from the group. Kasem was tall, dark, handsome, and brooding, *as always.* Nathan's leg was healing nicely, but he still limped and required a walking cane or crutch. Between that and his mild concussion, he would be working on the operation from the safety of his laptop screen.

Carlos waited until the team had assembled around the table and then tapped his tablet to project an enlarged map of Madagascar onto the table. "Okay, folks, let's get to this. We'll arrive at the Mahajanga Airport here, in the northwest of the island. The area used to be fairly run down, but there's been a construction boom in the past couple of years after several new solar plants were built in the area. We'll stay at the Antsanitia Resort about a half hour up the coast from the city. The main wedding party will be at the Lodge des Terres Blanches further northeast. Nguyen keeps luxury villas at the lodge for his friends and family, so that's where he and Seymour will be staying." Carlos indicated a series of four villas split over two small beaches on the east side of the island. "The rest of the resort is split across these larger two beaches and it's all booked, which gives us a legit reason to be further south at Antsanitia. Thankfully, the road running between the two resorts has just been redone, so it's only a half hour drive. Rachel has us booked in neighboring beach villas. While Kasem and Petra are attending the wedding events, the rest of us will be posing as wealthy tourists. We're arriving two days ahead of most of the wedding guests, so we'll have plenty of time to scope the area. We have two possible targets—Nguyen's storage unit and his beach villa. The point is to grab any information we can find, any financial records, where he hides the arms, travel records, etc. Remember, they took down Al Capone on tax evasion, so don't turn your nose up at anything. If the ledger exists then it'll be in one of those two places, but if not, we take whatever we can find, along with one of the security guards. Nguyen uses these guys all over the place, that testimony might be enough to cover for losing Madison's," his voice caught. "We go for the storage unit first since it's more secure, but if we don't find anything, we go for the villa. Maybe, *maybe,* at that point, we'll revisit a possible plan B that puts us inside the deal itself. The GPS tag Petra put on the arms that Nguyen had stored in London is now in Madagascar, somewhere near Mahajanga, although for some reason we can't get a precise location. If we get both the ledger and the guard, we can send the cavalry in for the arms and to pick up Nguyen—if not, we'll see if we can tag Nguyen to the arms sale." He looked at the team. "Any questions?"

Petra crossed her arms. "Nathan, have you already done a security evaluation of the hotel?"

"They use a localized server, so I can only get into the system once we're in range. It should work from our villa, but I can't be sure until we get there."

"What happens if it doesn't work?" Petra asked with a frown.

"I can set up at the main server station for the lodge here," Nathan pointed to the map farther inland from Nguyen's beach villa.

Carlos sighed, "If that's the case, Rachel and I will install a relay so that Nathan can still access the security system from the villa."

"My concern is that the actual wedding is on a different island, basically a sandbank." Petra indicated a small island off the coast of Mahajanga on the map, "Most of the wedding events will be at the lodge, but Janine said the wedding ceremony will take place on this cove island about forty minutes from there by boat." Petra tapped the screen, zooming in on the northernmost islands. "The wedding will be on this island," she said as she pointed to the map. "It's barely visible on the map since it's mostly underwater at high tide. That means the three of you will be on your own while Kasem and I are at the wedding."

"That's what makes it so perfect," Rachel interjected. "There's no way Nguyen is taking the ledger out to the wedding. He'll be gone. Seymour will be gone. We'll only have to deal with Nguyen's guards and hotel security."

"How are we neutralizing the guards?" Kasem asked.

"I already profiled the one I'm targeting," Rachel answered. "He's single and hits the bars pretty hard. He's arriving tomorrow afternoon. My plan is to get his access card to get us into the storage unit."

"Isn't that a bit reckless?" Kasem gave Petra a nudge.

Petra sighed, "Carlos, you'll have to be ready to go in in case things get dicey."

"I'll be ready." Carlos turned to Kasem, "It's no riskier than what you'll be doing. It might be our only shot."

"If you say so," Kasem agreed with an obvious grimace.

"Going back to the plan," Carlos said with another sigh. "Rachel is going to get us into Nguyen's storage unit while Nathan handles tech. I'll access the safe inside to see what we find. If that plan doesn't work, we'll reevaluate and come up with another plan."

Rachel drummed her fingers against the table, "Famous last words, boss."

Chapter 41

Mahajanga, Madagascar

Rachel placed her shot glass on the bar at the Maki Beach restaurant and waved at the bartender for another one, "Another round, please."

"If I didn't know better, I'd say you were trying to get me drunk," Petra said with a frown. "I can't keep up with you." She looked at the remnants of the fresh prawns she'd had for dinner. She wasn't hungry, but she wondered if she should order more food so that she would still be able to stand after trying to keep up with Rachel.

"This is the last one, I promise."

"That's what you said the last time," Petra protested as the bartender refilled their shot glasses.

"To girls' night," Rachel said raising her glass. She gulped it down before Petra even had the chance to put salt on the limes.

Petra followed suit. The liquid scalded her throat as it went down, and she shuddered, "No more. I mean it."

"When you're right, you're right." Rachel set her glass on the bar and swiveled her stool to look at Petra. "So, we're supposed to be bonding, right? What's your story? Why are you here?"

"Carlos is an old friend and my mentor. When he asked for help, I couldn't say no."

"What about his friend? Vik—the guy who died. Did you know him?"

"I met him a couple of times. He spoke to my class during training."

Rachel cocked her head to one side, "So you want justice for Vik too."

"Justice, sure. He was a good guy, and definitely a great operative."

"Come on, Petra. Aren't girls' nights all about telling secrets?"

"What do you mean?"

"Vik didn't just speak to your class. You knew him better than that, didn't you?" Rachel asked in a soft voice.

Petra kept her eyes fixed on the surface of the bar, "That is how I met him, but...how'd you figure that out?"

"Your personality type is tattooed across your face. You might have been with the Agency, but I'd hedge a bet that you left because it's not who you are. You care about people, not just assets or colleagues. Carlos, Kasem, Vik. You barely know Nathan and me, but you worry about us anyway." She raised her finger and pointed it toward Petra, "The only way you would stick Kasem's neck out that far is because it's personal. That's how I knew. What I'm really interested in is how *well* you knew him."

"Fair enough, but you've gotten enough out of me for one night. What about you? Why are you here?"

Rachel inhaled sharply to conceal her reaction. *You really stepped in it.* "I'm on assignment, remember? I'm here on orders."

"Right. You didn't pull any strings to get us on this op? To get clearance to have two former Agency operatives, and one foreign operative on your team? Along with a private plane, a swanky flat in London, and two villas at a posh resort in Madagascar? *On assignment?* Absolutely." Petra sat up straight and pointed a finger, mimicking Rachel, "I can see right through you too. Why fight for this so hard, especially with Nguyen's contacts within the CIA?"

"I'm just doing my job." Even as she said it, Rachel knew how unconvincing the words sounded.

"You don't want to talk about it. I get it. But Carlos told me that you freaked out at Hill Hearst when the safe was empty. It sounds like this is personal for you, and we should probably deal with that. If you react like that again, we're toast," Petra said with a shrug.

Rachel pretended to search for the bartender, "Where is he when you need him?"

"Talk to me," Petra said in a soft voice. "This is about someone important to you too, right?"

Rachel's voice caught in her throat, "I had a tough childhood. My dad. He worked for Nguyen, traveling all the time. My mom took care of me, but one day she was in a car accident. After she died, my grandpa raised me. Then when I was fourteen, my dad showed up out of the blue one summer. He said he was done traveling, was putting that life behind him. He just had one last job he had to do..."

"What happened?"

"He never came back. Nguyen killed him. Or Seymour. Maybe one of their henchmen. I don't know for sure, but they wouldn't let him leave the organization, so they eliminated him."

Petra placed her hand on Rachel's shoulder, "I'm so sorry."

"When I joined the Company, I did some digging and finally found out who my dad worked for. He had kept everything in his life separate to keep me safe." Rachel picked up the napkin next to her empty shot glass and began folding it over and over until it was a tiny wedge of a triangle. When she couldn't fold anymore, she unfolded it and started again. Petra watched in silence, letting Rachel decide when she was ready to continue.

"Anyway, that's when I put the pieces together. Since then, God, I've tried to get Nguyen so many times, but I never even got close. Then Nate joined me, and he found Carlos, and we've been so much closer to taking him down." Rachel's chest heaved, "I know I don't show it, but I'm so grateful to all of you. For being here, for doing this."

Petra knocked her shoulder into Rachel's, "No thanks needed."

Rachel was about to summon the bartender for another drink when her posture stiffened.

"What's wrong?" Petra asked.

"He's here. The security guard, Jonah Devlin."

"The security guard?" Petra's eyes darted toward the entrance to the bar. *Oh, right. The reason we chose this bar.* "Are you sure you're okay to do this today?"

"I'll be all right, but I'm going to go powder my nose. We won't get another chance before the wedding."

"I'll keep your seat warm."

******

When Rachel returned from the restrooms, she felt steadier. This was her chance. Her chance to avenge her father. She put on a flirtatious smile and made eye contact with Jonah when she sashayed past him, then took her seat next to Petra again. Moments later, he appeared at her side.

"Can I buy you ladies a drink?" he asked in a strong Northern Irish accent.

Petra flashed him a smile, "Sorry, it's girls' night. No boys allowed."

"You can't leave a fellow hanging like that. Just one drink? I need company, all by my lonesome tonight," he persisted with a charming smile and puppy-dog eyes.

"What do you think, Rachel?"

Rachel shrugged, "Free drink? Sure, why not? I say we let him join us."

"It shouldn't be this hard to buy two gorgeous women a drink. What's your poison?"

"Single malt," Rachel answered. "Show us how well you can pick."

"You're on." Jonah gestured to summon the bartender, "Three glasses of Lagavulin Distiller's cut? Neat."

After the first glass of whiskey, Petra excused herself, "I'm so tired and had way too much to drink. Plus, my husband keeps texting me." She giggled and held up her phone to accentuate the drunkenness that was only partially an act. "I'm going to grab a cab. Nice to meet you, Jonah."

Chapter 42

Mahajanga, Madagascar

Petra crossed the street to watch Rachel and Jonah through the large plate-glass window next to the entrance of the restaurant's patio. The shadow of the building awning provided cover, so she could watch unnoticed.

Rachel had turned her attention back to Jonah and placed her hand on his arm. Petra could hear the conversation through their earpieces as Jonah and Rachel joked and flirted. After watching for another fifteen minutes, she determined that Rachel would be fine on her own and retreated with an ache. She and Kasem hadn't been that relaxed since they'd left Kyoto.

After a restless night's sleep, Petra made her way to the neighboring villa to speak to Rachel. The walk was only a short distance, normally less than five minutes, but she took it at a leisurely pace, stretching it to more than ten minutes. She basked in the sparkling sunbeams that glinted off the surface of the ocean water. The Canal du Mozambique stretched out into the distance, pure azure blue against the paler cerulean of the sky scattered with only a few clusters of white clouds. Kasem probably would want to go to a place like this for their honeymoon, should they ever reach that point.

Petra lingered on the beach, flip-flops in hand, and the cool water splashed over her bare feet. The tide was in, so the shallow water splashed gently against her shins. It was just her luck that she would end up somewhere like this on yet another mission, instead of a vacation.

She tried to concentrate on her breathtaking surroundings, but too many thoughts raced through her mind. She could remember strolling hand-in-hand along a similar beach on Kish Island with Kasem in Iran, but her mind also had flashes of the weekend that she and Vikram had spent in Chicago. Why hadn't she told Kasem about her relationship with him yet? She knew that Kasem would understand about her having an ex, but the rest? Why was she still thinking about him, remembering him in that way?

"Hey!"

Petra spun around, "Hey, Rachel." Rachel was wearing the same outfit from the previous night, albeit with some additional rumples. Her hair, normally perfectly in place, was frizzy and matted. "How was your night? Was it a success?"

"I got the ID card, and the rest, was *not too bad*," Rachel answered with a twinkle in her eye.

Petra ran her fingers through her hair, "I'm glad someone here is getting some."

"You and Kasem aren't enjoying yourself a bit? I mean look at this place. It's made for people in love."

"Maybe if we weren't here on an op."

"I highly recommend it."

"Good to know," Petra said with a dramatic eye roll. "Your mark is a bit of a stud, huh? When are you seeing him again?"

"We're going on a hike today, and he's taking me out to dinner tonight."

"Great."

Rachel nodded, "After Nathan clones the ID card, I'll slip it back."

"I didn't realize you were going to lift it this morning." *Reckless.* Petra pursed her lips and gestured toward the villa, "Let's get that ID to Nathan so that he can clone the chip ASAP."

On their way inside, Petra sent Kasem a message about the impromptu team meeting. Fifteen minutes later, they were clustered around the coffee table in the living room. Nathan had his leg propped up on an ottoman with his cloning device plugged into the wall outlet. "The cloned ID chip will be ready in a few minutes," he said.

"Perfect. We'll be good to go tomorrow while you two are at the welcome cocktail," Carlos said using air quotes, "whatever the heck that is. How about an update for tomorrow now that we have the card and know we have access?"

Petra caught Carlos' gaze and he nodded at her to take the lead. "The wedding party arrived this morning. I checked in with Janine, and it sounds like the whole family will be busy running around with last minute prep—greeting guests, photos, the works, until the welcome reception tomorrow. That's when I say you guys hit the storage unit. Rachel can get the ID card back to Jonah today, you use the cloned one tomorrow evening to get into the storage unit, check out the safe and grab whatever you think could be useful."

Carlos nodded, "Rachel, are you good with that?"

"Yup."

Kasem glanced at her, "You might have to spend another evening with Jonah if he asks you to. You're flying fairly close to the flames. Is that okay?"

"Don't worry about me, pretty boy, I'll be fine."

I think she'll enjoy that, Petra thought in amusement. Rachel seemed completely unfazed by how much risk she was taking sleeping with Jonah. *I wonder if she's putting a good face on it. That's what I would do.* Petra looked over at Kasem, glad that she wasn't the one who was supposed to seduce the security guard. *Small mercies.*

Rachel took a deep breath and drummed her fingers on the table, "Let's get this moving, team. I don't want to give that bastard any chance to get away."

Chapter 43

Mahajanga, Madagascar – The next day

Carlos waited until he could hear the music from the cocktail reception before he and Rachel approached Nguyen's storage unit.

"I've deactivated surveillance on the storage unit. You're good to go," Nathan said over the coms.

"Thanks." Carlos looked over at Rachel, "Are you ready? Since we already scoped this place out yesterday, the entry should be a breeze. Unless you'd rather be out on another hot date?"

Rachel shot him a glance, "You're just jealous because you haven't been getting any. You talked to your wife lately?" She paused for a moment and sighed, "Sorry, that was uncalled for. After you, Mr. Poppins."

"Nathan, go live with the sound disruption," Carlos said.

Seconds later, Nathan set off the sound trap that they had created to sound like a family of lemurs on the other side of the storage unit. When the guard left to investigate, Carlos and Rachel crept forward. They scanned the cloned ID card and entered the dark storage unit. Once the door was closed behind them, they both donned their night-vision goggles.

"The safe's in the back," Carlos said.

They moved toward the back of the storage unit, passing two piles of stacked suitcases and boxes of wedding decorations. Carlos reached the safe and crouched in front of it while Rachel took up watch behind him.

"Hopefully, second time's the charm," she whispered.

"Keep your fingers crossed."

Nathan's voice came over the com, "Another guard joined the guard on duty. You may have to get out of there pretty quickly."

"Can you patch into their coms?" Rachel asked.

"Stand by." A moment later, Nathan continued, "It sounds like they're just investigating the noise. They haven't noticed anything inside so far but remember the access cards are logged. If something alerts them to that, you'll have to get out pronto."

"Got it." Rachel nodded to Carlos, "Make it snappy, Poppins." Over the com, she said, "Nate, can you tell if the other guard is Jonah?"

"It's Jonah," Nathan confirmed.

139

Rachel cursed under her breath and Carlos could hear the sound of her breathing as he zeroed in on the safe. For now, he couldn't afford the distraction of wondering what was going on with her. "Bloody hell," he said once he realized that he wouldn't be able to bypass the fingerprint access. "I can start by drilling, but I'll need fingerprints. Think your spy tech can make that work?" he looked back at Rachel.

"They can get it," Rachel said with a short nod as Carlos sent a message to Petra and Kasem to get Nguyen's fingerprints.

Carlos prepped his drill and triggered the noise eater switch, this time on maximum volume, "Nathan, turn on the white noise patterns to mask the drill."

Carlos waited for Nathan's signal before he turned the drill on low and watched the bit spin for a second to test it, "How does that sound outside?" he asked Nathan. Without the sound of fireworks outside, both the noise eater attachment on the drill and the white noise outside would have to provide much wider coverage than at Hill Hearst to mask the sound.

"The white noise is working," Nathan confirmed.

"Breaching the safe now," Carlos was about to place the drill against the surface of the safe when Nathan spoke over the com again.

"They're coming toward the entrance. Do you read me? Abort. Now." Even with the slight static of the com, the concern in his voice came across loud and clear.

Rachel moved closer to the safe with her Glock out and ready, "How much time do you need?" she asked as she attached a silencer to her gun.

"More than we have," Carlos snapped his toolkit shut. "Let's go."

"No!" She took a deep breath, "I'll distract them. You need to get this done."

"Rachel, don't—" Carlos whispered emphatically.

Before Carlos could stop her, she placed the gun on the floor next to him along with the ID card they had used for entry and took off toward the entrance.

Chapter 44

Mahajanga, Madagascar

Petra gave Nguyen a big smile as he sat down across from her at one of the tables at the welcome reception. "Congratulations," she said. "This is an incredible celebration. Thank you so much for having us."

He smiled in return, "This is the sort of thing that a man does for his son. He is priceless, after all. Even though he's still learning the ropes."

Petra nodded and waved for one of the waiters to bring them the tray of champagne glasses he was carrying. She wanted to avoid putting her foot in her mouth when it came to Nguyen's tumultuous relationship with Jim.

"Tell me, what did you and Amir do for your wedding?"

Something in his tone concerned her, but she disregarded it and handed him a glass, careful to handle it only by the stem. "Just a small family ceremony. We were going to have a larger reception later, but it got too complicated." She picked up a second glass and raised it, "To all of you. Thank you again for welcoming us into the family."

Nguyen acknowledged her cheers and set the glass down on the table after taking a sip. "Seymour mentioned that he couldn't find pictures of a Carlson Group wedding online. That explains it. You had a small wedding."

A lump formed in Petra's throat, "We practically eloped. We were caught up in the moment and it all happened so fast. My family wasn't too happy about that, so there wasn't much fanfare." She was tempted to search the rest of the attendees to seek out Kasem, Janine, or even Jim. Any friendly face would do, but she didn't want to give away that she was uncomfortable.

"We were fortunate that Amir was able to join our deal. It was quite serendipitous that we met him at that party at the Orangery." Nguyen held Petra's gaze and her stomach did a flip.

She fought for control of her two conflicting urges—one to flee and the other to punch him in the face, "It was. We're so grateful for that as well. Not just professionally, mind you. We've become quite close to Jim and Janine."

"Don't forget me. It's not only *their* friendship and trust that you've gained. Who would have thought you'd be out here in Mada with us now?"

Petra almost squirmed. His tone cut through her. *He knows. He knows something.* "We're very lucky they've been so welcoming."

"I must say, I've been very curious to find out how you arranged that fireworks show at Hill Hearst. You surprised all of us."

"We had some help bringing in everything and setting up, of course. We were already there early to help out, so Amir thought it would be a nice surprise to thank them." Petra gave him another smile, grateful that she was seen on the terrace throughout the fireworks show. *Could he have found out about the safe?* She dismissed the possibility. If Nguyen had known for sure that they were involved, they would already be dead. He was fishing—she just had to make sure he didn't bait her into revealing anything.

"Right," Nguyen looked at her with his black eyes that never betrayed a single emotion. "Did you and Amir ever go out to the stables? Jim said that you both ride."

"I wouldn't go that far. Amir's teaching me how to ride." She considered ignoring the question about going to the stables at Hill Hearst but decided against it since they had run into Seymour on their way out that morning. "Your trails are lovely. I felt like I was in an old Jane Austen novel, riding through the English countryside," Petra flashed him a doe-eyed expression.

The sides of Nguyen's mouth wrinkled ever so slightly in obvious disgust, "I should probably get back to our table."

Petra watched him walk away before she poured the rest of his champagne into her empty glass, slid the glass under the table, and used an image capture app that Nathan had uploaded on her phone to scan for his fingerprints. When she set the glass on the table, she noticed Nguyen speaking to Seymour before returning to the family table next to the dance floor. So far, he was buying it, but the team still needed to make it out of Madagascar before their covers came apart at the seams.

Chapter 45

Mahajanga, Madagascar

Rachel moved quickly toward the entrance to the storage unit. *This had better work.* She had a flash memory of her last conversation with her father—of him telling her that he was getting out. *This is for you, Dad,* she thought as she exited.

"Rachel, if you're doing this, you better hurry. They're almost on top of you," Nathan's voice ran through her earpiece.

"I'm on it." She caught the door to stop it from slamming and ducked around the corner. With her back against the wall, she dropped her sweatshirt to the ground and unbuttoned the top two buttons of her fitted black blouse. She loosened her hair so that it spilled across her shoulders. Rachel exhaled and removed a small bottle of breath freshener from the pocket of her sweatshirt. She turned the dial on the side of the breath freshener bottle to the alcohol setting and sprayed it into her mouth. The strong scent of booze made her wince, but she was grateful for it as a cover. Before replacing the bottle, she directed a few sprays at her clothes for extra effect and tossed the sweatshirt and bottle underneath a nearby bush.

"We should check inside," she heard Jonah say.

"Nah, it was just some animal. Go back to the party," another male voice responded.

Rachel deactivated her earpiece and stumbled with a loud giggle, putting on her best impression of a drunk. "Jonah?" she called out, "Are you here?" She giggled again, "I missed you."

"Er, Rachel, yeah. I'm over here." She could hear the obvious embarrassment in his voice and she continued to sell it.

"Baby, I looked for you at the bar tonight, but then I remembered that you were working since you showed me this place, you showed me, on our hike yesterday." She giggled, "I thought it would be nice to come see you." She swayed from side to side and he caught her arm.

"You can't be here. Let's get you back to your hotel," he said in a gruff voice.

"We should go back to your room." Rachel let herself fall into his arms so that her head rested against his chest, "It's closer. We could have some more fun."

"Jonah, why don't you go take care of that?" the other guard mocked. "I don't need your help here."

143

Rachel squealed as Jonah picked her up, cursing at his colleague under his breath.

"Where are you taking me?" she said.

"I'm taking you to bed," he grumbled. "You can't show up like this. If the boss found out, I could lose my job."

"I'm sorry, baby." Rachel kept quiet as he carried her back to his room at the main hotel lodge. He grunted a couple of times, but other than that, he kept his responses to a minimum. With her in his arms, the walk took about fifteen minutes.

When they reached his room, he dropped her on the bed and drew the curtains. "We'll talk about this in the morning. This was supposed to be casual, and then you show up at my work?"

After the door shut behind him, she waited a few moments before reactivating her earpiece. "Carlos, what's your status? Did I get the other guard off your scent? You've probably got another fifteen minutes to get out of there."

Chapter 46

Mahajanga, Madagascar

Carlos let out a sigh of relief when he received the fingerprint images from Petra. He loaded the image of Nguyen's left index fingerprint in life size onto the screen of his phone and prayed as he used an image relay to project it onto the access pad. A green light appeared on the safe, and the tension in his shoulders eased.

He moved on immediately to drilling past the combination lock and he could hear his heartbeat in his ears over the sound of the drill. He counted the seconds until he felt the drill bit give to indicate that he was through the exterior of the safe. He widened the hole as he had at Hill Hearst, praying that this time they would actually find something useful. *The ledger. It has to exist.*

When he inserted the scope into the safe, he caught a glimpse of a leather-bound notebook and his heart soared. *Almost there.* He could scarcely steady his hands as he triggered the magnetic insert on the other side of the lock. He shifted the tools on the outside of the safe until he heard a soft click as the locking mechanism disengaged.

"Rachel got Jonah to go with her," Nathan said across the coms. "The other guard is still outside. Hurry, Carlos. If he checks the entrance logs, he'll know someone's inside."

"Keep your shirt on. I'm working as fast as I can."

Carlos opened the safe door and pulled out the notebook, disregarding the jewelry cases on the other shelves. Even though he had expected it to be in code, his heart sank when he opened the notebook. The text was a series of words and numbers, but as far as he could tell, it looked more like gibberish. He sighed. It had been years since he had done work in cryptology—his major once upon a time. *Nathan will be able to handle this.* He used a pocket camera to photograph each page one by one, moving as quickly as possible. He was tempted to take the original, but there was no way they would be able to leave Madagascar in one piece if Nguyen realized that his ledger was missing.

Carlos thumbed through the rest of the pages and exhaled when he reached the end. "I'm closing the safe up now." Just like at Hill Hearst, he filled the hole in the door with putty and put a silver metallic cap that matched the surface on each side. He shut the safe door and prayed to himself. *If there's anyone up there, throw us a bone. We need to put Nguyen away and get out alive. Not too much to ask. Please.*

"Think you can help me out with that guard?" Carlos asked Nathan while he packed up his tools. "I'm on my way to the door." He holstered Rachel's gun in the back of his waistband and grabbed the ID card.

"I'm setting up another distraction. Stand by."

Carlos stood behind the closed door and waited for what felt like ages but was only a few seconds.

Rachel spoke over the com while he was waiting for Nathan. "Carlos, what's your status? Did I get the other guard off your scent? You've probably got another fifteen minutes to get out of there."

"I'm working on it," Carlos grunted.

"You're a go," Nathan said. "But keep it quiet. He's not far."

Carlos moved through the doorway and caught the door to stop it from making a loud noise. As he did so, he heard footsteps coming toward him from the other side of the storage unit. *Move.* He dove into the bushes just as the other guard poked his head around the corner.

Chapter 47

Mahajanga, Madagascar

Petra bit her lip in frustration, "Nothing?"

Nathan looked up from the copy of the ledger that Carlos had made, "I can't make heads or tails of this."

"Is it the resolution of the images?" Carlos asked.

"It's the code they're using. It doesn't match any cipher I've ever seen." Nathan sighed, "It could be a book-based code, where each of these letters and numbers map to a word in a book or something. If that's the case, there's no way to break it without knowing what book they used."

Petra slammed her fist on the coffee table, "We were so close! I thought we had him. There's actually a ledger, but we can't read it." A wave of guilt washed over her. *Why did I work with Obaidi? This is all my fault.* If she had never done that, Vikram wouldn't be dead, and she and Kasem would be far away from here. The guilt turned to anger as she thought of the Agency. *Without them, none of this would have happened.*

"We'll find another way," Carlos said. His words were confident enough, but the tone behind them sounded just like Petra felt.

"You don't understand. He knows something. You should have heard the way he spoke to me last night." Petra shuddered, "He must know about the skirmish in front of the stables. I know we wiped the cameras, but I swear he suspects. This is all coming apart." Her voice caught in her throat.

Carlos placed a hand on her shoulder, "We'll find another way, kiddo. I know we will."

For Vikram. Petra pictured his smile and bit her lip. She rubbed the back of her neck and stared at the copy of the ledger, willing it to decode in front of her eyes the way it would in a movie.

After several moments of silence, Kasem spoke up. "Has anyone heard from Rachel? I haven't seen her this morning. Did she even come back last night?"

"No," Carlos frowned. "She went off with that guard, Jonah. She saved my butt, actually—damn, she has balls. She pretended that she was drunk and came to see him so that he wouldn't check inside the storage unit. Nate, what's her twenty?"

Nathan tapped the screen of his tablet and the position of Rachel's tracker appeared on the map of the resort, "Looks like she's still in Jonah's room. That's fine, right?"

Petra checked her watch, "It's past ten. I think I should go check on her."

Carlos nodded, "Good idea." He motioned toward the door. "Kasem, go with her. If Nguyen's really onto us, she might need backup."

******

Petra watched the micro-expressions on Kasem's face as they made their way from where they parked their rental car a few hundred yards from Jonah's room at the lodge. "I'm surprised you decided to come with me," she said, focusing on keeping her voice soft and level. She felt like her skin was crawling, her guilt was eating her alive. Everything around her seemed to remind her of Vikram, of working with Obaidi, and of how she got Kasem captured, and Vikram killed. She avoided eye contact—they needed to talk, but right now, all she wanted to do was drive her fist through a wall.

He raised his eyebrows, "Why?"

"Lately, it seems like you've been avoiding me. We barely even sat down together at the party last night," she managed to keep her composure.

"I was just mingling for the cover."

She sighed and touched his arm, "Kasem, I'm sorry. I know this distance between us is my fault. I've been so wrapped up in this operation—"

He shrugged off her touch, "Petra, I know you're keeping something from me, and unless you're planning to tell me what it is, I don't want to hear it."

"You're right. I do need to tell you something, and I will. I promise." She gestured toward the lodge up the road, "Let's check on Rachel and then go back to the villa. I'll tell you everything." She blinked, and a single tear rolled down her cheek, "I'm sorry. I really am."

Kasem sighed and placed his hand on her cheek, "I'll hold you to that." He leaned forward and gave her a peck on the lips, "Thank you."

Petra's face broke into a smile as they covered the remaining distance toward the lodge. For the first time that day, she believed everything was going to be fine. The deep greenery of the bushes and trees sparkled against the bright blue sky as they strolled hand in hand.

They turned down a side lane to approach the lodge from the rear, where they would be less visible to anyone walking past.

When they were within fifty feet, they heard the sound of muffled yelling and quickened their steps. She reached under her bright green sarong and grabbed the Colt pistol from her hidden thigh holster. They neared the back entrance of the lodge a few feet from one of the windows to Jonah's room. Before Petra could peek in, she heard a woman scream followed by a loud thud.

Rachel.

Chapter 48

Mahajanga, Madagascar

Kasem reached Jonah's window on the side of the building with Petra trailing close behind him. It took only a second to take in what was happening. Rachel was on the ground curled up in the fetal position with Jonah kneeling over her.

Kasem pulled out his gun, pointed it at the window, and yelled, "Freeze!" but Jonah didn't notice them. Kasem glanced to the side and debated what to do. The small side window wasn't large enough to crawl through. The only entrances to the room were the door opening to the hotel's interior hallway or the sliding doors leading to the back patio. "Let's get to the patio."

They traversed the corner of the building quickly and reached the back patio door. The curtains were drawn across them, so they couldn't see what was happening. Kasem steadied his breath and gave the door an experimental shove. As expected, the door was locked. "Do you have your lock pick kit?" he shouted.

"No."

"This is going to draw attention, so we have to act fast." He unbuttoned the top two buttons of his shirt and pulled it over his head. He then pulled out his Beretta and held it by the barrel with his right hand before wrapping the shirt around it. "Take cover." He took a few steps back, drew his arm back, and slammed the butt of the gun into the center of the glass door, creating a spider web of cracks that spread throughout the pane. After another good punch at the center of the web, shards of glass went flying against the curtains. He quickly unwrapped the shirt and turned the gun around to grip it properly before entering. Kasem shielded his eyes as he stepped through the glass and pushed the curtains away to enter with his gun drawn and ready.

"Who the hell are you?" Jonah cried out with a pistol pointed toward Kasem. "Drop the gun, mate. You've got nowhere to go."

"I'll drop mine when you drop yours," Kasem said. He cocked the hammer and aimed the gun straight at Jonah's chest. "I'm a pretty good shot. I don't like your odds of dodging."

Jonah pointed the gun at Rachel, "Drop it, or I'll shoot her."

Kasem tried to compose himself and not look to his right. From where he stood, he couldn't tell how badly Rachel had been hurt, but Petra was still poised and ready on the patio and he didn't want to give her away. She would have to catch Jonah off guard. "All right," he said projecting his voice as much as possible, "I'm putting my gun down." He took a step toward Jonah and lowered the gun, catching a glimpse of Petra creeping toward the patio door. *That's my girl.*

"That's it. Nice and steady. Hands up and kick it to me."

Kasem kneeled and placed the gun on the ground. He slid it forward and to the right, careful to push it just enough. It stopped where he had planned, a couple of feet to Jonah's right. Kasem clasped his hands behind his head and stood, "Let her go and you'll never see either of us again."

"Wait. I've seen you before," Jonah frowned. "Weren't you at the party last night? Man, the boss is going to have a field day with this. Who the hell are you people?"

"I'm just a friend who was concerned about Rachel," Kasem said in a steady voice. He watched as Jonah moved toward the gun on the ground. *Come on, asshole. Kneel down and pick it up.*

Jonah leaned over to grab the gun.

"If you want to keep your head, I suggest you put both of those guns on the floor," Petra said as she marched into the room with her gun raised.

Chapter 49

Mahajanga, Madagascar

Kasem held his breath as Jonah looked toward Petra standing in front of the patio door. She glowered at Jonah with her feet planted firmly shoulder-width apart and had both hands steadying the gun in front of her. Kasem thought she looked like a character from one of those spy thriller movies she loved to watch. *But she's no character. She's the real deal.*

Jonah lowered both guns to the floor and Kasem approached him. "Turn around," he said with a shove to Jonah's shoulder, "on your knees, hands behind your back, *buddy*. Now!"

Petra tossed him two zip ties from the purse slung across her shoulder and Kasem yanked both of Jonah's hands behind his back and bound them together. He did the same to Jonah's ankles and stepped away.

"You had zip ties but no lock pick kit?" Kasem raised his eyebrows.

Petra shrugged, "I left it in my evening bag by accident. You got him?"

Kasem nodded and she slid Jonah's gun into her purse with her Colt pistol still in hand. She handed Kasem his Beretta and moved around them to Rachel, "Jesus."

"How is she?" he asked. Rachel looked unconscious and her face was bruised and bloody.

"She's got a knife wound to the stomach," Petra crouched over Rachel and set the gun on the nightstand to her left before laying her gently on her back. She pulled up Rachel's shirt to examine the wound, "The bleeding's not bad, but the knife's still in there. We need to get her to a doctor."

Holy crap, Kasem's back muscles tightened and he tossed her his shirt, "Put pressure around the wound, and tie the knife in place." *She's going to be okay.*

Petra kept one hand over the shirt applying pressure around the knife, and with her other hand felt around Rachel's neck, "Her pulse is off the charts and her breathing sounds off." She touched Rachel's head gingerly, which was also bleeding, but not profusely. "I'm sure she has a concussion, and those eyes are going to look like hell." She ran her hands over Rachel's ribs, "And she's probably got several broken ribs."

Kasem searched around the room until he noticed the ironing board by the wardrobe. "She might have a spine injury, let's get her on the ironing board."

Petra flattened the ironing board and laid it on the floor next to Rachel. "We have to do it together," she looked at Jonah and her body quivered. She took a step toward him and wrenched Jonah's head by the hair, "Are you happy with yourself?" She raised her fist and punched him in the eye, "You still won't look half as bad as she will."

Jonah grunted, and Petra grabbed his shoulders, "Take this, asshole," she said as she slammed her foot straight into his groin.

Jonah doubled over and collapsed on the floor. "You bitch," he yelled, followed by a series of expletives.

"That's right, I am a bitch. Don't ever even think of hurting another woman. Bitches don't like it," Petra kicked him again.

Kasem winced, "Come on, we need to get her to the hospital—now!"

"Fine," Petra brought the butt of her gun down on the back of his head and knocked Jonah out.

Kasem positioned himself by Rachel's head, with one arm cradling her neck and shoulders and the other hand stabilizing her lumbar spine. Petra moved to Rachel's feet and together they slid her off the floor and onto the ironing board. Once they had her on the board, Rachel's eyes opened for a second and she groaned.

"You're going to be okay," Petra squeezed her hand before she and Kasem lifted the ironing board up slowly. As they maneuvered their way out of the apartment, Rachel's breathing grew shallower and she passed out again.

"She might be going into shock," Kasem said when they slid her into the backseat of the car. *Thank god for this huge SUV.* He ran back into the room to pick up the still unconscious Jonah and tossed him into the trunk.

******

Over the drive to the clinic Rachel came in and out of consciousness—the fifteen minutes on the road felt like hours as they drove at breakneck speed. On the way, Petra called Carlos who directed them to a doctor that would handle things off book, while Nathan took care of the disturbance at the lodge. Fortunately, most of the people staying at the main lodge were tourists out at the beach or other security personnel who were already on duty. To provide further cover, Nathan blocked the lodge phones until they were on their way, and then made a false call to hotel security about broken glass on the patio. He even paid off the intern working at the front desk so that the incident would only be reported as a minor disturbance due to a drunken hotel guest.

When they arrived at the clinic, Carlos rushed Rachel inside and sent Kasem and Petra back to the beach villa to deal with the unconscious Jonah. During the drive back, Kasem felt his adrenaline coming down as his breathing slowed. His skin was crawling, he wanted so much to slam Jonah's face into a slab of concrete, to hit him, damage him, as much as he'd hurt Rachel—maybe even to put a bullet through his brain. Kasem glanced over at Petra in the passenger seat—she was staring straight ahead with her jaw rigid, as if she was barely holding on. *I've never seen that look in her eyes.*

Kasem focused on his breathing and forced himself to exhale slowly, trying to get control of his feelings. *Rachel's going to be okay. So is Petra,* he told himself. He wasn't sure how bad Rachel's condition was, only that going into shock was dangerous, but he couldn't let himself lose control. Killing Jonah wouldn't improve Rachel's condition, and he wasn't going to give into that darker side of himself again. *She still holds it against me,* he glanced at Petra again and recalled what she had said to Carlos on the flight to London. After he'd been captured in D.C., he'd taken the first opportunity to kill his captor after his escape, even though he'd no longer been in danger—consequences be damned. If he hadn't done that, they might have been able to use Anatoli's testimony to take apart the rest of the FSB operation that had set up the terrorist attack that they had barely managed to thwart in time. Much as he wanted to take revenge on Jonah for what he'd done to Rachel, he wasn't going to make the same mistake again.

Another glance at Petra made him shift in his seat. He wasn't sure how to process the rage he'd seen in her eyes, and he didn't want her to be consumed by anger the way that he had spent so much of the last few years. With every assignment he'd undertaken in Iran, with every kill that he'd made, and the loss of his previous identity, he'd given up a piece of his soul. It had taken years to claw back a semblance of it, and he couldn't bear the idea of that happening to his Lila. *Petra.* He saw similar emotions on her face now, but he didn't understand them, even though he felt like he should. That side of her seemed like a new person, he'd never seen her lose control in that way. In a way, he was grateful for her display of vulnerability in beating up Jonah—it proved that she too sometimes lost control of her emotions. Yet he didn't want that for her, he didn't want to believe that could be part of her. Just a little earlier that day, it had seemed like they were making progress, but that conversation felt like an eternity ago. Now all he could see was her anger, and how much of herself she must be hiding from him. Even if he didn't want it to be there, he could learn to accept it, but he had to see all of it. She had to trust him enough to let him see it. *Why can't she trust me?* He had obviously laid it all on the line for her over and over again, and he had never lied to her about what he had done as the Ahriman. *Why can't she do the same?*

Chapter 50

Mahajanga, Madagascar

Petra stared at the kitchen counter while she waited for Kasem to finish securing Jonah to a chair in their living room. "What's taking so long?" she snapped.

Kasem shot her a glance. "Almost done," he said, matching her tone.

She immediately regretted speaking to Kasem like that. She shouldn't take her frustration out on him, but she couldn't help it. The image she'd conjured in her nightmare of Gibran Obaidi telling Nguyen that Vik was an agent kept repeating in her head, followed by one of Vik being shot. She couldn't let go of the guilt that she had been Obaidi's original handler, that she had brought him into the Agency, which had ultimately led to Vik's death. *This is all my fault.*

Kasem pulled at the zip ties to test them before joining her in the kitchen, "He's all yours."

Petra was about to approach when her phone rang. *Carlos,* she thought as she almost leapt forward to grab it from her purse. "Carlos? Is she okay? What happened?"

"They gave her a blood transfusion and antibiotics that stabilized her, but they haven't removed the knife yet—they're doing some scans to see what organs it might have hit before they remove it."

"What does that mean?"

"I don't know exactly. If the knife hit something internal they'll have to do surgery to repair the hemorrhage, or repair the organ, I guess."

Petra's mouth went dry—Carlos didn't sound at all hopeful. "Okay, let us know when you know more," she choked and hung up.

"What did he say?" Kasem asked.

"They don't know yet—the knife might have hit something, so they haven't removed it yet. They gave her a blood transfusion but they're still doing tests before they take the knife out."

Kasem turned toward Jonah and smacked him across the head with the back of his hand. He grimaced at the pain in his hand, but ignored it as he hit him again and again.

Petra watched from the kitchen counter as Kasem continued to smack Jonah across the head, frozen in place. *I should do something,* but she couldn't move. Her eyes moved to her purse and she thought of the gun inside. Time seemed to stand still as she pulled it out, ejected the magazine and checked that there were no bullets in the chamber. With the pistol in hand, she stomped around the counter of their open kitchen, and when she reached Jonah, she raised her hand to stop Kasem from hitting him anymore. He backed away into the kitchen without a word.

She waved some smelling salts under Jonah's nose to wake him. "Wake up, asshole," she snarled. "Now!" She ripped the duct tape off his mouth, hoping to cause as much pain as possible.

His eyes flew open, but it took a couple of seconds before he recognized her. "Bitch," he said again.

Almost before he had the word out, Petra dealt him a hard blow to the ear with the butt of her gun. "Tell us what you know about Rachel and who you told, or there will be more where that came from."

"I knew that bitch was using me. She wasn't even a great lay."

Petra's skin felt like it was on fire and brought the butt of her Colt pistol down on him again, this time straight at his nose. Jonah cried out as blood dribbled over his mouth and down his chin, "You broke my nose?"

A coldness of spirit came over her as she spoke, "I can go all day, and you have a lot more bones to break." She shrugged and added, "My parents wanted me to be a doctor. I went in a different direction, but I picked up a few facts along the way. Did you know that the human body is comprised of 206 bones? Fourteen in the face alone." She traced his cheekbone with her finger, "So many bones and so many pain centers where the nerves come together."

"I'm just a freakin' security guard, lady." For the first time, Jonah's voice started to sound scared.

"And I'm Doctor Who." She placed the gun on the coffee table and picked up the pinky on his right hand, which was secured to the armrest at the wrist. "Did you know that phalanges are actually the bones of the fingers? There are fourteen phalanges on each hand." She wrapped her fingers around Jonah's pinky, "You have five seconds to start talking or you'll start to see what real pain is like." She waited for a second, but he stared at the floor. "One, two, five." She grabbed the gun once again and slammed the grip panel on the base of his right pinky.

Jonah screamed, and she did the same to his right thumb. "I can keep going with this hand or switch to your left," she said and crossed to his left side. "Right or left? Which will it be?"

"I'll talk."

Petra took a seat on the sofa on the other side of the coffee table. She placed the gun on the glass surface of the table and spun it around a couple of times, "Well?"

"I thought something was weird last night. It seemed like Rachel was only acting drunk. We drank a lot the other night, and she didn't act like that. And I couldn't figure out how she found me at the storage unit. I showed it to her on our hike, but it's not like I told her that's where I'd be." He spat out a mixture of saliva and blood, "You got a towel?"

"Not yet. Keep going."

"That's it. It didn't add up, so I checked the entry logs and noticed that my access code was used to enter the storage unit last night. She was the only one who could have lifted my ID." Jonah shrugged, "She really wasn't such a lousy lay. It's a shame. I was looking forward to having her again."

Petra pointed the gun at him with a look of disgust on her face. "Do you *want* me to move to your left hand? Or are you going to be a good boy?" After he nodded, she continued, "Did you tell anyone what you found in the logs?"

"I didn't want the boss to find out that I let some girl lift my ID." He paused and smiled through the blood dripping from his nose, "I'm looking forward to telling him about you people though. That'll be a regular treat."

Petra raised her eyebrows. They hadn't decided what they would do with him after he answered their questions. They had checked him for trackers, so he wasn't likely to be found in their villa. Unfortunately, a more remote safe house wasn't available on such short notice, and the only other villa nearby housed the rest of the team, so there was no one else to hear him scream. She doubted that he knew enough about Nguyen's operation to actually be useful, but she certainly wasn't going to let him go. *Maybe I could dump him into the ocean. Into a swarm of jellyfish.* The thought brought a slight smile to her face, "Good to know. But you'll have trouble talking with a broken jaw and no teeth."

"Who are you people?"

"Let's talk about your boss instead. What do you know about his deals? His buyers? Suppliers?" Petra kept her tone harsh and steady. *Maybe we can get something of use from this asshole after all.* Her phone vibrated on the side table and she checked it for messages. Carlos had used a contact of Rachel's to send a cleaner to Jonah's room, but they weren't sure if they could clean it before hotel security arrived to check out the commotion. *At least there were no gunshots.*

"What's there to say? Nguyen's a finance guy. I know nothing about finance."

"How long have you worked for him?" Petra set her phone down and made her way back to the kitchen to grab her tablet from the counter. She wanted to see how his answer compared to what they had on file about Nguyen. She caught Kasem's gaze as she walked back to the sofa. He was leaning against the refrigerator and watching the interrogation in silence with his arms crossed. She grimaced—by the look on his face she wasn't sure if he wanted to stop her or to join her, but she didn't know if she could handle either one. When he'd killed Anatoli, she'd held it against him, and now she was basically a hypocrite. Part of her wanted him to stop her, to end this so that she wouldn't keep going, but the thought of stopping, the thought of not making Jonah pay for what he'd done to Rachel seemed unfathomable. Kasem was angry too, but he seemed more in control—she couldn't stop herself from inflicting the maximum pain and long-term damage on Jonah. Even though Kasem had hit Jonah across the head several times, he hadn't done any permanent damage, but she wasn't so sure about what she'd just done to his hand. She just had to hope that Kasem wouldn't hold it against her, that he wouldn't bail on her after the operation.

"Two years," Jonah answered.

Petra nodded. The answer matched their files, although they had little information on where Jonah had served his security assignments. "How did you get set up? Where have you worked for him?"

"I met him through my commanding officer when I left the service two years ago. He said it was a good gig—good pay, some interesting travel, and a hands-off boss, so I took it. I needed the money."

"So, you became a mercenary." Petra could scarcely keep the contempt from her voice. Being a mercenary offered some benefits—clear incentives and a lot more money—but she had always struggled with the morality behind it. Working for the greater good already created more than enough shades of gray in a supposedly black-and-white profession, so a private entity had to be even worse.

"We're all mercenaries," Jonah growled. "What do you think the military had me doing? Black ops and hidden deals. Risking my life on a whim, and with nothing to show for it. At least this way I get paid."

"Risking your life?" Petra drummed her fingers against the table. Jonah wouldn't have said that if he hadn't served Nguyen during some sketchy deals. Finally, they might have something of value on Nguyen. "Tell me more."

"I stand on guard when he travels. That's it." Jonah clearly had realized his mistake and was now trying to backpedal.

"Where? Why? You're not one of his bodyguards here, so you're not protecting him. What is it that you're guarding?"

"I don't know. He wants a guard, so I guard."

His answer was so obviously a lie that Petra snickered, "You don't have a clue, huh?" She picked up the gun and transferred it between her hands as if to judge its weight, and then whirled it around her finger so that it pointed straight at him, "Are you sure about that?"

When Jonah didn't say anything, Petra approached him with a cunning smile. "I'm sure there are ways to make you more forthcoming." She grabbed his left hand and counted out his fingers, "How about a middle finger this time? It wouldn't be much fun to function without it, especially with broken fingers on both hands."

Jonah locked eyes with her defiantly, and she could tell that he was challenging her, daring her to keep going. Perhaps he thought that she wouldn't, that she was too soft to keep up the pain? Ordinarily, he would be right, but this was no ordinary day.

Petra yanked hard on his finger with one hand and slammed the side of her other hand on top of it. Jonah cried out in pain. She hadn't broken it yet, but she had most definitely demonstrated that she could. "The next one will break it."

A hint of fear entered his eyes. As a military operative, he had probably been trained to assess his captor, and at first glance, she was hardly to be feared. Now that she had started to prove his initial assessment wrong, she had a chance of getting some actual information.

"What does your boss have you guarding?" Her tone was quiet, calculating, and cold.

Jonah remained silent, and Petra picked up the gun and pressed it into his finger, "A bullet will hurt so much more. It's your call."

He shivered and nodded, "Okay!" He took a deep breath and the confession began, "Arms mostly. He buys them and then has security teams take them to conflict zones around the world to sell them."

Petra was pleased, "For example?"

"South Sudan. We were there three months ago to arm the rebels there."

"What kind of weapons?"

"Assault rifles, anti-aircraft missiles, napalm missiles." He shrugged, "All the newest stuff."

"Right." Petra glanced over to the kitchen where Kasem was still watching the conversation. She couldn't get a read on his face. She was tempted to stop and speak to him separately, perhaps to strategize about how they could use Jonah's testimony, but instead, she decided to press on. Putting Nguyen in prison hardly felt like justice for what Jonah had done. "Who does Nguyen deal with?"

"Different people, but Seymour's the only one who's always around. When we're guarding on-site, we report to him."

The mention of Seymour's name left a bitter taste in her mouth. "That's why he's not in London often." Petra tapped on her tablet to engage the voice recorder with automatic transcription and pushed it closer to Jonah, "You're going to go on record with everything you know. Every deal you've ever witnessed, every location you've gone to."

Jonah's eyes moved to the tablet and he blinked several times. Petra gave him a moment to start talking, but instead, he growled, "Kiss my ass."

Petra paused the recording. Without hesitating, she picked up the butt of the gun and slammed the metal into the knuckle below Jonah's left thumb. This time she heard the bone crack. Jonah screamed as his thumb drooped down at an angle that would have normally made her queasy.

"I think that if anyone's doing the ass kissing, it'll be you," she said.

Jonah stared at his thumb aghast. His eyes rolled back and he looked like he was about to pass out. Petra slapped both his cheeks multiple times, her head felt like it was on fire as she hit him again and again, "Get hold of yourself, talk and we'll give you something for the pain. But not until you talk." She took a step back and her chest heaved, she felt like she was outside of herself watching the interrogation. She couldn't get control of the emotions raging through her. The only thing that seemed right was to beat him, to hurt him, until he submitted.

He gagged, then recovered, "I'll tell you what I know."

"Good." She restarted the recording, "Who are his contacts? Who protects him at the CIA and other intelligence services? How does he keep his deals hidden?"

"He runs everything through his partners. Seymour. Sir Caleb. I don't know who else."

Petra sighed. Jonah's information confirmed her suspicions. They wouldn't be able to get Nguyen on paper without the ledger unless they could catch him red-handed, which was the plan that she had proposed in London. The problem with that, of course, was that

Kasem would have to go all in—try to take over the arms sale, basically becoming one of Nguyen's cronies like Seymour, or a patsy like Sir Caleb. "What were you guarding last night?"

"There's a safe in the storage unit. There's a lot of stuff in there. Jewels and documents mostly, but I don't know the specifics."

Petra paused the recording again and screwed the silencer onto the front of her gun. She moved toward him with a smile of disbelief. "Right. Poor Jonah. The big boss doesn't even tell him about what he's doing." She pressed the pistol to his knee. "I'll bet you have some idea about those documents."

His eyes grew wide and she nodded slowly, "If I fire this, you might never walk again. If you're lucky, you'll just have a really bad limp." She cocked the hammer.

He shook his head and kept silent.

Petra pulled the trigger on the gun and it clicked since the chamber was empty, "That was a warning."

"I don't know anything," he shouted in sheer panic. "I think it's company records. That's all I know. I swear."

"Get talking." Petra pressed on the tablet again to start recording. She put the pistol back on the table and took a seat across the coffee table. She listened quietly as Jonah began to recount the places where he had worked for Nguyen. Jonah had mentioned the names of three different cities in conflict zones. "Tell me how he brings the goods in. Every detail and the dates."

Petra gave him another ten minutes to talk before stopping the recording. "Thank you, Jonah," she said as she surveyed the transcription. They could use the information he'd given them to help track down Nguyen's suppliers and buyers with the location and timing of the deals. It still, however, wouldn't be enough to put Nguyen away unless they could decode the ledger.

"You've been very helpful. I expect we'll keep you around to testify against Nguyen." She was about to put the recording device away when she remembered Madison, how Carlos had found her body in her flat. Petra looked back toward Jonah—he was unlikely to know anything about that, but she had to ask, "What about Nguyen's assistant, Madison Blake? What do you know about her? Did he have her killed?"

A flicker of recognition at the name flashed through Jonah's eyes before he shook his head. Petra felt her torso turn rigid, *why would he know her?* "You're lying," her voice was icy. "What happened to her?" She pointed the pistol at the joint just in front of his left wrist this time, "One shot to that joint and I'll make sure you never use that hand again. The best surgeon in the world wouldn't be able to put it back together." Part of her wanted him to refuse to talk, she wanted to take that shot, she wanted to maim him permanently. Besides, she was afraid of the answer, afraid of what she would do if he confirmed what she knew in her gut.

Jonah spat at the floor, "Dammit bitch, what do you want from me? Seymour said take care of her, so I did. I followed my orders and I got a damn good lay out of it beforehand. Who cares? She was a nobody, just someone who got too much of a conscience working for Nguyen."

Petra stared at him, and a series of images flashed in front of her. Jonah confronting Rachel, then knifing her in the gut after she fought back, Rachel bleeding out on the floor, then lying in the hospital fighting for her life. Jonah with Madison, drugging her while she lay naked in bed. Petra blinked twice and the images changed—she now saw Obaidi telling Nguyen who Vikram was again, followed by Vikram at the docks. One shot to the heart and he fell to the ground.

Petra's body stiffened and she retreated to the kitchen counter where she grabbed the bullet that she had ejected from the pistol chamber. She took a deep breath, then dropped it and went for her purse instead. From a pocket on the inside of the lining, she removed a single blank and slid it into the chamber. Her jaw clenched as she moved back toward Jonah. "We do need to keep you around for your testimony—we can't let Nguyen get away with any of this. But you don't need your legs for that. In fact, you don't need your legs at all." She placed the silencer against his right kneecap and pulled the trigger.

Chapter 51

Mahajanga, Madagascar

Kasem watched in horror as Petra placed her pistol against Jonah's knee. Before he could react, he heard the muffled crack of the gun firing.

His mouth fell open. Time seemed to slow down, and it felt as if he was looking down on himself, like he was having an out of body experience. He crossed the room while Jonah screamed and passed out. Kasem grabbed a towel and pressed it against Jonah's knee. The blank was embedded in the kneecap, but it hadn't fully submerged under the skin. He applied pressure and looked around frantically. Petra was standing a few feet away with a dazed expression on her face. She dropped the gun and fell back into a chair.

"Petra," Kasem shouted, "get the first aid kit! We need tweezers and rubbing alcohol."

She sat there with a blank look. "Petra," he repeated, "the first aid kit. Go! Now!"

She blinked back at him and then rushed to the bathroom. A minute later, she returned with the kit in hand. "It was only a blank," she whispered. She opened the kit and pulled out the tweezers and a packet of alcohol wipes. After tearing the packet open with her teeth, she pulled the wipe out and ran it over the tweezers, "It's the best we can do."

Kasem grabbed the scissors from the kit and did the same, choosing to ignore her comment about the blank. They both knew a blank fired at close range was still incredibly dangerous. *What had come over her?* He steadied himself and grabbed the tweezers from her, "I'll need gauze. A lot of it."

Kasem took a deep breath and brought the tweezers toward Jonah's skin. His right hand shook, and Petra placed one of her hands on his to steady it. He looked at her and briefly tried to decipher what was going on underneath the surface. *There will be time for that later.* She let go and he guided his right hand toward the wound and grasped the sides of the blank with the tweezers. With another breath, he pulled straight upward. The blank remained still, and he pulled harder until it gave way. He dropped it on the ground as Petra pressed the sterilized gauze against the wound to stem the now free-flowing blood.

She kept pressure on the wound for what seemed like ages while they both sat in silence. Kasem wondered how Rachel was doing. Carlos had said that he would take care of her. Nathan was probably resting because he still hadn't fully healed. *If only Carlos were here.* Kasem wasn't sure what to say or do. He had never seen this side of Petra, and definitely not Lila. He'd never believed that such a side to her existed—he'd always placed her above the total loss of emotional control that he'd just witnessed. She had transformed into someone that he didn't recognize, someone that reminded him more of himself than the Lila that he thought he knew. While he understood her rage at what Jonah had done to Rachel, at Madison's death, Kasem could never have imagined her giving into it in that way. She had shot Jonah at point blank, even after he had talked, after he had given them what they wanted. Even if he couldn't blame her for the emotions—that would make him a full-on hypocrite since he felt the same way, shared the same dark side—he wasn't sure if he wanted to accept that side of her, especially since she wasn't willing to be open and honest about it with him. She might as well have been someone else. Perhaps Carlos could figure out what was going on with her. He couldn't, and he no longer knew if they could bridge this distance. There had been too many secrets and lies between them, too much baggage that they couldn't, or wouldn't, forget and leave behind.

Kasem watched the blood flow ebb and picked up the scissors, "I'm going to take off the gauze and clean up the edges. Get the Dermabond ready and some fresh gauze."

Petra followed his instructions and opened another packet of sterilized gauze, along with readying an ampule of Dermabond to seal the wound. Kasem shut his eyes for a second before he nodded at her. He took pressure off the wound and sprayed a temporary clotting agent on it before cutting at the jagged edges with the scissors. A few minutes later, the Dermabond was applied and the wound was covered with fresh gauze. He dropped the remaining gauze and disappeared into their bedroom, slamming the door shut behind him.

Chapter 52

Mahajanga, Madagascar

Kasem threw his clothes from the closet into his suitcase. His head was pounding, he didn't know yet what he was going to do, but he knew that he had to leave.

Petra opened the door, "Carlos is sending his medical contact to pick him up."

"Good."

"Why are you packing? We still have to go to the wedding later." Petra closed the door behind her and walked to the foot of the bed.

"I'm not going to the wedding, Petra."

"What do you mean? You heard what Jonah said. You know what Nguyen's done, what he's capable of. We still have a chance to get him. We can't blow the op now."

"I very much doubt that," Kasem sighed. "At least not without the plan you proposed, and I'm not doing that. I can't be your asset anymore."

"That's not it. You're not my asset—you never really were. I just want to catch him. Nguyen has to pay for what he's done," her voice quavered.

"I can see that. I can see that you're willing to do *anything* to catch him. Anything at all. Humanity be damned."

Her face turned grim, "That's easy for you to say."

"Maybe it is. I've done more than my share of inhumane things, but we're not talking about me. That guy out there? *You* tortured him. *You* broke his thumb, and you *shot* him. I don't recognize you anymore."

"He'll be fine," Petra protested.

"You shot him in the knee. He might never walk again."

"Didn't you see what he did to Rachel? And he killed Madison. He's lucky we didn't kill him."

"I saw what he did to Rachel. I don't begrudge you being angry. I'm angry. But the person I saw in that room? That wasn't you, or at least not the person I thought you were, and *you won't talk to me about what's going on with you*. We've been having problems ever since we left Kyoto, even before that. You're hiding things and you obviously don't trust me. I can't keep doing this. I'm done."

"Do you think I want to be here? I left this life behind after you were captured."

"What's happened since then? How many ops have you been 'pulled back' into?" Kasem asked, using air quotes.

"Well, we certainly wouldn't be here if I hadn't been pulled back into an op. For starters, I'd never have found you. What would you be doing? Still running around as Majed's puppet? Maybe you'd legitimately be working with Nguyen, not just undercover. Besides isn't this a bit of a double standard? You, chastising me for how I tortured Jonah with everything you've done?"

Kasem took a step back, reeling at what she'd said. Her words stung, they felt like a slap in the face. "This isn't about me and my sins. I've been trying to atone for what I've done. Hell, I've been here with you on this op. I know it will never be enough but I'm still trying to do the right thing. Don't turn this around on me just to win an argument. This is about what you did to that man in there. You and I both know this wouldn't be happening if you made a clean break from all of this. What is the deal anyway? Why do you have this psychotic need to capture Nguyen? You're acting like you've gone completely unhinged."

"Unhinged? You think I've gone unhinged? It's not that easy to just break away. This is about protecting the people I care about. It's about being there for them when they need me. I can't leave them in the lurch."

"If you made a clean break—I mean a *real* clean break, this wouldn't be happening."

"What do you think Kyoto was?" Petra threw her hands up. "Besides, these *people* have risked their lives for me, for you, for the Agency, and for the greater good."

"The greater good? Seriously?"

"I hate that phrase as much as you do," Petra paused, swallowing, "but that doesn't mean it doesn't have an appropriate meaning. I may not want to do this work anymore, but by stopping a terrorist plot in DC, we made a difference. Stopping Nguyen is important. You can't devalue that because it's inconvenient to our relationship."

"Inconvenient. Right." *Screw you,* Kasem could barely stop himself from yelling out the words. "I've put myself on the line again and again for you. You say this is about *people*? What about me? What do you think I've been doing for you? You take and take, but I get nothing back, not even the truth. I'm basically your glorified puppet. You still haven't even told me why you're so obsessed with this op." He sighed, "If you could just be honest with me, it would fix so many of our issues and—"

"A glorified puppet?" she kicked at the base of the bed frame. "You think I treat you like my puppet? I followed you to Kyoto, after knowing everything that you've done. Knowing all of that, I still love you."

"Knowing all of that? What is this, some kind of pity fest? What about you? I bet you haven't told me any of the crap you've done for the Agency. How many kills, how many people you've tortured. You keep putting this back on me, but I bet your hands aren't clean. Besides, as you so keenly seem to have forgotten, I would never have been in this mess if it weren't for you!"

"Forgotten? You think I've forgotten that? I carry that guilt with me every day, every minute. I buried you. I thought you were dead, and I buried you," she leaned over the footboard and tried to catch her breath. "You were dead, and then a few years later, you weren't. You were there, standing right in front of me in Kuwait, setting a bomb at the Emir's diwaniya." She lowered herself to the floor, sobbing, "You were alive, but you weren't the same person. You were the Ahriman, and I still loved you, and it was all my fault. General Majed would never have captured you, never have turned you into the Ahriman, if it weren't for me. Everything that you've done, is on me."

Kasem blinked twice and looked away, "We've been through this before. You couldn't have known what would happen, and my decisions were still my own. I'm trying to move on now, to leave that past there, where it belongs, but you won't let me do that. You won't let us do that—you can't forgive me, you can't forgive yourself. Maybe you don't see it, but you're still treating me like I'm your asset. I want—I wanted to be your partner, I was willing to let it all go. But it's done now, we can't go on like this."

He lowered his voice before continuing, "I know there must have been something between you and Vik, I figured it out ages ago. Why couldn't you tell me? You don't trust me, because of everything that I did. I can't let that go, can't get past it. It's done. We're done." As he said the words, the pain that came along with them flooded over him. "When we were in Kyoto, there were moments when I thought we'd figured it out, that we could make it work. It wouldn't be easy, but we could do it. I always said it was supposed to be an experiment, even if I wanted it to be more. That's my fault. You never agreed to anything more. But even with all that time together, you still can't trust me." He tried to move past her, "I have to go."

Petra looked up from the floor, "I'll tell you everything. Kasem, stop. I will. Everything. Just stay."

"It's too late. You obviously don't think we have a future." He raised his arm to stop her from interrupting, "I get it. I shot people in cold blood. I was someone else, an assassin, a terrorist, maybe even a slave. I'm not the man you fell in love with in Iran—what I did for General Majed changed me and I can't change back. I can understand why you wouldn't be able to get over them. I'm not over them myself, but don't forget that you weren't honest with me either, about who you were, *who you are now*. My past isn't an excuse for hiding things from me. It's not an excuse for treating me like an asset." His jaw set, "That's how it's always been. Once an asset, always an asset."

"That's not fair. And it's not true. You were never really my asset." Her voice caught, "Please stay. I'm sorry. I'm so sorry."

"So am I. I'm sorry that I pushed you so hard. It's my own fault. You would never have come to Kyoto if I hadn't pushed you. We could both be rebuilding our lives, doing what we want to be doing. You could be with someone you trust."

"I want to be with you." Petra moved in front of the bedroom door to block him from leaving. "Please don't do this. We need to talk. I can explain," she pleaded.

"It's too late." Kasem pushed past her with his shoulder bag in hand. He could hear her sobbing as he walked to the front door and let it slam behind him.

Chapter 53

Mahajanga, Madagascar

Carlos returned after taking Jonah to a local private clinic and found Petra sitting on the floor of her bedroom. It was his second trip to the clinic that day after he had taken Rachel. Nathan had arranged an off-book visit there for Jonah via a sizeable payment from the stash of cash Rachel had brought with her for the op.

He approached Petra with caution. After seeing the wound in Jonah's knee, he needed to find out the truth behind her behavior. Although she'd used a blank, such a close-range shot had done serious damage. Jonah wouldn't be walking anytime soon, nor would he be able to type or write until his fingers healed. While Carlos didn't give a damn about him, he couldn't imagine Petra inflicting that kind of damage on anyone.

Petra was leaning against one of the bedposts with her legs sprawled out in front of her and a bed sheet rumpled behind her. She was staring through the balcony screen door at the waves washing upon the shore outside. As he crossed the room, one look at the closet told him that Kasem was gone. *Poor kiddo.* Carlos exhaled and slid down to the floor next to her.

"That's one hell of a view—the stuff daydreams are made of," he said. He unscrewed the top of the bottle of vodka that he'd brought with him and took a swig, "How are you doing?"

"I don't know."

Carlos took another swig and handed her the bottle, "I hear you."

She winced with her first sip, followed immediately by another, "How's Rachel?"

"She's still coming in and out of consciousness, but the knife missed any vital organs, so she's going to be okay."

"Thank god," Petra's torso collapsed forward in relief.

"She's one lucky duck, I'll tell you that. An inch in any direction and this would be a very different conversation. She might have complications from the loss of blood, but they think that they stopped it in time. They're keeping her for observation now, but they might release her fairly soon—I think since she's off book, they want to get her out of there before anyone starts asking questions."

"And Jonah?"

"He has physical therapy ahead of him, but he'll recover. Mostly. He'll probably have a limp, and he won't be handwriting any letters for a while."

"He doesn't deserve to heal. He killed Madison, and what he did to Rachel... If we hadn't arrived in time, she might not..." Petra shuddered and gulped down some more vodka.

"I know, kiddo."

"He's gone, you know. Kasem's gone."

Carlos sighed at her confirmation, "I noticed. Are you okay?"

"No."

"Do you want to talk about it?"

"Maybe." A tear slid down her cheek, "It's my fault. I kept too many secrets, but it's what I've always done."

"Whatever happened between you guys, I know he loves you and that you love him." Carlos prodded her with his elbow, "You can work this out."

"I think it's too late for that. I messed it all up. I was too scared to tell him."

Carlos frowned, "That you had a relationship with Vik? You still haven't told him? Petra, we've been through this. It was before you even became involved with Kasem. Sure, it'd be a bit awkward to tell him, but come on."

"It's more than that."

"Care to share? I'll take it to the grave."

"I shouldn't have kept this from you either." Petra shook her head, "I'm so sorry, Carlos."

"It'll be okay. Whatever it is. It's not too late to tell me."

Petra took a deep breath and another swig of vodka while she built up the courage to find the words. With a sigh, she handed him the bottle, pulled her knees to her chest and wrapped her arms around them. She turned her attention back to the ocean.

"I met Kasem in Paris to cultivate him as an asset. It was all very flirtatious, even romantic, but I didn't think it would turn into anything serious. When I got back stateside, I met up with Vikram—Vik—at a bar in New York. We were just supposed to catch up, but it ended up being more. We spent this whirlwind week together, then he had to go to a conference in Chicago before he was supposed to leave on an op. I didn't know you'd be joining him on the op later."

"You went with him to Chicago?"

"I did. We had a great time. Romantic, fun. Just being in the moment."

"Sure. The plot of so many romantic comedies. Sorry—too soon." Carlos sidled closer to her and put his arm around her shoulder. "You'd only met Kasem once at this point?"

"Um-hmm."

"I don't think Kasem would love hearing about your week with Vik, but it was ages ago. He wasn't even your asset yet, much less anything more, so it's not as if you betrayed him."

"I know, and if it was just that, I would have told him." Petra reached for the bottle again, but Carlos moved it from her grasp. "I still think about Vikram sometimes, about how it would be easier to be with him. There wouldn't be this dark past to forgive or to put aside. Sometimes I think it would be easier to trust him. I actually thought about him after I found the ring, when I realized Kasem was planning to propose."

"That's heavy, but it's all based on fiction. You have no idea what your relationship with Vik would have been like. Do you still love him? Is that the issue?"

"Maybe I did, but it was so fast that it's not like I ever acknowledged it. It was just a blip—one that made me giddy like a lovesick teenager—but then it was over, and I fell in love with Kasem," she hesitated, "but there's more."

"What's the rest of the story then?"

"Gibran Obaidi."

Carlos' eyebrows furrowed. *It couldn't be. No.* He shifted away from her so that he could look her in the eye, "What about him?"

"I told you I'd never heard of him."

"And?"

"That was a lie. I was too ashamed to tell you."

"Tell me what, Petra?"

"He was my asset too, Carlos. Gibran Obaidi. He was another asset that I cultivated in Iran," she raised her hand to her mouth and looked at the ground. "Kasem was my asset too, but after he was captured, I had to get out of Iran immediately. I told Alex to pull in all of my assets who were still alive."

She yanked the bottle of vodka from Carlos' hand and took another sip, "I never trusted Obaidi. He always seemed slimy, but the Agency thought he'd be useful, so I worked with him anyway. After my exfil, Alex put me on emergency leave and reassigned my assets. I never checked in on Obaidi again."

"It's not your fault he was a bad apple."

"It's all my fault, Carlos. I was the reason that Kasem was captured, and now I'm the reason that Vikram's dead." The tears flowed freely down her cheeks and she wiped at them with the back of her hand. "I loved him, but everything I touch turns to dust. For three years, I thought that Kasem was dead, and he *was*. The man who he is now isn't the same person."

"Neither are you—not after everything you've been through." Carlos grabbed a tissue box from the bedside table and handed it to her, "Geez, kiddo, I thought you were going to say that you told Obaidi that Nguyen had a mole in his circle, and he passed that on to Nguyen. This isn't your fault. Sometimes assets go bad, shit hits the fan. That's what happened with Obaidi, and that's what happened with Kasem."

Petra sniffed and wiped her nose, "Don't you see? If Obaidi had never been my asset, then Nguyen wouldn't have learned the information that got Vik killed. He'd still be alive, and maybe the two of you would have found a way to put Nguyen away."

"Kiddo, do you know how many things would have had to be different for that to happen? How did you even come up with that? You can't play the 'what-if' game. It's not good for the psyche. There's no end to the blame game. I mean, *if* the Agency had never asked you to cultivate Kasem as an asset, then he wouldn't have been captured, but you also would never have met him. Even though things went to shit for him for a while, that has to be worth something. You're saying that *if* the Agency had never sent you in to cultivate Kasem in the first place, you would never have had to flee Iran because of his capture, and Obaidi might never have been reassigned and Vik might be alive."

"All the roads still lead back to me."

"Come on. Playing 'what if' is endless and pointless. It doesn't change anything in the present, and it seriously overestimates your role. If you really think about it, maybe Vik would still be alive *if* it weren't for *me*. I pushed us to stay under even after we feared that we might be compromised. We both wanted to catch Nguyen, so we didn't abort the mission. It didn't work out, and now Vik's dead. Trust me, I shoulder more blame for Vik than you do if we're playing this game."

"Maybe."

"And what about Madison? I recruited her as an asset, and now she's dead," Carlos looked down at the ground. "Rachel and I promised to protect her, but we failed. Part of me wants to blame myself, heck part of me does—but the real culprit here isn't Rachel or me, it's *Nguyen*. If you're looking for someone to blame for Vik's death, then look at him, or at Seymour, not at yourself."

"I guess…"

"Here's one for you, totally unrelated. When I was still with the Agency, I messed up on an op in Venezuela and got made. I was under diplomatic cover, so I was fine, but one night I didn't notice a tail when I checked on a drop. The Agency ex-filtrated me, no problem, but the secret police caught my asset. He disappeared into one of Chavez's jails. Maybe he was killed? I have no idea what happened to him. I played 'what if' a lot after that and learned that it does no good. Alex set me straight and said that I shouldn't feed my ego that much, I wasn't the nexus of all things in the universe." He rubbed her shoulder, "You're losing it right now. I get the guilt—I really do—but you can't let it define you. If you felt zero guilt, I'd be worried, but this much is only going to crush you. There's no way you could have known."

"That's what Kasem said," Petra bit her lip.

"Vik would say the same thing. In fact, he'd turn it into some weird South African proverb that no one else could understand."

Petra laid her cheek against her knees, "Thank you. I'm lucky to have you."

"Back at you." He stood up and held out his hand, "Now, you have a wedding to attend and gush over, so you need to get gussied up."

"The wedding? But Kasem's gone."

"He is? I heard he's just laid up with a stomach bug." Carlos pulled Petra up so that she stood in front of him. "We can keep your cover going a little longer. I'll do some more snooping while you're at the event. I figure if the code's that complicated, Nguyen must keep a cipher somewhere. Let's make all of this heartache count for something."

"I guess I better start gussying."

Chapter 54

Mahajanga, Madagascar

Petra stopped at the hospital to see Rachel on the way to the wedding. She was laying down with her torso propped up on a few pillows and frowning at her tablet.

"Aren't you a sight for sore eyes," Petra approached Rachel and gave her a gentle hug.

Rachel smiled in return, "You too."

"Thanks." Petra considered saying something about Kasem's disappearance but decided not to burden Rachel with it. She had already listened to about as much romantic advice as she could take for one day. She had tried to reach Kasem, but he wasn't answering his phone. Petra sighed and tried to push aside the emotions.

"Are you okay?" Rachel was giving her a knowing look, "Where's Kasem?"

Petra hesitated, "He left."

"You two are just the silliest geese in the bunch," Rachel paused, "Sorry, that's the morphine still talking. It's wearing off, but my filter's a little loose. Do you want to talk about it?"

"There isn't much to say. I should have told him everything."

Rachel nodded with a glint in her eyes, "You should have told him that you felt guilty about Vik and Gibran Obaidi."

"What?" Petra asked, taken aback. *How could she know?*

"I found a lot in my research before we started the op. Carlos told me that he had tracked the Agency leak to Gibran Obaidi, but he didn't get any further, so I asked my boss to get the whole file. The Agency sent over records on their asset recruitment of Obaidi and how he became blacklisted, but I never showed it all to Carlos."

"What did they say?"

"The records said that Obaidi was recruited in Iran by an unnamed female operative on a deep-cover op as an attaché at the French embassy. He was pulled into the Agency after she was extracted. They transferred him to a different handler who set Obaidi up as a large-scale middle man for arms deals."

Petra blinked twice, "When did you figure out I was connected?"

"I had an inkling. You're half-Persian, and you speak Farsi and French, plus you were so invested in this mission. At first, I thought maybe it was just because you and Vik had been involved—"

"No—"

"Petra, come on. I looked into Vik's past before the op to see if there were any clues from his personal life, or if someone might have turned on him. Romantic nights at the Drake Hotel, huh?" Rachel shrugged. "Then there was Kasem. He certainly wasn't trained by the Agency, so I figured he must have been an asset. I didn't know for sure until you suggested sending him into Nguyen's organization as a fellow arms dealer."

"What do you mean?"

"He was so sensitive about it, I just knew. If he'd never been your asset, he wouldn't have been so sensitive. With everything that I already knew about Vik and Obaidi, it was easy to put two and two together."

"I guess you're a pretty smart cookie."

Rachel chuckled, but a moment later her gaze turned serious. "My first CIA handler did call me a prodigy at reading people—I guess that double major in criminology and psych has to be good for something. Do you really think Vik's murder is your fault?"

"Sometimes."

"It isn't. If an op in Iran goes sideways, you get the hell out. I would have done the same thing. Besides, you had no way of knowing Obaidi would betray the Agency."

"But if we'd left Obaidi in Tehran—"

"Petra, if you'd never brought him in, he'd be dead, and that would be on your conscience instead. Carlos and Vik's op was shaky—lots of variables for something to go wrong, not just one Agency asset who ended up being a rat."

"I guess…"

"That's enough. I'm right, it's time to accept it and move on," Rachel said with a grin. "Now go. We can still get Nguyen and I need to get some rest. Besides, I'm counting on you."

Chapter 55

Mahajanga, Madagascar

Kasem ducked behind the nurse's station and watched Petra walk out of Rachel's room. She looked especially stunning in an ankle-length aquamarine dress with her hair styled so that it cascaded over one shoulder in a series of curls, but he resisted the urge to approach her. He still hadn't decided what to do—whether he should just leave Madagascar on his own or hide out and wait for the op to finish. Despite his fight with Petra, he couldn't abandon the team if they might need his help.

He waited until she was out of sight down the hallway before heading to Rachel's room.

"It must be visiting hour," she said. "You just missed your girlfriend."

"I know." Kasem leaned over to give her a hug, "It's good to see you this chipper. We were worried."

"You know me. I'm not made of glass." Rachel gestured toward a chair by her bed, "Have a seat."

"How are you feeling?"

"Right now? I feel like a thousand Oompa Loompas are shouting in my head, but I'll be fine in a few days." Her expression sobered, "I guess I got lucky, thanks to the two of you."

Kasem sighed, "Make sure you take it easy. Even if it didn't hit anything major, a stab wound can take some recovery. It'll get worse if you push too hard."

"I know, Dad."

After a moment of silence, Rachel crossed her arms, "I heard that you left, but here you are..."

"That's personal, between me and Petra."

"Right. Still, you should know that she was barely holding it together earlier. She needs you, even if she can't admit it."

Kasem swallowed and stared at the floor. *That's part of the problem.*

"You should give her a break. We're trained to keep secrets and it can be a hard habit to break. She's carrying a lot of guilt about you and about Vik."

About Vik? Kasem frowned, "What do you mean?"

"She thinks it's her fault. Maybe some of it even is."

177

"What are you talking about? How? I don't understand. What do you know? Please just tell me," Kasem said in a firm voice.

"She won't like it. You two are so stubborn. You really need to learn to communicate." Rachel hesitated, "At this point, I guess it can't do any harm if I tell you instead of her."

"I already left her and the op, so no, I don't think it can."

"I can't believe you haven't figured it out. Isn't it obvious? She and Vik were together. She loved him. They spent a weekend together in Chicago before he left for that undercover op with Car—"

Kasem kept his expression steady as Rachel confirmed what he had suspected, "Did she tell you that?"

Rachel explained how she had figured it out, then shrugged her shoulders, "Does it matter? She's with you now, or at least she would be if you hadn't left."

"But why wouldn't she tell me? I don't care who she was with before we got together."

"Oh, Kasem. It's not about you. She's weighed down by two tons of guilt. Carlos traced the leak that got Vik killed to an Agency asset named Gibran Obaidi. The Agency ordered Petra to recruit him when she worked in Tehran. Now she feels like Obaidi leaking that information is her fault. The Agency pulled her out of Iran so quickly—it must have been insane. Anyway, you already know that part since you were working together back then."

Kasem's muscles went rigid. They had never divulged that he'd been Petra's asset. "Back then? No, we met—"

"Please. I figured out you had been her asset ages ago. It's not like you were pretending to be Agency." Her voice dropped to a mocking whisper, "You do know that you don't have a pure American accent."

Kasem's eyes darted around the room, "Right." He didn't like Rachel knowing even that much about his past, but her ability to make those sorts of judgments is what made her such a strong operative. "Aren't you the observant one."

"Flattery won't get you anywhere. I just told you why your girlfriend kept secrets from you and you're not running out the door after her. Don't you think she deserves another chance?"

"It's too late." Kasem shook his head, "I can't believe she didn't tell me any of that. She didn't trust me enough to do that. If she doesn't trust me, then what's the point? We can't have a future together." *She knows everything about me. Everything I've done, and she couldn't tell me about this?* The thought reverberated through his mind, making his sadness even more profound.

"I think she would have told you if she could forgive herself. This is about a lot more than the death of an ex-boyfriend. This is about her relationship with you, and I'd say Obaidi and Tehran are at the root of it. She probably feels guilty about whatever happened to you out there."

Kasem's eyes widened. *Does she know?* Before he could express himself, Rachel waved her hand at him and said, "Don't worry, I still haven't figured that out, and I don't intend to go digging. It's not important to me or this op. I've seen you in action, and you can handle yourself. I'd trust you to back me up, and you've already done more than I can ever repay." She raised her hand to her mouth, "What's important is that you're here now. Petra needs you, as do Carlos, Nathan, and I. This is our last chance to put Nguyen away."

Chapter 56

Mahajanga, Madagascar

Petra tested her earpiece on her way to the dock. From there, she would catch the boat that would take her to the island where the wedding ceremony would be held. The wedding guests were organized into different boats by their last name. She searched for the surname Birch and made her way onboard. She spotted Janine's bridesmaids standing on the deck and approached to say hello. "Hi, Becca. Hi, Megha," Petra gave each of them a hug. "It's good to see you. I'm surprised you aren't on the boat with the family."

"Hey, Cara! We all got ready together, but Janine's parents wanted some alone time with her, so they're going over separately," Megha said.

Petra nodded and took a step back to survey their dresses, "Janine was right when she said that she wouldn't have ugly bridesmaid dresses. That color looks amazing on you both."

"It did work out," Becca smoothed out the long skirt of her chiffon sunshine-yellow gown. "Megha's looks even better with that gorgeous back and her tan. Um-hmm," she said in reference to the halter style of Megha's dress that featured an open back. "The single guys here aren't going to be able to keep their hands off her."

Megha rolled her eyes, "Are there even any single guys here? I think I've seen two and neither of them was very interesting." She tilted her glass back to drain the rest of her mojito. "I'm going to grab another drink. Would you like one?" she asked Petra.

"Sure, that would be great."

"All right. By the way, where's Amir? Is he going to ride out with Jim?"

Petra shook her head, "No, I'm afraid he's out for the count. He's running a bit of a fever and having some stomach issues. I fed him some soup and put him to bed."

"Oh no! That's such a shame. I hope he feels better," Megha said. "I'll be right back with those drinks. Keep an eye out for any cute single guys. None of those skinny metro guys that you like Becca. I want a man with some meat on his bones."

Petra chuckled as Megha walked away, "I guess she didn't meet anyone at the engagement party?"

"I think there was some guy she was interested in—one of the family friends, but he didn't make it," Becca said as they watched the late-afternoon sun glint off the water. "They've been texting since Jim introduced them, but I don't know what the deal is."

"What about you?"

"I'm single too, but I'm not looking right now." Becca looked down at the mojito glass in her hand. "I was with my boyfriend for seven years and then one day a few months ago he said he was done and just left. No explanation, nothing." She sighed, "We don't all have men like Amir in our lives. You hold on to that boy, he loves you."

Petra gave her another nod and was thankful for the change of subject when Megha reappeared with two mojitos in her hand.

"We're about to leave. Let's get inside before the wind messes up our hair," Becca said. "I'm so excited. Wait till you see the venue."

Petra followed the bridesmaids inside the cabin and they settled at a table by a window. She watched as the deckhand pulled back the access ramp to the boat and shut the gate. The boat shook for a moment as they started the engine. A few minutes later, they were speeding across the water with three other boats full of wedding guests following them. They moved away from the resort and headed out into the open sea.

Petra dipped her hand into her clutch and sent Carlos a quick text that she was en route to the ceremony. She had updated his contact information so that any stray glance would lead someone to believe that Cara was texting Amir. After she put the phone away, she fiddled with the wedding and engagement rings on her left hand. She'd been unable to imagine wearing them for real, but now she wasn't so sure. She wondered for a moment if Kasem had left the country yet. She could have checked up on him with his tracker, but she was trying to respect his privacy. If he'd already left, there wasn't much she could do about it, anyway. She had a job to do.

After they passed a series of choppy waves, the sea calmed down. *There it is.* Petra could see the island in the distance, a small dot of golden sand growing larger on the horizon.

They drew closer and Petra gasped aloud. The hotel staff had erected an altar made of bamboo, decorated with pink orchids and white hydrangeas. The closer they got, the more striking the single decoration seemed against the backdrop of the sun and sand with the blue of the ocean stretching out beyond as far as the eye could see. The boats passed the altar to stop at a temporary wooden dock on the far side of the island. The dock connected to a wooden path that had been laid out to lead the guests to the chairs in front of the altar. Each chair was marked with a white cloth embroidered with the name of a guest.

"Can you believe this? This is straight out of a dream," Becca said

Petra agreed, "I didn't think you could top the celebration at Hill Hearst, but here we are."

A waiter came by to offer them champagne flutes and Petra savored the sharp citrus taste. It was refreshing—the perfect match with their surroundings.

She touched her earring to reactivate her earpiece. Now that they were off the boats, Carlos would be able to follow the ceremony by listening in on her audio frequency. He was going to use that time to search Nguyen's and Seymour's villas to see if he could find anything to help decipher the coded ledger. Nathan had created backdoor access cards, but they would have to be careful of Nguyen's guards. Since Jonah's disappearance, Nguyen's remaining guards appeared to be on high alert.

"Here they come," Megha said in an excited voice. She pointed toward the dock where two more boats were approaching. The first one reached the dock and Jim and his parents climbed out.

"We'll see you later, Cara," Becca said. She grabbed Megha's arm and they returned to the dock to meet Janine's boat.

Petra searched the dock to see if Seymour had arrived with Jim and his parents. She couldn't see him, so she scanned the guests and spotted him toward the front of the seating area next to Sir Caleb. An involuntary shiver passed through her as she remembered their conversation at Nguyen's offices in London.

She directed her gaze back toward the dock and watched Jim and his parents approach the altar. His parents sat in the first row, while Jim stood to the right side of the altar where his two groomsmen and the officiant joined him. A small band set up on the left of the seating area played a soothing melody composed of a few chords while they waited for the second boat to dock. Once the second boat stopped, a deckhand opened the door for Janine's grandfather with her mother on his arm. After that, Janine's father appeared. Becca and Megha joined him as he took down the green flower screen that stood at the middle of the boat. When they were positioned in front of him, he folded the screen and placed it to the side. From where she was sitting, Petra could see a bit of Janine's white tulle skirt behind the yellow glow of the bridesmaid dresses, but she couldn't actually see Janine. The whole scene brought a bittersweet smile to her face—if they weren't on an operation, it would have been something really special for her and Kasem to enjoy together. She sighed and looked at his empty seat.

The music changed to a more traditional wedding tune. Janine's grandfather and her mother walked toward the altar, with Megha and Becca behind them walking single file, each taking slow elongated steps. For a second, Petra let herself wonder what kind of wedding she and Kasem would have wanted. Not something as elaborate as this, but some of the smaller sweeter touches were things that she would have wanted to adopt. She imagined Kasem's arm around her shoulders and stared straight ahead, willing away any tears.

"I'm heading to Nguyen's room now," Carlos' voice crackled through her earpiece. "Nathan thinks that the ledger might be in a book-based code, so I'm going to look for books that Seymour and Nguyen have in common."

Petra sent Carlos an acknowledgment text, glad for the distraction that his words had brought. She pushed past the sadness and watched Janine and her father approach the altar. Janine looked radiant in an ivory sweetheart A-line dress with a train that flowed out behind her.

Janine's grandfather and mother sat down on the front row on the left side of the aisle. Megha reached the altar first and stood to the side with Becca joining her a few seconds later. Both of them had bouquets of pink hydrangeas and white calla lilies that complemented their pale-yellow dresses, and the simplicity of the bamboo altar.

Petra glanced over at Jim's face as Janine and her father approached. He looked enraptured and content. Once again, an image of Kasem standing there appeared in her mind and she blinked it away. When Janine and her father reached the altar, he gave her a kiss on the cheek and took a seat next to his wife, leaving her to stand across from Jim.

The two of them looked so happy, it was both beautiful and painful for Petra to watch and listen. The officiant started the proceedings with a short speech on the value and meaning of marriage. Petra shut her eyes and the words washed over her in bits and pieces combined with the sound of the waves. The sun was about to set, and its warm rays touched her face. There were so many things that she wished for her life. She hadn't necessarily thought marriage was a possibility for her—not since Kasem's capture so many years earlier—but now, she couldn't stop thinking about it. Even if they could not repair their relationship, maybe she should still have hope that she could have such normalcy in her life. If not with Kasem, then perhaps with someone else, although once she had learned that he was still alive, she had scarcely been able to imagine a life with anyone else.

Carlos' voice came across her earpiece again as a bitter reminder of why she was actually there. "I'm entering Nguyen's suite now," he said. "I had to hold while I hid from one of the guards. I'll take video and pictures of everything I find."

Petra opened her eyes. The sun was setting behind the altar and she squinted with the glare in her eyes. The reddish hues of the sun spun out across the sky with the couple superimposed in front of the altar. *Wow.* She exhaled again as the officiant concluded, "Jim and Janine have written their own vows." He looked to Jim, "Jim, will you begin."

Jim took her hands as he began to speak, "Janine, I promise to be your love, your best friend, your confidant. I promise to be there when you are sad, and to celebrate in your victories. I promise to teach you to horseback ride, no matter how long it takes, and bake you a birthday cake every year. I promise to take your family as my own, and to go on as many adventures as we can together. From this day forward, my promise is that you will never walk alone."

Janine wiped a tear from her eye, "Jim, I promise to love you and take care of you, to be your best friend and to be your trusted accomplice as we go through life together. I promise to lift you up in your darker moments and shout your triumphs from the rooftops. I promise to force you to try new cuisines and to wear sunblock. I promise to eat all of my birthday cake and ride beside you on our adventures together. From this day forward, my promise is that you will never walk alone."

A tear rolled down Petra's cheek. She thought of Vikram, of the intensity of the time that they had spent together, *Maybe I did love him, but it's not the same as with Kasem.* Carlos' words echoed in her mind, *It's all based on fiction. You have no idea what your relationship with Vik would be like.* Looking on at the wedding, she realized how right he was. Vikram was just a moment of her life, an intense one, even a wonderful one, but still nothing more than a moment. They had never built a real relationship, never gotten through a tough time or tumultuous fight. They had never even shared in each other's triumphs. Even though her relationship with Kasem had started out as an asset that she was cultivating, it had been full of what makes up a real relationship. During their time in Kyoto, he had shared some of his darkest memories, and his hopes to move on with his life. They had lived together, laughed together, argued, and fought. *That's what makes a real relationship, not just a few romantic nights on the river in Chicago.* She wiped away one of the tears as the clarity sunk in further. *Kasem was right,* she had been holding back, hadn't been open and honest with him about her past and about what she wanted from her life. He was ready to take the next step, to commit that they would figure it out together, whether life took them back to Paris or anywhere else in the world. She'd been too scared before, but now she understood. *I'm ready.*

Once the vows were completed, the officiant took over again. He led the couple through the exchange of the rings. When he pronounced the end of the ceremony with the words, "You may now kiss the bride," the guests broke into applause.

Jim and Janine walked hand in hand up the aisle toward the dock and onto the boat that she had arrived on. A deckhand let them onboard and the boat sped away a few moments later.

"Congratulations to the happy couple," the officiant said. "Now, please make your way back to the boats that you arrived on. The reception will be at the main island resort. We look forward to celebrating with all of you. Please don't forget to take your embroidered cloths with you. They are for the good luck of the couple and will hopefully serve as a memento for all of you."

Petra looked at the seat next to her and picked up both of the cloths belonging to her and Kasem. *Cara Birch. Amir Birch.* She reread the names and felt another pang of regret. Their covers were so far from their real identities, but even undercover, they had not managed to attend this wedding together. Petra followed the crowd as the group returned to the dock and sighed—her realization that she was ready to move forward with Kasem had probably come too late. Twilight had set in and the sky had turned a deep shade of red with the sun disappearing across the horizon.

"Hello, Mrs. Birch."

Petra turned to see Seymour standing next to her, "Hi, how are you?"

"I'm fine. It was a lovely ceremony."

His voice chilled her to the bones even though his words were nothing out of the ordinary. It was the coldness in his eyes—the lack of emotion. Petra gave him a beaming smile, "It was, wasn't it? Absolutely incredible—the place, the sunset, the vows, everything."

"It's a shame that your husband couldn't make it."

Petra nodded, "Yes. He's in bed with a fever and nausea. He was so disappointed he had to stay behind."

"I see. Perhaps he spent too much time in the water and caught a cold."

"I don't know. Maybe. Whatever it is, he could barely get out of bed, but he still wanted to come. I tried to stay with him, but he insisted I come."

"I should have some soup sent over for him. Does he like chicken?"

Petra opened her mouth to protest, "He does, but really you don't have to. He did eat some chicken broth before I left. I refused to leave until he got something in him. He was hardly able to keep his eyes open, and I wouldn't want to wake him now."

"As you wish." The look in Seymour's eyes told her that he wasn't convinced. Petra swallowed, hoping that Carlos was catching this conversation over the earpiece. If Seymour sent anyone over to their resort, they would need to have a contingency to make sure that they wouldn't see an empty room.

"Cara, over here," Petra heard. She looked up to see the welcome sight of Megha waving at her from aboard the boat. In the throes of the conversation with Seymour, she had walked right past the entrance plank.

"It was great to run into you. I'll see you at the reception," Petra turned to Seymour before she hastily made her exit to climb aboard the boat. "Hey, thank you," she said to Megha.

"I thought you might need saving. That guy is such a creep. I don't know why Jim's father tolerates him."

Petra took a deep breath. *Because he does all of his dirty work.* "He does make me uncomfortable, that's for sure."

"At least he's not on our boat," Megha said with a wave of her hand. She pulled Petra into a hug. "Wasn't it beautiful? I can't wait for the reception. Apparently, there's going to be all this barbecued seafood. I'm so hungry. I haven't had a thing to eat since breakfast." She broke into a giggle, "I've had a few drinks, though. I'm not sure if it's me that's wobbling or this boat."

Petra chuckled, "You're all right. It's the boat. After dealing with that guy, I need another drink, too." She strolled toward the bar and spoke quietly into her earpiece while pretending to search her purse, "We're heading back now, Carlos. Nguyen's boat already left, so make sure you're out of the room in the next twenty minutes. I think Seymour's onto us."

The boat pulled away from the dock and sped off into the sunset.

Chapter 57

Mahajanga, Madagascar

Carlos heard Petra's voice come over his com link, "We're heading back..."

"Will do," he said in response. As the sound of the boat from her com filled his ears, he lowered the volume so it was just a soft hum.

He frowned and took video of the suite's interior, focusing on the bookcase, which he hoped would offer the clue that they needed to decode the ledger. Since the Nguyen family held an ownership stake in the resort, the room was designed in Nguyen's taste rather than in the standard hotel-room style. "I've got video of the living room. Nathan, stand by." He engaged the uplink on his phone to transfer the video to Nathan. An hourglass appeared on-screen, "Service is a bit spotty. You'll get everything once I'm out of here."

Carlos ventured into the bedroom, which featured a four-poster bed decorated with a white net canopy that draped the posts. He raised his eyebrows, *I wouldn't have taken Nguyen for a man with a princess bed.* He stifled a chuckle and checked the area around the bed for books, notebooks, newspapers—anything that could be used for decoding the ledger. He kept the video engaged—over the years, he had learned that sometimes the smallest detail, when seen once again in a picture or video, could trigger an idea. Still, Carlos couldn't help but feel lost. Madison, who he'd recruited as an asset, was dead. Nathan had barely recovered from his injuries at Hill Hearst and had been unable to make any progress with the ledger. His CIA colleagues were equally at a loss. Rachel was at the hospital recovering, lucky to still be alive. Kasem was gone, and now Petra seemed a bit off her rocker.

Jonah was the only real thing that they had gained from the operation. Carlos was tempted to throw in the towel and rely on his testimony, but it wouldn't be enough. Jonah couldn't definitively tie Nguyen to the arms deals, and Nguyen's lawyers would crucify him in court. If he were higher up in Nguyen's organization, that might have been a possibility, but as it stood, they were back at square one.

More like square zero. Carlos resisted the urge to slam his fist into the bedpost. *What am I even doing here?* Rather than sit around waiting, he'd taken it upon himself to investigate the book code possibility, although there wasn't any particular evidence pointing to that. The number of digits varied, so it was hard to tell what could be page, or word numbers.

Despite that, Nathan seemed sure that it had to be a book code. He and the decrypting specialists at Langley hadn't found any recognizable patterns to create a cipher, so what else could it be?

As he moved around the bedroom, he passed the doorway into the master bathroom and the walk-in closet. The closet looked similar to the one at Hill Hearst with one side sparsely lined with a few exquisite dresses and the other with a range of suits. He checked it briefly to see if a safe or anything of interest was inside, but he came up empty. A quick look into the bathroom offered up the same result.

When he finished taking video of the bedroom, part of him wanted nothing more than to lie in wait for Nguyen to come home and exact his vengeance. He exhaled and shook his head. Vik certainly wouldn't want him to go to prison for killing Nguyen, and that was exactly what would happen if he let his desire for vengeance dictate his actions. Besides, he was of the school of thought that true revenge on Nguyen would be a lifetime in prison—of watching the world go by and not being a part of it, rather than a quick death.

Carlos returned to the living room and checked the area one more time. He still felt like he was missing something, that there was some key in this room that he could exploit. At the end of the living room, there was a desk. Since there were no books on it, he hadn't paid much attention to it earlier, but now the desk called to him.

It was made of solid, aged walnut with an elegant finish. Clearly, as with the bed design, Nguyen had spared no expense in setting up his villa at the resort. Carlos ran his gloved fingers over the patterns in the wood. He slid his fingers under the tabletop and along the sides of the drawers beneath. All he could feel were the ridges on the wood—no buttons or anything along those lines. *That would be very Hollywood-esque,* he thought with a grin. *A button under the desk opens up a secret passageway that leads to everything that we need. If only.*

Carlos slid open each drawer. The top two on either side of the desk were empty. In the second one on the left, he found an array of office supplies including Post-its, a letter opener, and a stapler. In the third drawer, he found a box of blank greeting cards decorated with a painting of a red bird. He moved his hand around to the corners and caught a soft clicking noise on the inside of the drawer. He removed his hand and examined the drawer again. The inside had a depth of about three inches, but the outside looked about an inch deeper. *False bottom?* He pushed down on the bottom of the drawer again and it made the clicking noise again.

Compelled to investigate, he removed the drawer and pressed his left thumb hard against one of the corners. With his other hand, he grabbed the letter opener from the other drawer and used it to lever the edge of the particleboard upward. It took a few attempts, but eventually, the bottom of the drawer gave way. His heart leapt for a moment and then sank. There was nothing inside.

He was tempted to dwell on it, but a sound in his ear made him take notice. He could hear the putter of the boat that Petra was on and the sound of the waves, but it was slowing down. *They're back.* He chastised himself for not paying better attention.

He was about to slide the drawer back into the desk when he noticed something behind it. He squinted and adjusted his night-vision goggles. Something behind the drawers didn't match the desk's frame. Instead of replacing the drawer, he removed the remaining drawers and reached behind them.

His hand closed around a letter-size leather-bound book that was wedged against the wood panel of the desk, held in place by plastic brackets. Carlos' heart raced, he wanted to believe that it was *the* ledger. The book had to be valuable, didn't it? Why else would Nguyen hide it in his desk like that? It did seem a bit primitive and old-fashioned, but that jived with Nguyen's anti-technology mentality.

Carlos placed the notebook on the desk and flipped it open. Like the other notebook that they had found, its contents looked like gibberish—just a series of numbers. He flicked through a few more pages until he saw a page that laid out a series of numbers matched with letters. While it had been years since he'd studied cryptology, he was sure that he had found something. *This has to be the cipher.*

Petra's voice came over his com link, "Carlos, where are you? I'm about to head into the party."

Nathan's voice echoed the same sentiment as he joined the frequency, "Carlos, there's a guard on his way toward you."

"Roger both of you," Carlos said. "I think I found a cipher of some kind. I'm taking pictures of it. Can you buy me a couple of minutes?"

"I'll do my best, but hurry," Nathan answered.

Carlos' hands shook as he took pictures of each page in the book, starting with the cipher at the back and moving toward the front of the book. The seconds ticked by in his head. He had to move quickly, but he wasn't going to miss his chance to get the information they needed.

When he reached the front of the book, he heard a noise outside and a shiver passed through him.

"Carlos, you've got company," Nathan spoke over the com once again. "You need to hide. I'll get him out of there as soon as I can."

Carlos grabbed the book and crouched under the desk. He would be toast if the guard came behind the desk, but if he stayed on the other side of the room then he might stand a chance. He panted, but quieted his breath, as the main door to the suite opened.

The guard flipped on the living room light switch and Carlos held his breath. *Stay there.* Carlos heard the sound of footsteps and then objects moving around. For a second, he allowed himself to hope. So far at least, the guard was on the other side of the room and had stayed there.

Carlos typed frantically through his watch uplink to send a message to Nathan without making a sound, *"The guard is in here. Get him out."*

He waited for a few seconds before the response came over his com. "Stand by—working on it."

Carlos waited with bated breath. He recognized the voices from one of his wife's favorite shows—Agatha Christie's *Poirot*. From what Carlos could tell, Poirot was searching for a prime suspect who was hiding in a basement trash room. *Bloody hell. You've got to be kidding me.*

The sound of a phone ringing made him freeze until he realized that it belonged to the guard.

"Yes, sir. Right away, sir," the guard said in a meek voice. He turned off the television and Carlos listened to his footsteps move farther away until the door shut behind him.

Carlos sat still for a full minute after the door closed to make sure that the guard was indeed gone.

"You're clear," Nathan said. "Go now."

"On my way."

Carlos slapped the cipher into its position in the back of the desk and slid the drawers into place in front of it. "I'm leaving now." He checked his pocket for his phone with the video and took a quick glance around the room. He didn't think he had left anything out of place, but he didn't have time to do a detailed check. Nothing obvious caught his eye so he crossed the room to the main door.

He reached for the doorknob and was about to step out when Nathan shattered his hopes once again. "Carlos, stay put. The guard reengaged the alarm system with his lockup procedure. I need to disable it before you try to leave."

"Too late," Carlos saw the flashing red light above the door. The alarm had gone off.

Chapter 58

Mahajanga, Madagascar

Carlos looked to either side of him. Darkness had fallen over the beach, but he could see the beams of flashlights coming toward him on either side. He had to take cover and fast.

He looked up the slope behind him. There was some brush a few feet away, but his only real chance was to get to his car, which was hidden farther up the slope under a group of trees closer to the road. There was no straight shot without being out in the open, where they would be able to see him. He would have to risk it but stick to the trees and bushes as much as he could.

Carlos made a beeline into the nearest tree cover. He dove to the ground and crouched under the bushes. With his night-vision goggles, he could see the figures converging on the villa.

"Is there any way we could make it look like a false alarm?" Carlos asked.

"There's nothing I can do on this end," Nathan said. "If you left everything as it was, they might believe that, though."

"If I'm lucky," Carlos sighed. He had done a good job of leaving the beach villa as he had found it, so there was a chance that he wouldn't be found out, at least not until Nguyen or his wife returned. He just had to hope that the guards wouldn't want to disturb their boss during his son's wedding reception. Carlos quietly moved toward the main road, keeping to the tree cover as much as possible. Whatever he was going to do, he had to do it quickly.

Chapter 59

Mahajanga, Madagascar

Petra savored her first sip of champagne on shore. She was feeling good that Carlos' gamble for the cipher had paid off. When she heard the commotion, though, her stomach did a flip. She had to do something, but what? She couldn't get to Carlos without breaking cover, and that wouldn't help either of them.

Petra bit her lip. If Carlos were captured, Nguyen would recognize him, and he'd be as good as dead. *There's nothing I can do.* She pasted the smile back on her face. The seat next to her was empty, another reminder of Kasem's absence. She could certainly have used his support now. *I can't lose anyone else.* Madison was dead, and Nathan and Rachel were both lucky to still be alive. Kasem was gone, and she might never be able to tell him how she felt. She blinked several times to stave off the panic that was just over the horizon. If she let it in, she wasn't sure that she would be able to get it under control again.

"I'm heading toward the main road," Carlos whispered. "Keeping to the tree cover as much as I can."

You'll make it. Petra wished that she could say those words aloud, but she couldn't risk the other guests at the table overhearing her.

She continued her pretense of enjoyment as the emcee announced the wedding party's grand entrance. The music accompanying each person's entrance provided a fleeting distraction with the contrast of music choices—starting with the "Imperial March" from *Star Wars*, which was followed by Journey and then a Vietnamese folk song.

"I'm almost at the main road," Carlos said. "I only have about a third of a mile before I reach the car."

Petra let herself relax the tiniest bit as the emcee announced the newlywed couple's entrance. *He's going to be okay,* she told herself, attempting to face down the rising panic. She allowed herself to watch the dance, even though her mind remained focused on Carlos' trajectory toward the car. Jim spun Janine into a dramatic dip at the end of the chorus of "Unchained Melody." After a momentary pause combined with applause from the guests, the music shifted to a popular pop song from a few years earlier called "Shut Up and

Dance." The couple broke into a choreographed swing dance that captivated the audience.

Petra couldn't help but smile as she kept her eyes on the dance floor. The seconds ticked by, but she estimated that it would still take Carlos a few minutes to reach the car. *What if they block that road?* She didn't know how they could help him if that happened. The location of Nguyen's beach villa allowed for it to be both secure and secluded. The guard stations were all within a mile from each corner of the villa and the guards operated primarily on foot. That had been Carlos' best advantage to get in, combined with Nathan's hack of the security system.

"Some of the guards have started to patrol the tree cover behind me. I don't think they've seen or heard me yet, but I have to slow down to keep quiet," Carlos said.

Petra's throat constricted. *He's going to be okay,* she told herself again as she watched the end of the dance.

"The happy couple would now like to invite their friends and family to join them on the dance floor," the emcee said. The chords of "L-O-V-E" by Nat King Cole began to play and numerous couples ventured onto the dance floor.

Petra watched as her table headed to the dance floor in pairs along with a large portion of the wedding guests.

"Still making my way up the hill," Carlos said with a grunt.

Petra picked up her phone and thumbed through the apps on rote when someone tapped her on the shoulder.

"Would you like to dance, *Miss* Cara?"

Petra recognized the raspy voice and a shiver ran up her spine. Seymour's expressionless eyes looked as evil as ever. He was smiling, but the only feature on his face that seemed to move was his mouth.

"Certainly," she offered him her hand and forced herself to return his smile.

Seymour led her to the dance floor to join the couples already out there. Petra looked at them with a twinge of envy. Most of their faces were flush with love and romance, or at the very least friendship and enjoyment. That made her miss Kasem even more and highlighted the gruff contrast of her current dance partner.

Seymour placed her left hand on his shoulder and grabbed her right hand while Petra stopped herself from bolting. She wasn't sure how much longer she could keep up the charade that she was enjoying herself. With every moment, he seemed more and more repulsive.

"Where is your husband, Miss Cara?"

Petra was tempted to correct his use of "Miss" once again, but she decided against it. "I told you he's sick in bed at our villa. We're at the Antsanitia Resort because this one was booked by the time we tried to make reservations," she motioned toward the main building of the Lodge des Terres Blanches.

"Do you like dancing?" he asked.

"I do."

"I'm surprised your husband isn't here to dance with you."

"He loves to dance, but even dancing can't get him out of bed when he's sick." Petra swallowed. *His tone—somehow, he must know that Kasem isn't sick,* or even at the Antsanitia Resort any longer. Still, that wasn't immediately incriminating, unless he had found out about Carlos somehow. Why was Seymour so obviously suspicious all of a sudden? She steadied herself. *He can't be certain,* she reminded herself. *If that were true, we'd already be dead.*

She heard a spurt of static in her earpiece and she had to fight herself not to react. *Carlos must have gotten to the car.* She waited for him to confirm while she danced with Seymour in silence. It felt as if his eyes were boring into her, as if he could see right through her. As if he knew that she was working against him and he held all the cards.

Seymour pulled her in closer and she kept her gaze away from his face. *What is he playing at?*

"You're very attractive."

It took all of her self-control not to roll her eyes. "Thank you." *Is he really hitting on me?*

"Your husband doesn't appreciate you."

"Excuse me? Why would you say something like that?"

"I checked on your villa. He's not there. He could be anywhere. Off with some other woman."

"This isn't appropriate," Petra attempted to wriggle free of his grasp, but he held tight. She didn't push harder since she didn't want to cause a scene.

Seymour's eyes narrowed, "I think you know where he is. The two of you are up to something."

"I have nothing to hide." Petra shot a cold look back at him, "This dance is over."

"It would be rude for you to leave before the end of the song."

"Then I'll have to be rude."

"Don't be silly. Everyone here will be looking at you. I've known the Nguyens for twenty-five years. Do you really think they'd believe you over me?"

Petra was tempted to knee him in the groin, but instead, she maintained her composure. The song would be over soon enough.

Seymour's phone buzzed in his inner breast pocket, and Petra seized the opportunity. "Don't you need to get that?" she asked.

"It can wait."

They danced for the next thirty seconds until the last chords of the song faded away and he released her. "I look forward to seeing you again," he said. He looked her up and down, and Petra squirmed.

He moved away to make a call. Petra watched from a few feet away. His expression was disgruntled. *Carlos.* She grabbed a prefilled glass of champagne from the bar and took a few steps toward him, but the music was too loud for her to hear anything without being completely obvious.

Seymour ended the call, pocketed the phone, and disappeared.

Petra's eyebrows knit as he left. A lump formed in her throat. *What happened to Carlos?*

A wave of static came over the earpiece again. "I'm about to be caught." Carlos' voice struck her like a knife to the heart.

"Carlos?" She tapped her earpiece again, "Carlos?" She checked her frequency and adjusted the volume via the controls on her bracelet disguised as charms. "Nathan? Do you have a twenty on Carlos?"

"We're too late. He's been taken."

Chapter 60

Mahajanga, Madagascar

After making a hurried excuse at the party, Petra drove back to the villa to meet Nathan. Her hands shook as she gripped the steering wheel. Thirty minutes later, she pulled up in front of his beach villa.

He was sitting in the living room with his head in his hands. Petra walked inside and dropped into the chair across from him, "Tell me what happened."

"I don't know. When that guard went inside while Carlos was there, the alarm system reset, but it didn't show up on my screen. I should have noticed the stupid red light. I tried to warn him, but the alarm had already gone off."

"Not that. I know about the alarm. I heard all of that," Petra snapped. She wanted to stop her tone from sounding so harsh, but she kept thinking that Carlos might be dead. They had to get to him, and she didn't have time to assuage Nathan's guilt. "What happened after? How did they catch him? Where did they take him? We need to get him out before they figure out who he is."

"What do you think I've been doing?" Nathan slammed his fist on the coffee table. "I'm still tracking him, but I can't get anything on the building, damn it. I can't get inside." He stood up and kicked the base of the sofa. "I can't do anything. He's going to die in there, and it's all my fault. I never should have left Langley. I never should have agreed to do field ops. I'm not cut out for it. My supervisor was right. I'm such a fool."

Petra sighed. There was no way that they could get to Carlos without Nathan. She opened her mouth, but failed to find the words to comfort him. *You know it's not all his fault. Tell him that.* "Nathan, there's no point in beating yourself up." Even after psyching herself into it, she could not bring herself to comfort him. How could he have missed something as obvious and basic as an alarm reset? *Stop it.* "He's not dead, and he's not going to die." She said the words, but she didn't believe them. *He is going to die.* Seymour had left the party after that phone call. As soon as Seymour saw Carlos, he would recognize him and it would be over.

As if he could read her thoughts, Nathan stood up and started packing up his laptop bag. "You should get someone else out here. I'm no good for this."

"Nathan, you can't just leave. We need you. We don't have time to waste."

"You and Rachel can do it. You were trained for this."

"Rachel's still at the hospital. It's just you and me. We have to find a way to do this together." Petra followed him into his room and watched aghast while he threw his clothes into his suitcase. "You can't do this to us."

"Rachel can have another tech guy out here in less than a day."

"We don't have a day. If you feel guilty about this, then try to make it right. You can't just up and leave because things went wrong."

"Isn't that what your boyfriend did?"

Nathan's words struck her to the core. "He didn't abandon *us*," she said. "He left me. He made a decision about our relationship, not the op." She gave him a beseeching look. "Nathan, we need you. Please stay."

His shoulders shook as he met her eyes. "I messed everything up. If I'd only seen that icon."

Petra sank onto the sofa and watched him in silence. She needed to rally and find her resolve, but all she wanted to do was crawl into bed and cry. Kasem was gone. Rachel was injured. Carlos had been captured. *Carlos could die.* The thought was incomprehensible. "I don't know what happened with the alarm system. All I know is that Carlos could die. You made a mistake, but you're good at your job. Stay."

Nathan's eyes told her that her words might be getting through to him. *This is my chance.* "Nathan, please," she said again while she searched for better words. Inspirational words, something that could offer him more comfort. Anything that would remind him what they were fighting for.

Before she could come up with something, the sound of a keycard at the door made her jump. She pulled her Colt pistol from her calf holster and aimed it at the door. "Get down." She cocked her head toward the floor. Nathan followed her lead and crouched to the ground behind the sofa. Petra backed up toward the living room wall so that she had better coverage of the foyer. *Here they come.*

The door opened to reveal a disheveled Kasem. Petra lowered the gun but found her shaking hands unable to place it in her holster. She placed the gun on the windowsill and her face contorted. This couldn't be real. *He told me that he was done.* He approached her in silence and she looked him in the eyes. "What are you doing here?" she asked. She was afraid of the answer. *Is he really back?*

Kasem's eyes darted around the room, "Where's Carlos?"

Petra blinked twice and shook her head. She couldn't find the words to explain about Carlos, so instead, she repeated her question. "What are you doing here?"

Instead of answering, he covered the last few steps toward her. When he reached her, he put his arms around her and pulled her into his chest.

Chapter 61

Mahajanga, Madagascar

Petra's eyes opened in the middle of the night. She tossed and turned for half an hour before deciding to go for a walk on the beach. She peeked into the second bedroom and was relieved to see that Nathan was still there. Unlike her, Kasem had found the words that convinced him to stay. Rather than return to her villa, she had decided to spend the night in Carlos' room to keep an eye on Nathan. Kasem was asleep on the living room couch, so she tiptoed past him and out the door. After everything that had happened that day, she wanted to be alone.

The beach was lit by a bright, full moon. The stars above were scattered and visible along with the Milky Way. She wandered toward the water and removed her slippers so that the waves washed over her ankles. The water felt cool and welcoming, as if it could wash away her worries.

She walked along slowly, listening to the sound of the waves crashing. Her mind was cluttered with the myriad of issues that she needed to figure out. Based on data from his tracker, Carlos was still alive, but for how much longer if he was in Seymour's clutches? They were on the clock and they all knew it. She and Kasem still had so much to work out personally, but they had had to put that on the back burner. In tense situations, she had always been able to keep a cool head and compartmentalize, but this time she felt lost. The only thing that she could focus on was that she wanted to wake up from this nightmare.

Petra took a seat in the sand. With her knees bent and the waves washing over her ankles, she lay on her back and looked up at the sky. She remembered the last time that she had looked at the stars like this. She and Kasem had gone for a midnight stroll on Kish Island in Iran early in their relationship and fallen asleep on the beach looking up at the stars. They had planned on a future together that had disappeared right out from under them. Now that it was within their grasp once again, it seemed to be slipping through their fingers.

Then there was Carlos. He had built a real life outside the Agency. He needed more from life than just another mission, but he always came through for his friends. Now, because of that, he might die. If the tables were turned, Petra knew Carlos would do anything for her, he would move mountains to rescue her. She would do the same, even if part of her wanted to flee like the tides running out into the sea. Their relationship of mentor to mentee had become something far closer, he was family, more like an older brother than a former Agency colleague.

Petra shut her eyes and lay listening to the waves. The rhythm made her feel as if it were rocking her to sleep. She had just dozed off when she heard a voice calling out to her.

"Petra? Where have you been? I've been looking everywhere."

She squinted and opened her eyes to see a worried Kasem. The sun hadn't risen yet, but there was a glint of blue in the sky. She sat up, "Sorry, I took a walk to clear my head. I guess I fell asleep."

He glanced back at the villa and took a seat next to her, "How are you doing?"

"I'm a mess. I thought it was bad before, but now that Carlos—" her voice cracked, "now that Carlos is gone, it's like I can't even see."

"Jamal used to say that you have to be able to separate the forest from the trees. I never liked that saying, but sometimes it's apt."

Petra stiffened at the mention of his old friend from Tehran, "I guess so."

"Have you ever heard from him?" Kasem asked as he put his arm around her shoulder.

"Jamal? Not in a long time. The Agency forwarded along a Christmas card from him a couple of years ago. I think he's good."

"I went to see him before I set myself up in San Francisco."

"What? He knows you're alive?" She wasn't sure how to react. Kasem Ismaili was officially dead following his arrest in Tehran, so Jamal would be in jeopardy if he knew Kasem were alive.

Kasem shook his head and chuckled, although hidden within it she could sense the depths of his pain. "He never saw me, but I saw him. He seemed happy. I couldn't bring myself to shake that up."

"I'm sorry." Petra knew that the words were scarcely enough, but there was nothing else she could add to help with such a loss.

"I've told you so many times," he said in a soft voice, "that there's no way you could have known. I'm sorry for what I said earlier. You can't keep blaming yourself." He looked out at the water where a golden ball had appeared over the horizon. "I don't think we've ever watched the sunrise together."

"We've never been up early enough," she followed his gaze. "I'm sorry too, Kasem. I should never have said all of that."

He nodded, "I went to see Rachel at the hospital yesterday."

The abrupt change of subject made her sit forward out of his embrace. Rachel had said something to him. *Is that what made him come back?* "What did she say?"

"She told me about Gibran Obaidi, and confirmed that you and Vik were once involved."

Petra was stunned. *Is it really that simple?* "I should have told you myself. This whole operation—I felt so guilty. It kept compounding, and I couldn't talk about it. Obaidi was my asset, and he's the reason that Vikram died." She rubbed her nose and kept her eyes on the sand. "I'm so sorry."

"You should have told me. We have to be able to talk about stuff like that. You already know everything about my dark past. If we're going to make it, everything has to be out in the open."

"I know." She turned toward him, "It's all my fault, everything you went through, everything you did, everything you still deal with every day. I didn't know how to tell you about this too. Where to start."

When Kasem didn't say anything, she searched his face in fear. She was so afraid he would be angry, but there was only compassion in his eyes.

He reached for her hand and sighed, "You shouldn't have kept all of that inside. You never could have known about what would happen. If you want me to forgive myself for what I did, then you have to forgive yourself too. We can't live in the past if we're going to have a future. Together or apart, we have to move on or this will kill us."

Petra squeezed his hand. "Does that mean you still want a future with me? I would understand if you didn't come back for me. If you want to leave after we finish this op…"

"I don't know what I came back for, but I couldn't leave you guys in the lurch. I signed up for this, I have to be here to finish it. I understand now why you felt guilty, why you're so committed to the op. We have a lot to figure out if we're going to be together, if we even can be. We can't keep avoiding it and expecting it to work out."

"I feel the same way. I'm sorry I've been so bad at saying it."

"I didn't realize how much you cared about him."

Her eyes twinkled, "Are you jealous?"

"Of a dead guy? I think not. Although, I guess I'm dead myself." Kasem pulled her closer to him. "I'm just curious. Maybe a little jealous. I know I'm not the only man you've ever loved, and according to Carlos, there's always some guy lurking with goo-goo eyes for you. Vik, Grant, that French dude…and now Nathan."

Petra couldn't help but break out into a stream of laughter, "Nathan? Come on—"

"You know he's had a crush on you since the beginning. I'm pretty sure that's why he's still here."

"Actually, I think you're the one who convinced him." Petra's laughter started to subside and she tapped him on the nose. "You're cute when you're jealous. You should know, though, that I don't know if I loved Vikram. Maybe I did, I guess I probably did, but it happened so fast. It was intense and passionate, different from the kind of love that's part of a real relationship. There was potential for it to head that way, but it didn't have the chance. We really only spent a little over a week together. It was wonderful, but afterward, I went to London and fell for you instead. I guess the rest is history."

They sat in silence for a few minutes and watched the sun move upward from the horizon. Petra leaned on Kasem's shoulder and enjoyed the moment. When their eyes met later, he placed a kiss on her forehead.

"Kasem, there's more to say," she glanced down at her hands. "I've had so much trouble letting you back in, being open and honest with you. I think it's because part of me still can't believe you're alive, that we even have this chance to be together." Her torso shook, "When I found out that you'd been taken, I had to get out of Tehran so fast, and you were gone. That was it—for so long, I believed you were dead, so I did what I had to, tried to move on. Then when I found you in Kuwait, and—"

He interrupted in a dejected voice, "I know, you found out that I was the Ahriman and you couldn't believe what I had turned into—"

"No," Petra shook her head. "That's not what I'm talking about. There was all this baggage between us, and I felt so much guilt, that even when things between us started to change again, I couldn't let you in the whole way. I had—I have—all these walls up, and it's going to take me a while to bring them down. I thought you were dead, and it was my fault, but then you were alive, but all of the torture that you endured, it was still my fault." He pulled her into his chest and she let the tears flow freely down her cheeks.

When the sobs subsided, she looked up at him again, "We have to save Carlos, but I don't know how."

"We will. Nathan pulled some satellite imagery on the location where they're holding him. It's an old colonial property. He traced its ownership to a seed company that we think is connected to Nguyen."

Petra's mouth fell open, "We can get to him? Let's go." She started to stand up.

"We can't, not on our own, anyway. The facility is secluded and guarded. If we're going to get to him without being caught, we need more man power and more equipment."

"That's easy. We'll get Rachel to call Langley."

Kasem hesitated, "I really don't think it's that simple."

"What do you mean?"

"I could be wrong about this, but I don't think Langley's been funding our op."

Chapter 62

Mahajanga, Madagascar

Kasem opened the door to the beach villa and let Petra in first. His eyes lingered on her as she headed straight to the kitchen island, but he dismissed his longing with a deep sigh and zeroed in on the plan that they were about to carry out. He would need all of his wits about him. He knocked on Nathan's door, and when there was no response, Kasem entered.

"Rise and shine," Kasem said.

Nathan grunted. Kasem moved toward the windows and opened the curtains so that sunlight streamed into the room, "You can sleep after the op is over."

Nathan glared at him. "Who named you first officer?"

"Captain Kirk," Kasem answered without skipping a beat. "Come on."

"You might want to step outside."

"And let you go back to sleep? I think not. I need to be sure you're out of bed and ready to help save the day. No more dillydallying."

"You asked for it," Nathan pushed the covers back and jumped out of bed.

"Dude! Put some clothes on." Kasem turned around with his eyes burning holes in his eyelids. "You could have warned me."

"I asked for some privacy."

"Fine but get some pants on already. I'll see you in the living room in five minutes." Kasem shut the door behind him with a shudder. "Hey, Petra, guess what? That doe-eyed boy who's been mooning over you sleeps in the nude."

Chapter 63

Mahajanga, Madagascar

Kasem looked over at a fully dressed Nathan when he sat down across the coffee table. He was tempted to make another crack about Nathan's nudity but held his tongue. For now, they had to discuss the plan.

Kasem sighed. Although he had tried to put on a bold face for Petra, he was at a bit of a loss himself. He waited until she had joined them before they started.

Nathan gave her a bashful look. Part of Kasem wanted to roll his eyes in response to Nathan's crush, and another felt sorry for him. *She's trouble with a capital T. You couldn't handle it, dude. Trust me.*

Petra looked over at Kasem with a slight smile, "I checked on Carlos' tracker a few minutes ago, while you two were having your little slumber party." She grinned as Kasem and Nathan both gave her indignant expressions. "Carlos hasn't been moved yet. Nathan, can you get any intel on that location? We have to find a way in."

Nathan took the computer from her and tapped a few keys, "I can't get more than a high-level visual, but I did run a check on Carlos' vitals. He seems okay—blood pressure is a little high, but that's to be expected under the circumstances." He stopped, and his eyes shifted to the floor. "To get him out, we need direct, real-time surveillance."

Petra crossed her arms, "Can't we get it from the CIA?"

"We'd have to talk to Rachel, but I don't see why not."

"They're the ones who started this whole thing." Kasem drummed his fingers on the table, "We get image intel, find a way in, and get Carlos out." The sound of his fingers tapping reflected his trepidation. *It won't be that easy.* The answer appeared in front of him, but he didn't like what he saw, "I have another idea."

"What is it?" Petra asked.

Kasem hesitated, *She's not going to like this.* He stopped to consider for a second and continued, recognizing that his idea was their best shot, "I go to Seymour and tell him that I want in, and that I'll take what I know to the feds if they don't cut me in."

"But they could kill you," Petra's eyes were filled with fear.

"As I recall, it was your idea," Kasem countered.

"That was before they had Carlos. Before they suspected us," Petra said.

"It will buy us time to get Carlos out. The more time we waste, the more likely Seymour will kill Carlos. We can't let that happen. This is the only way to stop it."

"I don't get it," Nathan interrupted. "How is that going to stop Seymour from executing Carlos?"

Kasem exhaled and tried to catch Petra's gaze. She seemed more interested in the top of the coffee table. "Because if it comes to that, I plan on telling him that *I* hired Carlos."

"What?" Petra looked at him aghast.

"If I tell Seymour that I hired Carlos to get intel on Nguyen's operation because I want in, they won't execute Carlos."

"No, they'll kill you both!" Petra fired back. "It won't work anyway because we don't have anything on their operation to prove that's what Carlos was doing."

"We have the ledger." Kasem turned to Nathan, "Carlos sent us details on what he thought was a cipher. Can you use that to decode it?"

Nathan shifted his position, "I don't know. I thought I could decode the ledger the first time around, but I couldn't. That's why Carlos ended up in there in the first place."

The look on Nathan's face was one of total demoralization. Kasem thought quickly about how to rebuild his confidence. "I know you can do it now that we have the cipher," he said in a quiet but firm voice. "Rachel put you on this team for a reason."

"He's right," Petra added. "Rachel would say the same thing."

Nathan chuckled, "No, she wouldn't. She'd say that my forensic accounting skills go way over her head."

Petra raised her eyebrows at him, "All right. Maybe she'd add a funny crack, but you know I'm right. You're the best man for the job."

The living room door opened and Rachel appeared, seated in a wheelchair, "Damn right you're the best man for the job. How many cute accountants do you think there are in the world?"

******

Kasem stood to help Rachel as she maneuvered her way toward them, but she shrugged him off.

"Are you sure you should be out of the hospital?" he asked.

"Don't worry about me, cutie. They stitched me up, said I could go home if I promised to take it easy." Rachel's wheelchair hit the base of the couch a couple of times before she maneuvered herself to face the coffee table, "Phew. I wasn't sure if I'd hit the couch or not.

My depth perception is a bit off." She pulled at Kasem's cheek. "I'm glad you're back, pretty boy. I knew you'd come to your senses. You're too smart to ignore my sage advice."

Petra looked at Kasem with an amused expression. His eyes narrowed, and he chose to ignore her mocking, "It's good to see you too, Rachel. How did you even get here?"

"There are these special cars that you can call to take you places. You give the drivers money and they drive you anywhere you tell them to go. I think they're called taxis. No, I'm kidding—the resort arranged a special car for me, what with the wheelchair and all."

"Very funny," Kasem said with a scowl. "I assume you know about yesterday?"

Rachel's expression turned serious, "Nate and I talked, and I figured I needed to be here. I'm so sorry." She looked at Kasem and then Petra, "We'll get him back for you, kiddo."

"Thanks, Rachel." Petra took a large gulp of coffee.

Kasem wanted to move over and comfort her, but Rachel's wheelchair was blocking his way. "So, Rachel," he said in a soft voice, "to rescue him, we need real-time imagery on these coordinates and backup personnel. Can Langley help us out?"

Rachel ran her fingers through her hair, "I don't know. They might not go for it."

Kasem frowned. *This is what I was afraid of.* "What are you talking about?"

"They haven't been very supportive of this op."

Petra sat up straight, "What do you mean? We have a huge budget. The private plane? The flat in London? Your contacts at the clinic in London and here?"

Kasem's frown deepened at the memory of Petra torturing their captive, "Rachel?"

"I pulled some strings, but I think that well has dried up."

Petra's gaze hardened, and she picked Rachel's cell phone off the coffee table. "Call them and refill the well. We didn't need the Vera Wang evening gowns, but now we need them to come through. I don't care how many more strings you have to pull."

Rachel looked at her and then around the room. Her eyes stopped at Nathan, and Kasem noticed the pleading look in her eyes. "Nathan, can you call them?" she asked.

Kasem waved his hands, "Nathan, don't answer that. Rachel, I know this is hard, but Carlos is in real danger. If there were ever a time to pull strings, it would be now."

"All right, I'll do it." Rachel grabbed her cell phone from Petra. She skirted the coffee table and wheeled herself out the door of the villa.

Chapter 64

Mahajanga, Madagascar

Rachel made sure that the door had shut firmly behind her and moved the wheelchair a few steps down the path toward the beach. The sound of the waves would provide soundproofing for her phone call.

She looked at her phone with her finger poised to hit one of the names on her contact list. She could never have imagined that the deal that she had struck would have backfired this badly. Petra was right—she had managed to secure everything that they needed. The private plane, the luxurious accommodations, and all of the clothes and transport that went along with the fancy image to support Kasem and Petra's covers. They could have done without at least a portion of it.

Rachel sighed and dialed the number. Her superior picked up after two rings.

"Hi, Tammy."

The line was blank for several seconds before Tammy responded, "Rachel? I wasn't expecting to hear from you today."

"Something urgent came up. We need direct access to Langley's satellites and a backup team."

"I thought we set Nathan up with access?"

Rachel shook her head, "You used a link-in portal. It can pull lower-level imagery, but we need access to the original satellite feeds."

"That's not what we agreed on."

"I know, but it's what we need. One of my team members was captured by Nguyen's men."

"That is an unfortunate complication," the voice on the other end of the line remained cold and unsympathetic. "I'm sorry about that, but your objective is to obtain the ledger and any of Nguyen's records. We can't give you extra resources."

Rachel thought on her feet quickly to come up with a response. *They don't know we have the cipher.* "We have the ledger, but we have no way of translating it. He found what we think is the cipher, but he never managed to transmit the images of it. If we get him out, we'll have the cipher."

There was another long pause before Tammy's response, "We'll give you direct satellite-feed access, but we can't send you any personnel. Our contractors are all tied up."

"But we need backup."

"Nothing I can do about that. There's no one available."

Rachel swallowed, "We'll make do."

"Next time we speak, I expect to have the deciphered ledger in hand."

A shiver sped up Rachel's spine as the line disconnected.

Chapter 65

Mahajanga, Madagascar

Carlos raised his neck to give Seymour a defiant look. "I'm here on vacation," he repeated for the fourth time. He braced himself for impact as Seymour's goon wound up.

The impact reverberated from his face down his spine.

"This would be a lot easier if you just answered my questions, Anton," Seymour said in his cold and unnervingly calm voice. "What were you doing at Mr. Nguyen's beach villa?"

"I'm in Madagascar on vacation. Trust me, I would have avoided it like the plague if I'd known you'd be here." He spat out a mouthful of blood, aiming for Seymour's patent leather shoes.

Seymour stepped back, just out of range.

"What's the matter, Seymour? Can't get your shoes dirty?"

"If you don't cooperate, we'll have no choice but to kill you."

Carlos grunted. He knew that Seymour was only bluffing. Seymour wouldn't hesitate to kill him, but first, he needed to know who Carlos was working for, what he had found, and with whom he had shared it. Since he had managed to wipe his phone and ditch it in the woods, Seymour didn't know the answers to any of those questions. Carlos had been wearing gloves, so there weren't any fingerprints to reveal that he had found the cipher. That was his one shot to stay alive long enough for the team to rescue him.

Seymour turned to his goon and said something that Carlos couldn't hear, despite his best efforts. He then walked over to Carlos and whispered into his ear, "There's no rush. Everyone breaks. In a few hours, you'll be spilling your life story." Seymour headed to the door with a triumphant expression on his face, "Keep at it, Adam. His face doesn't seem to do it for him, so let's try his groin. That piece of pond scum doesn't ever need to have kids."

Carlos shuddered as the door slammed shut. He and Diane had been talking about starting a family before he left for Kyoto. The thought that Seymour might be able to take that away from him scared him far more than his capture. An image flashed in front of his eyes of Diane's face as he had said goodbye to her. "Take care of yourself, husband," she had said. "I love you."

She had always been so supportive of his career choices. When he had chosen to leave the Agency, and then a couple of years earlier Petra had asked for his help on the operation in New York, she'd accepted his assertion that he needed to do it. After he told her about Vik's death, she'd told him to get the bastards.

As Adam approached again, Carlos felt time slow to a crawl. The fear of never going home seemed ever more acute. He might never again see Diane's smile, hear her singing in the shower, or wake up with his arms around her. The thought of her pain if he died paralyzed him. The grit that he had shown Seymour shattered—as if it had turned from solid steel into glass. He braced himself for the weight of Adam's next blow, but this time without the resolve that had carried him this far.

I have to get out of here.

Chapter 66

Mahajanga, Madagascar

Petra rubbed the back of her neck while she waited for the updated imagery feed. Something about Rachel's demeanor didn't sit right. Perhaps Kasem was right? Why had it been such a big deal to call Langley? Something didn't add up.

Petra frowned. When she thought of it in more detail, none of it seemed to add up. She had taken it at face value because of Carlos. She would follow him to the ends of the earth if he needed it, as he would for her, but something was wrong with the operation. As part of Agency training, they had covered basic protocols for the other agencies they worked with, including the CIA. She had never heard of Langley providing such lavish accommodations to an entire team. Perhaps for her and Kasem as part of their cover—*but for the entire team?*

Why had she and Kasem been allowed to join the team in the first place? She could understand Carlos being brought in—he had worked undercover with Nguyen, but she and Kasem would hardly hold up against the CIA's scrutiny. She wished Carlos was around to explain. Had he forced their hand by saying that he would only play if he could bring in his own people? That still didn't make sense, though. This was Langley. Why would they agree?

Petra looked over at Rachel. She had always known that Rachel wasn't telling the whole story. She had assumed it was her father's connection to Nguyen, but how far had Rachel gone to ensure his capture? Who had she made a deal with to get their operation funded?

"Can we talk for a second?" Kasem tapped her on the shoulder.

Petra nodded, "Let's go outside."

After shutting the door behind them, Kasem turned toward her with a look of obvious concern. "I thought I was just being paranoid, but I'm positive Rachel's not telling us something."

"I agree," Petra said. "Why would the CIA approve us being here? I went with it because of Carlos, but now that I think about it, I don't get it. It doesn't make sense."

"What do you think it could be?"

"Maybe Rachel has a lot of clout with some higher-ups? They never vetted us, and they certainly wouldn't have cleared you, so she must have done something shady. Maybe Carlos said that he wouldn't play any other way?"

"Hmm. But why would that connection dry up now?" He scratched his chin.

Petra hesitated, "It's like you said. I'm worried someone else is bankrolling us."

"We could be working for someone else entirely. It wouldn't be the first time," Kasem sighed. "It would have to be pretty bad for Rachel to keep this a secret."

"Do you think Nathan knows?"

"If Rachel made a deal on the side, he might not know. He only just started field ops."

Petra looked out across the beach, wishing that it could offer her the answers. "What about Carlos?"

"He might have figured it out. He's sharp. It would be hard for Rachel to pull the wool over his eyes for long. I still don't understand how we missed it."

"That's a question for another day. If we assume that Carlos knew, then maybe it's not so bad? He wouldn't go along with anything too shady."

Kasem raised his eyebrows, "To put away the guy that killed his friend? I don't know what I would do under the circumstances. I haven't had that many friends and my operations under Majed were solo. But if something happens to Carlos? I'll do anything to get vengeance. I can see how he might look the other way at something shady to get Nguyen."

"Considering that I may have given a guy a limp for the rest of his life—if he's lucky—I see what you mean. What do you think we should do?"

"We could give her the benefit of the doubt."

"Maybe."

"You don't sound on board with that," Kasem said in a quiet voice.

"You could be right. Maybe I'm just too scarred by people doing the wrong thing for the right reasons."

"You almost sound like yourself again."

"It's a step in the right direction." She motioned toward the villa, "We should let her explain." Petra grabbed his hand, "If this goes badly, I'm going to say it was all your idea."

Chapter 67

Mahajanga, Madagascar

Kasem studied the imagery on-screen. The satellite map showed that Carlos' coordinates were located on a nearby island within an old four-towered compound. "That almost looks like a fort, but I've never heard of anything like that over there. Wouldn't it be a tourist magnet?"

Rachel shook her head, "It's all private property so it's off limits. It's owned by a company called Carlsville Holdings."

"I haven't been able to trace them to Nguyen yet, but I'm sure it's one of his front companies," Nathan added.

"Can we get there without tipping them off?" Petra asked.

"We can't risk it without backup." Kasem sat up straight, "The way over there is me. I have to approach Seymour."

He could see the reluctance on Petra's face and it comforted him, especially after their conversation on the beach. *I have something to come back for.* "Nathan, can you handle support remotely?"

"We'll find a way to get there," Rachel answered in a firm voice and gripped the armrests of her wheelchair to stand.

"No, *you* won't," Petra sat up with a new look of resolve that Kasem hadn't seen since they were all at the flat in London. "Rachel, I know you mean well, but I'm not even sure you can stand. We're better off with you here at the computer." She turned to Nathan, "And your leg hasn't fully recovered from what happened at Hill Hearst. You both need to stay here."

Rachel crossed her arms, "You can't extract Carlos on your own."

"You're right. We need backup." Petra looked around at all of them and stopped at Rachel once again, "Are you sure Langley can't even allocate one agent?"

Kasem's brow furrowed. Based on their discussion, they were certain Langley wasn't sending anyone. He had assumed that they would make it work, but Petra clearly had other ideas.

The muscle in Rachel's right cheek flinched. "No," she finally said after a few seconds of hesitation.

"Why not?" Kasem asked in a soft voice. "We're your teammates. Tell us the truth. There's more to this story."

"They pulled my funding, okay? That's it. There's no more story."

Petra placed her hand on Rachel's shoulder, "When?"

"A couple of months ago."

Kasem's heart sank into his stomach. That meant that her funding had dried up before Kyoto. He had hoped his instincts were wrong, "Rachel, who's funding us then?"

"Me. Through my personal accounts."

"Your personal accounts? All of this?" Kasem gestured around the beach villa.

"Everything."

"Did you know about this?" Kasem looked at Nathan, who shook his head with a blank expression. The look on his face told Kasem that it was indeed genuine surprise.

Petra let out a long exhale, "Does Carlos know?"

"I had to tell him when I brought him on board. He figured it out when I agreed to his terms."

"To bring the two of us on board," Petra nodded. "I see."

Kasem looked between the two of them. Petra seemed convinced, or at least convinced enough to let it go for the moment, but he wasn't so sure. His gut still told him that there was more to the story. *Where did Rachel get that kind of money?*

Rachel looked around the coffee table at all of them. "I'm sorry. I shouldn't have kept it from you. Nathan, I pulled some strings to keep you on special assignment. I should have told you."

Kasem considered letting it lie, but it still didn't sit right. He had to say something, had to get to the bottom of it. He wasn't an asset anymore, and he wasn't going to let others call the shots, "Rachel, where did you get the money?"

"It's my money."

She looked down at her hands, avoiding eye contact, and Kasem knew that he had to push harder, "Rachel?"

"From Gibran Obaidi."

Chapter 68

Mahajanga, Madagascar

Petra gasped, unable to comprehend what Rachel had just said. *Gibran Obaidi. We're being funded by Gibran Obaidi. The man who got Vikram killed.* She opened her mouth to speak, but she couldn't find the words.

The look on Kasem's face matched her shock. "I don't even know what to say. Rachel, you need to explain that."

"I had to go to him. I had just found Carlos when Langley pulled my funding. It was the only way to get Nguyen."

"I don't understand," Petra said. "Gibran Obaidi?" She was dumbfounded.

"It was my only shot. I went to one of Nguyen's competitors for funding."

Petra could understand Rachel's need for vengeance for her father's death, but at what cost? She absolutely could not understand getting into bed with Obaidi. She couldn't believe they were even having a conversation about it. Her throat constricted. "What about after the op? If we put Nguyen away, you'd let Obaidi be top dog?"

Rachel averted her eyes, "I figured we'd deal with him later. I was actually hoping I could turn him."

Because that went so well the last time, Petra kept the words to herself. There was no point in discussing it. Her mind backtracked to the morning that she'd woken up hungover in London—Rachel's tone had sounded off when she'd asked about the arms that they'd stolen from Nguyen. A knot formed in the pit of her stomach, "What about the arms we confiscated from Nguyen's storage unit? Did you hand them over to Obaidi?"

"Yes."

We already supplied Obaidi. Petra wanted to yell, she wanted to scream, but it wouldn't do them any good. They had to end their association with Obaidi, which left her with only one choice.

"We can't go into this now," Kasem said in a firm voice. "If we start questioning each other now, Carlos suffers. We need help, and we can't use Obaidi's funds anymore."

"Fine," Rachel nodded. "I can't be backup, but Nathan can. There's no one else. He's green, but he knows what to do. If I go to Langley again, they'll have us blindfolded in the back of a van in a

217

heartbeat. By the time we could convince them to help us, Carlos would be dead."

"*He* can speak for himself," Nathan interjected.

Petra placed her hand on Nathan's knee, "No." She looked at Kasem seeking his agreement. He had to be on board with this. She felt a modicum of relief when he gave her a nod. They might not like it, but it was their only option. "I'm not going to let Carlos die in there, and I'm not letting Nathan get hurt again to help us." She bit her lip, "I'll call the Agency."

Chapter 69

Mahajanga, Madagascar

Kasem gave Petra a few minutes alone before he followed her outside. She had just hung up the phone and had a blank expression on her face. He walked to where she was sitting on the ground in the shade by the pool next to the villa. "What did they say?" he asked as he parked himself next to her on the concrete.

"They're sending backup."

"Is the Agency taking over the op then?"

"Not exactly. Chris said he's willing to play it my way if we hand over the ledger and the cipher to the CIA as planned. He knows this is about Carlos, so he didn't push too hard." She continued to stare at the water in the pool as she spoke.

Kasem exhaled, "Who's he sending?"

"He's coming himself."

"From New York? That'll take forever. We need someone here now."

Petra shook her head, "He's not in New York. Evidently, he's transferred to the Nairobi station, but he was actually in Mauritius for a meeting. We aren't exactly pen pals, so I had no clue. He's taking an Agency jet and will be here in a few hours."

"I thought he'd been promoted out of fieldwork. First New York and DC, and now this?"

"He was, but once upon a time, he was an outstanding field agent, and he couldn't pull in anyone else without making this an official op. Chris is handling this off book. It seems to be his specialty these days."

"It really is hard for you Agency folks to let go of the thrill of the field, huh?" Kasem said with a smirk, hoping for at least a small smile from Petra. She solemnly kept her focus on the pool, though. Kasem took another deep breath, "Just him?"

"I think so."

"As long as he doesn't bring that Grant guy with him, we'll be fine."

"You're right about that," Petra raised her hand to her mouth. "Kasem, I really thought that I was done with them. It may not seem like it, but I've tried so hard to leave that life." She turned to him with pleading eyes.

"I know, Petra. I was just joking, trying to make you smile. I'm sorry." Kasem put his arm around her shoulders, "Chris might be Agency, but he isn't so bad. You guys might not always agree on things, but you were friends once and that familiarity could be helpful in a situation like this. It's good that he's coming." He gave her arm a gentle squeeze, "Let's go inside and prep for the cavalry." Kasem hesitated, "Can we even call him that? He's just one guy."

"If he comes with Agency resources? Absolutely, we can."

Chapter 70

Mahajanga, Madagascar

*P*etra walked up the dirt road that led down to the two beach huts to meet Chris. She was sweating from a combination of the noon sun and anxiety. Tonight would serve as their window to rescue Carlos. She couldn't imagine that Seymour would keep him alive much longer. Carlos would hold out on giving away any real information for as long as possible, but eventually, anyone could be broken.

She swallowed her fear as a silver Toyota Land Cruiser took a left off the main road and came down the slope toward her. As the SUV neared, she squinted. There appeared to be two people inside, but Chris had said he was coming alone. A glimmer of recognition washed over her as the SUV drew closer.

Petra fumbled for her phone to send Kasem an urgent message, "Grant is with Chris."

Her mind was moving at a mile a minute. Her ex-boyfriend Grant had helped her on an operation in Kuwait a few years earlier, where he had seen Kasem, or rather the assassin and terrorist, the Ahriman. Together, she and Grant had worked to stop the Ahriman from assassinating the Kuwaiti monarch, although in the end, Kasem had himself abandoned that plan. Since then, Kasem had done everything to turn his life around, but the people he had killed as the Ahriman would forever be in the ground, including the hundreds that had died in the attack on the Suez Canal. Would Grant recognize him? Kasem looked different now. At the time, he had been wearing a gutra head garb that had shielded part of his face, and he was thinner then with shorter hair and only a medium stubble. Could they do anything else to stop Grant from recognizing him now? The Ahriman was considered a dangerous terrorist, wanted dead or alive by governments all over the world. If Grant recognized him, the best that Kasem could hope for would be a lifetime on the run.

Petra stood on the road frozen in place—

"Petra, wake up."

She opened her eyes in a haze. "Kasem?" The room around her slowly came into focus, the bedroom at the beach villa. She'd been so exhausted that Kasem had suggested she take a power nap before Chris arrived. "How long was I asleep?" Petra sat up abruptly and saw stars.

"Don't worry, only about two hours," Kasem said with a chuckle. "But Chris called, he just landed, so he'll be here in about forty minutes."

Petra's throat constricted as the memory of her dream washed over her, "I'll go meet him up at the main road. By myself."

"If that's what you want, sure. How come?"

"I had this weird dream. You look different, right? Than you used to? You have those glasses for your cover, and your hair is even longer now, with a beard, not like you were..." Petra tried to recall exactly how Kasem had looked when she had seen him in Kuwait. *This is crazy. Stop.* "He didn't say that he'd decided to bring someone with him, did he?"

"No," Kasem frowned, "are you sure you're okay?"

"I'm fine. That dream was just a little too realistic. I'd better freshen up so that I'm not still half-asleep when he gets here."

"Okay."

Petra waited for a second, expecting him to leave. He didn't, so she got out of bed slowly. "Go on," she said. "I really am all right. I'm just going to shower. It'll help wake me up."

Kasem looked as if he didn't believe her, but he disappeared into the living room without another word.

Petra stood under the shower and considered her dream. She hadn't realized that she still had that fear—that someday Grant would show up and set her life with Kasem ablaze by outing him as the Ahriman. If the Agency found out about Kasem's past he'd be captured at best, or more likely killed, and it wouldn't matter what he had done since then to atone for his past. If she kept skating this close to the Agency, it was only a matter of time, and she wasn't willing to take that risk again. She turned off the water and shivered at the cold gust from the air conditioning as she stepped out of the shower. She had made the decision to leave the Agency behind because she had been forced into the field after telling them she no longer wanted that role. Once they had rescued Carlos, she would sever ties completely for a much more important reason. After their conversation on the beach, her future with Kasem was as clear as day, her doubts about him and their past transcended. Vikram was dead and she had to move forward. *I need more from life than just another mission, and I want that life to be with Kasem. I won't let the Agency take that away.*

She got dressed and opened the bedroom door a crack. Rachel was studying a printout at the coffee table, and Nathan was at his computer. Kasem was standing behind the kitchen island drinking a cup of tea. He was right. She had to stop treating him like an asset, like someone who worked for her—he was her partner.

No more Agency, never again. Petra sighed, *Carlos, why did you have to get captured?* She let out another sigh. When she thought of Carlos' capture, she also recalled why she was here in the first place. She remembered Vikram's smile for a moment—the memory was painful, but it no longer brought on a siege of doubt about Kasem. Her life had gone a different way, one that she was content with and wanted to move forward. *After this operation. We made a plan to do this for Vik, and Obaidi was my asset.* She had signed up to part of this op. While it might not be her fault that Vikram was dead, Obaidi was at least partially her mess, and she was going to clean it up and help get Carlos home to Diane.

Petra grabbed her hat and stopped at the kitchen to steal a sip of tea from Kasem on her way out the door. "I'll see you in a few minutes. When I get back with Chris, we'll have a short window to go over the plan so that we're ready for tonight."

She didn't wait for a response and trudged up the road away from the beach villa. The slope seemed steeper than it had in her dream, and she was both grateful and amused at the contrast between reality and fantasy.

It's going to be fine. Chris would show up, and they'd storm the castle and find Carlos, who would be shaken, but otherwise fine. Nathan would decode the ledger and they would have enough evidence to put Nguyen away for good. *And Seymour. Don't forget Seymour.* The memory of their last conversation still made her queasy. Those beady black eyes and that nasal tone, the way he hit on her even when he was throwing around accusations. She shuddered.

A silver Toyota Land Cruiser turned left from the main road and drove toward her. *The same rental car?* Her stomach turned at the sight of it. It was exactly like her dream. As the vehicle approached, she noticed that Chris was the only person in the car and her shoulders relaxed. *Phew. A premonition would be a bit much.*

The Land Cruiser pulled to a stop next to her and brought her stream of consciousness to a screeching halt.

Chris hopped out of the car and walked around the hood. "Petra," he said in his thick Scottish accent. "I wasn't sure if I'd ever see you again."

"Hi, Chris. Thanks for coming. It means a lot."

"I'm glad you called. It sounds like things really went into the gutter." He shielded his eyes and looked down the hill toward the beach. The two villas stood superimposed on the secluded beach with waves washing up on the white sand behind them, framed by the cliffs on either side. The view looked even more spectacular from this perspective.

"At least paradise is at our feet."

"You are right about that. Wow." Chris looked over at her and seemed as if he wanted to hug her, but was hesitant to do so, "Get in. You can ride back in style."

"Sure," Petra nodded and climbed into the passenger seat. She was still thanking her stars that it was empty.

Chapter 71

Mahajanga, Madagascar

Carlos could barely keep his head upright. After several hours of being beaten and tortured, he felt like a rag doll. His arms had turned a mottled spectrum of pink and red from the beating, soon to be black and purple as the bruises changed color. His left eye smarted and his cheek stung from an open cut—the bleeding had stopped, but he could feel the dried blood crusted down his cheek. He could no longer tell where his body ended, and the pain began.

Seymour had given him some reprieve by instructing his goon to stay away from Carlos' head other than the initial shiner and a few hard punches to the jaw. He wanted Carlos to have the mental capacity to tell them what they wanted to know. As the beating continued, Carlos had given away bits and pieces, but he had been able to maintain enough presence of mind to stick to details of limited value. He told Seymour that he had heard about the wedding and wanted to steal Nguyen's wife's jewelry collection. He explained that he was a private investigator that Vik had hired for backup. He stuck to the fact that he didn't know who Vik had worked for and had become an upscale thief after his death.

The web of lies had grown thick and he wasn't sure how much longer he could keep it up. *Petra won't let me die in here.* He had repeated the words to himself so many times that he no longer knew what they meant. Would he be able to walk by the time they rescued him? How long had he been there? Based on the light coming in through the window near the ceiling, not even a full day had passed since he had been taken prisoner, but that hardly seemed plausible. It had to have been days. How could one day stretch out for so long?

He gasped for air. His chest felt as if it were about to explode, but Adam had been careful to avoid his vital organs. Seymour also didn't want to risk him dying of an unexpected complication before they were able to beat the information out of him. *I think that's what he said.* Carlos racked his brain for what he had overheard. It was a faint memory, somewhere in the distance. *Did I hear those words? Or did I dream them?* His body trembled. He was losing his mind and he couldn't do anything about it.

Carlos pushed past the pain and panic to focus on his position. His hands were tied behind him to the chair, as were his feet. With his eyes shut, he searched his mind. He had learned how to handle this in training. Somewhere in his memory, he could find the instruction. *One step at a time.*

Carlos opened his eyes and looked around him, feeling strangely calm. This was his chance. He was alone. Adam had disappeared for the moment. *There is no pain.* He said the words in his head and then repeated them aloud, "There is no pain." He coughed and spat blood because of the punches to his jaw. Seymour's instructions had been precise—Adam had dealt several punches to the jaw, enough to cause severe pain without breaking it. *At least it's not broken.* The fact that he could form words told him that. His jaw wasn't radiating as much pain as the rest of his body, but that would change once the adrenaline wore off. An image of Diane floated in front of him again and his resolve strengthened. Somehow, he would find a way to escape, a way to get back to her.

He clenched his fists to release the stiffness in his fingers. The rope around his wrists had left his skin raw, but he had a decent range of motion. He felt around with his fingers as he tried to determine how they had tied the knot.

Carlos willed his fingers to start pulling at the rope. The frays cut into his skin. He wasn't sure what was more painful—the new cuts or the twisting motion of his wrists. *This isn't working. I need something sharper.* He looked around the empty hexagonal room. The walls were covered in wood paneling and there was a small window a few feet overhead. The afternoon light would be fading soon. He would need to figure something out quickly before it became too dark. The nearest wall was a few feet away, so it would be quite a feat to get close enough to use it for stability, but he had to try.

He moved his arms to the left to clear his hands over the side. They were still tied together but removing them from their position wrapped around the chair might give him more to work with. After several attempts and a stream of grunts, he managed to wrench his right shoulder enough that it passed over the corner of the chair. He leaned forward with his chest to his thighs for a second, panting, and attempted to catch his breath. His shoulder throbbed, but he could tell that it wasn't a severe wound. *It's not dislocated. Not yet anyway.*

Carlos braced himself for the next step and grasped the back of the chair with his hands. He placed his feet flat against the floor. In order to stand up, he would have to lean far over them, but not so far that he tumbled onto his head. He inhaled and exhaled, and then pushed his weight forward over his feet. He made sure not to hesitate too much since that would ruin his balance. He remembered from gym class as a teenager that you were never leaning as far as you needed to be until you thought you were way over your goal. He let out another grunt as his feet picked up the weight and the back legs of the chair lifted off the ground. As soon as the weight of the chair hit his back, he wobbled. He saw the ground in front of his head and backpedaled so that he landed hard on the chair once again. The chair skidded backward, and his upper arms slammed against the back of it. *That didn't go so well.*

By some kind of miracle, he was actually a couple of steps closer to the wall. He considered repeating the same motion, but instead, he elected to skid toward the wall. It took three attempts, but on the third, he managed to slide the chair a step closer to the wall. He did it again, each time getting closer. By the fourth time, his right shoulder could touch the wall if he leaned against it.

Once he reached the wall, Carlos racked his brain to remember why the wall had seemed like such a desirable location. The metallic taste of blood permeated his mouth and his head felt like a throbbing mess. He still had to figure a way off the chair. *How do I get out of this?* He was searching the wood paneling in a daze when a screw sticking out of the paneling caught his eye.

Carlos pivoted the chair and used the wall as leverage to turn the back of it away from the paneling. After so many attempts at skidding across the floor, the pivot felt easy enough. He turned to his left and pushed his wrists as far as he could the opposite way. From where he was, he could feel the rusted metal of the screw head against his skin. *It's a good thing I've had my tetanus shot.* He breathed in and out. He would have to hold the position over his left side long enough to fray the rope. *I have to remember to thank Diana for forcing me to go to yoga with her.* She had been worried about his health and had been taking him to her yoga class for the past year.

He breathed through the pain and moved his wrists against the jagged screw threads. The sores on his wrists felt as if they were on fire with the increased motion. He looked ahead and imagined walking down the beach outside with Diane. *That's why you're doing this.* Eventually, the rope started to split. He moved faster—up and down, up and down. After a while, his adrenaline took over.

When he finally got to the last thread, it caught on the screw head. *Pull!* He wrenched his wrist against the screw and it finally split. With his hands free, he collapsed over his thighs. He was tempted to rest there, but his mind pushed him to move. *Get up. Move faster.* He gave himself until the count of ten to catch his breath and then went to work on his ankles. With his hands free, he could grope at the knots. The poorly tied knots gave way after a few strategically placed pulls. *I guess Adam was no Boy Scout.* He looked at the screw again, thankful for its existence. For a moment, he wished he could add it to his collection of Agency souvenirs—reminders of why he had left that life behind—but he chose not to waste the energy to pull it from the wall.

Carlos stood up gingerly, stretched his sore muscles, and looked up at the window. The walls were too steep for him to climb. He repositioned the chair underneath the window and stepped up on it— he could almost reach the window, but not quite. He would have to find another way to escape.

His gaze shifted to the door. It was made of metal with a hinge on the inside. He pulled at the handle to try his luck, but as he expected, that got him nowhere.

He felt around his jacket. Adam had stripped him of his lock pick kit and other gadgets, but then he remembered a foldable metal device that he had stitched into the sole of his left shoe.

Vik had shown him that trick when they first started working together. Most searches missed the inside of the shoe, so it was an ideal hiding place. Because it was small and lay flat like a foldable nail file, it easily went undetected. Carlos had brought it with him as sort of an homage, not expecting to ever have to use it, especially given how many other gadgets he normally carried.

He knelt on the floor, took off his shoe, and rooted for the device, excited to feel the hard surface against his hand as he pulled up the inside of his shoe's sole. *Woo-hoo!* Once he'd retrieved it and put his shoe back on, Carlos slid the mechanism on the base of the device so that it ejected a longer metal rod that he could insert into the lock.

It's too bad Petra's not here. She'd have us out of here in three minutes or less. He smiled at the recollection. Petra had always been a champ at picking locks, both with and without a lock pick kit. It was as if she could see the inside of the mechanism in her head.

Carlos took a deep breath and imagined the old lock diagrams that they had studied during Agency training. He slid the rod of the device into the lock and moved it around. He looked upward. *Please, if there's anyone up there, I could use a bit of luck right now. Thank you.*

Carlos twisted the device and the base bent toward the door. He had a vague recollection that the device bent into a makeshift Allen wrench. *Is that what I'm supposed to do?* Vik had shown him how to use it, but it had been so long ago. Carlos let his instincts guide him and twisted the device around in a circle. He kept his ear close to the doorknob and waited until he heard a soft click. *Maybe.* He kept his hopes at bay and twisted the device again. This time the knob emitted a louder click. *Now I've got it.* With the wrench in place, he used his other hand to turn the doorknob.

The door gave way and swung toward him.

Chapter 72

Mahajanga, Madagascar

Kasem watched in silence while Petra took Chris through what had transpired on the operation. She seemed reticent, but after the conversation progressed past the first couple of minutes, she started to relax. He could even see bits of her rapport with Chris emerge. Although they had worked together for years, their current relationship was incredibly strained. Kasem had seen little of Chris during the operation in New York and D.C. a year earlier—Petra had made sure that his contact was mostly limited to her and Carlos.

Once they covered the background, Kasem took a seat on the floor next to them. He intended to be a full participant in any planning for the next phase. Plans that sent him into the fire would not be made without his input. *Never again.*

"Based on his tracker data, Carlos is being held here, in the compound at the center of this island?" Chris pointed to the map on Nathan's computer screen.

"Yes," Nathan answered. "It took a while, but I managed to access their perimeter cameras with your codes." He switched the view on-screen to show four camera views split into quadrants. One overlooked a pool and patio area of the compound. Another watched over the main road leading uphill into the central courtyard from the beach. The third focused on the interior courtyard, and the final one looked out on the beach that was the main access point to the island.

"As you can see, they closely monitor the interior of the compound and the main access point on the beach, which is a good distance downhill from the compound. They also have an airstrip to access the island." Nathan switched screens to show the camera view of the airstrip. "It's for small planes only, and Nguyen does own a small jet that he keeps at the lodge. It's only about ten or fifteen minutes by air, but about an hour by boat from here depending on the tides." He switched the screen back to the multiple-camera view and looked around the group.

Kasem scrutinized the camera views in detail, "Now that we have access to these, what do we know? Is Nguyen there now?"

Nathan shook his head, "Nguyen's been at the main reception hall at the lodge visiting with guests who are still in town after the wedding. He's hosting some small parties, stuff like that. I haven't seen Seymour on camera at the lodge yet, so I'm betting that he's on the island. I don't have as many viewpoints, though, so I can't be sure."

Chris studied the computer screen and a hard-copy map that he had brought with him. "What do you think Nguyen uses this island for? He and his wife live in London, and they have a beach villa here that's part of the main resort. So why keep that island?" he frowned. "In your intel, you said that the arms deal was supposed to go down shortly after the wedding, right?"

Petra raised her eyebrows and nodded.

Chris crossed his arms, "What about the arms that you guys tagged in London? You said they were near Mahajanga but you couldn't get a precise location. Is there any chance they could be there?"

"I guess," Nathan shrugged. "I don't know why our GPS would be blocked, but it's possible, if they have some kind of dampening field on part of the compound."

"Do you think that's where he's planning to do the deal?" Chris looked at Nathan again. "Have you found anything in the ownership papers on that compound?"

"Nothing definitive yet. He's hidden his tracks well."

Chris nodded, "Petra, what if we had Grant look into it? I still use him for contract jobs since I know he's trustworthy. He's outside the Agency, so we wouldn't raise any internal flags, and I did ask him to be on call. He can do all the analysis remotely."

Kasem could tell from the expression on Petra's face that she shared his hesitation about involving Grant despite the assistance that he could offer. He gave her a noncommittal shrug and watched the look of relief spread across her face. *I'm not that unreasonable,* he thought with a twinge of indignation.

"Okay," Petra said.

They waited a few minutes as Chris directed Nathan on how to send the information to Grant.

Petra tapped her fingers on the table in a sign of obvious impatience. Kasem couldn't help but agree with her. Information on the ownership of the island and how they might be able to tie it to Nguyen would be useful, but it wasn't their biggest concern. They needed to concentrate on how to rescue Carlos.

Chris looked up from the screen with a sheepish expression on his face, "Sorry, that took longer than I expected. Let's get back to the plan for tonight. Petra, what do you propose?"

"We obviously need to get to the island after dark." She tapped on Nathan's screen to enable the map projection from a camera on the side of the computer monitor. With the map of the island magnified across the table, she pointed to the main beach. "Like Nathan showed us, they monitor this main beach with cameras. I propose that we dock on the other side of the island here," she said indicating a cove secluded from the main beach. "It will be a steep climb up this cliffside to get to the compound, but the cover will be worth it."

Kasem leaned in, "There's another access point?"

Chris tapped on Nathan's screen again and the projection switched to a contoured view of the island so that they could see the slope from the beach. "We would climb our way up the bluff here." He traced the course from the cove Petra had indicated up the cliff face.

"Exactly," Petra added. "There's a fair amount of tree cover so we wouldn't have to worry about being seen."

Chris fiddled with the zipper on his hooded sweatshirt, "And that will be you and me, Petra? Since Nathan has a remote hack on the cameras, he can stay here." He turned his gaze toward Kasem, "What about you? You're our access point to Carlos?"

"Yeah. I'll distract Seymour so that you can get to Carlos."

"Great," Chris said with a nod. "We'll leave the boat anchored in the cove and get to the shore, then climb up the cliff."

Rachel frowned, "Are you sure? There's a reason they don't use that beach as an entry point to the island. The satellite feed shows that there are currents coming in here and here," she said and pointed to the east and north of the beach.

"I don't think we have a choice. We can't stow away on Kasem's boat and docking on the main beach is impossible." Chris surveyed the team, "Petra, Kasem, what do you think? Are you guys in?"

Kasem felt the words on the tip of his tongue. He would have to convince Seymour to see him, go to the island, provide cover long enough for them to extract Carlos, and get out of there before Seymour realized he was a fraud. *You can do this.* His eyes moved between Chris and Petra before he gave them a slow nod, "I'm in."

Chapter 73

Mahajanga, Madagascar

Petra strolled along the beach in silence with Kasem. She wished they had an alternative to the new plan, but she saw no other way. Kasem had made his choice to help Carlos, and it was the same choice that she would have made had their roles been reversed.

Kasem took her hand, "How do you feel about this?"

"I don't want you to do it. I wish I'd never come up with the idea." Her voice caught, "But I don't see another way. We can't leave Carlos in there."

"I know. I wish we'd been able to talk about it before, but we didn't have the chance."

"I couldn't have stopped you. No more than I can stop myself from doing my part. This is who we are. Helping someone like Carlos, that *has to be* who we are."

He stroked her hair and planted a kiss on her forehead. "We should get ready."

"In a minute," Petra wrapped her arms around his waist and stood there in silence with his arms around her as they drank in the beach and the sound of the crashing waves. The sun was lower in the sky now, but they still had some time before sundown. She stared at the cliffs on either side of the beach, and the azure waterscape that washed over the white sand. She closed her eyes and challenged herself to remember every detail. If everything went to hell, she wanted to be able to recall this moment. Every vivid detail.

******

When they returned, Rachel sat up and looked at them with a twinkle in her eyes, "Since the lovebirds are back, I guess we're a go."

Chris's gaze moved between Petra and Kasem, "Right?"

"Right." Petra took her seat on the floor again. She hadn't told Chris about her relationship with Kasem. His expression made it clear that he didn't approve. *It's not like we need his blessing.* Despite that, she felt uncomfortable under the weight of his gaze. What did he know about Kasem? She thought through what she and Carlos had revealed on the last operation in New York. He knew that Kasem was a former Iranian spy and that he had worked for General Majed. Chris also knew that Kasem had risked his life as part of an Agency op to put an end to a Russian terrorist conspiracy that couldn't have been stopped without his help.

Where does he get off judging us or Kasem? Petra resented Chris for it, especially since he had done many questionable things in service of the Agency. Whom she chose to date was none of his business. She had left the Agency and was out of his purview, and from a personal standpoint, his opinion no longer held water. Although they had made intermittent strides to restore their soured relationship, they were far from being the friends that they had once been. It wasn't easy to recover from the fact that he had given her no choice but to return to the field on the operation in Kuwait two years earlier.

Petra pushed those thoughts aside, "Kasem, the next step is for you to contact Seymour. Do we have a twenty on him?" She turned her gaze toward Nathan.

"Not yet, but he should be at the lodge for the goodbye cocktail party," Nathan answered.

"That's my best bet anyway. If Seymour isn't there, I'll talk to Sir Caleb, or even to Nguyen," Kasem stood up.

"Isn't that a bit brash?" Chris looked at him in concern.

Kasem raised his eyebrows, "No. I'm the one who established contact with Nguyen at the beginning of this op. If it weren't for my work forming a connection with Jim and our meetings with Sir Caleb and Nguyen, there would be no op." He hoped that Chris understood the intention of his words—*you are just now joining our team and don't run this show.* "What I need to deliver now is a meeting. We don't have time to discuss it in committee. Get the boat ready and keep an eye on Carlos' vitals. Even if things don't go as planned with Seymour, you'll have to be ready. As soon as it gets dark, if you haven't heard from me, proceed with the original plan. I'll try to be as much of a distraction as I can to give you the time that you need, whether I'm here or there."

Or being tortured, Petra thought. She let out a long exhale and nodded, "Go change your clothes. You can't show up at the hotel in what you're wearing."

A smile crossed his face, "That's right. I need brand-name shorts and boat shoes to interact with that crowd."

"I'd go with the white linen suit," Petra said.

Rachel had procured the suit for the trip, but Kasem had taken one look at it and sworn that he wouldn't be caught dead in it. *And I still won't.* He made a show of bowing, "I live to serve, milady. The linen suit it is."

Chapter 74

Mahajanga, Madagascar

Kasem adjusted his white linen jacket as he emerged from the car at the Lodge des Terres Blanches Resort. He rounded the car to give Petra his hand as she exited, "Have I told you how much I like it when you wear sundresses?"

Her eyes sparkled, "I don't think you have. I'll have to remember that." She took his hand and stepped out of the car, "Are you ready?"

"I'm ready."

"I'll leave to help Chris prep the boat once you've established contact with Seymour or Nguyen. Good luck."

"You too."

"Please be careful." She gave him a hesitant look, "I'd go to the ends of the earth for Carlos, and I'll do the same for you, but let's not let it get that far."

"I'll do my best."

They walked hand in hand toward the evening happy hour that Nguyen had planned for any guests who had remained in the area after the wedding.

"Sir Caleb," Kasem called out as they approached him. The tall Englishman was speaking to a much younger blonde woman. Kasem could hazily recall meeting her at the engagement party.

"Amir, Cara, it's good to see you," Sir Caleb shook his hand and gave Petra a kiss on the cheek. "Have you met Katherine? Her father and Nguyen go way back. Where did they meet again?"

"They went to boarding school together. It's good to see you both again," Katherine said.

"Lovely to see you too," Kasem replied.

"Are you feeling better?" Sir Caleb asked. "We were so sorry not to see you at the wedding yesterday."

"I am. It was an uncomfortable experience, but I feel much better now," Kasem placed his hand on his belly. "I can't believe I missed it. I hear it was a beautiful ceremony and a great party."

"It was. Cara, I'm glad you were still able to make it. I know Jim and Janine were as well," Sir Caleb said.

"I'm glad too! He wouldn't let me miss it." Petra gave him a beaming smile and linked her arm with Kasem's. She gave him a peck on the cheek before releasing it.

236

Kasem straightened up, "Sir Caleb, may I borrow you for a moment?"

"Of course. Katherine, I will leave you in Cara's capable hands."

"Thank you," Kasem said as he and Sir Caleb ambled away from the two women. Once they were a few steps away, he started his pitch. "I wanted to speak to you and Seymour about getting more involved with the deal. I believe I've found a buyer for your merchandise. I know that we raised a portion of the financing, but now Carlson wants a larger piece of the pie…"

Chapter 75

Mahajanga, Madagascar

Petra checked her watch for the third time as she and Chris finished outfitting the boat.

"It's not going to bring Kasem back faster," Chris said in a soft voice. "He said he'd try to be here. If he doesn't make it, we have to go."

"I'm just worried."

"You'd be worried either way. He is who he is, and he'll get here when he can."

She could hear the tone of judgment in his voice and couldn't stop herself from lashing out. "What are you trying to say?" As soon as the words were out, she regretted them. She might as well have opened Pandora's box.

"Nothing. If he can't get here in time, we'll have to go without him."

"Right." Petra remained silent for a few moments, both surprised and annoyed that Chris hadn't taken the bait. She wanted to fight with him, to call him out, to have it out with him. He had no right to be judgmental or passive aggressive.

"He knew the risks and he was trained for subterfuge—probably along with all sorts of stuff we don't know about."

Petra's jaw clenched. *What about you?* She did a final check to make sure that they had brought all of their communications equipment onboard. "I think we're all set," she said in a curt voice. "I'm going to get some extra ammo for my Colt and I'll be good to go."

"While you're inside, can you make sure we have Carlos' remote tracker data from Nathan? He said he was setting the app up for us. It uses a GPS satellite feed, so it'll still work even if we lose phone service out there."

"I'll ask him to check on Kasem's as well." She took a deep breath to gain control over her worries. *What if Kasem had approached Seymour and been taken too? What if they took him somewhere else?* She remembered when he had been abducted in DC and her stomach did a flip as she walked away from the boat.

She was halfway up the beach toward the villa when she noticed Nathan hobbling toward her.

"Hi, Petra," he said when he reached her.

"Hey, I was just coming in to get the remote tracker."

"I thought I'd bring it out to you. Here you go," he said in an out-of-breath voice as he touched his phone to hers to upload the app data. "I also brought you an extra charge pack so there's no chance of losing power while you're out there."

Petra gave him a smile and a nod, "Thanks. You've been a big help."

"I'm so sorry about before," he blinked several times and looked down at his feet. "I care about Carlos, and I care about you—"

"It's all water under the bridge. You're here now. That's what matters."

"I feel so stupid. I don't know how I messed up so badly."

Petra could see the distress on his face, "We've all been there. The blame game gets you nowhere. Carlos actually just reminded me of that. It's easier said than done, but you have to forgive yourself. Blaming yourself won't help Carlos, but it will make you miserable. Like I said, you're here now. That's what counts."

"What about you and Kasem?"

"What do you mean?" she frowned. Was he asking about her relationship? She knew that he had a crush on her, but she had maintained boundaries to ensure that he didn't get any ideas.

"How are you guys doing? He left—"

Petra raised her palm to stop him, "Nathan, Kasem and I are fine. What happened between us is our business, and ours alone. He's helping us get Carlos out, just like you."

"Sorry, I didn't mean to overstep."

"Thanks for the tracker. Go ahead and give it to Chris. I need to grab some more ammo." Petra moved past him with her emotions bubbling. She was overreacting—Nathan's question didn't deserve such strong irritation—but after her exchange with Chris, her patience had worn thin. *When did they become such busybodies? What gave them the right?* She opened the door to the villa and was tempted to wake a napping Rachel because only another female perspective was worth its salt for the moment.

Instead, Petra made herself a cup of green tea. The warm liquid helped calm her nerves. Her emotions had already been running high with Kasem taking such a risk. *Did Chris and Nathan really have to poke the bear?* She steeled her frustration. A few minutes later, she felt calmer and grabbed the extra ammo for her Colt pistol. She pulled the pistol from her holster and checked the magazine before putting it back. She hoped that she wouldn't need it tonight.

******

As soon as Petra returned to the boat, Nathan made a hurried exit and disappeared toward the villa.

Chris looked at her with a grin, "The guys you work with are always running after you, aren't they?"

Petra frowned. She could tell from his tone that he was only teasing, but it still bothered her. She ignored the question and looked over the inside of the boat once again. The sun was starting to set, and the first tendrils of dusk were at their doorstep.

"He should have been here by now. We have to go," Chris's words echoed her internal clock.

"Let's give him another five minutes. It's not quite dark yet."

"Fine."

Petra detected that his tone mirrored her own frustration. With a deep breath, she told herself not to react. *There's no point.*

"When did you start seeing him?" Chris's tone was gentler now.

Petra exhaled and answered, "October." He didn't have to know that she and Kasem had dated in Tehran when she was with the Agency, and he certainly didn't need to know that she had run into him again in Kuwait when he was still being forced to be the Ahriman as part of the deal that he had struck with General Majed.

"Is it serious?"

"It is, but there's a lot we still have to work through."

"I'm sure you do," Chris said. His voice was so quiet that Petra almost didn't catch the words.

"What did you say?" she asked with a glare.

"You heard me."

"What's your problem, Chris? My relationship is none of your business."

"But you used to talk to me about your love life all the time."

Petra shook her head, "A lot has changed. Back then, I never thought you would try to send me back into the field after all the PTSD I went through. I wouldn't have believed that you could prioritize a mission over a person."

"What do you think I'm doing now? I'm here because *you* asked me to be."

"I—" Petra bit her lip. He was right and they both knew it. He had dropped everything to help her, to help Carlos. "You're right. I really do appreciate you coming, and I know Carlos will too, but that doesn't give you the right to have an opinion on my personal life."

"We're friends, Petra. I'm only trying to protect you."

"Protect me from what?"

"Do you really know this guy? You've known him for what? Five minutes? He was an Iranian spy. You are literally dating an Iranian spy. Have you gone totally mental?"

"He was an Iranian spy, but he also went out on a limb for us when we needed him in New York. Besides, I don't care about who he *was*. I care about who he *is*. He takes good care of me, and he loves me."

"Do you really mean that? You don't care about who he was? I can't possibly believe that. You've never wondered about what he did in his past?"

"Of course, I have," Petra started to raise her voice as her emotions boiled over once again. "We've all done some terrible things. Don't you remember the operation in Kuwait? How you sent me in there even though I was supposed to be retired because of severe PTSD? What about every asset you've ordered your agents to burn?"

"We're not talking about me. We're talking about you and Kasem. I don't doubt that he's in love with you. Any idiot could see that by the way that he looks at you. But you're talking about a serious relationship. Can you trust him? Would you introduce him to your family? To your friends?"

Petra grimaced. There was some truth in what he was saying, which is why the words stung so much, but it wasn't because of Kasem. "I don't have much of a family or friends anymore, thanks to you. I've been in hiding from my life and the people I love. Do you have a clue what that is like? I hardly ever even call my mom and dad because the Agency won't leave me alone. You can't let me live my life."

"But here you are on an op that has nothing to do with me or the Agency."

"I came here to help Carlos. This was important to him, so when he asked for my help, I gave in without resolve. He's never tried to put this operation above my own health or sanity. Unlike some other people I know." Petra cringed, "Besides, he knows how toxic the Agency can be and has done everything to protect me from it."

"If you want us out of your life so badly, then why did you call me?"

"Because Carlos was captured. I had no choice. He's the closest thing I have to family right now. I wasn't going to let him die out there because I didn't want to pick up the phone and talk to your sorry ass."

Chris sighed, "I don't want to fight with you, Petra. I was just concerned, but you're right. It's not my place. I'm sorry."

Petra wasn't sure how to react. He had silenced her protests, but not her anger. The only way forward was to put the past aside. "I need a minute and then we can go," she jumped off the deck and walked out across the beach. She wanted Kasem to show up, to help prove Chris wrong, but it was a pointless exercise. Even if they could get Chris to believe that he was on their side, that wouldn't erase his past.

Why should I care what Chris thinks? Deep down, she did care because, in a way, he was right. She wanted a life with Kasem, and although she had done everything to push her doubts aside, she wasn't sure if that was possible. Petra kicked a pebble in the sand. She would feel comfortable talking to only one person about this—Carlos. They had to get him out in one piece.

Her phone buzzed with a message from Kasem.
On my way to the island with Sir Caleb.

Chapter 69

Mahajanga, Madagascar

Kasem watched as the sun dipped into the horizon over the water as they sped along on the boat. He glanced over his shoulder at Sir Caleb who was on the phone with Seymour. Approaching Sir Caleb rather than Seymour had been the right call—Sir Caleb was new to Nguyen's organization and more open to bringing others into it. He also didn't have the same instinctual distrust that Kasem had seen in his interactions with Seymour.

Kasem strained his ears, but he couldn't hear much over the sound of the boat's engine, although he could get the gist. Sir Caleb was trying to convince Seymour that he had made the right call on bringing Kasem to the other island.

Kasem wondered what they used the island for as he looked out through the rapidly gaining darkness. He would have preferred to see the approach during daylight because he needed every advantage to get away. He certainly didn't relish the idea of being stuck on the island with Seymour. A small part of him even worried that Seymour would throw him into the same holding cell with Carlos as soon as they arrived. He kept his heart rate steady with a series of breathing exercises. His training in Iran, for all its faults, had beaten the panic response out of him.

They reached the island half an hour later after a combination of silence and small talk with Sir Caleb and the deckhand. Kasem would have preferred some time alone with the deckhand since he suspected that he could get more information out of him, but by the time he had a moment alone with him, they were already reaching the beach. He toggled to the app on his phone and homed in on Petra's tracker. She and Chris hadn't reached the island yet, but judging from the distance, they would be there shortly.

"Where are we meeting Seymour?" Kasem asked as Sir Caleb reappeared at his side.

"He's up the hill."

Kasem deactivated the tracker application on his phone and did a mass delete of all messages. He didn't want to take any chances. He had one shot to escape alive.

He followed Sir Caleb down the dock and onto the beach. There was a path laid out in two-by-four wooden planks that kept them from sinking into the sand as they walked. When they reached the top of the beach, the path changed to a stone stairway leading up the hill. Kasem kept his eyes peeled for any of the offshoots Nathan had identified on the map. Given the stone structure of this path, the map application wasn't able to differentiate between a true trail through the wooded area around him and a well-built path. Luckily, Sir Caleb's slow pace and wheezing breaths gave him plenty of time to survey the surroundings.

Kasem kept the map in his head as they traversed the steep staircase. When they crossed the first ridge, they could see the different towers of the old fort compound. He tried to recall the relative positions on the map for where Carlos was being held. His eyes moved between the three shorter towers that surrounded the primary tower. *I believe it's that one,* he thought as he looked toward the one farthest from the primary tower.

"Where are we going?" he asked Sir Caleb again in an effort to play dumb.

Sir Caleb motioned toward the primary tower. It took him a few seconds before he was able to speak. "Seymour's office is on the third floor." He bent from the waist and panted, "Unfortunately, there's no elevator. I should spend more time at the gym."

Kasem clapped him on the shoulder. "Shouldn't we all? We're almost there."

"Youngblood. So much enthusiasm."

They passed two security guards on the ground floor when they reached the tower and another one on the first-floor landing. "A lot of security for an island in the middle of nowhere," Kasem said. He kept his tone upbeat with a hint of mockery, as if he were teasing Sir Caleb.

"Seymour doesn't take any chances. We store the goods here when we're between sales."

"Ah, that makes sense. How long does that usually take?"

"Moving the merchandise usually takes about two months," Sir Caleb answered with a shrug. "Sometimes more, sometimes a little less. Perhaps this time we can speed that up with your help."

Kasem detected a hint of excitement in Sir Caleb's voice and felt a twinge of remorse. Of all the people that he'd met as part of his cover, he'd become quite fond of Jim and Janine. He hoped that they wouldn't suffer too much for what they were about to do to Nguyen. Even Sir Caleb wasn't so bad. *If I didn't know he was a black-market arms dealer, I'd like the old man.* Kasem squashed those feelings by reminding himself why he was there and followed Sir Caleb up the remaining stairs in silence.

"I bet if I spent more time here, I'd be in better shape," Sir Caleb caught his breath when they reached the third floor.

"You and me both."

They sat down in a sitting room with two blue couches. The room had long, narrow windows that reminded Kasem of arrow slits, and quite possibly may once have been used for such defense. "Wow," Kasem couldn't help but say.

The windows overlooked the top of the bluff that descended behind the tower where he suspected Carlos was being held. Even through the narrow windows, the view was both magnificent and incredibly useful. To the far left of the cliff, Kasem could see a path that led into the forest. If he had to guess, that would be his best bet to hike down to the cove where Petra and Chris would dock. Since Petra and Chris would have climbing equipment, he might be able to use their equipment to repel directly down the cliffside, but the forest path would be a safer, albeit slower, bet if his timing didn't match. As he studied the landscape, Kasem worked to keep the expression of marvel on his face.

"I see you made it here in one piece," Seymour's nasal voice pierced the silence as he entered the room.

Before Kasem could answer, Sir Caleb took the lead, "We did. That seasickness medicine Janine recommended worked like a charm."

"Of course." Seymour turned his gaze toward Kasem once again, "I heard you have a proposition for us."

Chapter 77

Mahajanga, Madagascar

Carlos peered beyond the doorway and looked to the left and right. The hallway stretched out on both sides but moved at a slight upward incline on his right. He figured his best shot was to go left. *Hopefully, that corresponds to down.* If he had to guess, he was at least three or four floors up.

He stepped out and shut the door behind him as quietly as possible. To stay in the shadows, he pressed against the exterior wall of the hallway. He passed doors on both sides before he reached a landing with a stairway that led downward. Carlos steadied himself against the railing closest to the wall and crept down.

He counted the number of flights in the stairway while he sped downward. He was four flights up, then three, then two. At the halfway point, he passed a window that looked out over the surrounding area. Unlike the window in his cell, this one was low enough for the view to be accessible. Carlos kept to one side to shield himself from possible exposure and looked at the grounds. They were at the top of a hill with a cliff that dropped off in front of him, and forest that stretched out to the right. The entire view was surrounded by water. *Another bloody island.* He'd been unconscious when he'd been transported to his holding cell and he'd held out hope that he was still on the mainland. He kept his reaction in check as the direness of the situation dawned on him. He was on an island small enough to be owned and dominated by Seymour's men, and the only escape was to find a way off the island. *Am I in a Bond movie?*

After running down another half-flight, he found another window and crouched by it to get the view of the other side. He could see three other towers, and one seemed to be larger than the other two. There were three guards stationed between them—one closest to the entrance of the two smaller towers and the other two in front of the main tower.

He observed the area for a second longer and was about to move when he saw a group of people appear. He tilted his head to the side in surprise. *Kasem?* The limited light of the courtyard lanterns made it difficult to see, but he could tell the group consisted of Kasem, Sir Caleb, and a man he didn't recognize—most likely a guard, judging by his stance and posture. Carlos hesitated—even if Kasem was part of their rescue attempt, Petra would have to get them both out, and that seemed like a tall order.

He shook off his concerns and proceeded down the last full flight. He had to find the way to the beach, or at least decent cover in the forest until Petra could get to him. The best way to help Kasem would be to extract himself first. He clung to that.

Chapter 78

Mahajanga, Madagascar

Petra hopped off the boat into waist-deep shallow water along the beach. She shivered as the water seeped in through the gaps in her swim shirt and leggings. They had anchored there for fear of running the boat aground. She placed her waterproof pack on top of one of the swim motors that Chris had sourced through the Agency and let it propel her to shore. The motor emitted a soft humming sound, but the crashing of the waves drowned out any sounds of their arrival. Chris reached the shore with his own motor pack a few seconds after her.

"Are you ready?" he whispered.

"I'm ready."

They dragged the motors and their packs through the sand and stashed them behind some large rocks at the edge of the beach. Petra adjusted the focus of her night-vision goggles using the toggles on the sides. They were even more sophisticated than the goggles that she was used to—they didn't weigh much more than sunglasses and provided crisper outlines of the objects in view.

"I see you're enjoying those night-vision goggles. Pretty cool, huh?" Chris said in a cheeky voice. "The Agency isn't all bad, is it?"

Petra cringed. She was indeed impressed by the Agency's gadgets, but she would rather not admit that to Chris, "They're not too bad." Rather than continue the conversation, she checked the magazine in her pistol and nodded at Chris.

"Didn't you check before we left? Where would your ammo have gone between then and now? Do you think it teleported to another planet while we were in the water?"

"You can never be too sure." She pulled her climbing gear out of her pack and fastened it across her torso and shoulder so that it wouldn't tangle with her gun holster. With the climbing gear ready, she crossed the front of the beach toward the base of the cliff. She looked up and swallowed—the cliffside was steep and rocky and would have been a challenge to climb even during the day.

Before she started to scale it, she checked Carlos' tracker data and frowned.

Chris moved across the beach to join her, "Sorry, I haven't had to pack climbing gear in a long time," he said in a sheepish voice.

"That's fine," Petra said. "Look at this," she pointed to the screen on her phone to show him Carlos' GPS tracker.

"He's at the top of the hill, right? Let's get up there."

"Look closer. He's moved." She pointed at the screen again, "He was over here on this side of the tower when I looked earlier, but now he's on the other side."

"Do you think they're moving him? Or that he escaped?"

"I'm not sure." Petra watched the screen with her eyes wide. If Seymour were moving him, then they would have to revamp the plan, but if Carlos had escaped, they could reach him at the top of the cliff. "We have to intercept him, but either way, we don't know where he's going. Even if he managed to escape, we have no way to communicate with him." She cursed under her breath.

Chris surveyed the face of the cliff from top to bottom, "Our best shot is still up there." He fastened his first tread into the jagged wall of rock a foot above his head and clipped his carabiner into it.

Petra shut her eyes and exhaled. *Here goes nothing.*

******

When they reached the top of the cliff, Petra heaved herself up to the ground and collapsed onto her back in the cover of some bushes. Although their ascent had only taken ten minutes, it had felt like hours of reaching, grabbing, and praying that their treads would hold. It took her a few seconds to catch her breath before she was able to roll over into a crouch. Her heart pounded in her ears as she pulled her phone from its pocket on her holster. The red dot that noted Carlos' position hadn't moved while they had been scaling the cliff. She tapped the screen to change the settings so that it showed his location relative to hers, then tapped it again to add Kasem's tracker to the map as well.

"Kasem's in the central tower, but Carlos should be just over there," she whispered to Chris who had joined her in the bushes. She pointed toward one of the smaller towers.

"He's still in the same building?"

"I think so." Petra thought for a second. "They either moved him to a different room or he's watching the guards for an opening."

Chris looked at her, then through the bushes, and back at her again. "If we get closer on the perimeter, it's a straight shot to him." He pulled his Beretta from his holster and attached a silencer, "I'll cover you, but hopefully that won't be needed. There's only one guard in front of that tower, and it's dark." He lined up the shot and gestured toward the tower.

Petra sighed, "Use the tranq gun. It'll be quieter."

"Good idea."

With another quick nod, Petra retrieved her tranquilizer gun from her pack. She didn't normally use it on ops because it was less effective and speedy at taking down an opponent. In the field, that variability was dangerous, but as far as stealth, the tranq gun worked best.

She checked the cartridge and disappeared into the bushes without looking back. Although she and Chris had their differences, she still trusted him to back her up. *Here I go.*

Chapter 79

Mahajanga, Madagascar

Carlos watched the shadows from the ground floor of the tower. He had to move. The longer he waited, the more likely he would miss his window of opportunity. The guard stationed at his tower was occupied with a cigarette and talking with another guard over his com. *Now!*

He tiptoed over the threshold of two large stone French doors, one side of which had been left open, and pressed against the shadows along the building. Thankfully, he was still wearing black from his foray into Nguyen's beach villa. He sidled along the side of the tower for a few feet and then crouched to the ground and scurried into the bushes.

He kept low and looked behind him. On one side was a cliff and on the other was dense forest, but he wasn't sure which way would get him closer to a beach. The other option was the airstrip; he had heard the sound of a helicopter landing while he was in his cell. He considered attempting to steal an aircraft, but he quickly dismissed the idea. That sort of thing only worked in movies where stolen aircraft strangely and miraculously were fueled, ready to go, and made hardly any noise.

He was about to take his chances in the forest when he heard something coming toward him. He pulled out the device that he had used to pick the lock and ejected the slim rod. Whatever was coming, he wasn't going to take any chances.

He was about to lash out when he heard Petra's voice. "Carlos, it's me," she whispered.

"Thank God."

"Are you okay? I was so scared."

Carlos wrapped his arms around her, "Me too, but I'm all right, kiddo."

"I've never been so grateful for Rachel's damn trackers. I have to admit, it made it a lot easier to find you." Petra gestured behind her, "This way, toward the cliff face. We have a boat at the cove below."

"But Kasem just went into the middle tower."

Chapter 80

Mahajanga, Madagascar

Kasem's eyes darted around the room as Seymour and Sir Caleb stepped aside after he had made his pitch. He had to admit that, despite his fears, it had gone reasonably well. All that was left now was to either close the deal or leave. The room was set up as an open concept sitting room, with the stairwell and hallway on his left and windows overlooking the grounds to his right. He counted the paces to the stairwell and considered either option. To get away, he'd have to get past the guards outside and into the tree cover as quickly as possible. It would have been an easy enough feat in his days as the Ahriman, but he wasn't sure if he could do it now. He also didn't know how capable either Sir Caleb or Seymour were with weapons. While he didn't believe they were carrying, he had no doubt that Seymour had something within easy access.

His gaze wandered to the window again and he caught movement in the shadows. He wasn't completely sure, but he could have sworn that someone had run into the bushes from one of the smaller towers—the one where he had guessed that Carlos was being held. *Is he out?* He watched the bushes in his peripheral vision. He couldn't see any movement, but the spot was close to the cliff face that led to the cove where Petra and Chris should be docking. He considered making a run for it now, but his gaze glided to Seymour and Sir Caleb once again, and he decided to give them a few more minutes. The best way to escape would be to take them by surprise on their way out of the tower when he was already on the ground floor.

******

"We've come to a decision," Seymour said in his nasal voice.

Seymour's eyes didn't give anything away, but Kasem detected a note of discomfort in Sir Caleb's posture. Kasem pretended not to notice and leaned forward to pour himself a fresh cup of tea from the teapot on the table, "Can I give my father-in-law good news?"

"Let's not get ahead of ourselves," Seymour said with a wave of his hand.

Sir Caleb gestured outward, "Your proposition to bring in a buyer is interesting, but we'll have to evaluate it with Nguyen. We take it very seriously when we bring new people into our partnership. Could you tell us more about the buyer? I'm assuming he's one of Carlson's investors?"

"Of course." Kasem could see that Sir Caleb was pushing to salvage the opportunity. He had to get out of there before they asked too many questions. He had only a brief skeleton of a prospective buyer. Because of the urgency of Carlos' capture, he hadn't had enough time with Nathan to put together a more complete profile. "The buyer we have in mind is—"

"The fact that you discovered the nature of our investments is troubling," Seymour's tone cut through Sir Caleb's optimism like a knife. "I'd much rather hear about that than your mythical buyer. How did you find out about our business? We pride ourselves on operating under the radar. Not even Sir Caleb knows who we've lined up as our next buyer or where the negotiations are to take place."

Because you're on the radar of every major global intelligence agency, even if they're in your pocket. Kasem crossed his arms and portrayed as much confidence as possible, "It's my job to know. You have your sources, and we have ours."

"I see." Seymour stood up and poured a drink from a glass decanter of whiskey on the sideboard a few steps away. "We have a special guest here on the island. Did Sir Caleb tell you that?" He looked at them with a cunning smile, "I believe there's a reason that you showed up at that party and met Nguyen in London. Such a serendipitous occasion, wouldn't you say? Such timing."

Kasem swallowed the last of his tea, "It was fortunate."

"Indeed. You invested with us and became close friends with Jim and Janine. It all happened so quickly. Your wife even helped organize the engagement party. And now you want to set us up with a buyer. Quite the coincidence, wouldn't you say?"

Sir Caleb glanced at Seymour and made an obvious attempt to defuse the tension, "What he's trying to say is that we're glad to have met you. You've certainly proved your worth, but sourcing a buyer is a big step."

Kasem looked from Seymour to Sir Caleb, unsure of how to react. Should he pretend to be offended? To be understanding? Was this the moment to feed them the story about hiring Carlos? He chose instead to go with disbelief. "As you wish. I'll provide any information you'd like on the buyer. I don't have it on me since we left in such a rush, but I can send it over once we're back." He stood up and nodded at Sir Caleb.

"Not so fast. While I was waiting for you, I did a bit more research on Amir Birch of the Carlson Group," Seymour crossed his arms and gave Kasem a pointed look.

The look froze him in place. *What could he have found?* Everything on Amir Birch was supposed to check out. Kasem returned Seymour's pointed gaze, "You didn't do that before you took us on as an investor? I find that hard to believe. If that's true, I'm not sure I want to work with you."

"Right. That's why you approached Sir Caleb," Seymour tapped his skinny fingers against the top of the wooden sideboard.

Kasem could tell that he was calling his bluff. *Time to go.* He moved toward the landing and shook his head, "Sir Caleb, thank you for bringing me here, but obviously Seymour's not interested in making a deal. I think I'd better go before this sours our existing relationship."

"I'm afraid that's not going to happen. Take a seat," Seymour turned to face Kasem with a Glock in his hand.

Chapter 81

Mahajanga, Madagascar

Rachel looked over Nathan's shoulder at his computer screen and her stomach did yet another flip, "How are they doing?"

"The same as they were a minute ago. Carlos and Petra are still in the bushes just off the towers. Kasem is still in the main tower."

"Can't you do anything for them?"

Nathan shook his head. "There's nothing I can do from here. I already looped the cameras, but they can see the actual images on their screens. All we can do is be a lookout for activity on-screen."

Rachel's shoulders slumped. "Right, which is what you asked me to do." She sighed and a grin formed on her face, "This is an interesting role reversal—you bossing *me* around."

"It was inevitable." He returned her smile and gave her a playful punch on the arm, "I know you'd rather be out there, but what you're doing *is* helpful. I swear. Plus, since you're watching the cameras instead of me, I can work on decoding this damned ledger, which is what you brought me on to do in the first place."

"How's the decoding coming?"

Nathan shot her a look that silenced her. As she could see, constantly prodding him with questions wasn't helping either of them but staring at the screens was boring. There was a reason she had avoided desk work as much as possible.

"Are you sure there isn't anything else I can do to help?" Once the words were out of her mouth, she regretted them. "I'm sorry," she said with another sigh.

Rachel picked up her com device and radioed Petra, "There's no new activity on the cameras. You guys are clear if you want to head back to the boat. How's Carlos?"

"He's okay, as good as can be expected," Petra answered. "Carlos saw Kasem enter the central tower. We're deciding if we should wait for him. Can you give us a read on his vitals?"

Rachel frowned and switched screens. "His blood pressure was fine until a couple of minutes ago when it spiked a little. It's steady again now but—" Her screen went blank. "I think my screen froze, hold on." She reopened the tracker data and it came up blank once again. "I don't understand. There's no data. It's blank."

Nathan looked at her in concern. "Check the tracker map. Can you still see his position?"

Rachel switched the screens as Nathan had shown her. The map opened, and she could see the red dots for Petra's and Carlos' positions near the towers, along with Chris's position near the edge of the cliff. The dot for Kasem in the main tower had disappeared.

Chapter 82

Mahajanga, Madagascar

Petra stared at the screen where Kasem's tracker had been marked. "He's gone," she slumped backward and said the words again, "He's gone." A sense of despair overtook her.

Carlos grabbed her phone, "Not necessarily. They could be jamming the tower." He tapped on-screen to enable the com. "Rachel, tell me good news. Do you have him?"

"Negative. We can't find him."

"Copy that. We'll look for him on-site." Carlos tapped the screen again and turned off the com. He looked at Petra and squeezed her forearm, "This doesn't mean he's dead, kiddo. You got me back, didn't you? I was gone for a hell of a lot longer."

"I know, but we could see your vitals, track you." She swallowed and glanced at the tower again. It took her a few seconds to regain her focus. *Now isn't the time to lose it.* "If he's in there, he needs our help." *If he's still alive.* She refused to say the words. *He's not dead. He can't be dead.* Perhaps if she told herself that enough times, she would be able to convince herself.

"We could set up a distraction," Carlos said with a nod. "If he's able, it might give him the chance to get away."

"Take care of it. I'm going in to get him."

******

Petra steadied herself against the ground as she watched Carlos scurry into the bushes with her kit. The plan was for him to set a fire in the brush and use the distraction to shoot the guards circling between the towers. That would be enough of a distraction for Petra to get through to the main tower. They weren't sure where Kasem was in the tower, so she would have to search for him as quickly as possible. There were other guards at the airfield, which was less than a ten-minute drive, so the distraction would only give them a small window.

She squatted on the ground, ready to move as soon as she could see the fire.

The seconds ticked by until she saw a small flame start to flicker in the distance. *Just a few more seconds.* Carlos would have rigged the flames with the fire starter in her kit so that it would catch the fire

257

propeller device when he was a few feet away. Petra counted down in her head. *Ten, nine, eight…*

The small flames erupted into a six-foot inferno, and she ran for the entrance to the main tower.

Chapter 83

Mahajanga, Madagascar

Kasem glared at Seymour and the barrel of the gun pointed at him.

"How did you know we were dealing in weapons?" Seymour asked. "If your story checks out, we might let you go."

"I already told you. I did my due diligence. I wouldn't be much of an investor if I hadn't," Kasem answered.

Sir Caleb looked between the two of them, "Seymour, is this really necessary? Amir invested with us, trusted us. Don't we owe him the same?"

Kasem could tell that Sir Caleb's protests were having no impact on Seymour. *Why didn't I leave when I had the chance?* He kicked himself for even approaching Sir Caleb. The reasoning behind it seemed hopelessly flawed now. It had made sense when he thought that he could use it to get open passage for Petra onto the island, but that hadn't been necessary. *What am I doing here?*

He shoved those thoughts out of the way and kept his breathing constant while he searched for an escape route. Although this situation might be one of the worst, he had been in enough sticky spots to know that there was always something if you looked hard enough. He had allowed his cockiness and stubbornness—if he admitted it to himself—to lure him into a false sense of security about this meeting. He had known Seymour would be skeptical, but he had hoped that the greed that had kept him in Nguyen's outfit for so many years would supersede it. Clearly, he had been wrong. Risk aversion had won out.

Kasem judged the distance between himself and the gun. If they were still standing, he might have been able to wrestle it from Seymour's hands. Even out of practice, his training would carry him further than Seymour's skinny frame. Unlike the movies, though, that was both dangerous and reckless. Now that they were sitting again, he wouldn't even have the chance to try.

He looked at the coffee table to judge if it could stop a bullet. The oak was thick, but it also would be heavy, and he wasn't sure if he could flip it on its side fast enough. He was evaluating other alternatives when Seymour, who had been whispering to Sir Caleb, gave up on him. "Get out. Caleb, you don't have the stomach for this."

Take your boat and leave my island." Seymour's piercing eyes returned to Kasem, "I've had two unexpected visitors to this island in the past two days. Do you really think that's a coincidence?"

Kasem kept silent and watched Sir Caleb shrink away. He caught a few mumbles as he left, "...Nguyen will never stand for this...Can't believe you've treated me this way...Incredibly improper."

Judging from Sir Caleb's tone, he wasn't going to stand up for himself. Seymour outranked him within Nguyen's organization. Kasem's heart sank as his advocate disappeared down the stairs.

"What do you know about my other visitor, Amir? I find it hard to believe that you would both show up without any connection to each other. Tell me—did you hire him? Is that why he was snooping in Nguyen's home? I barely got anything out of him, but I have a second chance with you. You're not built of quite the same stuff, are you? A posh man like yourself? Handling torture isn't one of your skillsets."

"I don't know what you're talking about. I came here because I saw an investment opportunity." Kasem kept his gaze focused on the ground. When he'd explained his plan to the team, explaining that he had hired Carlos to spy on Nguyen's outfit was a last resort to keep Carlos alive. Instead, his association with Carlos was about to get him killed, with Carlos most likely following suit. Why hadn't he brought a weapon? He had thought about stashing something, but he'd been too concerned about being searched. He had only deigned to risk keeping his tracker since they hadn't managed to deactivate Carlos'.

"I have all the time in the world for you to talk. What you've failed to realize is that we aren't in a rush to move the merchandise. We already have our buyer lined up. We weren't greedy enough to go with your on-the-fly proposal." Seymour gave him an unnerving smile, "I knew I was right about you. Nguyen was so happy that his son had brought in an investor that he didn't listen to me. You managed to charm him—I'll give you credit for that. He won't be too disappointed, though. He's never had much faith in Jim. But Jim and Janine, they'll be devastated. The way you and your wife wormed your way into their hearts. I haven't seen a con duo like that in a long time. It's impressive—being in love and working together."

Kasem couldn't believe that Seymour was paying him and Petra a backhanded compliment. *Is this a movie monologue?*

"Did you know that she never budged when I solicited her? I had to try. You can't blame me, after all. She's just my type—a fiery raven, completely different from the other women at the party. You don't really appreciate her—letting her go to the wedding all by herself, vulnerable to all the single men there."

Seymour's words about Petra made Kasem want to punch him in the face, but he clung to his self-control. A flicker of light at the window caught his attention. *A fire?* Kasem kept his peripheral vision on the window. His instincts told him that this was his way out.

"Interesting." Seymour raised his eyebrows, "Perhaps she isn't your wife after all. Any real man would have said something to me for soliciting her. If that's true, your outfit is even more impressive than I thought. Amir, how do you know the man I have stashed in my tower? He went by Anton Garcia when I last knew him, but who knows what he goes by now."

Kasem only kept half of his attention on Seymour as he watched the fire. *Come on, Petra.* He willed the fire to be part of her plan. *It has to be. It's too much of a coincidence,* he thought, mirroring Seymour's words. He watched and waited.

The fire delivered. With a loud crash, it exploded into an inferno several feet high. Seymour turned toward the window and Kasem dove forward. He wasn't going to miss this opportunity.

Chapter 84

Mahajanga, Madagascar

Petra ran, her senses crowded with the sound of the initial explosion and the sharp cracks of the fire as it consumed smaller bits of the explosive that had set it off. She kept low to the ground to keep safe from the smoke. With her night-vision goggles, the path seemed eerily clear. She took down two guards who came toward her before they shone their flashlights at her, each with a single shot from her tranquilizer gun.

She passed by the smaller tower where Carlos had been held and moved as quickly as possible toward the entrance of the main tower. Staying low hampered her speed and the tower seemed farther away than she had judged, but she kept moving forward. Eventually, she would get there.

Amid the sound of the flames, she heard a loud crack whip through the air and she almost stopped. Her blood turned cold—the sound of a bullet in the tower ahead, followed by another one. *Kasem...*

Petra willed her legs to move faster. *Please be alive.* She reached the entrance after hitting another guard with the tranquilizer gun, he was too distracted by the growing fire to see her coming. She disappeared into the building and searched the ground floor. There was a foyer and a hallway, with only two conference rooms on either side, all of which were empty. She cursed aloud and ran for the stairs at the end of the hall. *Where did the shots come from?*

She was three steps up when she heard another four shots. The sound almost stopped her in her tracks again, but adrenaline and will maintained her momentum.

She reached the first floor. She couldn't see any light down the hallway, but she did catch the sight of light up the stairway. She followed her instincts and skipped both the first and the second floors. As she ascended, she placed her tranquilizer gun back into her holster and pulled out her Colt pistol. She wasn't going to bring a tranq gun to an actual gunfight.

Chapter 85

Mahajanga, Madagascar

Carlos used the climbing gear to lower himself down the cliff as he watched the explosion that he had set burst into a much larger fire. Much as he disliked the Agency, he had to give it to them for their tech. That piece of gear from Petra's pack, which he felt certain Chris had supplied, had been just what the doctor ordered. He was a few feet down when he considered going back for Petra. They didn't know what she was running into. He looked down at the base of the cliff and waved his arms. His vision could hardly pierce through the darkness, but Chris was most likely wearing night-vision goggles like Petra, which would make his descent visible.

Carlos tapped on the earpiece that Petra had given him, "McLaughry, I never thought I'd be grateful for your sorry ass." He was only half-joking. The two of them hadn't been able to mend their relationship when Carlos cut ties with the Agency years earlier.

"I'm not sure if I'm glad to hear your voice or not," Chris's thick Scottish accent came over the com. "Where are Petra and Kasem? I'm assuming it was your reckless idea to set off that explosion."

"If you didn't want her to use it, then why did you supply the tech?" Carlos grunted as he lowered himself another foot. "Jokes aside, thank you."

Chris was silent for a moment. "I know you'd do the same." After another pause, he asked, "What's happening with the lovebirds?"

"Petra went into the main tower after Kasem. She still has her secondary earpiece, so she'll let us know when they're on their way." Carlos hesitated, "Unless we go in after them—"

"Don't go getting any funny ideas."

Carlos sighed as he made his way down the rest of the cliff. Much as he hated to admit it, Chris was right—he would have done the same. He looked up to the top of the cliff and considered going after Petra. Emotions told him to go back, but reason propelled him downward.

He was halfway down when he heard the sound of two gunshots through his earpiece over the cacophony of the fire and the waves. He stopped cold and started to pull himself upward. He tapped on his earpiece, "Petra, do you read me? Petra?" He looked down the cliff again and grimaced, "Chris, I heard gunshots. I'm going back up."

Chapter 86

Mahajanga, Madagascar

Kasem slammed his weight into the side of the coffee table as the fire exploded outside. The table rolled on its side, knocked Seymour back, and landed on his leg. Seymour cried out in pain and the gun fell from his hand. Kasem scrambled to grab it and barely got his fingers around it.

While Seymour was still trying to crawl out from beneath the hefty oak table, Kasem slammed the butt of the gun into his head and ran for the stairwell. He had only made it few feet when a shot whizzed by him.

Kasem cursed as he dove into the first doorway across the hallway and another shot passed over him. *Damn.* Seymour had reached another gun faster than he had expected. Kasem sent off his own shot but missed. He fired off another one, and this time almost managed to catch Seymour in the shoulder, but he ducked behind the table.

Kasem grabbed his advantage and fired four shots in Seymour's general direction behind the table before he jumped into the stairwell. He didn't have clear enough sight lines and the table was too big to find a kill shot but the bullets bought him enough cover to run. Killing Seymour would be a plus, but he wasn't going to lose his chance at escape.

******

He almost ran straight into Petra on the landing halfway down the first flight of stairs.

"Kasem!" she cried out.

Without a word, he grabbed her hand and pulled her along as he ran down the stairs. When they reached the second floor, they ducked into a room to the left of the stairwell.

The fire was starting to quiet and he could hear footsteps coming down the stairs toward them. He kept watch by the door as they waited for Seymour to descend. He was moving slowly because of the injury to his calf.

Kasem looked at Petra and saw her Colt pistol in her hand. She had lined up the shot for the opening of the stairwell. "You got another one of those?" he whispered, "Or bullets?" He gestured with his gun, which was now empty.

Petra tossed him a tranquilizer gun and he frowned, "A tranq?"

"We need him alive. We can get him to turn on Nguyen."

"Fine, but this guy's mine."

Petra raised her eyebrows and removed a pair of handcuffs from her belt, "Can you hit him from here?"

Chapter 87

Mahajanga, Madagascar

Petra kept her shot lined up on the stairwell as she switched positions with Kasem. He moved past her to the other side of the doorway so that he had a better shot with the tranquilizer gun. *Any second now.* She blinked twice as the footsteps reached the landing.

Seymour came around to the top of the stairs while she kept her pistol pointed at him. His right shoulder was bleeding, but it didn't look like more than a graze wound. *Let Kasem get him,* she reminded herself. *We need him alive.* Her right hand shook as she held the gun. He was in her sights. She could take the shot. She could end this. He had killed Vik, had tried to kill Kasem, and had almost killed Carlos. This man didn't deserve to live.

"Amir, did you really think that you could get away?" Seymour said as he hobbled forward. "How are you going to get off the island? I have ten men on their way from the airfield. You don't stand a chance."

Petra's index finger twitched, she caught her breath and steadied her gaze. All she had to do was pull the trigger and Seymour would be gone. She slowed her breathing and took aim. She was about to give in, about to release her finger, when a soft *whoosh* came from Kasem's side of the doorway. The tranq dart landed square in Seymour's neck. He fell forward down the stairs and his head hit the ground.

Petra looked down at the gun and tried to catch her breath as she engaged the safety. She slid to the floor with her back against the wall. *Thank God.*

******

Petra was so relieved that Kasem's shot had preempted her own that a few moments passed before she processed what she was looking at from her position on the floor. Neither of them had taken a good look at the room they had sequestered themselves in, just verifying that there were no immediate threats before they lined up their shots. She looked around now and gasped—here, on the far side of this random room on Seymour's island, was a pile of crates that looked suspiciously like the explosives that she had tagged at the

267

storage unit. "Are you seeing what I'm seeing?" she looked up at Kasem.

He helped her up and they approached the crates together. As soon as they were close enough, she could see the serial numbers listed that corresponded to the ones that they had found in London. They had found the store of explosives that they had lost track of, the set that they hadn't managed to dispose of. *Holy shit,* she looked over at Kasem. She could scarcely allow herself to breathe as she photographed the haul using a button on her goggles. *This can't be real.* They had the trifecta now—this haul, along with the ledger, and Seymour's and Jonah's testimonies, would finally be enough to put Nguyen away. *We can get these bastards.*

Chapter 88

Mahajanga, Madagascar

Kasem grunted under the weight of Seymour's body on his shoulder. He and Petra covered the distance between the main tower and the forest as quickly as possible, and he dumped Seymour's body on the ground before doubling over, gasping for breath.

"You might need to get back in the gym once we get home," Petra gave him a cheeky smile.

"He's heavier than he looks," Kasem shot her a glare from his position on the ground. He took a few more seconds to catch his breath, "How far to the cliff face?"

"We'll have to use the path. There's no way we can carry him down the cliff."

"You mean we can't just pitch him off the edge? The beach is sandy," he shrugged as Petra's grin widened. "I'm just saying..."

"Can you pick him back up? The path is about a hundred feet that way." She pointed behind him, "It's a pretty windy road down to the beach."

"Fine."

"Poor baby. I'll make sure there are places where you can stop and rest," she gave him her best innocent puppy-dog look and his eyes narrowed.

"That's enough."

"Sorry," Petra chuckled. "Let's go."

Chapter 89

Mahajanga, Madagascar

Petra tapped her earpiece twice on their way to the forest pathway down to the beach. "Carlos, we're heading to the forest path," she said. "Carlos, do you read me?"

His voice came over with a loud crackle that made her wince, "Glad to hear it. In that case, I'm heading back down the cliff."

"Back down?"

"I heard gunshots and thought you would need my help."

"We actually could use your help. If you're at the cliff face, turn east about fifty feet and that's the head of the forest path. We're approaching from the other side with cargo in hand."

"Anything for you, kiddo."

******

We have to move. Petra thought about saying the words aloud, but both Carlos and Kasem could hear the movement uphill. Seymour hadn't been joking about the men arriving from the airfield. She could hear the rumbling of a helicopter overhead. They had only just managed to avoid its spotlight at a couple of points on the path. Thankfully, the forest provided cover, so their biggest threat was the men themselves. Petra was tempted to lie in wait and take care of them, but she'd been overruled. Kasem was right—they didn't have enough ammunition to take out all of them and there might be more on the way. Their best shot was to get off the island as soon as possible.

Petra glanced behind her again, "They're getting closer." She checked the map as they paused so that Carlos could maneuver himself over a small brook that crossed their path. When he stepped over it, he placed Seymour on the ground and panted.

"Your turn, buddy," Carlos said to Kasem.

Without a word, Kasem grunted and hoisted Seymour back onto his shoulders, "Is it just me or does this guy get heavier every time I lift him?"

Carlos grinned and tapped his hand on his stomach, "Maybe he absorbed some of my belly fat on the way down."

"That's funny. I don't think you've gotten any thinner," Kasem grumbled. "Your head actually looks bigger."

Petra moved behind them in silence, amused at the banter between them. Somewhere in this mess, Carlos and Kasem had become real friends. She wasn't sure how she had missed it, but she couldn't help but smile at the realization. The sound of the footsteps on the path above ended the happy moment. "We're almost there," she said in a low voice.

They were further away than she wanted to admit because of how windy the path was, but she had to keep them optimistic.

******

By the time they reached the beach, Petra was expecting bullets to be whizzing by their heads. They made it to the swim motors, and once they hauled them close to the water, Carlos waded in. He and Chris set Seymour up on the other side of one of the motors. "You lovebirds take the other one. McLaughry and I will handle this bozo." He turned to Chris, "You ready, McLaughry?"

"Yup." They started the motor and when they were a few feet away, Petra and Kasem did the same.

They reached the boat a few minutes later, just as Seymour's men appeared on the beach.

Chris already had the engine started, "Everybody up? We've got to be out of here before that helicopter pilot realizes he should be searching the water."

"Let's go," Petra said with a shiver. The temperature had dropped from the time they had arrived, and she was soaked to the bone.

Chris revved the engine and the island disappeared into the distance.

Epilogue

Kyoto, Japan—Two weeks later

Petra opened her eyes and groaned at the sound of her phone ringing a few feet away. Kasem grunted and turned over as she reached past him to pick it up from the bedside table. She caught the caller ID before she answered with video enabled. "Rachel?"

"Hi, Petra. Sorry, I know it's late there."

Petra rubbed her eyes, "It's fine."

"I have good news."

"Hold on a second," Petra sat up and nudged Kasem before she raised her speaker volume. "It's Rachel," she said when he opened his eyes. "Go ahead."

"Lady and gentleman, we got him."

Petra couldn't stop herself from chuckling at Rachel's imitation of the speech announcing Saddam Hussein's capture over twenty years earlier, "That's great news. Thank god."

"I can hardly believe it. Seymour turned on Nguyen like a good old flip-flopper when we squeezed him hard enough—just like you said he would, and that's how we found him. Once we grabbed his peeps at the CIA, the whole operation folded like a house of cards. We picked up the arms you photographed and the rest of what he had stored on the island. Since Nathan's decoded the ledger and now we'll have Seymour's testimony, it should be a fairly airtight case."

Kasem squeezed Petra's hand, "Have you told Carlos the good news?"

"Yup, he was my first call—sorry, guys, you'll have to play second fiddle on this one."

"No worries. Vik was his partner, I would have called him first too," Petra said. "How are you doing?"

"I'm doing pretty well. I have to sit out of fieldwork for a while, which is going to be god-awful, but I'll get through it," Rachel answered with a shrug.

Petra nodded, "It's not so bad, I promise. You'll make it."

"I guess I can't coax the two of you into joining my team? I have a good budget to work with now that we put Nguyen away."

Petra exchanged glances with Kasem and shook her head, "No, we're heading back to Paris." She leaned over and planted a kiss on Kasem's cheek.

"You really are the cutesiest lovebirds ever."

"Thanks, I guess," Petra shrugged. "By the way, how's Nathan doing?"

"He leveraged decoding that ledger into one hell of a promotion. I tried to get him to stay on my team, but he says he's done with field ops." Rachel shook her head in obvious exasperation, "Carlos, Nathan, and you guys. What a waste of field talent. We could have a lot of fun together. I'll let you two go back to bed, or if I know you better, give Carlos a call. Tell him I still think he should come work for me."

"You know me well indeed," Petra said. "Say hi to Nathan if you see him."

"Will do. Also, would you mind calling McLaughry for me? If I call him, it has to be an official Langley communication, and that's a whole lot of red tape that I don't feel like dealing with right now."

Petra sighed, "Sure." She waited until the call disconnected and gave Kasem another kiss on the cheek, "Have I told you how much I love you?"

"In the past hour? I don't think so."

"Well, I do."

"I love you too. Go call Carlos and tell Chris you're still not coming back to the Agency. I'm going back to sleep." Kasem gave her a peck on the lips and flopped back against his pillow.

Petra padded down the stairs and called Carlos when she reached the living room.

"Hey, kiddo. Just like clockwork. Did Rachel wake you guys up to tell you?" His image on the video screen was beaming.

"She did. It's pretty exciting that Nguyen is behind bars. I almost can't believe it. Are you and Diane celebrating?"

"She's waiting for me on the patio." Carlos raised a glass of whiskey up to the camera, "To you both. We couldn't have done this without you."

"Hold on," Petra grabbed an empty glass from the living room cabinet and poured out a finger of scotch before raising it, "To avenging Vik."

******

Petra was back in her bedroom when she remembered Rachel's request to call Chris. She sighed and dialed him. She got his voice mail and sat down on the edge of the bed to leave him a video message. "Hi, Chris, it's Petra. Rachel asked me to call and let you know that they managed to catch Nguyen. She thinks it should be an airtight case. Anyway, I know things between us have been rough, and I'm sorry for my part of that. You sent me back into the field, and I lashed out at you—but I get it. Even if I don't like it, there is such a thing as the greater good, I'd just rather keep my distance from it going forward. Maybe someday we can go back to being friends. I really am grateful that you showed up to help us. Thank you. Take care."

******

New York City, United States

Chris replayed the message a couple of times and turned around to look at Grant. He paused the message and zoomed in on-screen to the image of Kasem sleeping behind Petra.

"You really think this is the guy you saw in Kuwait?" Chris asked. He waved his right hand, "I've got no love for the guy, but I find it hard to believe that Petra's boyfriend is the Ahriman. Are you sure this isn't some weird jealousy thing?"

"I'm over her, thank you very much," Grant scowled. "Like I said—I'm not sure, okay? I know I've seen him somewhere and when they left the airfield in DC last year, I had this weird dream where it was the same guy. After you told me that you and Petra were still working with him, I thought I had to say something. But I could be wrong." He raised both hands, "I'm not making any accusations. I just thought I should tell you. What you choose to do with it is up to you."

"Sure, but this guy went to bat for us with the FSB, and now helped the CIA put this arms dealer away. No way he's the Ahriman."

"You could be right," Grant said with a shrug. "I only know I've seen him. I didn't get a good look and that's not a clear image. Maybe I recognized him from somewhere else."

"I'll look into it."

"That's your call. I'll see you when I see you, Chris."

After Grant left, Chris looked at the on-screen image with a frown. Kasem had been an Iranian spy, yes, but he had done a lot of good since then. Besides, Petra wouldn't be with him if she didn't trust him. There was no way he could be the Ahriman. No way.

THE END

Dear Reader

I'm so excited that you read my book. It still feels kind of surreal, that I have readers who actually read my books! Thank you so much.

I would love to hear what you thought of Resurgence of the Hunt. Would you mind posting a review on Amazon?

Word of mouth and reviews are critical for any author to succeed. I would be so grateful if you would post a review! Even if it's only a line or two, it would be a tremendous help. The link to review at is below:

http://smarturl.it/Ahriman3

Sign up for my mailing list here:
http://smarturl.it/PujaList

I'll let you know about new releases, contests, and more!

Thank you again!

With all my best,

Puja Guha

About the Author

Puja Guha draws upon her experiences from traveling and living around the world in her writing. She has lived in Kuwait, Toronto, Paris, London, and several American cities including New York, Washington DC, and San Francisco, along with extensive visits to see family in Kolkata (Calcutta). Each of these places and many more show up in her writing as her travel to places such as Madagascar, South Africa, India, Vietnam, Sudan, and Afghanistan, inspire more and more story ideas. She also uses her experience working in international finance and development with the World Bank and Oliver Wyman to delve into global political and financial themes in both her thrillers and literary fiction.

Find out more by joining Puja's mailing list at:
http://smarturl.it/PujaList
www.pujaguha.com
pujaguha@pujaguha.com

Made in United States
Troutdale, OR
04/10/2025